Killer Of Stars

Killer Of Stars

Book One of the Immortal Vagrant Trilogy

Travis James Annabel

Sydney, Australia

Editor: Ruth Jobson

Proof reader: Tiffany Fillingham

Cover art by: igorzh/Shutterstock

Published by Motion Factory Pty Ltd

www.motionfactory.com.au

www.travisjamesannabel.com

facebook.com/travisjamesannabel

travisa@netspace.net.au

ISBN 13: 978-0-9945385-0-5 (Print)

ISBN 10: 0-9945385-0-2 (Print)

ISBN 13: 978-0-9945385-1-2 (Ebook)

ISBN 10: 0-9945385-1-0 (Ebook)

This book is dedicated to my amazing daughter Mia Grace. My absolute shining light, the most beautiful creature in the world. I will always be there for you, and love you unconditionally.

Also to my wife Ruth, who has put up with my whims, ever changing moods and temper tantrums when things don't go my way. Thanks bub.

And lastly, to my best mate, my dog Jett... after all, I named a character after him.

PART ONE

THE WEAPON OF TYRANTS

(IGNORANCE)

It was simple, really. The Great Solar War was fought for one reason: to satiate the basic human need for conflict. Of course, historians will argue. Resources, they claim. Ideology. But no. These are excuses, not reasons. If one truly has no desire for conflict (as many war-time leaders throughout the annals of human history have claimed) then they would find a way to over-come their different ideologies, they would share their so-called precious resources. Humans need conflict, just as they need air.

So why claim otherwise?

Strip away all the reasons you've heard about the causes of the Great Solar War, because they're all lies. Lies to make us feel good about ourselves... to allow us the illusion of rationality, and of reason. When I say 'us', I of course mean those who existed so long ago – those who were our ancestors, as far removed from them as we now may be. So long ago... but have we really changed? We live longer now. Our technology has become so advanced that those first days of emergence into our home solar system seem like prehistoric times to many of our children. We think we've changed, of course. And maybe we have in many ways. But there is one way in which we have not...

Conflict; our desire for it, our yearning for it. It really is a significant part of our psyche, perhaps the one thing that every single one of us truly has in common. We have a deeply ingrained need for it – we crave it. No? Think about it... two children in a schoolyard punch-up... two lovers quarrelling... bartering over the price of an apple... a simple sports tournament... democractic governance... judicial systems. These are all forms of conflict *that have ingrained themselves so deep within our culture, so deep within our evolved minds and bodies that we barely even consider these things as such.*

But I digress. You don't want to hear about such boring things as the human psyche, in all its glory. Post-humans are all the same. You want to hear about war! About great battles, brave heroes and violent endings! Be truthful, I know.

Now I'm sure you learnt all about The Great Solar War as a child. But I may have a different perspective than your people have, so listen well. The war, of course, was fought between two sides; The Global Union, and the United Alliance of Nations. The two mega-powers which ruled post-digital renaissance Earth at the start of the second space-race in the early to mid twenty-first century. It had been a need back then, you see... greed was the one constant (apart from conflict *wink*), and the very nature of greed compels us to do whatever is necessary to get more, more, more out of everything. The global economy was such that individual nations could not survive... so they did what they needed to do to get what they wanted... they joined one of the two global governments, which were in turn puppet governments for the biggest transnational corporations. Money was what ruled the Earth back then. For a while, though, things were calm. Earth had just emerged from the Digital Renaissance, which had begun at the end of the twentieth century, and the wonders that human kind was creating were enough to keep the population interested. They had their computers and AI's to think for them, they had their robotics to work for them, and they had their devices to entertain them. Cold-fusion gave them all the power they could ever wish for. It truly was a golden age.

So what happened?

Earth was old... humanity had discovered everything there was to discover, they'd climbed to the highest peaks, dived to the deepest depths. There was nothing to fight over, because there was nothing new. Really, our ancestors were like children; they would fight and squabble over a toy, until they became bored with it, and then they would fight and squabble over a different toy, until they had become bored with that... and so on. And that's what happened; humanity had fought and squabbled over Earth for millennia... suddenly it was boring, and was not worth fighting over. But then we decided to explore the solar system.

Suddenly we had things to fight over; Luna, Mars, the asteroid belt. New toys. New reasons to return to that primitive urge that never quite abated... the urge for conflict.

Both factions took steps into space, building Luna bases, constructing various orbital structures, and making plans for Martian colonization. The Alliance was the first to send a ship to Mars, though. It was planned as a two-step program, a small three man visit in a return craft to iron out the bugs for a second trip with colonists and infrastructure. The first vessel arrived safely, and the Alliance became the first to put a man on Mars (Evan Drake, since you asked). The Union didn't like the fact that the Alliance had beaten them to what was, at the time, the ultimate goal. So they decided to skip the first step, and send a ship packed full of colonists and infrastructure to the great red planet before the Alliance could do so.

They failed, spectacularly.

The vessel was wrought with bugs and computer glitches. Back then, space vessels used a technique called aero-braking to slow down for orbital insertion... it involved grazing the atmosphere of a planet at just the right angle and depth that the vessel would slow and draw them into an orbit, without destroying the ship. It didn't take much for it all to go wrong, and in the case of the Union vessel, it went spectacularly wrong. It's not clear precisely what happened, but it is believed that a computer glitch placed the vessel at the wrong angle-of-attack for the aero-braking, thus causing the vessel to burn up within the thin Martian sky. Of course, at the time the Union went crazy, claiming Alliance conspiracies and the like. Was it true? Doubtful. Technical error is a much more statistically plausible scenario, certainly over sabotage. But one can never be too sure.

The Union's Martian failure allowed the Alliance to take their time, and to do things right. And they did. In the year 2036AD, the Alliance established the first permanent human colony on another world.

The Union, of course, was not happy. Nevertheless, they continued on with a second attempt at sending Union colonists to Mars. Almost a year after the Alliance colonists had established their new home, the second Union vessel arrived in Martian orbit.

And this is where things get interesting.

After aero-braking into Martian orbit, the Union vessel was contacted by the first colony. They were advised that as per Alliance policy, the Union vessel would be fired upon if it attempted to enter the atmosphere of Mars. The vessel did not have enough fuel to return to earth – it was only ever designed for a single, one-way journey, so the Captain weighed his options: he could attempt to enter the atmosphere and call the colonists' bluff (if indeed it was a bluff), or contact the Union mission control back on earth's moon. He had enough food and resources to maintain Martian orbit for a week: then he would have no choice but to attempt atmospheric insertion.

The Union mission control on Luna, were of course furious. Union diplomats hammered their Alliance counterparts, trying to come to some compromise before the colony ship was forced to land. The Alliance would not budge, however. Two weeks after arriving around the red planet, the Union captain ordered the AI that ran the ship to begin atmospheric insertion.

They were destroyed.

The Alliance colonists had built two surface-to-space missile launchers, and though they had little ammunition, it only took one hit. The Union rulers condemned the Alliance colonists, as well as the leaders of the Alliance, suggesting that the Alliance was deliberately provoking the Union into hostilities. The Alliance responded by claiming that they had simply stopped an aggressive move by the Union to invade sovereign Alliance territory – Mars. The Union declared it preposterous to claim an entire planet, and advised the Alliance that they would retaliate in kind.

They did. A single week after the destruction of the Martian colony ship, the Union launched a full scale assault against the Alliance's Luna and Earth Orbital forces. They destroyed every single Alliance vessel and platform between the Earth and the Moon, and they occupied the Alliance Luna colony. This had left the United Alliance of Nations without a foot in space and with no way to send resources or supplies to their Martian colony, let alone any additional colonists.

The Alliance was forced to the negotiation table. After a year of frayed nerves, hostile tension and fierce negotiations, a deal was hammered out between the two mega-powers. The Alliance would allow the Union access to Mars, and the Union would hand back the Alliance's Luna colony. After all the death, chaos and destruction, they had come full circle, and were back to where they had started.

Now, I'm sure you would think that the two great powers would have learned from their mistakes. Surely more conflict could only be detrimental to humanity's continued expansion throughout the solar system? Not necessarily. Look back right across the landscape of human history – mankind's greatest achievements; the splitting of the atom, the invention of rocketry, ballistics, computing, even the simple wheel, were all created or achieved during periods of conflict. During peace time, governments have no choice but to spend their money on the basics: education, health-care, feeding the starving, clothing the poor and housing the poverty-stricken. It is only during periods of conflict that governments have the justification to spend big on something like research and development.

So, as you can understand, more conflict was inevitable. It was precipitated by the Union this time. They launched their third Martian colony ship and it arrived within Martian orbit without incident. Without incident that is, until its crew launched a missile at the Alliance colony with a cold-fusion warhead attached. The Alliance colony that had been built over the prior years ceased to exist and the Union claimed Mars for themselves.

The Alliance forces on Luna immediately began a fierce campaign against their Union counterparts, but the Union had prepared for this eventuality and had secretly garrisoned a brigade of mechanized troops on the moon's surface. The Alliance was once again booted from the surface of the moon.

The fighting, however, did not initially spread to Earth. After their loss of both Mars and the Moon, the Alliance had no choice but to withdraw from conflict with their tails between their legs and to take the time to rebuild their forces and re-plan their strategies.

For almost a year, the Union had complete control of Earth Orbit, Luna and Mars. During this period, they even began to mine the asteroid belt that sat between Mars and Jupiter. The Union was resource rich, and well and truly controlled every single off-earth asset.

The Alliance bided their time however, and when all their plans were complete, they set in motion the first real campaign of what would become known as the Great Solar War – yes, everything I have spoken of up until this point has been preamble. Incredible, wouldn't you say?

Why did they call it the 'Great' Solar War, you may ask? It goes back to what I said at the beginning. Conflict is a part of us. We see war as a platform for heroic deeds, honour, courage and loyalty. For one to bleed for their cause is for one to be a patriot... a hero. It has been the same since the first monkey picked up a stick and beat another monkey over the head with it. And look at us now: monkeys with antimatter... monkeys with starships... monkeys with the power to do whatever the hell we want.

Monkey gods.

I know, I'm a cynic. A sarcastic bitch with nothing better to do than teach you about the evils of ourselves. Anyway, back to it.

The Alliance initiated hostilities by attacking the three spaceports that the Union operated in Asia and Australia. At the same time, they launched a surface based attack against all of the Union's Earth orbital forces. The attacks were considered successful, but they failed in one major aspect – they were only able to destroy two of the three Union space ports. This allowed the Union to reinforce their orbital space forces as well as their Luna forces.

War raged. Ground and naval battles were fought on Earth. Low gravity battles on the moon and hugely epic space battles in the orbit of Earth. New weapons were being deployed on a weekly basis; such nasties as antimatter bombs, boson lasers and particle accelerator weaponry. Tactics improved on a daily basis. Thousands died. And then hundreds of thousands.

And then millions.

All the time though, Mars remained out of the fight. The Alliance did not have the resources to expand the conflict to a fourth front, and the Union likewise had no desire for the conflict to spread further.

Eventually, the Alliance gained the upper hand. They occupied massive portions of Union land on Earth; all of Australia, large portions of China,

South Africa. Luna was all but lost for the Union also. Still the fighting continued. The Union leaders promised their people there would be no surrender to the tyranny of the Alliance, no retreat! The Alliance leaders promised theirs that they would not stop until the evil of the Union was erased, the last Union patriot wiped out. But in reality, the war had been all but won.

It was then that the Union colonists on Mars began their most ambitious project. They knew that it was only a matter of time before the Alliance fleet would be heading for Mars. They knew that their enemy would wipe out any lingering trace of the Union, as they themselves had done upon their arrival to the red planet. So they decided they would leave.

Years before, the Union leaders had begun diverting their ore ships returning from the asteroid mines to Mars – resources that they did not want the enemy to get their hands on. The now one hundred thousand strong Martian colony built a reasonably sized fleet of vessels (some manned, some unmanned) to protect their planet. Then they started on their main project – the first human starship, which would be christened The Stargazer. It was to be a huge slower-than light sleeper ship, holding ten thousand cryogenically frozen colonists, and crewed by a small number of families, who for generation after generation would be the keepers of the great vessel.

Unfortunately for the Union colonists, their Earth brethren lost the war sooner than had been anticipated. Against their promises, the Union leadership had in fact surrendered when the Union capital of Tokyo had been sacked by a large Alliance force. The Alliance could finally begin their preparations to retake Mars.

The Martian colonists were disheartened by what they saw as their leaders' betrayal, but they would not give up. They pressed ahead with the construction of The Stargazer, doing as much as they could to prepare the vessel for departure before the Alliance task-force arrived in Martian orbit. They had three months – for that was the amount of time it would take the Alliance force to make the journey between planets.

In the end, they barely made it. The Stargazer was completed, but then began the arduous task of freezing the ten thousand colonists, and placing them aboard the great vessel. The leaders did the maths, and realised that they could not have the Stargazer fully loaded before the Alliance fleet arrived. They managed to have four thousand aboard by the time the Alliance fleet aero braked into Martian orbit.

The Martian defence fleet engaged the attacking Alliance fleet, and the battle was the bloodiest, most passionate fight of the entire war. Martian captains kamakazied their vessels into Alliance capital ships, Alliance commanders sacrificed their smaller vessels in order to protect the larger ones.

The battle lasted days. Eventually the Alliance fleet began to emerge as the victor, as everyone knew they would. But the Martians were not about to give up. They launched The Stargazer and another small escort fleet. The great ship and its escorts engaged the Alliance fleet, with the future hopes and dreams of their people the only motivation.

And against all odds, The Stargazer broke through.

The vessel had taken a small amount of damage, but their escorts had done an admirable job, and the great ship broke Martian orbit and engaged its ion drive. With the huge thrusters engaged, the Alliance fleet had no hope of ever catching it.

The Stargazer pushed on and on, leaving the chaos of its home system in their wake, and then leaving the Sol star cluster behind too. It travelled three hundred light years, further than necessary to find an inhabitable planet, but far enough that they hoped they would never be burdened by the legacy of their past ever again.

After six hundred years of travel, the great vessel arrived at its destination, a planet they named 'Eden' in a single star solar system, not too dissimilar to Sol. It was here that they planned to forget Earth, Luna, and Mars. It was here they planned to rebuild their society, only better. A society where everyone lived in peace and harmony.

But of course, if you've listened to anything I've told you, then you would know that peace and harmony was never going to happen. 'Eden' would not be the Utopia they thought.

After all, they were still human; and humans need conflict.

One

The Redeemer Temple, in the heart of Eden's biggest, and only true city, Avoca, was the largest and most ostentatious structure on the entire planet. It had been built (like most structures on Eden) using red ore, mined from out in the badlands, shipped to, and then refined in Avoca. It had been constructed almost thirty years ago, as a monument to the greatness of the Morphites and as a reminder to the people of Eden of the redemption they needed to earn.

The temple was a dark grey mass of spires, with a huge central spire that extended so high above the dark gloom of the city the very tip of it breached Eden's abnormally low atmosphere, which extended to only two hundred meters above the planet's mean ground level.

Lord Adjutant Imanre Hes strolled through the great Redeemer hall, the largest open space within the temple, glancing at all the beautiful pictograms depicting the history of Eden and the glory of the Morphites. It was the only place the aging man could find a moment's solitude, as speaking was strictly forbidden within the great hall. The Triumvir Adjutants rarely visited the great hall, and there were no Lesser Adjutants to hassle him with their reports and their concerns. In the great hall there were only the Acolytes who kneeled in front of the pictograms in silent prayer.

Hes passed the pictogram depicting the emergence of the Providencian Pilgrims and stopped to study his favourite – the one honouring first contact with the Morphites. The painting showed a huge white streamlined space ship landing next to the ramshackle slums that were now the 'Old Town' section of Avoca, a Morphite descending down the ship's ramp towards a group of Eden's citizens who were dressed in rags, holding their hands out to the Morphite in a plea for help. And they had helped.

That is why they are to be revered, Hes thought, saying a silent prayer.

The great double doors at the end of the hall opened, bringing unwelcome noise into the silence of the revered place. A large man with a black cape over the black and white ornamental Judge's uniform strode in, his polished boots pounding heavily on the stone floor. His head was bald and his goateed face was frozen in his usual frown. The praying Acolytes looked up in annoyance, then hurriedly went back to their prayers when they realised who was making all the noise.

The man's name was Drealon Rus and he was a Judge, one of the powerful (and feared) Redeemer law enforcement officers. There were five Judges at any one time on Eden and they were selected from the ranks of the Advocates by the Triumvirate of Adjutants as an upper echelon of Redeemer law enforcers of sorts, handling sensitive and serious situations, while the Advocates handled everyday law enforcement. The Judges reported directly to the Lord Adjutant and as a result, were often seen as Redeemer enforcers, carrying out the will of the Temple. It wasn't entirely true – the Judges had a fair amount of autonomy when it came to their operations – but nonetheless, they were feared.

Judge Rus was especially feared, after what had become known (unofficially) as the Massacre of Rusden. Rus had taken ten Advocates to the Techno town of Rusden in an effort to make the rebellious heathens tow Redeemer line. The Technos, of course, had resisted, and the situation had turned violent. Rus and his Advocates ended up burning the town to the ground and while it could hardly be considered good press for the Lord Adjutant at the time, Hes had to concede that the situation had made the citizens fear the Judges even more than they already had, which in turn made it easier for them to enforce Redeemer law.

Drealon Rus approached Hes and kneeled before him, bowing his head. Hes sighed and ran a hand through his balding grey hair. He touched Rus lightly on the shoulder and the big man stood, motioning for Hes to follow him out of the great hall. *Well, at least I managed a few moments of solitude,* Hes thought as the two of them marched out towards the exit. They reached the two huge doors and passed through, Rus closing the enourmous ornamental things behind them.

'I specifically requested to not be disturbed,' Hes said, his deep voice echoing throughout the hall's foyer.

'Apologies, my lord, but your presence is required urgently,' Rus replied, his serpentine voice a soft but menacing drawl.

'Urgently?' Hes repeated, slightly surprised. 'Very well, Judge Rus. Lead on.'

The Judge bowed his head, turned on his heel and led the Lord Adjutant towards the mechanical elevators that climbed up to the administrative offices midway up the huge central spire of the temple. The journey was quick; the elevator was one of the few pieces of technology that had endured since the landing of *The Stargaze,* which was a relief to Hes as he didn't particularly enjoy spending time alone with Rus. Before long the doors opened and Hes and Rus entered the large Adjutant reception area. They strode through the hallways, Rus evidently leading them towards Hes' own chambers. Outside the chambers the other two Triumvir Adjutants waited, appearing slightly nervous.

'Lord Hes,' one of the Triumvirs, Felden Yew, said by way of greeting. 'Why have we been summoned?'

'I have not the faintest clue,' Hes replied. He turned to Rus. 'Judge Rus?'

'You have a... guest, my lord,' he replied. He motioned to the office doors.

Hes sighed angrily.

'I do not appreciate the theatrics, Judge Rus,' he said opening the door and entering the office, flanked by the other two Triumvir Adjutants. Inside, an individual sat facing Hes' huge wooden desk, their back to the office doorway. Hes and the other Adjutants stopped in their tracks, Hes' eyes widening slightly. The individual's head was bald, and they were wearing a simple one piece white outfit which was devoid of any colour, logos or ornamentation. Rus walked around the three Adjutants towards the individual and kneeled.

'May I present to you Lord Adjutant Imanre Hes, sir,' He said.

The individual stood up, their figure far too thin to be that of a human. They turned, and peered at Hes, their hairless, wrinkleless and almost featureless humanoid face devoid of any expression.

A Morphite!

Hes and the other two Adjutants immediately kneeled, bowing their heads to the alien.

'Please,' the Morphite said in perfect English, his voice soft and fluid. 'There is no need for such formality.'

The four human men stood uncertainly. The Morphite held out a hand towards Hes who shook it after a momentary delay.

'Forgive me, my lord,' Hes said. 'It's just... you're a Morphite! There hasn't been a Morphite on Eden in almost seventy years! Forgive me, but I am somewhat... taken aback.'

'Indeed,' the Morphite replied. 'My name is Zesiro, and I come on behalf of my people in regards to a very serious matter.'

'Anything you need, you have our full support, of course!' Hes replied. 'Allow me to say, my lord that I am over-joyed that you have chosen my tenure as Lord Adjutant to return to Eden!'

Zesiro held up a hand to silence Hes, but his voice remained soft and non-threatening.

'Please,' the Morphite replied. 'Do not think that my people agree with this false religion you have built around us. To us, it is fallacy. It is no improvement to your world than when we left it all those decades ago. You have learned nothing as a people.'

'With respect, my lord,' Hes said, taken aback. 'We are trying to better ourselves. Redeem ourselves for what we did back then... how we behaved. Our contact with you and your subsequent departure from our world has helped us grow!'

'You still fight over us... over our technology.' Zesiro replied. 'You are infants playing with fire, and you continue to burn yourselves.'

'The Technos are a small minority,' Hes replied, dismissively. 'Surely you can't hold the majority of us responsible for the actions of a few bad eggs?'

'I apologise,' Zesiro said. 'In this shape, we Morphites have a tendency to be devoid of expression and emotion. People tend to misunderstand the precise meanings of what we are saying when we lack these things. Allow me to fix this problem...'

Zesiro's face began to ripple. The ripple spread across his body, and he began to change. Hair grew from his head, his clothing changed colour, texture and form. Within seconds, a young human man, dressed in heavy black clothing, with long black hair and vivid blue eyes was staring at Hes. Zesiro pointed at his own face, which was creased in an expression of anger.

'Now see this?' he said, the gentleness in his voice all but gone. 'This is not happiness to be here. Let me get one thing absolutely straight, Lord Adjutant. We... I find your ridiculous religion offensive and this draconian regime you have created for yourselves oppressive! We do not like it. We are offended by it! Do you understand?'

'Yes, my...'

'Do not call me "my lord"! For pity's sake! I am not your Lord! Don't you even understand your own damned form of communication?'

'I doubt you came here to insult us, Morphite,' Rus said, anger seeping from his otherwise calm tone of voice. 'So what exactly is it we can do for you?'

'You will be silent, Judge Rus!' Hes boomed.

'No, we're getting somewhere now,' Zesiro replied. 'Finally!

Someone who understands plain English. I am here, Judge Rus, because my people need your help in... acquiring someone.'

A piece of paper materialized in Zesiro's hand. He passed it over to Hes.

'This individual is very important to us. We want him alive, and in *one piece*.'

'May I ask why you need us, my... Zesiro?' Hes asked. 'With your technology, surely...'

'You don't need to know any of this.' Zesiro replied. 'All I need of you is to find this individual, and bring him to this very office. Once here, we will take him off your hands. That is *all* you need to know.'

'Then it shall be done,' Hes replied, bowing his head slightly at Zesiro.

Zesiro smiled, and his face began to ripple again. He reverted to his natural form. 'It is all we ask, Lord Adjutant Hes,' He said, his voice reassuming it's softness.

With that, the Morphite dematerialised and disappeared.

'Hope save us...' Adjutant Yew breathed.

'What are we to do?' the third Adjutant, Imelda Qes said in a stricken tone.

'We do as he asked,' Hes replied.

'But the things he said... how they think of us...'

'It's irrelevant!' Hes snapped. 'Can't you see? They are testing us! They want to see if we are ready!'

He ran a hand over his forehead, wiping away the perspiration. He turned to Judge Rus.

'Judge Rus,' he began. 'I am giving this assignment to you. You will find this individual the Morphites so desperately want.'

'I will, my lord,' Rus replied.

'You will find him and you will bring him here, as quickly as possible.' Hes passed the piece of paper over to Rus.

'I understand, my lord.' Rus replied. He glanced at the sheet of paper. 'By the end of the week, you will have Jonas Dresden.'

Two

Jonas Dresden, the man thought as he stared at his face in the glass of a half shattered window. *I know my name.* He turned and stared at his surroundings. *So why the hell can't I remember anything else?*

The town was small, dirty. A working class town unlike the city of Avoca, which with Eden's one and only Redeemer Temple was an altogether different cess-pool. *Hmm... I know the planet's name is Eden, I know the name of its largest city... what's happened to me?*

Jonas peered up at the sky. Eden's sun was high, but the sky remained black with a billion stars spotting it like a diamond strewn blanket. Jonas instinctively knew that Eden's human viable atmosphere extended to a mere two hundred meters above the average ground level, meaning it was too thin for light from the distant sun-like star to reflect off and create the various shades of blue that humans had lived with for thousands of years on Earth. Not that there was anyone on Eden who had ever been on Earth.

Jonas looked down the street and examined the town. The streets were only partially paved, and the buildings were mostly built with the pre-fabricated metal materials made from the ore that was mined throughout the badlands. The occasional transport trundled through the streets along with more frequent cruisers. Signage hung from the various shops and outlets, filthy and faded. The majority of people walking around the town were working class – miners, technicians and labourers. He spotted a sign hanging out the front of a central building; *Port Usharin Tavern.*

He was in Port Usharin, then. On the edge of the Badlands' Crimson Sea, named so because it was a wide, flat expanse covered in red ore that stretched for hundreds of kilometres across the surface of Eden before it petered out into the golden sands of the Desert of Forever. Port Usharin was a mining town, responsible for mining and processing the majority of red ore that was then distributed across Eden. It was one of many scattered towns in the badlands, still a thousand kilometres from the city of Avoca, the largest on Eden, and seven hundred kilometres from the planet's second largest city, Providence, which sat as the gateway to the mysterious Valley of Stars.

And Jonas Dresden had no idea how he had gotten there.

The tavern... that was the obvious place to get information. Jonas strode down the street towards the dirty looking establishment, a distance of no more than fifty meters. He crossed the street, hopping out of the way of a cruiser at the last moment. A bouncer stood next to the tavern's large iron door. He nodded at Jonas as he approached and opened the door for him.

Inside, the filthy place was filled with smoke from cigarettes and semi-legal narcotics. The stench of ale filled the air, and the slightly nostalgic tunes of the Providencian Symphonic played. The tavern was not quiet, but it could hardly be said to be buzzing either. A total of ten or twenty individuals sat or stood around the bar. A large bearded man stood behind the bar polishing glasses with a filthy look on his face, while a young woman served drinks. As Jonas approached the bar, she slapped away a patron's wandering hands and hissed a warning at him. The man took his ale and fled to a table, not quite taking his eyes off the bar girl.

'What can I getcha?' She asked as Jonas sat at the bar.

'I don't really know,' Jonas responded. 'What's good?'

The young woman grunted a sarcastic laugh.

'Yeah, funny,' she replied. 'One Crimson Ale coming up.'

She pulled the amber beer and sat it in front of Jonas.

'Three creds, man,' she said, sticking her hand out.

Jonas frowned. *Nice move,* he thought. *Do you even have any money?* He reached into his left pocket. Nothing. He grinned sheepishly at the bar girl and reached into his right pocket. Miraculously he discovered a small bundle of plastic notes, around fifty creds. He passed a five over to the bar girl.

'Keep the change,' he said.

'Thanks honey,' she replied, with a genuine smile. She stuck the note in the tiny cash drawer and deftly pocketed the change. 'I haven't seen you here before. You here to work in the mines?'

'You mean the red ore mines?' Jonas asked.

'Yeah, you know. The only reason this dirt-bucket of a town is on the damn map,' she replied.

'I... no. No, I'm not here to work in the mines,' Jonas replied. *At least I don't think so.*

'Yeah I didn't pick you for a miner,' the young woman said.

The big bearded bartender approached, a scowl on his face.

'This guy bothering you, Gala?' He said in a deep gravelly voice. The bar girl gave Jonas a quick smile.

'No more than anyone else, Darris,' she said winking.

'Then maybe you can get back to work,' he replied, throwing her a tea-cloth. She caught it with a grimace, the smile all but gone.

'Yeah, sure thing.'

She walked away towards a swinging door which led to a small kitchen. As she walked through the door, she spun her head and gave Jonas a wink. Jonas couldn't help but smile. The big bartender, Darris, placed his hands on the bar and leaned in menacingly towards Jonas.

'I'll give you a piece of free advice, stranger,' he growled. 'Stay the hell away from her.'

Jonas peered at the huge man, wondering how to act. He knew instinctively that if the man tried anything, he could easily defend himself. *And I know I could hurt him much more than he could hurt me...* He didn't see any point in starting a ruckus, though. He needed information, not grief.

'Is there an Advocate office in town?' Jonas asked, deciding to ignore the man's threat. The bartender frowned, taken aback by the change in conversation. He took a moment to answer.

'Why, you in some kind of trouble? Or you just lookin' to cause some?'

Jonas sighed, and raised his eyebrows in frustration. As he did so, the young woman emerged from the kitchen. He waved his hand at her, and moved down the bar towards her, ignoring the bartender's annoyance.

'Hey! Gala is it?'

She smiled an amused smile. 'Galatea,' she replied. 'Only my friends and Darris here call me Gala.'

'Galatea, then,' Jonas said. 'Is there an Advocate's office in town?'

'Yeah, there is,' she replied. 'Such as it is, anyway. Head down the street, take the next left. You can't miss it. Well, actually, you can. It's tiny. But keep your eyes open, and you'll do fine, honey.'

'Thank you, Galatea,' Jonas replied. He turned towards Darris. 'See? Now was that so hard?'

He left the bar to the sound of Darris cursing angrily, and Galatea laughing and teasing Darris. Outside, Jonas began strolling down the street. A huge transport moved down the dusty road, followed by an even larger, monstrously sized tracked ore-hauler, which Jonas knew were called Behemoths by the locals. The drivers of the vehicles yelled at stragglers in the street to move out of the way, and as they passed by, the ground trembled under Jonas' feet. He watched as a filthy man picked up a stone and hurled it at the Behemoth, screaming obscenities at it, apparently having just lost his job in the mines. As Jonas passed him, he could smell a strong scent of alcohol emanating from the man's tattered clothing. Jonas hurried past, unwilling to become the focus of the drunk's attention.

He turned left where Galatea had instructed, and after only a few meters almost missed the Advocate's office. Galatea wasn't kidding when she had said it was tiny. Jonas entered the small, scrappy structure.

The inside of the Advocate's office was surprisingly large in comparison to its frontage. There was a small reception desk with a hallway next to it which led down to the office itself. No-one manned the desk, but Jonas immediately noticed a button with a sign saying 'Press for attention'. He pressed it, and a faint ringing noise sounded from out the back of the office. There was no noise to indicate that anyone had heard the bell, or was even out the back. Jonas decided to investigate. He moved down the hallway slowly. There were black and white 'Wanted' posters lining the ochre walls, with the occasional anti-Techno propaganda poster interspersed between them. A framed Redeemer poem hung in the centre of the first door he approached. He knocked on the door quietly. No answer. He turned the knob and entered. It was the Advocate's office, a simple, sparsely furnished room, with an old pre-Morphite desktop computer sitting on a metal and composite desk that was littered with papers. A photo of a man who was presumably Port Usharin's Advocate standing with the previous Lord Adjutant, Hessan Meu in the Redeemer Temple hung on one of the walls.

Jonas moved out of the office and closed the door behind him. He moved down the hall to the second and last door. There was a barred window in the door. Jonas peered through. It was obviously a cell. A small, filthy toilet and an uncomfortable looking metal bench were the cell's only furnishings, and a man with short brown hair, a brown leather jacket, black pants and boots lay on the bench. Jonas knocked on the door, and the man looked up. He frowned at Jonas, not expecting to see a face other than the Advocate's.

'Who the hell are you?' he asked in an annoyed voice.

'I'm looking for the Advocate,' Jonas replied. 'Any idea where he is?'

The man was sitting up now. He grunted a laugh, and held his arms out wide.

'I can't help you, my friend,' he said. 'And to be honest, I'm not too sure you'll ever find...*him*.'

The prisoner leaned back against the filthy brick wall using his hands as pillows. He had an amused look on his face.

'You look pretty pleased with yourself,' Jonas said. 'Too bad you're the one behind the bars.'

The man raised an eyebrow, and leaned forward again. 'You offering to get me out?' he asked, a look of poorly concealed hope on his face.

'Why would I get you out?' Jonas asked. 'I need the Advocate's help. I'm pretty sure he wouldn't be too pleased if I let his prisoner go free.'

'I can help you,' the man said. 'You know the reputation of the Advocates, surely? They're not exactly the fairest group of people on Eden.'

Jonas felt a presence behind him in the hall, and moments before he turned, a female voice sounded.

'Now, now, Jett! Are you saying you *don't* appreciate my hospitality?'

Jonas turned to see a young woman wearing the black and blue uniform of an Advocate.

'Ah, shit...' the prisoner, whose name was evidently Jett muttered.

The woman approached Jonas, her short blonde hair fashionably worn, and her blue eyes drilling holes in him.

'And who the *hell* do you think you are?' she asked calmly.

'I'm sorry,' Jonas said, not realising he was staring at the woman. '*You're* Port Usharin's Advocate?'

Jett laughed in his cell, as the Advocate woman scowled. She raised an eyebrow.

'Yes, as hard as it is to believe, I am the Advocate,' she replied.

'Give him a break Tailynn!' Jett said with a laugh. 'There are only about three other lady Advocates on Eden, of course he's shocked!'

The Advocate reached the cell door and glared through it at Jett.

'I mean, I thought you'd be used to it, jeeze!' He leaned back against the wall.

The Advocate turned back to Jonas and looked him up and down.

'I am Tailynn Sar, Advocate of Port Usharin,' she said formally, the annoyance never leaving her eyes. 'And I repeat my original question to you: Who the *hell* do you think you are?'

'My name is Jonas Dresden,' Jonas replied. 'And I need your help... Advocate Sar.'

'Dresden?' she repeated. 'That's an odd name.'

'You ain't no Techno are you, Dresden?' Jett asked from his cell, suddenly growing suspicious.

'No, I'm not...I'm...' Jonas scratched his head. 'Well, that's kind of the problem.'

Tailynn Sar held a hand up to silence Jonas. She turned to the cell, and withdrew a bunch of keys from her belt, dangling them in front of the cell door's window. Jett grunted a laugh and stood, taking a couple of steps towards the door.

'Not so fast,' Tailynn said. 'Formalities, remember?'

'Come on, Tailynn!' Jett exclaimed. 'Aren't you getting a little tired of this?'

'Aren't *you?*' she replied. 'Jett Dor, on one count of drunk and disorderly conduct, how plead you?'

'Ah, Jesus...'

'Jett!'

'Fine!' he snapped. 'I plead guilty.'

'As a duly appointed Redeemer Advocate, I hereby fine you two-hundred and fifty Creds,' she said, inserting the key into the lock.

'*Two-hundred and fifty?*' Jett exclaimed.

Tailynn withdrew the key out of the lock with a shrug.

'You can stay in there, then,' she replied, beginning to turn away. 'Your choice.'

'Fine!' he snapped. She smiled, and unlocked the door. Jett pushed it open and walked out, dusting down his jacket. 'Anyone would think you were trying to teach me a lesson.'

'And anyone would know how futile that would be with someone like you,' Sar retorted. She turned to Jonas. 'Now, what was it you wanted again? Jonas, wasn't it?'

'Yes,' he replied. 'And I'm afraid I need your help. You see, I seem to have lost my memory.'

Three

Zesiro was melded with the control centre of his personal starship, the *Zenith of Desire*. His form blended perfectly with the bio-mechanical systems of the small vessel which was in a holding orbit above Eden, fully veiled. There was not a sensor system on Eden sophisticated enough to detect the presence of the *Zenith*; not even the Technos scavenged Morphite devices would come close.

Since arriving in orbit of the backwards pre-human world, the *Zenith of Desire's* systems had performed innumerable scans of the planet, attempting to locate any sign of Zesiro's quarry – all to no avail. Dresden had been very thorough in masking any sign of his existence.

Zesiro had gone through a short phase of uncertainty over his decision to reveal himself to those ridiculous Redeemers. Their backwards religion based around Zesiro's own people disgusted him, and he had not made the decision to visit them lightly. Truth be told, he had very little faith in their ability to find Dresden. Dresden had managed to elude Zesiro for years... the chance of an ordinary backwards pre-human finding him were slim to none – but he had no choice. If nothing else, sending the Redeemers after Dresden would force him into running again, and perhaps revealing himself to Zesiro and the *Zenith's* advanced scanners.

Zesiro instructed the *Zenith of Desire's* construct to open a communications line back to the Morphite Command Hub, having the top half of his body emerge from its blend with the vessel. A trio of Morphites appeared in front of him in the *Zenith's* control centre. Their faces conveyed no feeling, and their even blander clothing conveyed no indication of rank or hierarchy. They were, however, the three most important individuals within Morphite society, and considering Morphite society by definition was void of hierarchy, that was saying something. They were the Originators, those who had come before any other Morphite, bar one. They were revered by all Morphites – they were their leaders and the ones who had given Zesiro his quest to capture Jonas Dresden.

'Originators,' Zesiro said by way of greeting with a slight bow of his head.

'Zesiro,' the three of them replied in unison. The most feminine of the three spoke. 'How does your search progress?'

'I have tracked Dresden to Eden, Originator,' he replied monotonously.

'Eden, you say?' one of the masculine Originators said, what Zesiro could only articulate as a hint of surprise in his voice. 'That is... worrying.'

'I agree, Originator,' Zesiro replied. 'My vessel's systems have been unable to detect any trace of him. I have initiated contact to advise you that I have had no choice but to initiate contact with the pre-humans, specifically the Redeemer faction.'

'A risky choice you have made, Zesiro,' the second masculine Originator said.

'Risky and unwise,' the first added.

'Perhaps not,' the feminine one said. 'It has been some time since we have assessed the situation on Eden. And Jonas Dresden is undeniably elusive. That is, no doubt, why the Progenitor allied herself with him. I believe Zesiro has made the correct choice. I make the assumption that your reasoning was to set the Redeemers after Jonas, thus forcing him to reveal himself to you?'

'Yes, Originator,' Zesiro replied. 'That was indeed my plan.'

'Calculated,' she replied. She looked at each masculine Originator who in turn nodded at her. 'We are in agreement that you shall infiltrate the pre-humans. Your goals are to one; capture Jonas Dresden, and two; assess the situation on Eden. Are your instructions clear, Zesiro?'

'Yes, Originator,' he replied.

'Fare you well,' the three of them said in unison, before their images disappeared.

Zesiro was mildly surprised that they had given him permission to infiltrate the population of Eden, but their reasoning had proven logical and sound. It was certainly the best chance he would get of locating Dresden, and it had indeed been some time since the pre-humans had been assessed.

He took form and stood in the control centre. His body morphed into human form, with the same appearance he had taken when speaking with the Redeemer Lord Adjutant. He morphed himself clothing, something that the *Zenith's* intellect advised him would be suitable to blend in – black trousers, with a loose fitting ivory shirt and a black knee length jacket. He had the *Zenith of Desire* select an infiltration point – a small alley way in the city of Avoca – and he used the vessel's transit stream to teleport down to Eden.

There was, of course, no-one in the alley when he materialised. He was near some kind of markets – there were stalls everywhere, lining the streets. Humans bartered with the stall owners, buying foodstuffs, materials and medicines.

Zesiro was revolted by the place. They were like rodents, these pre-humans – scavenging in the filth for the slightest morsel. Truly, it was a wonder that the descendants of these things had made it all those light-years from Earth.

Reluctantly, he entered the hustle and bustle of people, going with the flow, allowing the river of pre-humans to carry him down the street. He passed a filthy, legless beggar, covered in muck, sitting on a wheeled contraption, his coarse voice calling to anyone within earshot, begging for the smallest number of creds. A few more meters down the street, he passed a stall with a man and a woman quarrelling. The woman spat in the man's face, who in turn slapped her across the face so hard she fell to the ground with a loud cry.

Zesiro put his head down and hurried as best he could, desperate to get out of the filthy hordes of pre-humans in the market place. He turned down an alley, searching for a short-cut. He hurried through the dimly lit backstreet, only to find himself at a dead end. He sighed, and turned to walk back to the street. Three men had followed him, and were now blocking his path. They were scruffy, with short beards and long messy hair covered by woollen hats. The three of them wore large coats, which were obviously concealing weapons. A quick mental scan confirmed his assumption – two were armed with short, primitive blades and one was armed with an ancient projectile pistol. Zesiro was not even sure the pistol was in working order.

'Going somewhere, pal?' the one with the gun said in an intimidating voice.

'Yes, in fact,' Zesiro replied placidly, as he calmed his mental state to a suitable pre-combat level.

'I think you're mistaken there, pal,' the man replied, which garnered gruff laughs from his colleagues. 'You see, you're wearing some fancy clothes there. I'm willing to bet that you've got a few creds to your name. Am I right?'

'No.'

'Doesn't sound too convincing to me. How about you, boys?' The other two men grunted single syllable replies.

Zesiro sighed, cursing the pathetic humans.

'Look,' he began. 'I don't really have the time or the inclination to go through this rigmarole with you three. You have one chance to turn around and leave this alleyway.'

The man's confidence faltered momentarily before his bravado kicked back in.

'Oh yeah? You going to make us?'

'Don't say I didn't warn you,' Zesiro replied, boosting the adrenaline levels in his own mind.

The man reached for his pistol, but was far too slow. Zesiro's arms took an instant to morph into two sixty centimetre blades, and before the man's gun had even cleared his coat, they were both impaling the man's chest, having surgically pierced the man's heart, and severed his spinal cord. The man was dead before Zesiro had withdrawn the blades from the body. By then, the other two men had drawn their own blades, nothing more than hand-crafted daggers, blunt and rusty. One man lunged at Zesiro, his blade swiping the air. Zesiro spun away from the man's attack and stabbed him in the spine with his left blade-arm. Two down.

The third man took a few steps back.

'You, ah... you win.' He turned tail, and began to run down the alley. Zesiro's arms morphed back to their human form, and he quickly leant down and picked up the second man's dagger. He deftly flicked it into a throw-hold, and hurled it down the alley at the third man. The blade stuck in the man's neck, severing the spine, and killing the man instantaneously. He hadn't even made it half of the way back down the alley.

Zesiro instructed the *Zenith of Desire's* construct to lock its transit stream onto the three bodies. They disintegrated into molecules and disappeared, their bodies deposited somewhere in the cold void of space.

He marched back down the alley and rejoined the flow of people, intent on leaving the filthy markets. He cursed in his mind – at the humans, at himself, at the Originators... and at Jonas Dresden. *Especially* at Jonas Dresden.

Curse him for leading Zesiro to such a hellhole.

Four

'So let me get this straight... you can remember nothing at all?' Advocate Sar asked.

She was sitting at her desk with Jonas on the uncomfortable chair next to it. She was typing notes into a tablet, perhaps one of the most advanced pieces of technology in all of the badlands, with the possible exception of some of the mining machinery. For some reason, her former prisoner Jett Dor had tagged along. He was standing in a corner of the room, leaning against the wall, having just strapped a twin holster belt to his waist that contained a pair of pulse pistols which had evidently been confiscated when he'd been arrested.

'I can remember my name,' Jonas answered. 'I can remember general things – like details about Eden, the Redeemers... I just can't remember details about my past. Everything before I woke up in the street a couple of hours ago is gone... as though it never happened.'

'Clean slate... it can't be all bad,' Jett said.

Sar rolled her eyes at Jett's comment, but Jonas got the impression that her exasperation was somewhat of an act.

'Why are you still here, Jett?' she asked.

Jett just shrugged, an amused look on his face. Sar turned her attention back to Jonas.

'What about your name?' she asked. 'Dresden is a very unusual surname... only a tiny percentage of people have one that is made up of more than a single syllable.'

'I know,' Jonas replied. 'But all I can tell you is that I know that's my name. I have no recollection from where it originated.'

'Your mother... father? Siblings?'

'No recollection.'

Sar placed the tablet on the desk, and leaned back in her chair with a frustrated sigh.

'I'll run your name through the Advocate data-hub. See if I can find anything,' she said eventually. 'Perhaps the Redeemer databases will have something on you. Are you a practicing Redeemer, Jonas?'

Not likely, Jonas thought. He couldn't articulate his feelings, but there was something about the Redeemers that made his skin crawl. Was it possible he *was* a Techno? That didn't feel right either. 'I don't think so,' he replied eventually. 'I don't particularly *feel* religious, anyway.'

'Ok, fair enough,' Sar said. 'But everyone knows the basic story behind the Redeemers, how they came into being. Can you remember any of that?'

'Sure,' Jonas replied. 'The Redeemers came into being after the Morphites left Eden.'

He felt a tingle down his spine when he mentioned the Morphites.

'And who are the Morphites?' Sar asked.

'Aliens,' Jonas replied. 'Aliens who came to Eden to help.'

'And why did they leave?'

'Because pre-humans drove them away.' He'd used the term "pre-human" instinctively, but as soon as the words had slipped from his mouth, he knew it was unusual.

'Interesting that you used the Morphite name for us,' Jett muttered, not missing the faux pas.

'Indeed,' Sar said, frowning slightly. 'And why did they come in the first place?'

'They told the people of Eden that they'd watched human civilization on Earth implode... that humanity had destroyed itself.

They said that the people of Eden were all that remained of humanity, and they wanted to help in our preservation,' Jonas answered. The answer had sprung out of him – almost as though he had been programmed to say it, and saying it had given him a strange feeling, one he could not articulate. Sar was satisfied with his answer, though.

'Well, you can obviously recall basic history. Just your own personal history is the problem. Do you remember your parents or grandparents ever having talked about those days?'

Jonas shook his head.

'Like I said, I don't even remember my parents or grandparents,' he answered.

Sar picked up the tablet again, and tapped a few notes into it.

'Right,' she said. 'That means we have nothing to go on apart from your name. The database search should be easy enough under those parameters, although it could potentially limit results. It will still take some time, though, Mr. Dresden. Where are you staying?'

Jonas thought about the question and realised he had no answer. Sar cottoned on quickly.

'The tavern has a few rooms – nothing flash, but the cost is low,' She said.

'Sounds like a plan,' Jonas replied, not too thrilled at the prospect of another run in with the gruff and surly bar man Darris. But then he thought of Galatea, the bar girl, and the Tavern didn't seem so bad. 'When can I expect to hear back from you?'

'Come back tomorrow,' Sar replied. 'I should have something by then.'

Jonas stood, and extended his hand towards the Advocate. She took it and shook firmly.

'It's what I'm here for, Mr. Dresden,' she replied. 'Do you know your way to the tavern?'

Before Jonas could answer, Jett stirred in his corner and pushed away from the wall.

'I'll show him the way,' he said. 'It's about beer o'clock anyway.'

'Jett, for hope's sake...'

'I'm just kidding!' he replied.

'Thank you again, Advocate Sar,' Jonas said, before allowing Jett to drag him out of the office. Out on the street, Jett turned to Jonas.

'I wasn't kidding, by the way,' he said. 'We're having a drink.'

There were fewer people in the Tavern than when Jonas had been there previously. The bar man was nowhere to be seen either, to Jonas' relief. Galatea stood behind the bar polishing glasses. She smiled at Jonas as he and Jett wandered over to the bar and took a couple of seats.

'Well, looks like you found the Advocate's office,' she said to Jonas with a wink. 'But you seemed to have picked something up along the way...'

'Come-on, Gala, sweetheart!' Jett said amicably. 'Two of your finest crimson ales!'

Galatea laughed a good natured laugh, and began to pull the beers from the tap.

'So are you going to behave yourself this time, Jett?' she asked, teasingly. 'You're such a trouble maker!'

'Darris over reacted,' Jett hissed, 'as usual. But this time it cost me big.'

Galatea turned to Jonas.

'So was Advocate Sar able to help you, honey?' she asked.

'That remains to be seen,' Jonas said, sipping the beer she'd just placed in front of him.

'She'll be able to help,' Jett said confidently. 'Trust me.'

Galatea grunted a good natured laugh, obviously well versed in interpreting her customers' nuances. She looked back to Jonas, and nodded towards Jett.

'He has great *faith* in Tailynn Sar,' she said, good naturedly. 'Why do you think he's always getting himself hauled in?'

'If you're suggesting I fancy the good Advocate, Gala, then how wrong you are. You should know that you're the only girl for me.'

'Yeah, in your dreams, Jett!'

Jonas continued sipping his beer, listening to the good natured exchange between Galatea and Jett. He laughed out loud when it was expected of him, but truth be told, his mind was far away from the dusty little pub. Who *was* Jonas Dresden? Where was he from? More importantly, what had happened to him to make him forget almost *everything*? He dug deep within his own mind, searching for answers, but coming up with absolutely nothing. Not even a flash of a memory was there. It was troubling to say the least. Even more troubling was the sense of dread he felt within... the sense that there was no explanation for his memory loss that could in any way be good. No, whatever had happened to him to cause his memory failure was something bad. He had a dreadful sense that whatever it was was going to cause him trouble sooner, rather than later.

He was drawn out of his reverie by Jett's hand slapping him on the shoulder.

'...Isn't that right, pal?'

Jett and Galatea were looking at him expectantly, evidently having asked him a question he had not heard.

'Sorry,' Jonas answered apologetically. 'I was miles away. What was the question?'

'Your memory loss,' Jett replied. 'I was just telling Gala how you can't remember a single thing. As in nothing. Nada.'

Galatea looked at him expectantly, a curious and vaguely concerned expression on her face. Jonas nodded sombrely.

'It's true,' he said. 'I don't even remember how I came to be in Port Usharin. Hopefully Advocate Sar can discover something about my past with her network queries.'

'Wow,' Galatea replied, wide eyed. 'Well, I have to say that if anyone can help you, it's Sar. I'm no fan of the Advocates, but Sar is probably the most reasonable one of them out there. If she can, she'll help you.'

Jonas hoped that the young bartender was right. He and Jett sat chatting for another hour or so, polishing off another couple of the dusty tasting crimson ales, while Galatea joined the conversation when she wasn't busy with her duties. Jett proved to be adequate company, and Jonas was surprised to find himself enjoying the other man's anecdotes and sarcastic sense of humour. And Galatea... well, Jonas could see her watching him when she didn't think he would notice. He wondered if she was noticing the returned glances he was giving *her* when he thought she wasn't paying attention...

The doors to the Tavern opened and the large and surly bartender, Darris, returned. He wore his typically filthy expression as he strode in, which became even filthier when he noticed Jonas, Jett and Galatea chatting at the bar. He strode over, and addressed Jett.

'You've got a lot of nerve showing your face around here, Dor,' he growled.

Jett and Galatea both tensed the moment they heard Darris' voice.

'Hey, ah, Darris,' Jett mumbled. 'Sorry about the other night, pal.'

Darris grunted something unintelligible in reply. His attention turned to Galatea. 'Don't you have some work to do, Gala?'

Gala muttered something under her breath and grabbed a tea-cloth before walking off. Darris' attention finally shifted to Jonas.

'You're that trouble-maker from before,' he growled.

Jonas decided he didn't like Darris. He didn't want to cause himself any trouble, but Darris just *pissed* him off. At least that shed some light on his own personality... he couldn't stomach imbeciles or bullies.

'If by trouble-maker you mean paying customer, then yes, that is I.' Jonas left the sentence dripping with enough sarcasm that even someone like Darris would understand. Galatea, who by now was at the other end of the bar polishing glasses stifled a laugh. Darris glared at Jonas.

'You gettin' smart with me, stranger?'

'You gettin' dumb with *me?*' Jonas retorted. 'Wait, don't answer that.'

Jett watched the two of them trading insults with an astonished expression. Darris growled. 'Get out,' he said menacingly.

By now, Jonas felt he had Darris figured out. He was a big man, sure. Surly and resentful for whatever reason, which Jonas didn't care to know. But his instincts told him that Darris was all bluster, a coward. He used his size and aggressiveness as a deterrent so he would never be forced into true conflict.

'Or what?' Jonas replied. 'You'll get violent? You'll call the Advocate? I've done nothing wrong. I'm sure Jett here will vouch for that. Galatea too.' He paused for effect, watching Darris do all he could to disguise the surprise and fear in his expression with anger. 'So no... I don't think I'll be leaving.'

'I'm warning you...'

Jonas leaned in close, his face mere inches from the other man's. His reply was barely a whisper, but it was filled with enough venom that it had the desired effect.

'Warn me then. I dare you.'

Darris glared at Jonas for a moment longer, and then turned tail and trundled off into the Tavern's kitchen, knowing full well he had lost. After a moment, an amazed Jett broke the silence.

'Holy shit! What in hope's name just happened?'

Galatea dumped her tea-cloth on top of the still moist glasses and moved up the bar towards them.

'If I didn't know better, I'd say that our new friend here just scared the hell out of Darris!' Jonas could tell that she wasn't as surprised as Jett. Perhaps she already had an inkling of Darris' true nature. Jonas decided that as much as he'd enjoyed Jett and Galatea's company, he needed some time on his own. He needed to *think*. He needed to be away from these distractions so he could try to begin understanding what had happened to him.

'Darris is a coward,' he said dismissively, before turning to Galatea. 'You have any rooms available?'

Galatea, not at all thrown by the quick change of subjects, shrugged. 'Sure.'

'I think I'd like one, if you don't mind.' Jonas turned to Jett. 'Thanks for the drinks... and the company.'

He held out his hand and Jett immediately shook it, still surprised at Darris' reaction to Jonas.

'Hey, no problem, pal,' he replied. 'Thank you for... whatever you just did to Darris!'

Galatea led Jonas up a set of rickety wooden stairs, away from the quiet voices of the bar patrons, and down a musty smelling hallway. She stopped at a door and inserted a key, opening the room.

'This is it,' she said, 'such as it is.'

The room was small, with a single springy bed in a corner, a desk and chair in another corner and little else. The room was a little dusty, but other than that it was clean and neat. And quiet.

'Perfect,' Jonas replied. He turned to Galatea, and relieved her of the room key. 'Thank you.'

'You're welcome,' she replied with a smile. He smiled back, and there was an awkward moment of silence. 'Well, I suppose I'd better get back to work, before Darris has another coronary.'

Jonas laughed and nodded.

'Sure,' he said. 'It was nice to meet you, Galatea.'

'Likewise,' she replied, she started to walk off, before thinking of something else. 'Oh! And by the way... call me Gala.'

Five

Judge Drealon Rus stood in a restricted data-chamber, which was hidden deep within the Redeemer Temple. Only the Lord Adjutant and the Judges knew of the chamber's existence as its contents were far too sensitive to allow even the Advocates or Triumvir Adjutants to get wind of it. If even a rumour of the room's existence were made public, it could spell the end of the Redeemer faith. The room and its contents were necessary, however. Without them, the Redeemers would never have been able to maintain their control over Eden's population.

The data-chamber was a small, spherical room, approximately five meters in diameter. It was only accessible via a single entrance, which was guarded around the clock by a duo of Advocates, and protected even further by a retinal scanner which had been stolen years ago from the Technos by a team of Advocates led by Rus himself. The chamber was void, bar a small metal table in the centre of the room on which sat a small metallic sphere. Judge Rus activated the security door which closed with a hiss, leaving him alone in the perfectly spherical chamber.

He took a step towards the table and reached out his hand to touch the small device. His skin made contact with the metallic object and the sphere immediately began to glow. After a split second the wall of the spherical chamber was illuminated with a plethora of scrolling data. After another split second, a computerised feminine figure appeared in front of Rus.

'Judge Drealon Rus,' the apparition said in a feminine voice. 'Welcome.'

'I require information,' Judge Rus said in his serpentine voice.

'Please state your query.'

The metallic spherical object was a relic from the days that the Morphites walked amongst the humans of Eden, and had been stolen from them during the unrest that had led to them abandoning the planet. The device was what the aliens referred to as a Construct, a semi-sentient artificial intelligence. Each Morphite space vessel was equipped with a construct, and it was Rus' understanding that this one had been no different. The construct was, without a doubt, the most sophisticated piece of technology on the entire planet. Capable of interfacing with almost any computer, data-pad or semi-digital device on the planet, it was the only reason the Redeemers had managed to maintain power for three decades. It granted the Lord Adjutant and the Judges the means to quell any potential problem long before it became a threat.

The construct's existence within the Redeemer Temple and its continued use were the reasons for the chambers' strict secrecy. The Redeemer faith strictly prohibited the use of any Morphite artefact. It was human abuse of such technology which led the Morphites to abandon Eden after all. Only the Techno heretics violated the Redeemers' laws and continued to scavenge Morphite technology. But even the Technos had never been able to find an operational Construct. The irony of the situation was not lost on Judge Rus as he stood before the device.

'I require you to search for the name of an individual. I want you to advise me of every mention of it you find.'

'How wide do you require me to search?'

'Planet wide.'

'What is the name?'

'Jonas Dresden.'

'Searching.'

As Judge Rus waited momentarily for the Construct's search results, a thought crossed his mind: was the Morphite Zesiro, who had given him the quest of finding Jonas Dresden, aware of this Construct's existence? The thought was troubling. Perhaps after his current query, he would recommend to the Lord Adjutant restricting the use of the Construct until they were certain Zesiro had left Eden and its surrounding space.

'One result found,' the construct's feminine voice announced.

'Advise.'

'Approximately one hour ago, Advocate Tailynn Sar inputted a query into the data-hub. She completed a wide ranging search, with the search parameters simply being the name "Jonas Dresden". There were no results to her search.'

Judge Rus let that sink in. Why would an Advocate be searching for information on an individual who was wanted by the Morphites? He pondered it momentarily, but could think of only one reason.

'Where is Advocate Sar posted?' he asked the construct.

'Port Usharin.'

Rus placed his hand on the metallic sphere, and the Construct deactivated. He turned and exited the data-chamber.

Half a world away, Advocate Tailynn Sar was astonished when her rarely used tablet buzzed with an incoming communications message. She hurriedly activated it, and was even more astonished when she saw the fearsome face of Judge Drealon Rus staring back at her. Her eyes widened slightly, and she was sure her reaction was noticed by the infamous judge.

'Advocate Sar?' the Judge drawled in his menacing voice. Tailynn realised she'd been speechless for a moment longer than was comfortable.

'Y-yes, Judge Rus,' she replied hurriedly. 'What can I do for you?'

'An hour ago you made a query into the Advocate data-hub,' he said. 'Your search parameters were a name: Jonas Dresden.'

Tailynn was astounded. Her search had provided no answers.

Jonas' name didn't come up once. Yet somehow, a *Judge* was aware of her search, and was querying her about it! Who the hell *was* Jonas Dresden?

'Yes, Judge Rus. That is correct.'

'Why were you searching for this individual?'

Tailynn frowned with surprise back at him. What could a Judge possibly want with the innocent seeming Dresden? *Was* he a Techno, after all?

'I wasn't searching for him,' she replied. 'He asked for my help.'

'He's there? In Port Usharin?'

'Yes.'

Judge Rus sighed deeply, which to Tailynn seemed awfully like a sigh of relief. She bravely decided to ask the fearsome Judge a question of her own.

'Is Jonas Dresden wanted for something, Judge?' she tried to inject as much innocence into her question as possible. Rus's eyes narrowed.

'How well do you know this man, Advocate Sar?'

Tailynn cursed her curiosity.

'Barely. I met him for the first time a few hours ago.' Her instincts told her not to reveal the nature of their meeting, and why she was searching the data-hub for any mention of him. To Tailynn's relief, the Judge seemed to accept her statement.

'Very well,' he replied. 'I will be leading an Advocate strike force to arrest Mr. Dresden. We will be departing Avoca within the hour. Do not approach the target, but ensure he does not leave town. Do you understand, Advocate Sar?'

No, she didn't. Tailynn prided herself on her ability to read people. What the hell could Jonas have done to warrant being pursued by a Judge led strike force? Had she misread the man so completely?

'I understand,' she replied.

'Good.' The Judge's fearsome face disappeared from the screen of the tablet, and was replaced by the text that had filled the screen prior to the call. Tailynn placed the unit down, her mind racing. What the hell was going on? An Advocate strike-team, led by a Judge was never a good thing. There was always collateral damage when they were deployed.

Tailynn sat back in her seat and sighed. She wasn't a practicing Redeemer, which wasn't necessarily unique within the Advocates. She'd joined the Advocates because she'd believed that it would be the best way to *serve* Eden's populous. She'd wanted only to help people, to offer them the aid she had needed so long ago. But the fearsome Judge's aggressiveness had unnerved her. She was well aware of Rus' reputation. She knew without a doubt that the reasons *she* served as an Advocate were far removed from the reasons *he* had joined. Tailynn had always trusted her instincts, because they'd almost always proved to be right. They were almost like a sixth sense. And her instincts told her not to trust Judge Rus.

She ran her hands through her hair and sighed again, wondering what she was going to do.

Back at the Redeemer Temple, Judge Rus strode into the elegantly decorated chambers of Lord Adjutant Imanre Hes. He kneeled before the leader and bowed his head.

'My lord.'

The Lord Adjutant anxiously motioned for him to stand up. Rus was acutely aware of the man's uneasiness since the Morphite's visit.

'You have news, Judge Rus?' Hes asked, a hint of hope within his tone.

'Yes, Lord Adjutant. I have located Jonas Dresden.'

Hes' relief was almost palpable. His expression softened, and he actually smiled at Rus.

'I am pleased, Judge Rus,' he said. 'As always, you have proven your aptitude for your work. Where is Dresden hiding?'

'Port Usharin, my lord,' Rus replied. 'A small mining town on the edge of the Badlands and the Crimson Sea.'

'I presume you are preparing a strike-team?'

'You presume correctly, my lord.'

'Good.' Hes turned away from the Judge, and picked up an

intricately engraved crystal decanter, which was filled with a dark liqueur. He poured himself a small glass, and raised it to his lips, allowing himself to savour the spicy aroma of the locally manufactured beverage. He sipped the drink, and the bitterness flowed down his throat. He licked his lips delicately and then turned back to Judge Rus. 'I cannot stress enough how important it is that we bring this man in. The future of the Redeemers, indeed the future of the entire population of Eden is relying on your success in this endeavour. And I do not want Jonas Dresden harmed, Judge Rus. He must be brought in alive.'

'And should he resist, my lord? Should he have... companions? Friends who would lend him aide?'

'Dresden himself is not expendable,' Hes answered carefully. 'However, *he* is our target and he alone. Should anyone else intervene, or attempt to prevent his capture, they are enemies of the Redeemers, and you may treat them as such. Do you understand, Judge Rus?'

'I understand, Lord Adjutant.'

The Lord Adjutant dismissed him with a nod. Rus turned on his heel and strode out of the chambers. He had a strike team waiting for him, made-up of his most loyal and trustworthy Advocates. They would depart for the Badlands immediately.

Rus smiled in anticipation. These strikes were what he lived for... they were the reason he accepted the offer to become a Judge, why he had suffered his fool mentor's training for as long as he had. As a mere Advocate, he had always been bound by the instructions of his superiors, specifically those of his mentor, who had sought only to inhibit his growth within the organisation. But then the fool had lost his passion for his role, and when he had resigned they had made Rus his successor. As a Judge, Rus answered to no-one except the Lord Adjutant. And Imanre Hes had always allowed him a long leash to complete his tasks as he saw fit. Hes understood the fear that Judge Rus put into the population. If a bloodbath was required to make a point, then Rus never shied away from it. He thrived on the fear that he left in his wake.

As the Judge approached the strike-team's assembly point within the Advocate wings of the Redeemer temple, he found himself hoping against hope that Dresden would resist. All he needed was an excuse... and he prayed that Dresden would give it to him.

Six

Zesiro sat in a quiet corner of a tavern in the new sector of Avoca. The tavern was smoke filled and the strong stench of ale filled the air, but it contained a quieter clientele than some of the others he had passed since progressing to the new sector from the slums.

The Morphite sat in a trance-like state, his mind linked to the construct that controlled the *Zenith of Desire*. The intelligent vessel had contacted him after it had detected a fellow construct in operation on Eden's surface. Zesiro was only mildly surprised; there had been a lot of technology left behind when the Morphites had abandoned the world. He was more surprised, however, to discover who was using the construct. The signal was coming from within the Redeemer temple, rather than the Techno city the *Zenith* had detected hidden deep within the badlands. Zesiro grunted to himself. The pre-human Redeemers were such hypocrites. Did they honestly think that they could fool the Morphites so easily? Far from earning themselves redemption in the eyes of Zesiro's people, they were simply digging their own grave. And from Zesiro's point of view, it was a very deep grave indeed.

He had seen much since infiltrating the planet's population on his quest to find Jonas Dresden. The Originators had requested that he assess the current situation on Eden... assess how far the pre-humans had come since the Morphites had left the world.

Zesiro was less than impressed.

As he had travelled through Avoca, he'd learnt more and more about the pre-humans. The new sector of the city – that which had been constructed after the initial arrival of the Morphites on Eden around a century ago – was laden with wealth. An aristocratic upper-class had emerged here along with the Redeemer administration shortly after the Morphites had abandoned the lesser race. The Redeemers ruled from here with an iron fist, using the Judges and Advocates to enforce their laws, and the wealth of the aristocracy to prop them up. They justified their draconian regime by claiming that they sought redemption for the entire population of Eden – redemption for the vile acts that had driven the Morphites away from the backwards world. On one hand, they claimed to benevolently rule the population, coaxing them towards the redemption they said they needed to attain in the eyes of the Morphites. On the other, they used the feared Judges to quell any form of dissent, be it justified or not. Zesiro was aware of entire towns that had been razed by the law enforcement officers, massacres that had left thousands dead. Yet they refused to acknowledge their own hypocrisy. When it came down to it, it wasn't the fact that they had *done* these things... the massacres or the draconian control of the people; after all, they *were* just pre-humans. No, it was the *hypocrisy* that irked Zesiro so. The first Redeemer law that had been pronounced by the administration had been the law that forbade the scavenging or use of any Morphite technology that had been left on Eden. They claimed that that was the first step towards the redemption that they sought... yet it was a step that the administration was willing to ignore when it suited their purposes. It disgusted Zesiro. He found the arrogance and hypocrisy of the aristocrats and the Redeemers reprehensible.

But the old sector – the slums he had first arrived in – had disgusted him even more. The old sector contained the less fortunate individuals, those who weren't born into wealth, or lacked the required strength or intelligence to succeed in life. They were the down-trodden, the used and the abused. And he was intensely repelled by them. They were like rodents – turning on each other for the last morsel of scrap. He had witnessed much as had traversed the slums... theft, extortion, assault, rape, murder. It seemed to Zesiro that it didn't take much for the pre-humans to turn on one another. In fact, they seemed to revel in the ability to inflict a level of pain on others that was slightly more intense than the pain others inflicted on them.

The pre-humans were a long, long way from attaining the redemption that they claimed they sought. Zesiro doubted they would ever be able to attain it. Not that it even mattered to the Morphites, of course. No, Eden's inhabitants had had their chance. They wouldn't be getting another.

Zesiro returned his attention to the *Zenith's* construct, as it monitored its fellow artificial intelligence hidden somewhere deep within the Redeemer temple. The report his construct had made caused the Morphite to frown in surprise.

The Redeemers had located Jonas Dresden.

The *Zenith's* intelligence relayed the conversation between the Redeemer construct and Judge Rus, and then the conversation between Rus and the Advocate from the badlands. *Port Usharin.* Jonas Dresden was in Port Usharin.

Zesiro was aware of the Judge's plan to lead a strike force to the small mining town to capture his quarry. Regardless of what he had asked of the Lord Adjutant and of Judge Rus, he could not let the Redeemers get their hands on Dresden. The fugitive was far too important, and Zesiro had no faith in the Judge's ability for restraint. He would have to move quickly. He stood from his table, leaving his bitter tasting ale half drunk. He exited the tavern, and quickly strode down the street, urgently seeking an isolated spot. He found one quickly, another dark alley stretching to a dead end between two buildings. He moved quickly to the end of the alley, before mentally commanding the *Zenith of Desire* to open a link to the Originators.

The link was not an audio or visual one. Zesiro simply sensed the presence of his contact in his mind. Zesiro was surprised when he realised that he was communicating with only one of the three originators, the more feminine of the three.

'Originator,' he communicated after a slight pause, taken aback by the lack of the other two leaders, which was in his experience unusual. The Originators usually acted only as a trio. But then again, the feminine Originator had always been the more assertive of the three. Still... 'Is something wrong?'

'I ask of you the same question, Zesiro,' the Originator replied. 'You are the one who contacted me.'

'My apologies, Originator,' Zesiro communicated. 'I am unaccustomed to addressing but one of you.'

'The others are... occupied. What is your report?'

'I have located Jonas Dresden,' he replied. 'He is hiding in a small town in the badlands region of Eden. I will momentarily be travelling to this town in pursuit.'

'You have performed well, Zesiro,' the Originator communicated. 'Apprehend him immediately, however we maintain that he must not come to harm.'

'Yes, Originator.'

'What of the pre-humans?'

Zesiro thought about what he had seen of Eden's population. Unimpressive to the point of offence.

'They have learnt nothing, Originator. They are... as pre-human as ever. Hypocritical, arrogant, selfish and violent.'

He remembered all he had seen, knowing that the originator would take his memories and understand. After a moment, the Originator's disappointment came flooding through.

'Pity.'

'My instructions, Originator?'

'You have adequately assessed the pre-humans. They are no longer of relevance to us. You are to devote your full attention to the apprehension of Jonas Dresden.'

'Yes, Originator.'

'Fare you well, Zesiro.'

The Originator's presence melted away, and Zesiro found himself alone once more. He was close to capturing Dresden now, he could feel it. He knew his long chase was coming to an end. In a way, he was disappointed. Dresden had been a worthy adversary... he had led him on a long pursuit. But that pursuit was coming to an end, as Zesiro always knew it would. It was only a matter of time before Dresden was in custody. After all, Dresden was only human.

The Morphite connected with the *Zenith*, and instructed the ship to immediately stream him to Port Usharin.

It was time to put an end to this game of cat and mouse.

Seven

Jonas dreamed. It was an extremely vivid dream, void of the chaotic narrative usually associated with the subconscious mind. In the dream, Jonas sat in a sterile white room, opposite another figure, a woman who he felt as though he knew, although he could not put a name to her face. She was older than he, attractive in a motherly way. Her dark hair was lined with silver, and her brown eyes were bright, bursting with an intelligence that seemed almost super-human. Her caramel skin was slightly lined and creased, wrinkles that in no way betrayed her true age. He listened as she discussed ancient human history. She talked of historical instances that Jonas knew of, although from a perspective that seemed vastly removed from what he remembered learning. After what simultaneously seemed both an instant, and an eternity, her expression changed. Her historical narrative ceased and her tone changed to one of concern.

'You're in trouble, Jonas. Time to wake up.'

Jonas woke. After taking a moment to gather himself, he scanned his surrounds. *The room I rented at the Port Usharin tavern*, he recalled. He took a deep breath and centred himself. The dream remained unusually fresh in his memory. *You're in trouble, Jonas...* He stood from the bed and walked over to the small sink in the corner of the room. The tap was tight, and when he twisted it, only a small trickle of water came out. He splashed what he could on his face, and then quickly dressed.

Downstairs, the tavern was empty. A large clock on the wall indicated it was early morning... Jonas had managed a decent night's sleep, although truth be told, he didn't feel like he had.

'You're up early,' Gala's voice echoed slightly in the openness of the empty tavern. Jonas peered up to see her walking down the stairs. He frowned.

'You live here?' he asked.

'One of the perks of the job,' she replied. 'Free board. If you can call it a perk that is.' She went behind the bar, and began brewing a pot of coffee. 'So... restless night's sleep?'

'Actually, I slept rather well,' Jonas replied, before frowning slightly. 'At least, I think I did.'

'Could have fooled me. You're a talker, that's for sure.'

Jonas frowned again. The last time he remembered seeing Gala was when she had given him his room key. Had they... spent the night together? He certainly felt an attraction for the young bartender, but he couldn't remember anything happening. Did his memory continue to fail him?

Gala laughed at the expression on his face.

'Don't worry honey, you're memory isn't playing tricks on you again,' she said, good-naturedly. 'The walls in this place are paper-thin... I could hear you talking in your sleep from my own room all the way down the hall.'

'Oh... sorry,' he grunted.

'It's all good,' Gala replied, before frowning slightly. 'One question, though: what does *Immortal Vagrant* mean?'

A memory flashed in Jonas' mind. It was there, and then gone as quickly as it had come. *Immortal Vagrant*. It meant something to him, he was certain. It was important, but the memory remained elusive. He strained his mind to recall the flash, but no matter how hard he tried, he just couldn't recall the meaning of those two words. Gala watched him with a concerned look.

'Did you remember something?' she asked.

'Almost.'

A loud groan emanated from under a medium-sized billiards table that sat in the corner of the tavern. Gala and Jonas both turned their heads and watched as Jett Dor crawled out from under the table, clutching his head as though he were in great pain. He stood and looked at them with squinted, bloodshot eyes. Gala sighed loudly in annoyance.

'Do you two have to talk so loudly?' Jett groaned. 'Some of us are trying to sleep.'

'Damn it, Jett!' Gala cursed. 'You are so lucky that I'm the one who had the morning shift today, otherwise Darris would have hauled your ass right back to Advocate Sar's cell!'

Jett looked like he was about to protest (or vomit – Jonas couldn't tell which), but he was interrupted by a great roar from overhead. Despite his memory loss, Jonas recognised instinctively the sound of multiple thruster engines. He dashed for the tavern's front door, and wrestled with the lock before flinging it open. Raising his eyes to the dark sky, he watched as a trio of immaculately preserved pre-Morphite Dusters passed overhead and circled the mining town for a second time. He took note of the rather distinctive Advocate insignia plastered on the sides of the light attack/transport craft.

Even without being able to remember a thing from his past, Jonas knew instinctively that they had to be here for him. He watched as the three craft descended towards the street in perfect formation, their thrusters forming clouds of dust beneath them.

Jonas slammed the door of the tavern and locked it. He turned to see Gala and Jett standing behind him with concerned looks on their faces.

'What is it?' Gala asked.

'Three Advocate dusters containing what is probably a Judge-led Advocate strike-team,' Jonas replied.

Gala's eyes widened in what was obviously fear. 'A Judge?'

'You know, for someone who claims to have no memory, you seem to know a hell of a lot about what's going on,' Jett grumbled, working hard to overcome his hangover.

'Why would a Judge come to Port Usharin?' Gala wondered aloud. 'There's nothing here.'

'A truer statement has never been spoken,' Jett muttered.

Jonas looked hard at them both. He had to make a snap decision on whether or not to trust these people he had just met. Without any useful memories, he was running on instinct, and his instincts told him that he *could* trust both Jett and Gala. He hoped against hope that he wasn't about to make a huge mistake.

'I can think of only one reason a Judge would be here,' Jonas said. 'And that reason is me.'

Gala frowned, while Jett gave Jonas a look of distrust.

'Is there something you want to be telling us?' Jett asked. 'Did you lie to us about your memory?'

'No,' Jonas replied. 'Everything I've told you is the truth. I remember nothing.'

Gala gave him an uncertain look. Jonas could tell that she desperately wanted to believe him; however the logic of Jett's queries had made her wonder. She opened her mouth to speak, and her words came out in a tone Jonas had not before heard in her... fear, uncertainty. 'Then how do you know that...'

'I know because it's the only thing that makes sense!' Jonas interrupted, trying to minimise the urgency in his tone. He could tell that Gala was scared, and he needed her thinking clearly. 'Think about it: I wake up in the street with no memory other than my name, which is in itself an unusual one. I have the local Advocate search for any information she can find on me, and within less than twelve hours, an Advocate strike-team arrives. There's such a thing as too much coincidence.'

'You're right,' Jett said quietly. 'But if they're here for you, then what is it you've done? Are you a Techno after all?'

'I don't think so.'

'Then what?'

'I don't know!' Jonas knew the situation was urgent. He needed Jett and Gala's trust, and he needed it now... not just for his own protection, but for theirs too. 'Look, we can discuss this later. Right now, the three of us have to leave here. We can't let them find us. I'm sure you both know the reputation the Judges have.'

Gala remained silent, uncertainty plastered across her face. Jett, however was simply not willing to take Jonas at his word.

'Are you insane?' Jett exclaimed. 'Why the hell would we help you? I like you, Jonas, but I'm not going to mix it up with a Judge to protect you.'

'I'm not asking you to help me!' Jonas replied. 'I'm asking you to help yourselves! The first thing that a Judge is going to ask Advocate Sar is where I am, and who I'm associating with. And she is going to give them *your* names!'

'Tailynn's a good person,' Jett protested. 'She wouldn't sell anyone out.'

'Not knowingly,' Jonas replied. 'But she's an Advocate, and if she does her job, then we are fucked.'

Gala turned to Jett. 'He's right, Jett. If what Jonas thinks is true, and the Judge is here for him, then Sar will have no choice but to aid the Judge.'

'And if they're not here for Jonas?'

'Then it won't matter if we escape, because they won't be looking for us,' Jonas answered.

Jett gave them both hard looks, deep within thought. After a moment, he withdrew one of his pulse pistols and handed it to Jonas, before withdrawing the second and keeping it for himself.

'I don't know why, but I trust you Jonas,' Jett said, the drunken bar-fly persona all but gone. 'Where are we going?'

Jonas checked the pistol's charge, which was full. He then turned to Galatea.

'Is there a back door to this place?' he asked.

'Not on the ground floor,' Gala replied. 'There's a balcony on the second floor, though.'

'We'll go that way,' Jonas said, before turning to Jett with a questioning expression, indicating the pistols. 'By the way, what's with the arsenal?'

Jett gave him a grave look. 'I'm a bounty hunter.'

Jonas raised his eyebrows in surprise, to which Jett shrugged.

'Okay, I'm a *drunken* bounty hunter,' he said. 'Can we get a move on, for hope's sake?'

The trio rushed up the stairs towards the second floor. As they ran down the hallway, Galatea in the lead, a door swung open. As they stopped in their tracks, Darris, the large and surly bartender emerged from what was obviously his room. The large man gave them a confused look. Jonas' mind raced with options. Within a split second, he'd made his decision. He moved Gala aside and rushed down the hallway towards the big man. He tackled Darris to the ground, and then hefted the pulse pistol by the barrel and brought the grip down on Darris' temple, hard enough to knock him out and leave a pretty bruise, but not hard enough to inflict any serious injury. As much as he disliked the man, he hoped that the bruise would be enough to convince the Judge and the Advocates that Darris had had nothing to do with Jonas' escape. Behind him, Gala gasped in surprise. Jonas turned back to her.

'He'll be fine,' he promised. 'Lead on.'

Jett chuckled at the unconscious man as they moved past him towards a door at the end of the hall. Gala approached the door, and withdrew a key from her pocket, unlocking it quickly. She swung the door open, and entered, Jonas and Jett close behind. The room was a small indoor conservatory, where Darris evidently grew a number of herbs and vegetables – and other, less legal flora – that he used in the tavern's kitchen. Gala led them to the other side of the room, which had another door, this time a screen door which allowed air to flow feely into the room. Jonas indicated for Gala to stop, and he passed her. He opened the door quietly, and peered out cautiously. He could see the three Dusters which had come to rest in the middle of Port Usharin's main street. Spotting a few of the town's people peering out of doors at the Redeemer craft, he could sense the fear in the air.

As he watched, the troop doors of the craft opened, and each of the three craft expelled five advocates, all wearing extravagant body armour, and brandishing assault rifles, some energy based and some projectile based. The advocates moved calmly, establishing a perimeter around the dusters. Once the three craft were secure, a huge, bald-headed judge emerged from the lead duster. He wore a black and white Judges armoured combat uniform with a black, ground length cape over his shoulders. Attached to his belt, Jonas could see the hilt of the traditional gun-blade weapon used by the Judges.

'That's Judge Drealon Rus,' Jett muttered, peering out the door behind Jonas. 'One of the less friendly Judges, if you can believe there's such a thing. He was responsible for the Massacre of Rusden.'

'Where's the closest red ore mine?' Jonas asked.

'About twenty to thirty kilometres away, deep within the crimson sea,' Jett replied. 'There's a transfer depot a lot closer, though. Bound to be a lot of vehicles there, and not a lot of people at this time of the morning.'

'We go there, then,' Jonas decided.

'How do we get past that Judge and his men?' Gala asked, her fear evident.

Jonas turned to her and gave her a reassuring look.

'Just follow my lead, and do as I say,' he said. 'Trust me, and I'll get the three of us out of here. This is what I do... I think.'

Eight

Tailynn Sar strode down the dusty main street of Port Usharin, directly towards the three Advocate dusters that had just landed. Swirls of red dust still clung to the air, slowly rising above the group of advocates, and their Judge leader. Tailynn inadvertently brushed the small standard-issue Advocate pulse pistol strapped to her belt with her hand – the gesture comforted her. She had worn her newest and best uniform, the blue and black fabrics crisp and un-faded and the gold trim still bright. Tailynn was nervous, having never dealt directly with a Judge before, especially one with a reputation such as Drealon Rus.

Judge Rus stepped forward away from the Advocate strike-team, watching Tailynn approach. He appeared as fearsome as his reputation implied, his white and black body armour polished to a shine and his black cape waving behind him in the breeze that still remained after the dusters' landing. His gun-blade was visible, strapped to his black belt, folded up in its rifle form.

Tailynn stopped a few meters in front of the Judge and bowed slightly.

'Welcome to Port Usharin, Judge Rus,' she said.

'Advocate Sar,' Rus replied by way of greeting. 'I expect you have Jonas Dresden's location?'

Tailynn hesitated. She'd joined the Advocates to help people... and she wasn't convinced that she was doing the right thing. Rus noticed her hesitation and she was sure he would make a mental note of it.

'Mr. Dresden is at the tavern,' she replied finally. 'If I may ask, Judge Rus, what is it that this man has done to warrant apprehension?'

Rus smiled a serpentine smile and ignored Tailynn. He turned on his heel to face his strike-team, all anonymous Advocates wearing armoured helmets that covered their faces, with breathing vents in the approximate areas of their mouths.

'Squad A you will maintain the landing perimeter. Squads B and C, I want a secure perimeter around the tavern. No-one goes in or out.' The three groups of Advocates immediately sprung to action, ten of them advancing towards the tavern, using dramatic hand gestures to indicate positioning. Rus turned back to Tailynn. 'Who has Jonas Dresden been associating with in Port Usharin?'

Tailynn frowned. She had a very bad feeling about the situation. She was well aware of official Advocate procedures; it was common practice to apprehend any individuals that were known associates of wanted criminals, for questioning if nothing more. But there was only one person she was sure of that had in any way "associated" with Jonas Dresden: Jett Dor. As much as Jett annoyed her at times, she couldn't bring herself to name him. He was her oldest friend – if friend was indeed the correct term to use – and they had been through so much. She still thought of the days they had spent back in Providence, not to mention the reasons they had turned their backs on their pilgrimage and fled to establish new lives in the Badlands, away from the memories that still to this day troubled them both so. As haunting as they were, those memories were always bitter-sweet – these days she sometimes hated Jett as much as she cared for him.

But she would never sell him out.

'To the best of my knowledge, Dresden is new in town and has made no associations,' she lied, as convincingly as she was able to.

Tailynn couldn't tell if Judge Rus believed her, but he didn't bother questioning her any more. He withdrew his gun-blade from its black leather sheath. Its silver body glinted in the light from the over-head stars, and she was acutely aware of its lethality. The weapon was in its gun form, complexly retracted and shaped akin to a standard pulse rifle. Rus extended the stock and held it as such, grasping the trigger grip in his right hand, the under-barrel in his left.

'You will accompany me, Advocate Sar,' Rus instructed.

Tailynn nodded, although she remained uncomfortable. Striding off, Judge Rus led her towards the entrance to the tavern. Although Rus held his weapon in hand, she refused to draw her own, unsure of her superior's motivations towards Dresden.

Rus strode up to the tavern's entrance and without even pausing, lifted his leg and kicked in the timber doors as hard as he could, the metallic lock splitting the jamb as they flung open. Rus propped his weapon's stock against his shoulder and, taking a cautious yet aggressive stance, moved into the darkened tavern with Tailynn following at a reasonable distance.

It took a moment for the pair's vision to adapt to the tavern's dark interior, but Rus scanned the main bar area with his weapon quickly. The room reeked of ale and tobacco and Tailynn could also smell the sweet remnants of a mild narcotic called Fantasia which had become quite popular in the badlands. The drug was not exactly legal, but neither was it strictly illegal. Still, Tailynn hoped that Rus was too focused on his current assignment for it to concern him.

Rus looked at Tailynn for directions. She pointed up the stairs, and Rus again led the way, his weapon constantly scanning for a target. They slowly climbed the wooden stairs. At the top they reached a long hallway with a trio of doors lining the walls either side, and a seventh at the end of the hallway.

Tailynn immediately noticed what appeared to be a body midway down the hall. From the figure's size, she was reasonably certain that it was Darris, the tavern's owner and operator. She hadn't been expecting that. Breathing heavily, she decided to withdraw her pulse pistol. Just as a precaution.

Rus led her towards Darris and upon reaching the big man,

Tailynn bent down and checked his pulse. Still there. She looked up at Rus.

'Unconscious, not dead,' she whispered.

He nodded and then indicated the first doorway back down the hall. They quickly moved back to it and one by one checked each room. Galatea Loc's room was the first one. Tailynn knew the bar-girl reasonably well through Jett, who was a mutual acquaintance. Tailynn was surprised to find the young woman's room empty.

The room across the hallway was a guest room, but it looked as though no-one had stayed there in some time. The next two rooms were a supply closet and a bathroom respectively, both of which were empty. Darris' room was next which was, understandably, empty as well. As they exited the room, Darris' limp form let out a groan and Tailynn bent down to check him over again.

'Leave him,' Rus hissed.

Tailynn stood, doing as she was told, even though the Judge's orders grated on her. She was an Advocate – it was her *job* to help people. She was uncertain of the extent of Darris' injuries, but in her opinion they should have been seeing to him before resuming their search for Dresden. Rus, however was focused to the point of being single minded. She reluctantly did as he instructed, and followed him to the next door.

The room they entered had evidently been the one Jonas Dresden had boarded in. The bed was unmade, and the room's small sink trickled water, the room's occupant having failed to turn the tap off properly. There was no way to tell how long it had been since Dresden had been in the room, however.

The pair exited the room and turned their attention to the last door at the end of the hallway. Rus approached it with haste and flung it open, letting his weapon lead him in, the need for cautious approach abandoned. The room was Darris' herb garden, and the air was moist and heavy. With horror, Tailynn noticed a number of plants growing in pots with bright blue flowers – Sapphire Jahara's, the plant and flower from which fantasia was extracted. While it may have been a bit of a grey area as to the legality of the drug itself, the Sapphire Jahara had been outlawed years ago by the council of Adjutants, when it became clear to the Redeemer faction that the plant had been engineered by the Technos. Possession of the plant was strictly illegal.

Judge Rus, however didn't seem to notice the plants. His attention was fixated on a door leading to a small patio. He spoke into a small communicator attached to the cuff of his left arm.

'Squad B, converge on the western face of the target structure,' he ordered his Advocates. 'Our target has escaped the tavern. I want an outward sweep of the adjacent buildings.'

The big Judge turned and strode back to the hallway, with Tailynn following immediately. She saw Darris struggling to stand up, having regained consciousness. She darted ahead and helped him to his feet.

'Darris Ban, it's Advocate Sar,' she said. 'Are you alright?'

The man seemed to be dazed, but otherwise unharmed.

'I'm fine,' he grunted in reply.

'Who did this to you?' she asked.

He looked at her with an angry expression.

'That out-of-towner. Dresden or whatever the hell his name is,' he answered. After a moment, he added: 'Gala and that dumb-ass Jett were with him.'

Tailynn's blood turned cold, and she sighed in annoyance. *Hope-damn it, Jett!* she thought. *Why did you have to get yourself involved?* Rus gave her a curious expression.

'You know the people he mentioned?' he asked. Tailynn nodded.

'Galatea Loc is the bartender of this establishment. Jett Dor is a local Bounty Hunter.' Rus narrowed his eyes as she spoke, evidently more attuned to human nuances than Tailynn had given him credit for.

'You are close with this Jett Dor?'

Tailynn nodded reluctantly.

'Yeah, we go way back,' she admitted.

Rus stared at her momentarily, and she knew that the Judge was assessing her competence then and there. Her instincts told her that he didn't trust her any more than she trusted him. His mouth curved in a vicious grin, and she heard the sound of his weapon shifting into its blade form. She looked down and watched as the gun-blade shifted its parts until rather than the pulse rifle it had been mere seconds prior, it had quickly become a large, gleaming broadsword with a complicated mechanical hilt and a long, slightly curved blade. Tailynn's mind raced, and she gripped her pulse pistol tight. She knew instinctively that the Judge was about to do something bad. She looked up and realised that he'd turned his attention back to the big bartender.

'You are the owner of this establishment?' Rus asked, his tone menacing enough that even Darris appeared cautious. After a moment, Darris nodded. 'Are you also aware that a number of years ago, the council of Adjutants declared it forbidden to grow or maintain the plant Sapphire Jahara?'

Darris' breathing became erratic. He knew he'd been caught red-handed. He stuttered as he replied to Rus with what Tailynn *knew* to be an outright lie.

'I... It wasn't me,' he stammered. 'She... she grew them, so she could sell fantasia to my customers. Gala. They're Gala's.'

Rus let out a deep laugh, which seemed to boom through the hallway. Tailynn again gripped her pistol tightly, uneasy at the situation. Rus' laughter died down, until his face had become twisted in a look of disgust.

'Such a big man, yet such a lack of courage,' he hissed. 'I despise cowards.'

He lifted his blade, and slashed across Darris' torso. The big man let out a cry, but was dead before he hit the floor, the Judge's blade having sliced a two inch gash into his body from his shoulder to his waist.

Tailynn's pulse pistol was suddenly in her hands, pointed at the Judge.

'Drop the weapon!' she screamed at him.

He turned to her with an amused expression on his face.

'You are overstepping your bounds, Advocate Sar,' he said, menacingly.

'And you just murdered a man in cold blood!' she hissed back. 'You may be a Judge, but you don't have the right to kill an unarmed man who should have stood trial for his crimes!'

'That is where you are wrong, Advocate,' he replied, his voice dripping with contempt. 'I answer only to the Lord Adjutant, which means as far as you and *anyone* else is concerned, my word is law.'

Tailynn breathed heavily as the Judge's gun-blade retracted back into its rifle form. She hadn't lowered her own weapon; it was still pointed directly at Rus' head, but she knew she'd made an error in judgement by threatening the Judge... a potentially fatal one. She wasn't going to shoot the man, and she was sure he was well aware of that fact. Rus clipped his weapon back onto his belt, and then turned and walked back down the hallway to re-group with his Advocates. He left her with one last serpentine grin as he disappeared down the stairs.

Tailynn lowered her pistol and ran a hand through her hair, trying to think desperately of what she should do. She'd just made an enemy of the most dangerous Judge on Eden, she was sure of that. She doubted after what had happened that she'd be an Advocate much longer, but one thing was certain – she had to know what it was that Dresden had done to warrant being chased by a Judge and an Advocate strike team. She strode back towards the herb garden, intent on finding an alternate route out of the building. She'd find Dresden and question him. Tailynn had always trusted her instincts in her work as an Advocate and her instincts told her that Dresden was not a bad man. If she had indeed burnt her bridges with the Advocates, then she had to have answers.

And if she found Dresden, then she would find Jett, and she could give him the whack across the head that he deserved.

Nine

Jonas peered out the door of Advocate Sar's office, looking towards the street where the three Advocate dusters were landed. What better place to hide than the one place the Advocates would never think to search? Jett, however was of a different opinion, believing Jonas' plan reckless.

'This is crazy, Jonas!' the man hissed in a whisper.

Jonas shushed him quiet. He was waiting for the Advocates that were guarding the dusters to be drawn away, but they stubbornly obeyed their instructions to the letter and did not budge from the landing perimeter.

'We need a distraction,' he muttered.

'Can't we just circle around them and emerge at the far end of town?' Gala asked, nervously.

'Too time consuming,' Jonas replied. 'By the time we're on the outskirts, they'll have already expanded their perimeter, and we'll have nowhere to go. It's straight through the middle or nothing.'

He closed the door, and took a deep breath, mentally examining their options. Sar's office was a good place to hide short term, but eventually the local Advocate, maybe even the Judge would use the place to regroup when they inevitably failed to locate Jonas. They really needed to get to the other side of Port Usharin's main street, but the three dusters, guarded by a squad of Advocates proved far too much of a risk for such an attempt. They could try to create a distraction, but that would require splitting up, and Jonas wasn't entirely comfortable with Jett's level of sobriety to allow that.

The office door opened.

Simultaneously, both Jonas and Jett whipped out their pistols, as Gala went scrambling back from the door. The entering figure stopped in their tracks as they realised in shock that they had two pulse pistols pointed at their head, only centimetres away.

Tailynn Sar slowly raised her hands in the air as she absorbed the situation. Out of his peripheral vision, Jonas saw Jett lower his gun. His own didn't waver.

'Tailynn?' Jett exclaimed.

'Shut up, Jett!' Jonas hissed in a whisper. His attention never wavered from the blonde, uniformed woman. He continued in the same urgent whisper. 'Advocate Sar, close the door quietly behind you, and enter the office.'

Sar did as she was told, seemingly careful not to antagonise Jonas. Once the door was closed, she turned back to him.

'They're looking for you,' she stated, matter-of-factly.

'I know,' Jonas replied. 'Whatever it is they say I've done, it's not true.'

'That's just it,' Sar replied. 'Judge Rus refuses to say why they're after you.' She paused momentarily, and Jonas could tell she was torn as to whom to trust. 'I have to say, having a gun shoved in my face isn't exactly filling me with a desire to hear your side of the story.'

'Your saying I should trust you? You're an Advocate,' Jonas replied. 'Just like the people outside with the big guns, who are looking for me. As if I can allow myself to trust you.'

Sar looked at Jett momentarily before peering back at Jonas.

'I doubt I'll be an Advocate for much longer,' she said.

Jett took a step towards her, a frown on his face. 'Why,' he asked. 'What happened?'

It was only now that Jonas realised how shaken Sar was – and he didn't think it was because of the gun he still pointed at her. Something had happened that had turned her world upside-down and had made her question her convictions. Jonas was impressed that she'd been able to maintain such composure; it was perhaps that precise moment when he decided she was a person of honour – a person he *could* in fact trust, regardless of what he had just told her.

'Judge Rus,' Sar began. 'He killed Darris.'

Gala stepped forward in shock.

'What?' She asked. 'Darris is... dead?'

'I'm sorry, Galatea,' Sar replied. 'Rus discovered Darris' little plantation of Sapphire Jahara, immediately declared him guilty and executed him without blinking. That's why I'm here now.'

She explained what had happened afterwards.

'You pointed a gun at a *Judge?*' Jett exclaimed, shocked. 'I thought you always claimed to be the smart one!'

'Judge Rus murdered a man,' Sar replied. 'I don't care what his motivations were. Darris deserved a fair trial.'

Galatea had sat down on the floor and was sobbing. Jonas's heart went out to her. He lowered his gun and crouched down beside her, placing a hand on her back comfortingly.

'I'm sorry,' Jonas said quietly. Gala sniffed loudly.

'I don't know why I'm crying,' she said. 'Darris made my life hell most of the times. I guess now I don't have to lock my door at night.'

Jonas rubbed her back once more and then stood. He didn't have the heart to tell her that if things happened the way he though they would, she'd never be sleeping in the tavern again. He turned towards the Advocate.

'It would seem that we all share the same goal,' he stated.

Sar nodded firmly. 'Indeed. What was your plan?'

'We were going to try to make it to the transport depot,' Jett said.

'Not a bad idea,' she replied with a nod. 'We'd have to get past the squad of Advocates at the dusters first, though.'

'Yeah, that's what we were discussing before you scared the shit out of us,' Jett replied. He turned to Jonas. 'You were talking distractions?'

Even with an extra member added to their little group, Jonas still wasn't comfortable splitting up. He was certain, however, that a distraction would be their best possible chance for their escape. He turned to Jett.

'Are there any vacant buildings in town close to our position?' he asked the bounty-hunter, as Sar moved over to the office's door and opened it, peering out carefully.

'Nothing exactly vacant,' Jett replied.

Out of the corner of his eye, Jonas saw Sar close the door hurriedly. He turned his attention to her. 'What is it?'

Her eyes were wide with fear as she motioned towards the back of the offices, back where the small cell was.

'Get out the back!' she hissed. 'Judge Rus is coming!'

Gala sprung to her feet and Jett grabbed the young woman by the arm, directing her down the small hallway. Jonas however, remained planted and staring at Sar, a hint of uncertainty clouding his judgement.

'Trust me!' she whispered pleadingly.

After another split second, Jonas decided he didn't have a choice. He followed Jett and Gala, rushing to the back cell. Jett opened the heavy door, careful to flick the locking mechanism to ensure their ability to escape the room if need be. As the cell door closed behind them, they heard the front door of the Advocate's office open, listening as a booted figure came striding in. Jonas risked peering through the small barred window that was centred on the cell door and looked down the hallway. He could see Sar in front of the huge Judge, standing her ground. He could also see at least two more armoured Advocates beside Rus.

'Dresden is nowhere to be found,' the Judge's voice boomed.

'Perhaps he fled Port Usharin during the night,' Sar replied. 'He could theoretically have made it to one of the mines, or a transport depot.'

'Yes,' the Judge's voice hissed. 'And perhaps you helped him flee.'

Inside the cell, Jett tugged at Jonas's arm urgently. 'We have to help her!' he hissed, almost silently. Jonas nodded and withdrew his pistol, as Jett did the same. He held up three fingers to Jett, indicating the number of opponents in the office. Jett nodded.

'I did nothing of the sort,' Sar replied to Judge Rus. 'I am an Advocate, Judge. I know my duties.'

Rus laughed a harsh laugh.

'You are not an Advocate!' he proclaimed. 'The moment you drew your weapon on a Judge, was the moment you resigned your position.'

Jett made to exit the cell, but Jonas stopped him. 'Not yet,' he mouthed. Jett's anxiety regarding Sar's situation was evident.

'I am hereby placing you in custody, *former* Advocate Sar,' Rus said. Sar scoffed at the man, trying to prove herself unintimidated.

'On what charge?' She spat back at him.

'Dereliction of duty, and intent to disobey a direct order,' the Judge replied. 'On your knees.'

Jonas watched as the Judge relieved Sar of her side-arm and pointed it at her head as she defied his order to kneel. Jonas willed her to do as she was told.

'Give me a reason,' Judge Rus said quietly, a serpentine grin on his face.

Reluctantly Sar did as she was told, and kneeled on the ground. Satisfied with himself, Rus grunted a laugh and turned his back to her. He motioned to the two Advocates with him.

'Take her into custody,' he ordered.

It was time to act. Jonas motioned for Gala to stay put. The young woman nodded, and Jonas turned to Jett. The bounty-hunter gave a slight nod, and Jonas moved to the door. As quietly as possible, he turned the handle and flung the door open. He and Jett barrelled out the cell door and down the hall.

Jonas didn't hesitate. He fired a single shot at one of the Advocates, knowing somehow to aim for their neck, which was the weakest point of their armour. The energy bolt blasted through the man's protection and killed him instantly. Jett didn't hesitate in following suit, and took down the second Advocate just as quickly.

As the two Advocates dropped to the floor, they took up position either side of Sar, their weapons pointed directly at Judge Rus's head.

'Move and you're dead,' Jett said.

The huge Judge immediately defied him, and turned to face them. Jonas was surprised to see a vicious grin plastered across the big man's face. Sar reached forwards and relieved him of her own weapon.

'Jonas Dresden, I presume,' he said slowly.

'You presume?' Jonas asked in surprise. 'You don't know your own quarry?'

The Judge remained silent. How long did they have before the other Advocates came looking for their leader? He needed to formulate a plan of escape, but he also realised that this might be his first real chance to get some answers; he couldn't pass up the opportunity to potentially discover the reason for his memory loss, not to mention why he was being hunted by a Judge.

'On your knees,' Jonas ordered. When the man didn't respond, he turned to Jett and nodded. Jett, still pointing his gun at the Judge, moved around him, and kicked Rus in the back of the legs, forcing him to the ground. Rus's gun-blade fell from his belt, and Jett kicked it away from the man's grasp. Jonas continued his questioning. 'I want answers. Why are you after me?'

Judge Rus just stared at him, silently defiant. By now, Galatea had emerged from the cell and had come to stand by Jonas, using his proximity as a comfort mechanism.

'Answer me!' Jonas hissed. 'What have I done to become of interest to the Redeemers?'

'You can torture me, and still I will not answer,' Rus replied, a firmness in his voice convincing Jonas that he was telling the absolute truth. 'My oath to the Redeemers means more to me than pain, or the threat of death.'

Jonas sighed angrily and at the exact same moment, something clicked in his head. It was as though an outside influence had entered his head and was now pulsing a warning directly into his brain. It wasn't painful, rather a bit of a shock, as it had not been something he'd been expecting. It took him a moment to compose himself, and Gala looked at him with concern.

'What is it?' she asked in a whisper.

'We've got to get out of here,' he replied, so certain of that fact, yet unable to articulate why he was so certain.

'Why?' Tailynn asked in surprise.

'And what are we supposed to do with him?' Jett added, motioning towards Judge Rus.

'It doesn't matter,' Jonas said, his desperation growing. 'The Judge is of no significance. A far greater enemy is closer. I think we're about to get our distraction.'

It was at that moment, that the small undetectable craft that had been approaching Port Usharin opened fire on the Advocate Dusters.

Ten

Zesiro watched from a rooftop on the outskirts of Port Usharin as the *Zenith of Desire* entered Eden's low-lying atmosphere and opened fire on the Advocate dusters. A visible red beam shot from the bow of the small vessel and hit the nearest duster – nevertheless intense enough to cook a pre-human alive, the red beam was but a targeting primer, and was not powerful enough to damage the dusters on its own. Zesiro watched as a condensed burst of energy shot from the *Zenith,* down along the beam and destroyed the armoured duster in a single blast. The nearby Advocates who had been assigned to maintain the landing perimeter were thrown away from the intense burst, their armour smouldering. He watched as they all stood, more or less intact, and looked to the sky in desperate search of a target.

The *Zenith* was in full stealth mode, and Zesiro knew the Redeemer troops would not be able to destroy it, even if they could see it. The on-board construct had its orders, and it would fulfil them with the utmost efficiency before withdrawing to planetary orbit.

The small Morphite vessel came in on another attack run, targeting a second duster. As soon as the red beam struck the atmospheric vessel, the nearby Advocates wisely chose to retreat to the false safety of nearby structures. A couple of the Redeemer law enforcers fired off random energy bolts into the sky, but none came close to Zesiro's personal ship, nor would they have done any damage even if they had hit their marks.

As the Advocates retreated in an attempt to regroup against the invisible attacker, Zesiro took the opportunity to move. Remaining in his pre-human form, he dived off the rooftop and landed on the dusty ground between two structures. His attack on the Redeemer forces was an attempt to lure his prey out from whatever hole he was hiding in. He knew that Jonas was no fool – he'd been chasing the man far too long to underestimate him – but by attacking the Advocate strike team, he was goading them into burning the entire town to the ground, a tactic the Judges (especially Rus) had never shied away from before. Jonas would have no choice but to attempt escape.

The *Zenith's* construct contacted him mentally to advise that its task was complete. Two of the three Advocate dusters had been destroyed, and now the intelligent ship was returning to a holding orbit above Eden.

Zesiro moved out into the street.

Port Usharin was eerily quiet, the only sound emanating from the burning wreckage of the two dusters, and the occasional cry of a terrified townsperson. Zesiro strode down the dusty main street, in full view of anyone who may have been watching. Two armoured Advocates emerged from their hiding place beside the Tavern and challenged him. Zesiro ignored them and continued walking towards the dusters. The Advocates opened fire, one using a projectile rifle set to automatic, the second using a semi-automatic energy pulse rifle. Zesiro had already activated his personal armouring – a force-field barrier which covered his entire body – and the energy bolts absorbed harmlessly into the invisible energy field, while the bullets from the projectile weapon shattered into millions of pieces upon impact. The two Advocates, confused at their weapons' ineffectiveness yelled for him to halt, then continued shooting when they realised their instructions were being ignored.

As he neared the remaining duster, more Advocates emerged onto the street until Zesiro found himself surrounded. He stopped in his tracks and looked around at what remained of the strike team. They all pointed their assault weaponry at him, but he was secure in the knowledge that there was nothing on Eden (with the possible exception of some of the Technos' salvaged machinery) that could ever come close to penetrating his invisible armour. One of the Advocates yelled for him to get to his knees. After a few moments, when Zesiro had not complied, the Advocate yelled for his comrades to open fire. A combination of projectiles and energy bolts slammed into him to no effect.

'Cease fire!' yelled a booming voice.

The Advocates complied immediately, and Zesiro turned to see the huge Judge he had met in the Lord Adjutant's office, Drealon Rus, striding towards them. He stopped a couple of meters in front of Zesiro, a look of barely concealed rage on his face. He was smart enough to lower his voice so the members of the Advocate strike-team could not hear their conversation, however.

'You did this,' he hissed, accusingly.

'I did,' Zesiro replied, matter-of-factly. 'Your men require incentive.'

'You may be a Morphite, but alien or no, I don't suffer fools,' Rus said angrily. 'I was just about to take Dresden into custody when *you* gave him the distraction he needed to make his escape. What possible incentive could destroying our only means of transport bring, anyway?'

'Dresden is near,' Zesiro replied. 'I know that for a fact. He has not yet escaped the town. Burn the buildings, slaughter the residents. I know you were only looking for an excuse to do so and I have now given you one. Dresden will emerge in a misguided attempt to save these so called innocent people.'

Rus thought that over, and Zesiro knew immediately he could see the logic in it. It was more than logic though – the big man was excited at the prospect. The Judge's blood-lust sickened Zesiro to the core. Where Zesiro himself used such tactics as a means to an end, taking no joy in the actions (even if they *were* just pre-humans), Drealon Rus *enjoyed* slaughtering his own kind. It was because of people like Rus that the pre-humans of Eden would never gain the redemption they sought (or so they claimed) from the Morphites.

'I bow to your superior wisdom,' Rus replied eventually, although Zesiro was not so ignorant to miss the sarcasm in the big man's tone. Rus turned to his men. 'The town's people have evidently risen up against the Redeemer faction,' he announced in a loud voice. 'Burn the buildings to the ground; execute all residents for obstruction of justice.'

Even though their faces were covered by armoured helmets, Zesiro could tell that the Advocates were giving each other uncomfortable looks. One brave (or foolhardy) Advocate stepped forward.

'Judge Rus, I believe it to be an error of assumption that the residents of Port Usharin are responsible for the destruction of the dusters,' he said, his voice distorted through the helmet. 'The weapons used... I have never witnessed such fire-power before. My only guess is that the attackers were Technos, utilizing scavenged technology.'

'You are correct,' Rus replied to the Advocate. 'The Technos are indeed responsible, but they have only attacked us because the residents of Port Usharin have allied themselves with the heathens. The residents of this town are traitors to the Redeemers.'

Zesiro had to admit that he was impressed with Judge Rus' ability to adapt to a situation on the fly – and in his ability to lie. His men accepted Rus's explanation, completely satisfied with his reasoning. Zesiro turned back to the big man as the Advocates sprung to action.

'Where did you last see Dresden?' he asked.

'The local Advocate's office,' Rus replied. 'He has already established a small group of followers, and they are armed.'

'Yes,' Zesiro began. 'Jonas is very good at that. He inspires confidence in people. He is a born leader.'

'Who is Jonas Dresden?' Rus asked, his curiosity finally getting the better of him. 'You speak as though he is not from Eden. Is he too a Morphite?'

Zesiro decided to indulge the man. In a moment of weakness, he felt sorrow for the pre-humans and their inherent ignorance. But then he remembered the city of Avoca, and the disgust he felt towards its residents, and he knew he could never truly feel pity or sorrow for any of them. The fact was that the pre-humans only had themselves to blame for the ignorance and tyranny that corrupted Eden.

Still, he chose to indulge Judge Rus – at least a little bit.

'No, Dresden is not a Morphite,' he replied. 'But you are correct in a way.'

'Then what…'

'Enough questions, Judge Rus,' Zesiro said, interrupting the big man. 'Concentrate on the job at hand. Burn the buildings, kill the residents. Flush Jonas *out!*'

Rus smiled his vicious smile.

'There won't be a heart left beating.'

Eleven

Jonas, accompanied by Jett, Gala and Tailynn Sar moved quietly through the back-alleys of Port Usharin. Small gaps between the dusty buildings meant that they had to travel single file most of the time, with Sar leading the way, and Jonas and Jett taking up the rear. The mental warning that had alerted Jonas still pulsed in his head, but the initial shock of it had worn off as he had become accustomed to it, although what it was he still had no idea. He tried to rack his memory for anything, but there was still nothing but a blankness that he was finding more and more disconcerting. He had his instincts still, and thus far they had served him well. But the warning in his head was far from instinct and he was really beginning to wonder who the hell he was to have acquired such an ability. The memory loss was once again proving to be a liability – he wasn't sure who it was he was fleeing from, and who could be a greater danger to him and his little group than the fearsome Redeemer Judge, who he had insisted they leave behind in Sar's office. He was careful not to allow himself the luxury of dwelling on his failed memory, however. *First things first*, he thought. *Get to safety.*

Sar had managed to lead them to the outskirts of the town, having used the surprise attack on the Advocate Dusters as the distraction they'd needed to escape. She stopped the group at the edge of the building, still well covered from any of the Advocates who were bound to be still searching for them. Especially now, after they had killed two of their comrades.

At the edge of the building, the dusty, lifeless landscape dropped away from the town's perimeter, gently sloping down into the valley beyond. They could see kilometres of terrain from their position, and dotted across it was the occasional structure or automated vehicle. From the hill they had a superb view of the Pandora Nebula hanging in the sky, all deep blues and contrasting reds which blended together to form swirls of purple. Sar pointed to a small group of structures that sat down in the middle of the small valley.

'That's the transport depot,' she said. 'It's about a kilometre away. There should be plenty of vehicles there.'

'And a lot of open space,' Jonas pointed out. 'If that remaining Duster takes to the air, they won't have much of a challenge spotting us.'

There was a scream some way behind them, a woman. The scream was long and blood-curdling, and it ended abruptly. The group of four turned back towards the town, just as a second scream sounded, followed closely by a third. They could see a cloud of dark smoke rising from a building.

'What's going on?' Gala asked, the fear prevalent in her voice.

'Another attack?' Jett wondered out loud. 'Who was it that attacked those Dusters, anyway?'

Jonas snuck back down between the two buildings, until he had a view of one of the town's secondary thoroughfares. He watched as an Advocate dragged a ragged looking woman out of a structure by her hair. A second Advocate emerged from the structure, tossing a flare back through the open door. Fire took hold immediately, and the structure started to burn, the intensity of the bright flames indicating that the building's insides had been doused with an accelerant. As the first Advocate struggled with the hysterical woman, the second approached and levelled his rifle at her. Without even hesitating, the Advocate pulled the trigger and the woman's head exploded, a projectile spewing blood and brain matter all over the dirty ground.

Jonas cursed silently, and retreated back to his little group.

'What's going on?' Sar asked anxiously.

'The Advocates are burning down the town, executing the population,' he replied, matter-of-factly.

'What?' Jett exclaimed. Gala let out a cry of disbelief.

'We have to do something!' Sar said, forcefully. 'This isn't right. The people of Port Usharin are innocent bystanders.'

'I know,' Jonas replied quietly.

'What can we do?' Jett asked dismissively. 'There's thirteen more Advocates out there, Tailynn, not to mention the Judge. And hope only knows who the hell that guy talking to Rus was. It'd be suicide to return.'

'We can't just save ourselves and do nothing to help!' Gala exclaimed. 'Those people are being murdered out there!'

'You're right, we can't do nothing,' Jett replied. 'But we should be using this as an opportunity to escape! This is the perfect chance.'

'Oh please, Jett,' Sar scoffed. 'Even you can't be so callous as to allow all these people to be sacrificed simply to allow our escape!'

The problem was, Jonas reflected, was that both Sar *and* Jett were right. It would indeed be suicide to return to the burning town in an attempt to stop the Redeemer sponsored massacre. But how could he ever sleep at night knowing the sacrifice that had been made to allow his escape? Despite the fact that he had no recollection of who he was, he *knew* that he'd never been the kind of man that would allow the mass-murder of civilians to go unanswered. He turned to the others.

'Jett, Gala,' he began. 'You're heading to the depot. Advocate Sar and I will do what we can here.' Jett was about to argue, but Jonas raised a hand to silence him. 'If we have any chance of survival, then we need a way out of here. And I can't send Gala on her own.'

Jett conceded the point with a curt nod. 'And once we reach the depot?'

Jonas turned to look down the valley again, assessing each of the structures he could see from their high-point. He pointed to a small one that sat on the hill leading down to the valley, about a third of the way to the depot.

'Bring whatever vehicle you find back to that structure. Hide it and yourselves in there. Wait two hours from now – if we're not there by then, chances are we'll be dead. Oh, and make sure you get the fastest vehicle you can.'

'And if the Judge sends Advocates to that structure?' Jett asked.

'The bulk of the strike-team will remain in the town,' Tailynn interjected. 'If Rus sends anyone it'll be two Advocates at the most. Use the element of surprise and take them out.'

'And you're okay with me taking out two Advocates?' Jett asked quietly.

'They're not Advocates anymore,' Sar replied firmly, 'they're murderers.'

Jett nodded, and grabbed Gala by the arm, dragging her with him. Gala gave Jonas a desperate look.

'Please don't die,' she said, to both him and Sar.

Jonas nodded, and then motioned for them to go. She and Jett ran off down the hill, using rocky outcrops where they could as cover. Jonas turned to Sar as he withdrew his borrowed pulse pistol.

'You ready?' he asked.

Sar nodded confidently, and withdrew her own pistol. Jonas led the way, weaving a route back through the town's buildings. They emerged on the secondary thoroughfare where Jonas had witnessed the civilian woman being murdered. Her disfigured body lay limply in the middle of the street. He noticed the expression on Sar's face harden as she saw the body.

Further down the street, another two Advocates had rounded up a family: a man, woman and two young boys. The children were crying, while the woman was pleading with the Advocates to spare their lives. One of the Advocates knocked her on the back of the head with the butt of his rifle, and she fell to the ground with a cry. The man yelled in anger, and grabbed the weapon of the other Advocate. He was unable to snatch the rifle, however, and the two wrestled over it momentarily. Jonas and Sar rushed over as the first Advocate raised his weapon towards the man. Jonas raised his pistol and fired, hitting his target in the abdomen. The Advocate's armour absorbed the brunt of the shot, but the man still fell to the ground in pain, his grip on the rifle faltering. The weapon fell to the ground. The second Advocate was still wrestling with the man as Sar rushed over and pointed her pistol at the base of his neck, as Jonas's gun remained trained on the first.

'Let go of the weapon,' Sar said, quietly, but forcibly. The Advocate, startled at the newcomers, did as he was instructed. The father of the family snatched the rifle away from him. Jonas addressed him.

'Take the gun, protect your family,' he instructed. 'Get them the hell away from Port Usharin.'

The man nodded thanks, as he helped his wife to her feet, and rounded up his crying children. They fled between two buildings, heading towards the valley that Jett and Gala were traversing.

'What do we do with these two?' Sar asked.

Jonas didn't hesitate. He pulled the trigger of his pulse pistol, and killed the Advocate at point blank range. Sar gasped, but Jonas didn't stop. He walked over to the second Advocate, who was desperately pleading for his life, and executed him.

'What are you doing?' Sar exclaimed. 'They were unarmed!'

'They were liabilities,' Jonas replied, mildly surprised at his own lack of remorse at the death of two individuals by his hand. 'If we're to survive this, then we cannot take prisoners.' His firm tone relaxed momentarily. 'I realise this is hard for you. And I realise that you've probably never killed before...'

Sar's eyes flared at what she evidently took to be Jonas' patronisation.

'I have killed before,' Sar replied in a quiet, yet firm voice. Jonas instinctively knew that she was telling the truth and that whatever event in her past had forced her to kill another human being still haunted her to this day. She continued: 'We cannot just murder these men, though! How does that make us any better than Rus?'

'It's not murder; these men were combatants,' Jonas replied calmly. 'Not only that, they're killing civilians. They were going to execute that family if we hadn't intervened. The father, the mother *and* the children. Those people *weren't* combatants. We can't hesitate, Tailynn.'

Sar knew he was right, but Jonas could tell she didn't like it. Until an hour ago, these men had been her comrades. She gave him a curt nod and Jonas motioned towards an unburnt building which had the door wide open. As Sar began to stride towards the structure Jonas bent down and retrieved the weapon of the Advocate who lay dead at his feet, before following her.

The building was empty and Jonas led Sar to the top floor, peering out of a small, grubby window in a vacant bedroom. The window looked out across the main street of the town. The two destroyed dusters lay in the middle of the road, still smouldering, while a single Advocate guarded the remaining Duster. Peering down the street, Jonas could see the remaining Advocates storming into buildings. Judge Rus stood in the middle of the street, barking orders. The mysterious man he had been talking to after Jonas and his people had escaped Sar's office was conspicuously absent. Jonas watched as the Advocates dragged another couple out of a building; an older woman and a man that Jonas recognised from the tavern when he had first visited it. The woman was screaming, hissing, biting, while the man was quiet, perhaps still drunk from the previous night spent at the tavern. The couple were dragged over to Judge Rus, who withdrew his gun-blade, flicked it into blade-mode and struck them both down stoically. Even from a distance Jonas could tell from the man's body language how much he had enjoyed the task.

Sar looked at Jonas with an urgent expression. He knew how desperate the woman was to stop this massacre, however he was also acutely aware of the fact that the Advocates both severely outnumbered, and out-gunned them. Jonas made a snap decision.

'We have to assault Rus head on,' he said. 'It will draw the attention of the other Advocates and take the pressure off the town's people. If we can hold our own long enough, a few of them might be able to slip away to safety.'

'We'd be sacrificing ourselves,' Sar replied quietly.

'Our odds of survival wouldn't be high,' Jonas admitted. 'But they never were to begin with.'

Sar hefted her pistol and gave Jonas a curt nod, accompanied by a firm look. Jonas knew that she still felt she had a duty to fulfil, having been Port Usharin's Advocate. Jonas checked the rifle he had acquired from the dead Advocates and hefted it. More than enough ammunition.

'Let's move,' he said.

The duo snuck down beside one of the buildings and cut into a narrow walkway that ran between it and a second structure. Jonas glanced at a broken window and when he saw his own reflection in it realised that this was where he had first woken up, coming to terms with the fact he had no memory. It occurred to him that if he had never woken here, then there'd be a lot fewer dead bodies scattered throughout the streets of Port Usharin.

Forcing this unsettling thought out of his mind, he led Sar down the walkway and paused at the point before the town's main street opened up before him. Across the street, a building burned, its bright flames emitting a searing heat that he could feel from a distance of fifty meters – no doubt somebody's home. He peered around the edge of one building, trying to spot the Judge and his lackeys. They'd moved further down the street and a number of Advocates were storming another residence while Rus barked orders, his back turned to Jonas. The guard who had been posted by the Duster had been called down to assist in the massacre. Jonas recognised the tactical error made by Rus instantly – the big man had grouped his forces, put all of his eggs in the one basket as it were.

This was it.

Jonas gave a quick nod towards Sar, and then strode out onto the street, his commandeered assault rifle leading the way. A couple of Advocates emerged from an alley way nearby, and Jonas fired a single shot at each of them, dispatching them instantly. Rus had ignored the two gun shots, evidently assuming that they had come from his own men. Jonas and Sar closed on the Judge, and from a distance of roughly seventy-five meters, he opened fire in full-automatic mode. A large number of the metallic projectiles went wide of Jonas's target, but a fair amount peppered into Judge Rus's back. The huge man fell to the ground with a yell of surprise. As Jonas continued to stride towards his target, two more Advocates emerged from a nearby building and Sar dispatched them with a barrage of energy pulse fire from her pistol. Jonas ceased firing, however he did not take his attention off Rus's seemingly limp form that was lying face down in the dusty street. He trusted Sar to cover him from other threats while he focused on the primary target. Another Advocate emerged from a building, firing his energy-pulse assault rifle wildly. All of the shots missed their targets, and Sar finished him off with a well placed shot to the throat.

Apart from the Judge and his mysterious companion, there were only a handfull of remaining Advocates – five at Jonas's count – and they had a fair idea of which building they were in; a small house a few structures up from the Tavern. Sar covered the building carefully, while Jonas closed in on the judge. As Jonas closed to within twenty meters of the body, the Judge began to stir. Jonas realised that the man's heavy armour had held against his barrage. The Judge groaned and got to his feet, turning to face Jonas. His gun-blade was still attached to his belt, but he evidently realised the futility of making a grab for it while Jonas pointed a rifle at his head, finger on the trigger. Jonas stopped about ten meters away.

'You've gone too far, Dresden,' Rus growled.

'Says the man who just slaughtered half the innocent population of a town,' Jonas replied.

Rus grunted a laugh. 'There is no such thing as innocence.'

Two of the remaining Advocates burst out of the building behind

Rus, and were quickly dispatched by Sar who had been waiting for them. Their bodies fell limply to the ground. Sar took the opportunity to acquire her own rifle, tucking her Advocate service pistol into the holster strapped to her belt. Jonas's attention had not wavered from the big Judge.

'What are you going to do? Execute me?' Rus wondered aloud. 'You would kill a Redeemer Judge in cold blood?'

'Yep,' Jonas answered simply.

He fired a single projectile at Rus's head, and it was as though he was seeing things in slow motion: the bullet left his weapon, travelled the distance between the barrel and Rus's face, and then shattered into a million pieces ten centimetres from its target. Belatedly, Jonas realised that the mental warning that had alerted him earlier, was now blaring within the confines of his head, more urgent than it had ever been. Rus had not flinched, but he had not been expecting this turn of events either. As Jonas frowned in surprise, Rus's face twisted in a grin of understanding.

In his peripheral vision, Jonas saw a figure move. He allowed his attention to be drawn momentarily towards the newcomer, as the man they has seen earlier talking with Rus emerged onto the street and strode over to Rus's side.

Jonas's memory flashed, a split second of recognition. He knew the man, he was sure of it. He watched the man curiously, his weapon still pointed at Rus, although he was aware that it was probably useless.

'Hello Jonas,' the man said, his long black hair blowing in a light breeze that had kicked up.

Jonas stared at the man, begging his own memory to reveal more. Sar was anxiously watching on, her weapon flicking between Rus, the newcomer and the building where three Advocates still remained, unsure what was going on.

'I know you,' Jonas said finally.

'Yes, you do,' the man replied, an amused expression on his face. 'You know me quite well, actually. What was it you said to me last time we were in a position to converse? "Know your adversary". Wise words indeed.'

'Who are you?' Jonas asked, desperate for information. The man gave him a surprised look that vanished after a moment when Jonas' situation dawned on him.

'You initiated a memory wipe on yourself,' he said, matter-of-factly. 'Impressive. You have managed to elude me for so long, I knew you were capable of extreme measures, but this is ingenious.'

'Jonas, who the hell is this guy?' Sar asked anxiously.

Jonas didn't have an answer for her. He was certain that he knew the person, but he couldn't remember specifics. The man laughed, and took a step towards Jonas.

'Let me introduce myself,' he began. His body began to ripple, and the man *changed* right in front of them. One second they were staring at an human man of average build, with long dark hair and dark, unassuming clothing. The next, they were staring at a featureless being, entirely hairless, impossibly skinny and completely expressionless. The figure wore plain while clothing. Sar gasped loudly.

'A Morphite,' she whispered in disbelief.

'My name is Zesiro,' the figure said, and then rippled back into its human form. 'And you, Jonas Dresden, are the man I've been chasing for years.'

Both Jonas and Sar stood there unmoving, silent, thrown by this revelation. Rus laughed out loud, and his hand moved down to his gun-blade. He unhooked it from his belt, and, with a press of a button, the weapon shifted itself into blade form.

'Dresden lives,' Zesiro instructed the big Judge. 'But you can kill the Advocate.'

Rus's grin was perhaps the most vile thing Jonas had ever seen. The Judge took a step towards Sar, gripping his blade gleefully.

'Former Advocate,' the big man corrected his ally in what was almost a whisper.

As he strode towards her, Jonas switched the aim of his weapon back from Zesiro, and began spraying bullets towards Rus. Sar was doing the same, stepping backwards as she did so. A hundred bullets were fired and all hundred shattered against the force-field Zesiro had projected around his momentary comrade. Three strides away from Sar, Rus hefted his blade over his head, and Jonas watched in horror has he began his swing.

Out of nowhere, a missile ploughed into the ground a dozen meters away from where the four of them stood, the resulting explosion sending them all flying away from its impact point in the middle of Port Usharin's dusty main street. Jonas rolled on the ground, dazed by the surprise attack. He took a moment to orient himself, and stood. A smoking crater sat directly in front of him, and his gaze lifted to the sky. Half a dozen colourfully painted airships sat in the sky above the town, each with two big rotors attached via struts on either side of the huge central helium bladders and crew decks. The airships were known as Skimmers, due to the fact that they skimmed the edge of Eden's low laying atmosphere and the void of space beyond.

Hurriedly, Jonas darted over to where Sar lay dazed and confused by the explosion. On the edge of his vision he could see Rus struggling to his feet. Zesiro had seemingly disappeared. Jonas grabbed Sar by the hand and hauled her up.

'Quick, we've got to get out of here!' he yelled.

Sar stumbled as Jonas dragged her, leading her towards a building that the Advocates had never gotten around to setting on fire. He barged through the door, and closed it behind them, peering out the window to see if Rus had followed.

'What the hell just happened?' Sar said, still dazed.

Jonas looked into the sky at the colourful skimmers, and grinned.

'The Technos happened.'

Twelve

Rai Ashima stood in the centre of the bridge of her skimmer, what she and her crew had (unofficially) named *The Rust-Bucket*, or *Rusty* for short. She watched as Port Usharin's residents used the Technos attack on the Redeemer forces as a distraction for escape. People littered the side-streets and alleys, running away as fast as they could, fearful that an Advocate, or the Judge himself would be right behind them. She could also see the bodies of the unlucky few who had taken Advocate bullets to the head before the Techno rescue force had arrived. From a height of a hundred and fifty meters above ground level, the bodies looked so small, so... irrelevant. Rai had to remind herself that they had in fact been people. And she wouldn't forget that fact – the Technos, unlike the Redeemers, valued life.

She turned her attention back to the main street of Port Usharin. The Judge had survived the missile that the lead Skimmer – captained by her father, Sid Ashima – had fired, and had managed to take cover. Her crew were using *The Rust-Bucket's* salvaged Morphite scanners to search for their elusive enemy, but the technicians back at Rho's Sacrifice had never been able to reverse-engineer the technology in a way that would garner a true understanding of how it worked, which meant that the scanners were far from completely effective. Every once in a while they detected something moving back along the street, seemingly using the unburned buildings as cover. She assessed the direction the potential target was going and realized their goal almost immediately. She hit a button on the console directly in front of her and a communications channel opened directly to her father on board the Technos lead Skimmer, a grainy, holographic image of him appearing before her.

'Pops, I think I have a target,' she said. 'Looks like he's heading for the remaining duster.'

The older man had a completely bald head, his forehead creased with wrinkles caused by a combination of age and excessive frowning, and wore a typically colourful, yet utilitarian jump-suit.

'Well what are you waiting for?' Sid replied, his gruff, drawling voice filled with excitement, and a little anxiety. 'Take the damn thing out!'

'I'm on it, Pops.' She turned to her crew. 'You heard the man! Full starboard turn, one-eighty degrees. I want *Rusty's* nose pointed directly at that duster! Arm missiles!'

The Skimmers were not the fastest or most manoeuvrable craft on Eden. It took some time for the hulking air-ship to turn and by the time it was pointing in the opposite direction, a number of skimmers had landed in the street and were attempting to round up the fleeing towns people. Simultaneously, a squad of armed Technos had engaged three Advocates who had holed up in one of the buildings, Rai realising that the latter was proving to be the easier of the two tasks. The problem was that the town's people didn't trust Technos any more than they trusted the Advocates who had been slaughtering them. Redeemer propaganda had been most effective at painting the Technos as a rather unsavoury group of renegades – all lies, of course, but the slanderous campaign had proven most effective.

The Techno faction had been formed a few years after the Redeemers had taken ultimate control of Eden. They had formed out of necessity, really – for a decade and a half they had made their living salvaging the technology of the Morphites who had been kicked off the surface of Eden by a large number of the human population. It was of no coincidence that the same portion who had forcibly removed the Morphites from the world had become the Redeemers, and were now using the concept of 'redemption in the eyes of the Morphites' as a way to control the population; the Techno faction had believed all along that kicking the Morphites off Eden had been a well planned move to grab power. Indeed, that ascension to power had affected the Technos more than perhaps any other group on the planet. The first Redeemer law to be implemented had been the law that prohibited the scavenging and use of any Morphite technology – a law that instantaneously ruined one of the largest markets on Eden, and bankrupted a good number of people.

When the Techno faction had formed as an opposite to the Redeemers, they didn't hide their existence. In those early years, no-one could have foreseen how brutal and ruthless the Redeemers would become. The Technos publicly opposed them at every opportunity, while shunning their laws and continuing to salvage Morphite tech. Back then, Technos were wide spread. They co-inhabited the main cities of Avoca and Providence and they had numbers in almost every town on Eden.

They did, that is, until the Redeemers had unleashed the Judges and the Advocates.

Suddenly, anyone with a suspected link to the Technos were arrested and imprisoned – and in some cases even executed. Back then there were no courts (not even the kangaroo-courts the Redeemers had since established), and the Judges and Advocate's had a very loose leash when it came to determining the guilt of their suspects. Many individuals who had been arrested had never even had a link to the Technos. The leaders of the Techno faction got to work building a safe-haven for their people and over the years the Technos left the major cities and towns, fleeing deep into the badlands, where a hidden city (eventually named Rho's Sacrifice after one of the Techno's who had been killed during the massacre of Rusden) had been established.

The Technos, out of necessity of survival had hidden, unwilling and unable to fight the might of the Redeemers. They exiled themselves from Eden's population centres and chose a life of solitude, continuing their work salvaging any Morphite tech they could find and adapting it to create a better lifestyle for themselves. To the Redeemers, the Technos had become the perfect distraction; an invisible enemy that could be blamed for everything and anything. Their propaganda machine was relentless.

Thus, it was really no wonder that Port Usharin's population didn't trust them – they'd been fed so many lies over the years. Even after the massacre of the Techno town Rusden (one of the few settlements they had chosen to establish away from their hidden city), the Redeemers had painted the Technos out as terrorists, that the massacre had been *necessary*. Since that dark day, all Technos agreed on one thing: they would never let another Redeemer sponsored massacre go unpunished. It didn't matter whether it was another Techno town, or not.

So here they were.

Rai ordered one of her bridge crew to target the single remaining duster with a missile. The crew member did as he was instructed, and announced that a missile was armed and ready to fire.

'No time like the present,' she replied.

The crewmember gave her a confused look. 'Huh?'

'That means "fire", dumb-ass,' she said, rolling her eyes. Good help was hard to find.

The crew member nodded, and hit a button on his console. The missile streaked away, curving slightly before dropping down to the stationary duster. Rai watched as it flew, dead on target, the duster moments away from being converted to little more than scrap metal. Then something strange happened – the missile simply exploded in mid-air, ten meters from the duster.

'What the hell just happened?' Rai yelled, instantly annoyed. 'Jep, I swear if you screwed that up I'm going to...'

'It wasn't me, Rai!' The crewman replied. 'The missile hit something!'

'Don't give me that crap!' Rai snapped. 'I was watching it, it hit nothing.'

Suddenly, the Judge was in the middle of the dusty street, making a run for the duster. Rai stabbed a finger towards the front of the bridge, where the whole crew could see the huge man through the clear, curved diamond-laced windows that started from the bridge's roof and curved around the front of the skimmer, to a meter under the front of the bridge. Rai slapped a hand against a console.

'Damn it, target the Judge!' she yelled. 'Forward pulse turret!'

She watched as the pulse cannon charged up and then let loose a barrage of blue-white energy bolts that peppered into the running Judge. Her entire crew gasped when the bolts all seemed to dissipate in mid air, centimetres from the Judges body. She gritted her teeth as the man looked up at her with a snarling grin.

Judge Rus himself. *You die now*, Rai thought, her hatred for the butcher of Rusden burning in her mind.

'He's got some kind of shielding,' one of the crewmen exclaimed.

'Missiles!' Rai yelled. 'Arm two of 'em, and fire immediately!'

Her crew did as they were told, and after a moment, two missiles streaked away simultaneously. Again, the missiles exploded in mid-air. Rai gritted her teeth and cursed loudly as she watched the Judge climb into the duster. *So, the Judges are using Morphite tech now*, she thought. *Fucking hypocrites.* She watched as the dusters' engines fired up, and the craft lifted off the ground. It hovered momentarily, and then spun around, its nose coming to bear directly on *The Rust-Bucket*. Rai's eyes grew wide as she saw the Gatling-gun which hung under the ship spooling up.

'Evasive manoeuvres!' she yelled.

The Gatling-gun belched fire, and a hail of bullets peppered the front facing surface of *Rusty*. Her crew dived behind their consoles, shielding themselves, but it hadn't been necessary – the diamond-laced window had held, a crack forming right in the middle, impact points dotted all over it. Rai jumped to her feet and darted over to the starboard porthole, immediately seeing a plume of smoke and flames emerging from the engine that powered the skimmer's starboard rotors. The scavenged metal sheets that the body of the airship was made from were nowhere near as strong as the window.

Darting back to her command console, Rai noticed that Judge Rus's duster had sped off, targeting a second skimmer. She yelled at her crew.

'There's a fire in the starboard engine! Get the extinguishers online!'

Her crew were efficient, even though they were unaccustomed to combat. The engine fire was quickly extinguished, and one of her crew assessed the damage.

'We're damaged, but lift is holding,' the crew member said, eyes wide, fearful. 'Another hit, though and we're toast.'

'Better get ready for breakfast, then,' Rai muttered. 'Come about! Target that damn duster!'

'Did you not just hear what I said?' the crewman exclaimed.

'Just do it!' Rai yelled, hitting her console with a fist. 'Everything we've got! We all know that Morphite defensive shrouds aren't completely invulnerable! If we hit it with enough firepower, then we might just break through.'

By now, the Judge's duster was darting in on a strafing run on one of the landed skimmers. It's Gatling-gun spun-up, and a cloud of bullets erupted, peppering the defenceless skimmer with white-hot slugs. The grounded skimmer wasn't as lucky as *The Rust-Bucket* had been. It exploded, spewing flaming wreckage across the street, the airship's crew clearly dead. Rai gritted her teeth, and screamed at her crew to fire. Two more missiles streaked away, followed with a barrage of energy bolts from the two forward facing pulse turrets. A second skimmer, the one captained by Rai's father added their firepower to the attack, his ship also equipped with a Morphite pulse beam. The red beam shot out from the bow of the skimmer and locked onto the duster. Three red/white energy pulses blasted down the beam and struck the Morphite defensive shroud that surrounded the duster. The first two pulses were stopped by the shroud, the third however broke through. It struck the duster on its left wing, sending it in a tumbling spin towards the ground. Judge Rus somehow managed to recover the out of control aircraft however, and he pulled up only meters from the ground.

Rai watched in annoyance as the duster lifted into the air again, and fled Port Usharin, no doubt heading back to Avoca to rally his Advocates.

'Damn it!' she cursed, moments before her console beeped with an incoming message. She hit a button, and her father's holographic image appeared in front of her.

'You let him get away, hope-damn it!' her father drawled in annoyance.

'*I* let him get away?' Rai squeaked incredulously. Her father dismissed any further protest with a wave of the hand.

'It doesn't matter,' he said with a sigh. 'Land your skimmer and begin loading people.' He cut the communication, and Rai gave her crew an incredulous look.

'*I* let him get away?'

Thirteen

Jonas and Sar peered through the window of the house they hid in, watching in relief as Judge Rus' duster fled Port Usharin, and the Techno airships began to land in the streets. The colourful skimmers kicked up a lot of dust as they neared the ground, their huge rotors spinning up dust-devils every few seconds. Jonas looked over at Sar.

'I suppose we should go and introduce ourselves,' he said.

Sar frowned. 'But they're Technos,' she replied, quietly.

'They're also the people who just saved us from the Judge,' Jonas replied. 'I know the kind of things that the Redeemers say about them, and I understand why you're hesitant. But after what we've just endured, I'd be inclined to give them the benefit of the doubt. Besides, are you really in the mood to take anything the Redeemers have ever said as gospel?'

'No, I suppose not,' Sar replied after giving it some thought.

Jonas nodded at her, and stood.

'Jett isn't going to like this,' she muttered as Jonas led her out of the building.

They exited the house and moved out into the dusty, chaotic streets of Port Usharin. A number of Techno skimmers already sat in the middle of the wide main street and the remainder were beginning to land. Unarmed Technos moved through the street, trying to coax the terrified town's people to safety. Many had already fled the town, not willing to trust the Technos any more than they had the Judge and his Advocates. The Redeemer propaganda machine had conditioned them well. A small percentage of the townsfolk, however, were smart enough to take the situation at face value, and had accepted the Techno help with thanks. The rest were slowly coming around to the idea that the Technos only wanted to help.

Jonas and Sar moved out into the street slowly, holding their weapons in a non-threatening manner. It didn't take long for their rescuers to notice them. A group of unarmed Technos spotted them, and pointed dramatically, yelling for their comrades in their cowboy drawls before fleeing. A few seconds later a squad of three armed Technos approached at a run, and aggressively levelled energy weapons at them both.

'Don't move, Advocate!' the squad's leader, a petite and surprisingly young woman with strawberry blonde hair snapped. 'Weapons on the ground, hope-dammit!'

Jonas and Sar did as they were told.

'Neither of us are Advocates,' Jonas said to the woman calmly. 'We were fighting the Judge, surely you saw that when you attacked?'

'You're not Advocates? Could have fooled me,' the woman said, indicating Sar's uniform.

'I was an Advocate,' Sar explained, attempting to mimic Jonas' calm. 'In fact, I was the Advocate for Port Usharin, until Judge Rus attacked the town.'

The young Techno woman touched her hand to a hidden earpiece, and after a few seconds looked up at them again.'Port Usharin's Advocate is a woman named Tailynn Sar. That you?'

'That's me.'

The woman grunted a laugh. 'Popular lady. A planet wide alert just went out across the archaic old Redeemer data net. You are now Eden's most wanted, along with someone called Jonas Dresden.'

'That's me,' Jonas said quietly.

'Look at that, two for the price of one.'

Jonas sighed, uncertain what angle to play with the Technos. He thought it through momentarily, watching the other Technos round up more of the townspeople. Eventually he decided the best course of action was to be upfront.

'Look,' he began, 'regardless of what the Redeemers have to say about us, we are not criminals. We're just a couple of people that have found themselves in a messy situation.'

'Hey, you don't have to preach to me,' the Techno woman replied. 'Any enemy of the Redeemers is a friend to the Technos, at least in principal.'

'So we're free to go?' Sar asked, uncertainly.

Before the Techno woman could answer, another Techno came rushing over.

'Rai!' he called desperately, before stopping nearby and panting momentarily. 'Rai, your father sent me for you.'

'What is it?' the young woman snapped. 'I'm busy!'

'The fires in the buildings are spreading quickly. They're beginning to threaten the skimmers. Pretty soon this whole town is going to be a smouldering pile.'

'So? What the hell does he want me to do about it?'

'He's issued a withdrawal order,' the man replied as though he'd already made it clear.

Jonas and Sar watched on as Rai rolled her eyes and cursed at the man.

'Why didn't you just say that?' she asked rhetorically, and then muttered 'Why is good help so damn hard to find?' She looked at Jonas and Tailynn and motioned cynically towards her damaged skimmer. 'If you don't mind, time appears to be of the essence.'

Jonas and Tailynn began to follow the young woman, as she quickly headed for the boarding ramp of her airship.

'We have some friends on the outskirts of town,' Tailynn mentioned. 'We need to pick them up.'

'Sure thing,' Rai replied, nonchalantly. 'But first things first, let's get the hell out of here before we all become walking matchsticks, huh?'

She led them up the ramp of the big, rusty skimmer, up through its metallic innards until they reached the command deck. They passed a handful of rescued townspeople on the way, all of whom shied away from Sar, her Advocate's uniform acting as a ward.

The command deck of the skimmer was brimming with technology: computers, holographic projectors and the like scavenged and adapted from decades old Morphite technology. During the year long unrest which led to the Morphites abandoning Eden, many Morphite vessels were either damaged or stolen by the human rebels. Long since abandoned, these vessels were rediscovered by the Techno faction, along with a number of Morphite built structures that dotted the planet; atmospheric stations that had been installed by the Morphites to synthesise and pump gasses into the sky which had formed Eden's low lying atmosphere. The technology that the Technos had scavenged from these stations, and from the abandoned ships had been studied, and it had been determined that there was little possibility of duplicating the tech. This was due to the limited resources available on Eden and the intricate and advanced nature the technology. In fact, many of the components and materials in the alien machinery could not even be identified, even utilising the ancient databases that had travelled all the way from Earth aboard the *Stargazer*. Thus, the Technos were restricted to utilising the scavenged machinery, coupling components together where they could, or relying solely on intact systems and machinery. For these reasons, the technology that was scavenged was obviously finite, valuable beyond any amount of money.

Jonas and Sar watched as Rai gave her crew instructions. Within moments, the huge rotors on either side of the skimmer's fuselage were spinning and they were quickly airborne. They flew slowly over Port Usharin, witnessing the damage caused by the Advocate assault on the town. Pillars of smoke rose from the fiercely burning buildings, and then flattened out like mushroom heads as they reached the edge of the low lying atmosphere. The fires in the town had well and truly taken hold and were spreading rapidly. Jonas estimated that it would be a matter of only an hour or two until all that remained of Port Usharin was a pile of smouldering ashes. He could still see bodies in the streets and occasionally a living person fleeing the town. As he watched a young couple dashing over open ground attempting to hide from the overhead skimmers, he found himself filled with guilt. If he'd never been in Port Usharin, all these people: the dead, the living, the rescued, the fleeing would be living their boring lives uninterrupted, oblivious to the hurt and suffering the Advocates and the Judge would never have caused.

Why had he come to Port Usharin? The fact that he couldn't answer that question – nor the myriad other questions that were plaguing him – was driving him mad. *You initiated a memory wipe on yourself,* the Morphite had said. *Why?* Jonas asked himself desperately. *Why would I do that? And who was I to even be able to do that?*

Sar was directing Rai towards the town's outskirts, singling out the small structure that Jonas had instructed Jett and Galatea to hide in. The Techno pilot banked the skimmer (which Jonas learned was aptly named *The Rust Bucket*) towards the structure, moving away from the bulk of the skimmer fleet that was evidently heading directly to some hidden Techno base or city.

As *The Rust Bucket* neared the structure Jett and Galatea had fled to, a stream of energy pulse blasts erupted from a window, peppering the fuselage of the skimmer.

'Hope-dammit!' Rai exclaimed. 'Who the hell's shooting at us *this* time?'

Jonas and Sar gave each other a knowing glance.

'Jett,' they both muttered simultaneously.

'Your guy?' Rai asked in annoyance. 'Doesn't the dumbass know we're trying to help him?'

'Probably not,' Sar replied. 'Jett's never been a big fan of Technos.'

'Ah, you gotta love Redeemers,' Rai muttered. 'Send a little propaganda their way and they'll believe anything.'

'Do you have a loud speaker or anything that I could address them with?' Jonas asked.

Unimpressed, Rai hit a button on the console in front of her. A holographic soundwave image appeared in the air in front of her.

'Better talk quickly,' Rai said. 'I don't want to risk the very remote possibility that his aim will improve and he starts to do some damage."

Jonas stepped forwards and spoke.

'Jett! Hold your fire! This is Jonas. I have Tailynn with me. The Technos have rescued us.'

It took a bit of convincing, but eventually Jett and Galatea emerged from their hiding spot into the open, and Jett placed his weapons on the ground. Rai ordered *The Rust Bucket* to land, and as the rotors wound down, Jonas and Tailynn emerged from the ramp, with Rai a few steps behind them.

'Jonas? Tailynn?' Jett asked with a confused look on his face. 'What the hell are you doing on a Techno airship?' Jonas and Tailynn updated them on everything that had happened since they had split up.

'Wait a second,' Jett said once they had finished. 'You expect *me* to get aboard a Techno airship? No. No way.'

'Fine,' Rai interjected. 'It's only about a two hundred kilometre walk to the nearest town, jackass. You'll be fine. Oh, and I'm sure that the local Advocate will give you a nice big warm welcome too!'

Jett frowned at the logic of Rai's statement.

'She has a point,' Jonas said with a shrug. 'They've already put out a "wanted" listing for Tailynn and I, it's not going to be long until your name gets added to it.'

Jett conceded the point with an annoyed sigh.

'Fine,' he said. 'But don't expect me to like it.'

He walked off heading towards the skimmer's boarding ramp. He gave Rai a frown as he passed her.

'Techno rabble,' he muttered as he passed her.

'Redeemer sheep,' she replied, and then bleated.

Fourteen

Lord Adjutant Imanre Hes paced behind his desk anxiously. He had heard reports of Judge Rus' actions in Port Usharin, and was brimming with anger. Didn't the fool Judge know what kind of publicity nightmare he had caused? And word was he *still* hadn't been able to apprehend Jonas Dresden – had, in fact, lost an *entire* Advocate strike team in the process, not to mention a number of dusters! And only moments ago, he had received reports of Techno involvement in the region. Just what the Lord Adjutant needed. How would the Redeemers (and their leader) appear in the eyes of the Morphite Zesiro now? What chance did they now have of *ever* achieving the redemption in the eyes of the aliens they had so desperately sought?

The door to his chamber swung open, and Judge Rus strode in, his combat uniform still covered in dust, debris and what could only be blood spatter. He stopped before the Lord Adjutant's desk and kneeled, bowing his head.

'Lord Adjutant,' he said.

Hes scowled, and paced anxiously behind his large desk, still uncertain as to how he should deal with the situation. Rus had failed, that much was clear. Should he assign the task of Jonas Dresden's apprehension to another Judge? In Hes' experience, Rus had always been the most capable of the current Judges. On one hand, he was hugely disappointed in the huge man's actions. It wasn't the fact that he had destroyed an entire mining town, nor the fact that he had no doubt murdered a large number of faceless individuals – the nature of the mission had always meant that civilian casualties could potentially be expected. Rather, it was the loss of the Advocate strike team and the Dusters, coupled with the fact he had *failed* in his task altogether that enraged Hes. On the other hand, he knew enough of Rus' capabilities to know that if he had failed, then any other of the serving Judges would have done so too.

The Morphite had been coy as to revealing anything about this Jonas Dresden. Who was this man that had seemingly *singlehandedly* wiped out an entire Strike team? Was he somehow in league with the Technos? And what could the Morphites possibly want with him?

Rus, impatient with Hes' silence, raised his head slightly.

'Lord Adjutant?'

'Be *quiet!*' Hes snapped.

He paced for another few moments, before stopping and sighing loudly.

'You failed in your task, Judge Rus,' he began, putting on his most displeased tone of voice. 'You have made all Redeemers appear as fools in the eyes of the Morphites.'

'I was admittedly unprepared for Dresden,' Rus replied, still down on one knee. 'But we were not given all the information by the Morphite, and neither did any of us anticipate Techno interference.'

Hes sighed loudly. What Rus said was undoubtedly true. It had been many years since the Technos had emerged from their self-imposed exile.

'Tell me about the Technos,' Hes instructed. 'What was their involvement in the incident?'

'The Technos interfered at the moment we were about to apprehend Dresden,' Rus explained. 'It was their intervention which was directly responsible for Dresden's escape. I believe they are a larger threat than we could have ever imagined. They assaulted my forces with what could only be described as a small army, including large skimmers built with Morphite technology.'

Hes gasped slightly, an involuntary reaction to this revelation. The Technos had an army? This was not good. Not good at all...

Rus rose to his feet, evidently not awaiting instruction to do so, which would have irked Hes had he not had bigger problems to deal with. The big Judge peered closely at the Lord Adjutant. His gaze was serpentine, and sent chills down Hes' spine.

'It is possible that Dresden has taken shelter with the Technos,' Rus continued. 'I desire authorisation to seek out the hidden Techno city and wipe it out.'

Hes stared at the big man incredulously. Could he be serious?

'Your Advocate strike team has been lost, Judge Rus!' Hes exclaimed. 'From where would you get the manpower?'

'I would form an assault force utilising a combination of serving Advocates taken from districts of Avoca, Providence and any nearby settlement,' Rus said. 'In addition, we should conscript a number of Redeemer citizens.'

Hes couldn't believe his ears. *Conscript* citizens?

'Have you lost your mind, Judge Rus?' Hes asked. 'If we remove even a small number of Advocates from their posts, who would police their areas? There would be chaos in the streets! And conscript citizens! Who would train them? How would we arm them? How would we quell any form of resistance to the conscription process?'

'The Technos pose a clear threat to Redeemer interests, Lord Adjutant. The simple fact is that they have an army, and we do not,' Rus hissed. 'We must stop them, before they destroy everything that the Redeemers have built. We must strike first, and we must strike hard. We *must* deliver a killing blow to them pre-emptively. It may take weeks, even months to build an army. But we *must do so!*' His voice changed tone at this point, his edge of dogged insistence taking a dark and menacing turn. 'If you do not see that, *Lord Adjutant*, then you are a fool.'

Hes stared aghast at Rus, as the big man caught his breath from his rant.

'You *have* lost your mind,' Hes said, his own tone one of complete shock. 'You are out of line, Judge Rus!'

Rus sneered, and he looked up to the roof.

'Do you hear this?'

At first, Hes thought that Rus was talking to him, but the question didn't seem to make sense. Then after a moment, the Morphite Zesiro was standing next to Rus, materializing in the same human form he had taken upon his first meeting with Hes and the other two triumvir Adjutants. Hes gasped unconsciously, and bowed his head immediately. Zesiro just sighed an annoyed sigh.

'You just do not learn, do you, Lord Adjutant?' the Morphite asked rhetorically.

'My... my lord?'

Zesiro sighed angrily as Hes belatedly remembered the Morphites extreme distain for the title. His mind raced. Had Judge Rus been in contact with Zesiro after he himself had been?

'You are an *imbecile!*' Zesiro roared, making Hes shudder in fear. 'Nothing but pre-human vermin! A rodent! Nothing more!'

Rus stood next to Zesiro an amused smirk on his face. Hes could tell he was immensely amused at the situation, taking joy in his own fear. At that moment, Hes hated the man, and made a mental decision that Rus would be *disciplined* for this act of insubordination.

'This whole world is populated with nothing but rodents!' Zesiro continued to rage. 'You are unworthy of redemption in our eyes! You have never been worthy of it, and you never will be! The best you can hope for is that your *pathetic* civilisation survives long enough on its own for you to understand that you are nothing! And that your existence is *insignificant!*'

Zesiro finished his rant, a look of pure anger still plastered across his face. Hes peered up at the Morphite, his fear only now beginning to give way to something more akin to indignation, perhaps even anger. He peered directly into the Morphites eyes. Had he, and every other human on Eden been wrong about the Morphites? They had always been seen as a benevolent species, their only intent to help the Edenites. Had they *really* been so wrong?

'If we are so insignificant, then why did you come to us in the first place?' Hes asked quietly. 'Why did you help us build this world into something that could sustain us? Why are you now here, requesting our help to find this Jonas Dresden?'

Zesiro sneered as Rus remained completely still and silent, staring across at Hes with an arrogant smirk.

'Perhaps all those years ago, in a moment of weakness we felt pity for you,' Zesiro replied. 'Or perhaps it was a sense of nostalgia for what we once were, and a desire for some kind of historical preservation.' Hes frowned in confusion at this last sentence. Historical preservation? Zesiro continued 'But there is one thing that I can guarantee you with all certainty, Lord Adjutant Hes: I do not need *your* help to find Jonas Dresden.'

Hes watched on in confusion as Zesiro turned to Rus.

'Dresden is with the Technos, Judge Rus. Build your army. Find him. Capture him. Wipe the Technos out if you desire, I do not care.'

'And what of the Lord Adjutant?' Rus asked the Morphite. 'I find it unlikely that he will give me his blessing to do what I must.'

'I think you underestimate the good Lord Adjutant,' Zesiro said with a smirk.

His face began to ripple, and Hes watched in adbject horror as Zesiro's face morphed into a precise facsimile of his own. He gasped.

'You *will* help us Lord Adjutant,' Zesiro said. 'Whether you choose to do so or not.'

Hes watched as the alien who had taken his appearance turned to Judge Rus.

'You can kill him now.'

Rus smiled his serpentine smile and withdrew his gun-blade, flicking the switch that made it fold itself into blade mode. The Judge raised the blade above his head and brought it down towards Hes' neck with gusto.

Hes felt a sting, a split second of disconcertion, and found himself staring at his own headless body. And then there was oblivion.

Fifteen

Rho's Sacrifice lay deep within the Badlands, well past the Crimson Sea in a region known as the Desert of Forever. As the fleet of skimmers glided over the desert's golden sands, Jonas, Galatea, Jett and Tailynn stood on an observation deck on the upper hull of *Rusty*, the air on the edge of the planetary atmosphere light and cool, the stars in the sky bright, and the Pandora Nebula hanging over them vividly. They watched as the fleet approached a huge rocky mountain in the middle of the desert, one of many outcroppings scattered throughout the region. This one was different than the others, however. Rai had explained to them how her people had hollowed out the nameless mountain and built their hidden city there. Far from any Redeemer town or city, the Techno exiles had made their home here deep within the vast and inhospitable badlands – and it was here that they had prospered.

The Techno city was now home to over twenty-five thousand individuals, and was constantly growing. They were wholly self-sufficient Rai had told them, having constructed huge underground hydroponic farms to grow food, and utilising three salvaged Morphite quantum reactors to power the mini-metropolis (overkill, Rai had admitted – but Technos loved the safety that came with installing multiple redundant systems). Hard-to-come-by components and resources could usually be created in one of five salvaged Morphite synthesisers, although Rai had indicated that the

Technos preferred salvaging (or occasionally stealing) these resources, as the synthesisers were extremely delicate devices, and the chances of ever replacing them should they fail was slim to none.

As the fleet approached the mountain, huge camouflaged hangar doors began to open in the side – five in all – and the fleet split up, each skimmer heading for its designated landing area. One of *Rusty's* crew members emerged on the observation deck and instructed the four of them to return to the skimmer's internal decks, as they would be docking shortly. They did as they were instructed and returned to the bridge, where Rai was throwing commands around, ensuring her crew got the damaged skimmer home safely. Jonas watched through the huge viewport on the bridge as the airship approached the open hangar. Inside he could see dozens of dock workers running around preparing berths for the incoming ships, and hurriedly mooring the ones that had already docked. Jonas was impressed with the Technos' efficiency and as *The Rust-Bucket* moved slowly through the huge doors and touched down on metallic struts he complemented Rai on her and her peoples' skills. Jett, Tailynn and Galatea watched on in amazement, having never seen anything like it. Jett especially was quiet, having come to the realisation that the Technos weren't exactly the rabble he had always been led to believe they were.

Once the skimmer was safely moored and the engines had completely spun down, Rai led Jonas and the others down the airship's boarding ramp and across the hangar floor, towards a bald older man who had emerged from one of the other craft and was now striding towards them, an unhappy look on his face. As he approached, he waved a hand at Rai.

'This was a hopedamned disaster!' he exclaimed when he was in speaking distance. Rai simply rolled her eyes at him. 'The committee's going to have my ass!'

'Calm down, Pops,' Rai replied, somewhat condescendingly. 'We saved a hell of a lot of people today.'

'At the expense of some of our own!' the man replied, running a hand over his smooth forehead. 'Not to mention the hardware we lost, or the fact that we – sorry, *you* – had the Butcher of Rusden in your sights, and you let him get away!'

'There was more going on that any of us knew, Pops,' Rai replied. She turned and indicated Jonas. 'This here is Jonas Dresden. He's got one hell of a story for you. Jonas? This is my dad and the head of our so-called militia, Sid Ashima.'

Sid just looked at Jonas without a word, his face filled with annoyance.

'Rai's right,' Jonas began to explain. 'The Judge had an ally that you couldn't have anticipated: a Morphite.'

'A Morphite?' Sid replied incredulously. After a moment of silence, he turned back to Rai. 'Rai if you're going to have someone lie for you, at least tell 'em to make it believable.'

'I'm not lying,' Jonas interjected.

Jonas began to explain everything to the older man, with Tailynn and Galatea interjecting their own snippets every so often. Jett remained silent, evidently still unsure about the Technos. After they had finished their tale (which, admittedly *was* sounding rather absurd), they waited for a response from either Rai, who hadn't heard the full story yet, or her father. Both, however were silent.

'It's the truth,' Jonas insisted. 'I know it's hard to believe that the Morphites have returned to Eden, but they have.'

'Actually,' Rai began slowly, 'it's not as hard to believe as you think.'

'What's that supposed to mean?' Jett asked suspiciously, finally breaking his silence.

Rai and Sid gave each other a look.

'There's someone we need you to meet,' Rai said to Jonas. 'His name is Haldon Cos.' Tailynn pricked her ears up, and Rai regarded her with a nod. 'I see you recognise the name.' Tailynn nodded.

'Who is he?' Jonas asked.

'I'll let him explain that to you,' Rai replied.

Sid let out an impatient sigh.

'This is all fascinating,' he began, 'but I have a report to make to the committee.'

'Enjoy yourself, Pops,' Rai replied.

Sid muttered something under his breath as he turned around and strode off.

'Is he going to be in as much trouble as he seems to think?' Jonas asked Rai.

'Probably,' she replied with a shrug. 'But knowing my dad, he'll tell 'em that if they don't like it, then they can stick it where the stars don't shine.'

They followed Rai through the streets of Rho's Sacrifice, allowing her to act as tour guide as they journeyed to the location of the mysterious individual. The huge hollowed out mountain had been lined with structures built out of a wide variety of materials the Technos had been able to salvage, but rather than appearing slum-like as Jonas had anticipated, Rho's Sacrifice was an immensely colourful place and came across as festive and exotic. Its inhabitants buzzed around the streets like bees, busy but happy and Rai stopped often to talk to colourfully dressed friends, introducing Jonas and the others as she went. The city was structured somewhat open-plan, with no specific districts. Rai explained that in Techno culture work was life, and this philosophy had been reflected in its planning, meaning there was no separate business district or residential district, rather the blend of both. The exception to this rule lay at the centre of the city, where a wide open market-place and entertainment precinct resided, what Rai said her people referred to as the Grand Promenade. As they walked through the Promenade, passing food stalls, commodity vendors and entertainers (not to mention Sapphire Jaharas planted freely throughout in gardens with a mix of various other exotic flora), Jonas had a quick memory flash – this place reminded him of somewhere. A name came to his mind fleetingly – and he almost lost it, but just at the moment of its disappearance, the name solidified in his mind: Olympus. Everything else vanished from his mind – the fleeting glimpse of memory, the feeling of similarity... but the name remained. This place reminded him of somewhere called Olympus. Where was Olympus? Why did the name of the place bring him such comfort? He closed his eyes tightly, trying to squeeze more out of his mind. After a moment, he felt a hand brush his arm.

'Are you alright?'

He opened his eyes to discover Galatea standing in front of him, a look of concern plastered across her face. Jonas smiled.

'I just remembered something,' he said, excitement in his voice. 'I remembered a place. This city reminds me of it.'

He laughed loudly and Gala did likewise, surprised by Jonas's show of emotion. He stopped abruptly when he realised Rai, Jett and Tailynn were staring at him in surprise, having not heard his revelation about his fleeting and momentary return of memory.

'You alright?' Jett asked slowly.

Jonas grunted a laugh, and shot a smile at Gala who smiled widely back at him.

'I'm fine,' he replied. 'Let's keep going.'

On the other side of the Promenade, Rai instructed them to climb aboard a small tram which ran along a magnetic-levitation monorail, heading off towards a cluster of buildings built high above the main section of the city on a rocky ledge which stuck out from the inside wall of the hollow mountain. Rai explained that the district they were heading to was, in a way, a sort of prison. Those who were convicted of a crime in Rho's Sacrifice were sent there, she told them. It was not a prison in the traditional sense of the word, though. There were no cells, or chains or restraints of any kind. The residents of the district had their own apartments, and they all worked jobs assigned to them, mainly jobs in waste processing and other undesirable fields. Rations were distributed on a weekly basis, and health care was provided by a guarded clinic. They were forbidden, however to travel back to the city proper at any time. Only authorised individuals had control over the tram which was the only way in or out of the district, and Rai, being a member of the militia had such

authorisation. Officially, the district was referred to as the Ledge,
however Rai told them that its residents had a different name for it:
Purgatory.

The tram stopped at the small station upon reaching the Ledge
(Jonas didn't miss the ironically wonderful view of the rest of the
city that the Ledge's inhabitants would be privy to), and Rai led
them off into a small receiving area, manned by two armed militia
guards. They were both friendly to the group (sucking up to the
boss's daughter would get them nowhere, Rai assured them), and let
them through the secured checkpoint without a problem.

Purgatory proved to be a rather apt name for the Ledge. It was,
of course, a very different place to that of the city below. There
was no colour, no festive atmosphere. Just industrial greys, and an
overwhelming sense of hopelessness. Shabbily dressed people
roamed the streets, some obviously mentally ill, while others were
behaving somewhat predatorily. No one bothered Jonas's group,
however, Rai's presence serving as a ward, although she wore no
uniform and displayed no insignia or anything else that betrayed her
as being a member of the militia that Jonas could identify.

Rai led them to one of the apartment complexes nearest to the
rocky wall of the mountain, and once inside led them up a short
flight of stairs before stopping in front of a door. Before she could
knock on the door, however, Jonas stopped Rai.

'I have a question,' he began. 'Who is this person, and why is he
here?'

Rai darted a glance at Tailynn.

'You say you know who Haldon Cos is?' she asked, receiving a nod
from Tailynn in reply. 'Then you can guess why he's here.'

'I suppose so,' Tailynn replied.

'Okay, is someone going to let us in on this little secret?' Jett asked
in annoyance. Rai winked at him.

'All in good time, sheep-man,' she answered, which garnered a
scowl from Jett.

She knocked on the door loudly. There was no answer. After a moment of waiting, Rai nevertheless opened the door and strode in, Jonas and the others following. The inside of the apartment was sparsely furnished, and dimly lit. A smoky aroma filled the air, and Jonas couldn't decide whether he liked it or despised it. Rai led them into the main living area, where a man sat on the floor, facing away from them, dressed in a black, form fitting sleeveless shirt and plain black pants with heavy leather boots beside him, and a big red trench-coat draped over a nearby chair. The aroma was coming from a small glass filled with incense that was smoking lightly.

'It's been a while, Rai,' the man said in a deep, calm voice. He still hadn't turned around.

'It has been,' Rai replied. 'I've brought some people you're going to want to talk to.'

After a few moments when Jonas had just about assumed he hadn't heard her, the man stood, and turned around to face them. His face had a scar running down a cheek just below one of his eyelids which seemed lazy. His short, dark hair was greying.

'It's been a while since I've had visitors,' he said, looking over Jonas and the others. 'Welcome to Purgatory.'

'This is Haldon Cos,' Rai said to them. 'He used to be a Redeemer Judge.'

'Used to be, being the operative word,' Cos interjected. 'I left my position willingly a number of years ago, and essentially defected to the Technos. Yet I'm still left on the Ledge with the rabble of Techno society.'

'Come on, Haldon. Give me a break. You know if it were up to me, you'd be out of here.'

'So you keep telling me,' the big man replied calmly. 'Yet here I remain.'

'Why *is* he here?' Tailynn asked Rai, the young woman shrugging in response.

'He's a former Judge. For most of my people that's reason enough,' Rai said. 'Need I mention the guy he was once mentor to?' When

Tailynn returned a blank, uncomprehending stare, Rai added: 'Oh, I wrongly assumed you knew.'

'Why are you here, Rai?' Cos asked, although there was no hint of impatience in his voice. Rai motioned to Jonas.

'I'd like to introduce you to someone. This is Jonas Dresden. He's got no memory of who he is, or where he's from. Or why the Redeemers are after him... or the Morphites.'

Cos frowned slightly.

'Morphites?' he muttered. Rai nodded firmly.

'He needs to hear your story,' she said.

Cos remained silent for an uncomfortable amount of time. He stared at Jonas as though evaluating him and Jonas stared right back, doing the same, unsure why their young Techno rescuer had arranged for them to meet. Eventually, Cos was the one who broke the silence.

'Take a seat.' They all sat down where they could, Jett doing so with an irritated sigh. 'You all know of the Providencian pilgrimage?'

All of them – Jonas included – nodded. 'Completing the pilgrimage is the ultimate goal of most practicing Redeemers,' Tailynn said. Jonas hadn't missed the uneasy glance that she and Jett had exchanged. Cos nodded.

'Yes,' he replied. 'It might be interesting for you all to learn however, that contrary to popular belief, the Redeemers were never the instigators of the pilgrimage.'

In essence, Haldon Cos' story began over ten years ago. He had been a loyal Redeemer Advocate, regarded as one of the brightest and most loyal. It was no surprise really, when his name had been put forward as a potential Judge's candidate, and when the Triumvir Adjutants announced that the position was his, he took his new role and made it his own. Cos had been widely regarded amongst Redeemer circles as the most efficient of the five Judges at the time: firm but fair, uncompromising and with a loyalty that was unwavering. He was responsible for tracking and executing the leaders of a large crime syndicate that had spread throughout

Redeemer settlements, including both Avoca and Providence, and he had quelled three minor civil uprisings within Avoca.

A few years into his tenure as Judge, the Lord Adjutant at the time had secretly assigned him to investigate the Providencian Pilgrimage. Each year, hundreds of Redeemer citizens travelled to Providence and embarked from the city on a pilgrimage through the Valley of Stars. The reason behind the pilgrimage was simple: those who were successful in reaching the end of the roughly seven hundred and fifty kilometre long valley were said to receive Morphite redemption, and were to be taken from Eden in the care of the aliens. Indeed, the few who it was believed had completed it were never heard from again. To the believers, the pilgrimage was the ultimate show of faith, while to the unbelievers, it was just another Redeemer trick.

The thing was, however, the pilgrimages had begun without official Redeemer knowledge.

This was a secret that had been guarded by the Adjutants fiercely, fearing that it would look as though they had lost control of their people (or their own religion) should it become public knowledge. So they'd had no choice when the popularity of the pilgrimage had increased but to endorse it and encourage it as though it had been part of their teachings all along. For years, the pilgrimage had been plaguing the Redeemer leaders, so the Lord Adjutant at the time, a popular man called Dosan Ren had assigned Haldon Cos to investigate.

Haldon had begun his investigation by examining reports of the region that the pilgrimage took place, specifically the Valley of Stars. It was said that the pilgrimage had to be completed on foot, rather than by vehicle. He was amazed to discover that earlier investigations of the area had found an energy dampening field surrounding the entire valley, almost exclusively restricted to the precise length and width of it. An Advocate duster which had attempted a flyover of the valley a few years prior had in fact crashed there, all of its old *Stargazer* era tech having failed simultaneously. Upon salvaging the vehicle, no fault could be found which could possibly have led to its complete system failure.

He made the decision to travel to Providence incognito, disguised as a pilgrim himself. He travelled to the city from Avoca via the old, mechanically unreliable rail link, keeping to himself and staying out of trouble. Upon his arrival at Providence, he went through the expected rigmarole, bartering for supplies and planning his journey before finally departing through the large concourse that opened up into the valley. True to the earlier Advocate reports, his data pad stopped working a few kilometres out from Providence.

The journey had been long and gruelling. Spaced along the Valley of Stars were a handful of tiny settlements. These settlements were little more than camps, really, with the exception of the final one and had been established by entrepreneurial individuals who saw a buck to be made out of catering to the pilgrims who were on their journey. The camps only sold food, medical supplies and beds for the night (at highly exorbitant prices, of course), but nevertheless, Haldon found himself eagerly anticipating these respites as he journeyed.

Along the way, he encountered many pilgrims. Initially, he had attempted conversing with them, discreetly conducting his investigations into the pilgrimage. But it quickly became apparent that the majority of them were too blinded by their faith to be of any help to him. After this became apparent, he travelled in solitude, resisting any overtures of camaraderie or friendship that the other pilgrims made toward him.

After the first couple of hundred kilometres, Pilgrims began dropping like flies. Some were under-prepared, and were unable to bear the gruelling trek any longer. They would stop over at the camps along the way to regain their strength, the plan being to return to Providence. Indeed he had witnessed a considerable number of people trekking through the valley in the opposite direction to him. Others were not so fortunate: many would succumb to injury or illness. The lucky ones would survive; the not-so-lucky would perish, and be buried in unmarked graves along the main route through the valley. Haldon had seen many of these graves along the way.

Still, a surprising number of those who began the pilgrimage soldiered on. The further they progressed, the greater the number of individual travellers and small groups who merged to become larger groups, following a "safety in numbers" philosophy. Haldon though, remained alone. At the four hundred kilometre mark, he reached the final, and only true settlement along the way, which was aptly named Eden's End. He had taken a full day to rest here, and had stocked up on supplies in preparation for the final three hundred kilometres. He took the opportunity to question the settlement's proprietor, but the man was as oblivious to what lay at the end of the valley as the pilgrims were; his only concern was making enough money from his venture to one day retire to the wealthy new sector of Avoca. Haldon left Eden's End and continued on. The valley gradually narrowed and increased in depth over the last three hundred kilometres, becoming a deep, narrow canyon. The rocky cliff edges towered over him oppressively and despite (or perhaps because of) the fact that very few pilgrims made it this far, he found himself in low spirits.

Eventually, he came to the end of the Valley.

It was unspectacular; simply a dead-end in the canyon, with hundred meter high cliff-faces surrounding him. He could see twenty meters ahead of him, where the well worn path simply stopped. There were no other pilgrims around, which baffled him, as he knew for a fact that a small group had left Eden's End the day before he had and he had not passed them along the way, or seen any sign of them on a return trek. Confused, he reluctantly walked to the end of the track.

And suddenly, he was in the canyon no longer.

Sixteen

The huge area out the front of the Redeemer temple, known as Stargazer Square was packed with people. *Probably in excess of three thousand*, Zesiro thought as he peered out of the sole window in the Lord Adjutant's chamber. He was minutes away from addressing the people in the guise of Imanre Hes, announcing Judge Rus' plan of conquest against the Technos. He had convinced the other two Triumvir Adjutants to go along with Rus' plan, and he was amused by the respect they showed for this newly resolute Lord Adjutant. Likewise, the Council of Lesser Adjutants had agreed to the plan unanimously, not that he had needed their consent, but it *did* make things a lot easier.

Zesiro rose from the desk he sat at, and moved over to the chamber's door, locking it so as to prevent anyone's intrusion. He returned to the desk, and then sat down behind it again, and his upper body shifted shape, his form becoming the smoothed skin, hairless form the pre-humans had initially witnessed. He activated a link to the originators, and again, the only one to enter his mind was the feminine one.

'Originator,' Zesiro greeted her, hiding his surprise this time.

'Zesiro,' The Originator replied. 'I am encouraged that you have contacted me at this time.'

If Zesiro could have frowned in this form, he would have.

'May I ask why, Originator?'

'There has been a... change on Alpha One,' she began. 'Allies of the Progenitor have attempted a takeover. They have failed, but a consolidation of power has taken place.'

'A consolidation of power?'

'Yes. My fellow Originators have turned, and were advocating unity with the Progenitor. Their influence has been removed. I am now the sole Originator.'

Zesiro was shell-shocked. The Progenitor had, for a long time, been a destabilising force on the Morphite homeworld. But to have caused this much disruption? For centuries the Morphites had been led by the trio of Originators. To know now that only one remained was almost incomprehensible.

'Do you understand now, Zesiro, why it is so important that you apprehend Jonas Dresden?' the Originator continued.

'I have never doubted it,' Zesiro replied. 'It is clear that if the Progenitor and Jonas Dresden are to meet, then there can only be more destabilisation to our people.'

'Indeed,' the Originator replied. 'When will you have Jonas Dresden in custody?'

'He has gone into hiding again,' Zesiro replied. 'I have been forced to take the guise of Eden's Lord Adjutant in an attempt to corner him.'

'I am disappointed, Zesiro.'

'He will not elude me again, Originator,' Zesiro said with a bow of his head. 'I now have the resources of this entire planet at my fingertips; he has nothing.'

'Not true,' the Originator replied. 'He has an ally in the Progenitor, and even if they have never met, and are light years apart her influence should not be taken lightly.'

'I understand, Originator.'

'Fare you well, Zesiro.'

The Originator's presence slipped away. Zesiro sat in his chair for an indeterminate amount of time, stunned by the developments on his homeworld. A heavy knock at the chamber doors snapped him out of his reverie.

He hurriedly shifted back into the form of Lord Adjutant Hes, and moved over to the door. He opened it, revealing Judge Rus, his uniform pristine and his gun-blade prominent.

'It is time, Lord Adjutant,' he said.

Zesiro nodded, belatedly realising that the other two Triumvir Adjutants stood a few paces behind Rus. He followed them out of the chambers and they took the lift down to the ground floor of the temple. He strode through the large foyer, Rus and the Triumvir Adjutants in tow, and as he hurled open the huge doors that led to Stargazer Square, there was a roar of applause from the crowd that had formed. He moved over to an ornamental lectern that had been set up on the stairs above the square, a small microphone sitting atop it. Rus and the Triumvir Adjutants took their places on either side of him. Looking over the crowd, Zesiro's resolve was absolute.

'Redeemers,' he began once the applause had died down. 'By now many of you will have heard about the massacre of Port Usharin in the Badlands. Many of you will also have seen the footage of Techno Skimmers attacking the town,' – doctored footage, of course – 'and its people being massacred by these heathens!'

There was a huge uproar. The majority of the crowd had, of course seen the footage (the Redeemer propaganda machine had been, as usual, relentless), and they were all furious. They wanted vengeance... blood for the poor dead souls in the Badlands that none of them had ever known. Zesiro continued, encouraged by the crowds animosity.

'We cannot allow this attack on the innocent people of Eden to go unanswered!' Cheers. 'We must respond in kind!' More cheers. 'Thus, I have instructed Judge Drealon Rus to begin the construction of a Redeemer Army. This army will be made up of existing Advocate personnel, but we will also be enlisting volunteers. Those who volunteer for a tour with this new Redeemer Army will be trained, and will be handsomely compensated for their loyalty and the faith that they will no doubt demonstrate. The Techno heathens have always worked against us to prevent what is best for Eden. They have defied the Redeemer teachings! They have hampered our attempts at redemption in the eyes of the great Morphites. Now they openly attack us! No more! My answer to this act of aggression by the Techno faction is this Redeemer Army. If it's war they want, then its *war they'll get!'*

The crowd roared. Zesiro's speech had done just the trick. They would not have to conscript anyone now, there would be more volunteers than they could use. As he raised his arms towards the crowd in a gesture of hope and unity, the disgust he felt for these people was amplified far beyond anything he had previously felt.

Pre-human rodents, he though. *You deserve this.*

Seventeen

After the unexpected conclusion to his pilgrimage, Haldon Cos had awoken in a sterile, featureless white room. He had stood from the platform upon which he'd been resting, and looked around. A woman sat in the room a few meters away, dressed in plain white clothes that tended to blend with the room itself, so that it appeared somewhat as though her head were floating. She smiled at Haldon, her brown eyes bright with intelligence. Her dark hair was unassuming, and she had caramel-coloured skin.

'Hello,' she had said.

Haldon had taken his time responding. He examined her closely, and in his mind, he knew who – rather *what* – the woman had to be. Truth be told, he had never really been a believer in the Redeemer faith. He had long been of the opinion that the population of Eden didn't necessarily deserve redemption for what they had done to the benevolent aliens that had only ever tried to help them.

But here he was.

'You're a Morphite?' he asked eventually.

'You could say that, yes,' the woman had replied, a gentle amusement in her eyes.

'Are... you here to take me away from Eden?'

'Isn't that what you want?'

Haldon had had no idea what he wanted. He had never expected to actually meet the Morphites at the end of his investigation. He had been expecting some kind of Techno trick, perhaps, or some kind of criminal element. He had never once believed that the end that all pilgrims expected to come to could be... well, *real.*

The Morphite woman had sensed his uncertainty.

'You are not a pilgrim, are you?' she had asked, knowingly.

'No,' Haldon had replied, uncertainly. 'I came... to investigate.'

'An Advocate?'

'A Judge.'

The woman nodded, understanding. She looked him over again. 'So, now that you are here... is this what you were expecting to find?'

Haldon shook his head. The Morphite smiled at him.

'And what do you want to do now?' she asked.

'What do you mean?' he asked, with a frown.

'Well, you're here. Do you want to know what happened to all the other pilgrims? Where all the thousands who have travelled here over the years have gone?'

He did. So she explained. Her people, those who had come to Eden a century ago had not been entirely truthful with the planet's population. They had told the pre-humans that Eden's population were all that remained of the planet Earth, that the people they had left behind when the *Stargazer* had left its home system all those centuries ago had continued to wage war against each other, and in the end they had destroyed the Sol system, along with themselves. But that was a half truth. Humanity had indeed destroyed its home solar system, but they had not destroyed themselves. The Morphite woman explained to Haldon that there was a multi-system human empire that spanned the stars, built by those whom had fled the destruction of Sol. They had built new homes, and they had prospered, becoming an important part of the galactic community, which consisted of a number of alien races.

Haldon had questioned her fiercely. Why had the Morphites lied to the people of Eden? Why had they never allowed the humans that had created this empire to contact them?

The Morphites, she had explained, were at war with this human empire. They had originally come to Eden not as benevolent creatures that had only wanted to help the pre-humans out of the kindness of their hearts, rather as scientists: the humans on Eden were *specimens* to the Morphites, specimens of a race of beings that they were at war with. Specimens that could be studied for their weaknesses.

'Is that what you're doing now?' Haldon had asked desperately. 'Is that what this pilgrimage thing is? A way for you and your people to get your hands on more *specimens*?'

'No,' the woman replied. 'I do not stand with my people anymore. In their eyes, I am a criminal, perhaps even a traitor.'

'So why? Why do you do this?'

'Because Eden, and its people are more important than you could ever imagine.'

But that was all the mysterious Morphite would tell Haldon. To learn more, he would have to make a leap of faith. She had asked him the question again: what did he want to do now? Did he want to take the next step on the pilgrimage and learn what had become of all those who had come before him, or did he want to return to his life on Eden?

'I took the coward's way out,' Haldon told Jonas and the others. 'I asked to be returned. Not through a feeling of loyalty towards the Redeemers, no. I was simply afraid.'

Jett, Tailynn and Galatea sat with stunned expressions on their faces. Jonas however, stared directly at Haldon, his mind racing. The man's story made an eerie sense to him.

'You see why I wanted you to meet him?' Rai asked Jonas, who simply nodded once.

'What happened... after you were returned?' Galatea asked in a small voice.

'The Morphite sent me straight back to Avoca, and I tried to fit back into my normal life and my role as a Judge,' he answered. 'I was given a new apprentice, a young Advocate who the Lord Adjutant wanted me to train to become the next Judge. But my heart wasn't in it. I couldn't stop thinking about the secret I knew. I had decided not to reveal it to the Lord Adjutant or any other Redeemer. My report to him was a completely fabricated tall tale – to be honest, I'm not sure why I didn't come clean. I just *knew* that the Redeemers couldn't be allowed to know.

'My apprentice proved to be... problematic, to say the least. I believe you all know of him...'

'Judge Rus?' Tailynn asked with wide eyes, the penny dropping. 'He was your apprentice?'

Haldon nodded. 'Yes. After a year back in Avoca, I was unable to stand it any longer. I resigned as a Judge. The Lord Adjutant wasn't happy with me, and immediately promoted Drealon Rus to my post, and then sent him after me. I had always known that Rus was unstable. I should have done everything I could to prevent him from ever becoming a Judge, but after my experience in the Valley of Stars, I was unable to focus on anything, let alone my apprentice's training. I attempted to travel to the Badlands, but Rus came after me with orders relating to my assassination. He failed, however, and eventually I sought out the Technos, and defected. I thought they could help me. But of course, they could never bring themselves to trust me, especially after what Rus did at Rusden. That's why I'm here in Purgatory.'

'What did you think the Technos could help you with?' Tailynn asked.

'Finding the Morphite,' Haldon replied, as though this were obvious. 'With all their salvaged technology, I thought they'd be my best hope.'

'Why didn't you just travel down the Valley of Stars again?' Galatea asked.

'Because I wanted to find her on my *own* terms,' he replied forcefully. 'I had to be sure that what she had told me was the truth. She'd made it clear that she'd told me all she was going to until I committed to the next step in the "pilgrimage". And that was the problem: she wanted me to commit on *faith*. And I couldn't. It was unacceptable. I just... couldn't commit until I knew exactly what I was committing *to*.'

The group sat in silence for a long time, processing what they had just learnt. Jonas's mind raced. Images flashed in his mind, images that until Cos has finished his tale had remained stubbornly buried. It was as though the very act of learning about the greater galactic community and humanity's involvement in it had unlocked bits and pieces of his memory. Not everything, not by a long shot. But he knew something important about himself now. And he knew what they had to do next.

'I have to go to Providence,' he said, breaking the silence. 'I have to find this Morphite.'

'But the Morphites are the ones after you!' Galatea exclaimed.

'I don't think this one is,' Jonas replied.

'You remember something,' Jett said knowingly. Jonas nodded.

'Yeah,' Jonas admitted. 'I think the Morphite that Judge Cos encountered is the reason I'm here. She's the reason the other Morphite is chasing me. She's the reason I wiped my memory.'

'You remember all this?' Jett asked cautiously.

'Not exactly,' Jonas said. He took a deep breath before continuing. 'It's the only thing that makes sense, though. You see... I remember where I'm from now. And it's not Eden.'

PART TWO

REVEALING THE PAST

(WONDER)

Humanity learned one lesson from the Great Solar War: Diplomacy does not work. Diplomacy is compromise, and compromise is fallacy. I may sound like a cynic in saying this, but this understanding – this lesson we learned – was perhaps the best thing to come out of the war, and indeed all of the twenty-first century. No, really.

It was Jacob Harrison, the president of the Alliance at the conclusion of the conflict who said: "When it comes down to it, when you get past all the false diplomacy... all the false promises, there are only two ways a conflict such as this can be concluded – by fighting to the bitter end, or by capitulating to your enemy. Well, we fought to the bitter end, and we won!" Of course he didn't really believe what he was saying – he was probably reading a teleprompter with words that had been written by some intern... and the humanitarians had almost crucified him for saying it.

But he was right.

Whether our ancestors believed it or not, they took those words to heart. They embraced their basic need for conflict – but not to quench their thirst for blood. They embraced it to save lives. Seriously.

Over the next three hundred years, much happened in humanity's home system. Wide spread expansion occurred – we colonised the moons of Saturn, the moons of Jupiter, Uranus and Neptune. We even colonised Venus. City states sprung up throughout the asteroid belt, huge habitats that were themselves hollowed-out rocks the size of continents. The United Alliance of Nations didn't last long into this period, claimed by another bloody war, and another ten conflicts after that one claimed millions more lives. A dozen global governments rose and fell.

But this is how we thrive. We learnt from the Great Solar War of the fallacy that was diplomacy. So we changed. Wars were fought on smaller scales, fought in fact to achieve a specific goal or to acquire a specific resource. Without diplomacy, quarrelling governments had no way to expand their quarrels... no way to discover the others' subterfuges and misleading, nor to garner hatred for an enemy. This meant that there was no real venom to the conflict, no animosity between rivals. In a way, those three hundred years were good for humanity. But of course, there was always something just around the corner which threatened to throw humanity's development off on another unexpected tangent.

The twenty-ninth of June, 2353AD, was the day that everything changed. It was a coincidence of cosmic significance that on this day, two key events that would have everlasting repercussions occurred. The first was a breakthrough of our own. Scientists in Buenos Aires became the first people ever to splice a strand of human DNA with artificially engineered zeptites – machines that were one trillion times smaller than a nanite. Those zeptites were rather crude compared to the machines that we employ these days, and they actually did very little, and offered negligible uses. But it was a huge step in developing a synthesis between organic and artificial engineering, and it was without a doubt the first step that was taken to make my people what we are today. To use an ancient analogy, it wasn't just a small step or even a giant leap for mankind; it was as though we had grown wings.

The second event was just as monumental – it was also the day that we made first contact with an alien species: the Ingrelden.

I wonder: did they teach you this when you were a child on Illium? Is accepted history the same for you as it is for us? Curious... but I digress.

The Ingrelden; the first alien species that humanity had ever encountered. Proof of what humanity has suspected for millennia – that we were not alone in the universe. The Ingrelden, of course, were a benevolent people. They weren't what we had envisaged aliens to be, really. They weren't little green men, or vile monstrous beings. They weren't so alien that we didn't immediately recognise them as sentient life-forms. They were rather like us, actually. Bipedal, oxygen breathing humanoids. Of course, you know that that is where the similarities ended... apart from the fact that they had *two arms and two legs, their physiological features could never have been mistaken as human. But you know of the Ingrelden, of course. You deal with them on a semi-regular basis, I imagine.*

What is of significance is what they did for us. They were wary of making things too easy... they were never going to give us their technology outright, rather they would give us hints; point us in the right direction. The arrival of the Ingrelden heralded a new era for humanity, short lived as it was. For two centuries we lived in peace, conflict free. We advanced in ways our ancestors had barely imagined – medical technology became so advanced that old age essentially became a thing of the past, disease and illness all but unheard of.

This of course, became our undoing. For generation after generation, the human race grew. With the abolition of death came another huge problem: sustainability. Generations of people, who should have been long dead, continued to live. Earth reached its capacity... and then so did Mars, Luna, the moons of the gas giants...

Sol was full.

Humanity was aware of the simple solution to this problem. The Ingrelden had told them stories of the millions of terra-compatible worlds that littered the galaxy, and the aliens of course had the means by which to reach these distant worlds; how else had they come to Sol? But their Faster Than Light technology was not something the Ingrelden would share – not even hint at as they had done with so many other technologies. Their motivations were not selfish; they had no desire to bottle humanity up in the one system. They wanted Humanity to expand, and become part of the galactic community... but development of an FTL drive was a vital step in the development of a galactic species, and one that the Ingrelden claimed we had to make on our own. To them, the ability to travel faster than light was like a rite of passage, it was not something a sentient race could be gifted with, rather it was something they had to earn.

The Ingrelden had been incredibly foolish. Or perhaps they had just been ignorant or naive. By essentially providing us with the means to live such long lives, but then to withhold from us the technology to sustain it... they had created a monster, one which would have no qualms with biting the hand that for a century had fed it. Perhaps by helping us develop long life and genetic immortality they were attempting to give us an incentive to develop FTL travel. Honestly though, I don't particularly care to speculate as to the motives of the Ingrelden. They made the foolish choice they did – and they payed for it.

Could humanity have launched generation ships, the same way the Global Union had all those centuries ago? Entirely unfeasible. All projections indicated that even five hundred years after the launch of the Stargazer, the great vessel would still not have reached its destination planet. No, there was only one way we could guarantee our continued sustainability and expansion, and it was by following a path that was well trodden over the course of human history...

We waged war.

It was entirely logical and reasonable, really. Centuries past, we'd even justified it scientifically with such philosophies as Darwin's Law; the survival of the fittest. Really, I may sound sarcastic here, but this is where our genetic need for conflict helped us as a species: kill the weak, gain the power and cull the needless. It was evolutionary.

The small number of Ingrelden enclaves that were scattered throughout Sol fell quickly. We destroyed their planetary and orbital structures within our system, and captured their vessels, executing the crews. The Ingrelden as you know are a benevolent people, non-confrontational. They never stood a chance.

Ingrelden technology was far removed from ours, so it was never going to be as simple as pulling an FTL drive out of an Ingrelden ship and putting it in one of our own. The technology had to be studied, reverse engineered, and re-designed to suit human ships. This was inevitably a lengthy process.

Humans by the masses are not patient people. Especially when their comfort is taken away from them. The population knew that the FTL technology was what would allow them to expand, which in turn would allow them to survive. A number of different factions worked on cross-engineering the Ingrelden FTL drives, and the race was on – a new type of space race that would not just unlock the solar system, rather the entire galaxy itself.

Once again, conflict thrived. The race to successfully produce a starship led to human civil war throughout the solar system. We called this one the Omega War, for obvious reasons. As had happened prior to the Great Solar War, now centuries past, myriad human factions coalesced into two alliances. Due to the exploding population, individual human lives as a commodity were void of value. Entire cities on earth were razed, entire space cities destroyed, entire colonies wiped out.

As the two sides fought intensely, their scientists worked to cross engineer the drives they so desperately needed. But that was not all they worked on. They integrated Ingrelden technology into weaponry, utilizing their ingenuity for destruction, rather than the peaceful purposes for which it had initially been designed.

In the end, however it wasn't Ingrelden technology that had proved a turning point in the war. It was technology developed by humans the very same day that they had first encountered the alien species: zeptites.

The faction that had, over a century prior, developed the technology began to advance it, and they quickly found applications it could be utilised for. It turned out to be a far more useful, far more advanced technology than anything the Ingrelden had ever helped the humans develop. The zeptite technology was utilised by the faction that had created them for many varying purposes. They used the machines to increase the mental acuity of their strategists, intelligence officers, leaders and scientists. They used them to vastly increase the strength of their soldiers.

It was one woman, however, who took the first step to realising the full potential of the zeptite technology. You may perhaps have heard her referred to by a specific title before. To my people, she was more than any single name could ever convey, but she had been born as Haleh Madani sometime in the twenty-sixth century in Tehran. The legend goes that Madani had been a brilliant, if unpredictable scientist. From time to time she had a tendency to forgo any reasonable safety precautions in order to produce results. Luckily, for the faction she was a part of, this was one of those times.

Madani staunchly believed that the zeptites could change the very nature of human existence, so she went about altering her own DNA and allowing the zeptites to invade the very fabric of her being. What the zeptites had done to Madani's body was described differently by many people. Some claimed she was no longer human, perhaps having become some kind of cybernetic synthesis between human and machine. Others claimed she had transcended humanity. Some believed she had become a god.

Laughable really, the legends that humans create, regardless of their background. Believe me when I say, Madani was – is – far from a god.

She was studied by her people, and they adapted her principals into other willing volunteers and improved on some of what she had done, although they were particularly wary of experimenting to the extent that Madani herself had done. After months of her new, transcendent existence, Madani disappeared from the public eye, and from the research that had been her life until it had reached its pinnacle. History is uncertain where she went during that period, but she had appeared to have simply vanished. Many thought that it had been a result of her transformation; that she had just ceased to exist... And that that had been her plan, all along.

The zeptite enhanced forces in the end proved to be far too powerful for the forces of their opposition. The secrets of the Ingrelden FTL drive had, by now, been revealed. However, rather than utilise it to do what both sides had initially planned – you know, expanding to the stars in order to sustain themselves – it became a new weapon in the war. Just like children in a school-yard punch-up, they had forgotten their motivations for conflict, blocked out all external distractions and were focused solely on each raw act of violence. FTL capability had granted both sides the ability to almost instantaneously send their fleets across the solar system. This ability, in effect, increased the speed at which the war was fought. No more months' worth of preparation and travel for a fleet engagement, no more withdrawing of forces to await reinforcements.

The war, in reality, should have been won by the zeptite enhanced faction, even though they had been by far the smaller of the two warring factions. But, unlike the Great Solar War of the twenty-first century, there was no clear-cut victory. Something happened that prevented the zeptite enhanced faction from pressing their advantage and claiming victory...

That something was Haleh Madani.

Madani's return was as mysterious as her disappearance had been. No-one was certain where she had gone. And why she did what she did upon her *return is still to this day debated. Many think that she had gone insane, while others believed she had felt responsible for the human race as a whole. Take it from me: it was probably a bit of both.*

There is no debate, however as to what she did upon her return.

What I know (if you even care) is that she had seen something in herself. She had seen the true potential of the human race, but at the same moment had also seen what the human race was doing to itself. The one true legacy that humanity has always had is conflict. It has driven us to become what we are today, and it will drive us even further into the future towards what we will become. I think that Madani believed that an end to conflict would propel humanity (both – apologies – all three of its factions) even further into that future, and to a point in time where we'd evolved away from the residual instinct to engage in conflict.

So she flew a ship into Sol's star – Earth's sun.

Ask anyone, and you will discover that no-one knows exactly what she did (bar one person *wink*), if she had taken some kind of device with her, or if her own body was capable of initiating what had occurred, but whatever the method, she had extinguished the sun. Within days, the star had begun to dim, and as each week passed, it dimmed a little more.

The two warring factions had no choice but to cease hostilities and divert their forces to humanitarian (funny word, that) endeavours, for the star of the Sol system was dying, and earth and all the human colonies throughout the system would become uninhabitable.

It was not a fast process that which Madani had initiated. The two factions had plenty of time to evacuate their entire populations. It took each of them years, almost a decade but eventually the two factions set off in different directions, towards new (and separate) solar systems.

Nine years after Madani's flight into the sun, the final flicker of light winked out of it. The home-system of the human race was dead.

And that, my friend, is how humanity became known as the killer of stars.

Eighteen

Jonas woke from another of his unusual dreams, slightly disoriented, but well rested. It had been just over a month since he had arrived in Rho's Sacrifice. Haldon Cos' revelations about the Valley of Stars and the truth about the Providencian pilgrimage had spurred him to action, and he knew without a doubt now what it was that he had to do. He'd spent the last four weeks preparing to complete the pilgrimage himself, gaining what support he could from the Technos, which had been considerable thanks in no small part to the influence of Rai Ashima.

A week after Jonas and his group had been rescued by the Technos, the faction had sent a skimmer to the region near Providence, utilising their scavenged Morphite technology to scan the area around the Valley that Haldon had claimed was surrounded by some sort of energy dampening field. They had indeed detected a high density energy field enveloping the entire valley, and their assessments of the readings indicated that it would be no safer for their skimmers to approach the valley than it had been for the Redeemer duster that had been sent almost a decade prior. This had disheartened Haldon Cos, who had been hoping to learn more about the mysterious Morphite he had met, and to discover a way of contacting her.

Haldon had finally been released from Purgatory and was now living in an apartment down in the Promenade, near the one Jonas had been assigned. Upon learning of Jonas' plan to complete the pilgrimage, he requested that Jonas allow him to join him, and Jonas had immediately agreed, realising the advantage in having someone who had already completed the trek accompanying him. They were only days away from departing Rho's Sacrifice to complete the pilgrimage, and Jonas was anxious. Now that he had an inkling of why he had wiped his own memory (and of who he was), he was keen to continue on his adventure in order to release more of his memories, which still stubbornly refused to reveal themselves to him.

Gala stirred beside him. He glanced down at her naked form lying in bed next to him and smiled. It had been a natural progression, really. He'd felt an attraction for the young woman the first time they had met in Port Usharin, and it hadn't taken long for them to consummate their mutual feelings once they had settled into Rho's Sacrifice. She really was a sweet person, but also strong and wilful. She hadn't responded well to Jonas' refusal to allow her to join him on his pilgrimage, but she had eventually accepted it.

Jonas climbed out of bed, careful not to wake Gala. The apartment he had been assigned by the Technos was fairly basic: one bedroom with a separate living room, a small bathroom and a basic kitchenette off to one side. It did have a window that looked over the Promenade, however, and it was comfortable enough. He dressed in the colourful clothes that had been given to him by the Technos and left the apartment, planning to surprise Gala with breakfast in bed.

He exited the building, and strode though the streets towards the Promenade. It really did remind him of Olympus, the exotic space city that lay between his homeworld Illium, in the system of Tau Ceti, and Proteus which was the third planet of the Epsilon Eridani system. Olympus had been just as colourful, festive and exotic as Rho's Sacrifice, and it gave him an odd sense of nostalgia as he walked through the streets. He couldn't remember ever actually having visited Olympus, nor any specifics of the place. Rather, it was more of a general recollection and flashes of imagery. Little of his memory had returned in the month he had spent at Rho's Sacrifice, and what had returned was light on specifics... but there was undeniable progress which had been a huge positive.

He went to a small food stall and bought two servings of Bakava, which was a sweet pastry that both he and Gala adored, and two steaming cups of Ora, a hot beverage made from the ground root of a locally genetically engineered plant, which the Technos said they had created as a local analogue to an old earth beverage called coffee.

Back at the apartment, Galatea lay awake in bed, the sheets pulled up over her naked body. She smiled at Jonas as he entered, carrying breakfast.

'Hope's mercy, where have you been all my life?' she asked playfully.

Midway through the meal, the smartpad that Jonas had been assigned by the Technos buzzed and he answered a call from Sid Ashima, who had managed to retain his position as head of the militia after the less than successful operation in Port Usharin. The gruff older man was summoning him to an urgent meeting at the Techno militia's headquarters, and he wouldn't tell Jonas why. Jonas advised him he would be present and severed the link. The old man seemed more worked up than usual. *Not a good sign*, Jonas thought. He just hoped that whatever it was that had Sid worried didn't have anything to do with his pilgrimage.

Jonas and Gala left their apartment for the meeting. They walked through the Promenade and then took a maglev tram up to the militia HQ, which was part of a small group of structures clustered around the skimmer docks. There were no guards at the tram station to greet them (Techno security in Rho's Sacrifice was almost nonexistent with the exception of Purgatory), so they continued on to the building they had both been to multiple times before. On the way they encountered Jett and Tailynn who were heading in the same direction.

'Let me guess,' Jett said to them. 'That hyperactive old git summoned you two as well?' Tailynn elbowed him in the ribs disapprovingly and he reacted with a slight yelp.

'He did seem more worked up than normal,' Jonas admitted.

'He did,' Tailynn agreed. Before the four of them could continue on their way, she took Jonas by the arm, firmly but gently. 'Do you mind if I have a quick word with you?'

Jonas nodded, with a surprised look on his face. Tailynn gave Gala and Jett a look that indicated she wanted it to be a *private* word. The two of them continued on to the militia HQ with a minimum of grumbling.

'What's wrong?' Jonas asked, still surprised.

'I feel... that I owe you an explanation,' she began awkwardly.

'For what?'

'For why Jett and I refused to accompany you on your pilgrimage,' she answered after a moment's hesitation.

When Jonas had made his intentions of completing the Pilgrimage clear, he had initially asked both Jett and Tailynn to accompany him (much to Gala's chagrin). To his surprise, they had both declined, and would not give him a reason why. Jonas had not pushed them – there was obviously something in their past that was stopping them, and he had admittedly put them both through enough already.

Jonas shook his head.

'You don't owe me a thing, Tailynn,' he said. 'If anything, it's the other way around. After everything I've dragged you into...'

Tailynn shook her head firmly.

'No,' she interrupted. 'You've opened my eyes, Jonas. Jett's too. Without you we'd have never seen the true nature of the Advocates, nor the Judges or the Redeemers. We'd have never discovered that the Technos weren't the terrorist troublemakers we'd always been told they were, or the fact that the Morphites are already on Eden. Nor the nature of the wider galaxy,' she gave a slight laugh. 'We were so ignorant.'

'It wasn't your fault,' Jonas said.

'Perhaps not,' she replied. After a moment: 'So let me explain to you something that *you* don't know.'

Jonas nodded slowly.

When Tailynn had been a teenager, she had been a true believer. Her parents had seen to that. As a family they had visited the Redeemer temple in Avoca religiously, praying to the Morphites, whom they believed would one day come to save them, and all of the humans of Eden. The Sar family were not well off; they lived in the old section of Avoca and all three of them worked hard, every day of the week, saving as much as they could from their earnings, and spending as little as possible on the necessities. Their goal was simple: to one day have enough money to buy transport to Providence and then the supplies they would need to embark on the Providencian pilgrimage. One day, Tailynn's father had come home from work in a festive mood. They'd done it! He had declared. They had enough money!

A week later, two days shy of Tailynn's seventeenth birthday, they had departed their shack in the Avoca slums, and travelled to the new sector of the city and the rail station where they would depart on one of the fancy trains that were the only viable travel link between Avoca and Providence. The train ride had been long, but Tailynn had enjoyed it thoroughly – it had been unlike anything she had ever experienced before. After two days of travel (thanks to a breakdown mid-journey – all too common with the limited maintenance that the train received), they had pulled into Providence's grand station and disembarked.

Tailynn's father had immediately begun the arduous task of sourcing the supplies they would need for their pilgrimage. It would be a long trek, and a tough journey, especially for one as young as Tailynn. Few people her age ever embarked on it. It took her father another three days to acquire all the resources the family would need. Meanwhile, they had rented a room in a cheap inn. The room had only one small bed, a tiny grubby window and shared kitchen and toilet facilities, but to Tailynn it could well have been a suite in the Avoca Grande; the shack they had just left in Avoca had been smaller and dirtier and did not even have a flushing toilet, which was not uncommon in the city's old section.

It was during the days that she had stayed in this inn in Providence that she had met another young pilgrim, a twenty year old former junior acolyte of the Redeemer church called Jett Dor. He had been bunking in the room next to the one her family had rented, and Tailynn had immediately fallen in love (or at least, she thought she had). Jett had had a great sense of humour, was big and strong, and was full of faith in both himself and the Morphites. He had spent three years studying to become a full fledged acolyte with the church, but after having passed all the exams, he had made an eleventh hour decision to reject the church's offer and commit himself to the pilgrimage, as he felt it was the best way to prove himself in the eyes of the Morphites.

Much to Tailynn's dismay, her father had been better at bartering for supplies than she had anticipated, and they left a day early, well before Jett had been ready, so Tailynn's (admittedly silly) hopes that he could travel with them were dashed. As her parents loaded themselves and her up with bags and supplies, and led her through Providence, across the grand concourse and out into the Valley of Stars, she sulked. But as they progressed down the rocky valley, the stars and the Pandora Nebula bright in the sky above them, she managed to overcome her angst, realising that both she and her *darling* Jett were ultimately going to the same place.

The first few days of travel were easy, but by the third day she was exhausted, so it had been very pleasant indeed when they reached the first of the wayside camps along the valley. That night she had slept on a soft air-bed, and eaten a hot meal – a well deserved break that had been rejuvenating, even if she did spend much of their one night layover keeping an eye on the entrance to the camp in the hope that Jett would appear. He didn't though, and the next morning her family had packed up their things and departed the camp. Before they had left, however, she had overheard a conversation between her father and the camp proprietor; something about "outlaws", and having to pay their way to progress down the valley. Her father had laughed the proprietor's comments off, however, so Tailynn had put it out of her mind.

The next few days were straining, but rewarding, and they progressed a good distance down through the valley, the Pandora Nebula hanging overhead like a guiding star from the Morphites themselves.

The ambush came on their sixth day of pilgrimage.

Masked outlaws had emerged from a rocky outcropping on the western edge of the valley, and had quickly surrounded them. They were armed: some with makeshift clubs and bats, others with swords or knives and one or two of them with clockwork fire-arms. There were ten of them all up, and they had quickly grabbed the family of pilgrims and spirited them away, back to a hidden network of caves, it's entrance shrouded by the rocky outcropping Tailynn had first spotted them emerging from. There were another dozen or so outlaws in the caves, and few of them could have been considered sane. There were both men and women varying in age from about their mid-twenties to around their fifties or sixties, although Tailynn couldn't be sure. The bandits had immediately raided their supplies and were tucking in greedily, while a couple of them tied Tailynn and her family to a grouping of wooden posts that had been stuck securely into the rocky cave floor. Tailynn's father begged and pleaded with the outlaws, imploring for their release. They could have the supplies, he'd cried over and over.

Eventually one of the older outlaws, a large bulky man wearing a particularly scary mask which Tailynn had belatedly realised had been made from human remains ventured over, and sat down in front of them. His gravelly voice was deep and menacing, and as he spoke, Tailynn was more afraid than she had ever been in her life.

'You got to pay your way through this valley, 'deemers,' he drawled, munching on some tinned soya strips he had acquired from their supplies. 'We ain't inclined to let people like you pass for a pittance.'

There was a roar of insane laughter from his cohorts. He silenced them with wave of the hand.

'You had no creds in your shit, which means you been hiding it,' he continued. 'How much you got?'

Tailynn's father stuttered his answer.

'We... we have n... no creds,' he said. 'Pl... please, you must believe me!'

The big outlaw scoffed at him.

'You fuckin' lie to me 'deemer?' He spat in Tailynn's father's face. 'You didn't travel with zilch creds. Only a fool do that. How you expect to get back if you don't make it all the way? All 'deemer pilgrims have creds!'

'We d... don't!' her father cried. 'I swear!'

'So you just a fuckin' dumb cunt, then?' There was a howl of hysterical laughter from the other outlaws.

'Please don't hurt us! Please!' Tailynn's father grovelled. 'There must be something we have that you need other than creds!'

The big man turned to Tailynn, and gave her a look that she had, to this very day, never forgotten. After a moment of silence, he answered.

'Yeah,' he drawled. 'Yeah you got somethin' I need.'

Tailynn could remember at that moment the horrified look that passed between her parents. And she could also remember the precise moment when that look turned from horror into resignation, and then into ashamed acceptance. Tailynn had not really understood what was going on at that point. Perhaps she had been naive, or perhaps it had just never occurred to her that her parents could have been so flawed, so full of cowardice to do what they did. But it had not been until her parents restraints had been released, and they had fled the cave weeping uncontrollably, but never looking back at her, that she had realised what had happened.

And almost immediately, the raping had begun.

They had all had a go, the men and the women, and when she had cried out in pain, or in fear they had beaten her. After the first few hours it seemed as though her entire naked body had been covered in blood, tears and other revolting bodily fluids, but her senses had numbed. She had been on the verge of insanity at that point, and as the big man who had made the abhorrent deal with her parents raped her savagely, he whispered in her ear that she would be one of them very soon.

Eventually, the savage outlaws became fatigued, and they tied her limp, naked form back up to one of the poles while they went about scavenging through the supplies they had taken from her and her parents.

Tailynn fell into an oblivious sleep.

She was unsure exactly how long she had been asleep for, but when she had woken, the outlaws were asleep, and a new form had appeared, tied to the post next to her, beaten and bruised, unconscious but alive. Her heart skipped a beat: it was *Jett!* She whispered his name urgently, over and over again, willing him to wake, which eventually he did. He saw her face and moaned quietly, his mouth gagged. Tailynn tugged at her bound hands, and realised that her restraints were not as tight as they had initially been when she had first been captured, but in her numb state she simply hadn't noticed. She tugged and tugged, her wrists burning against the coarse rope, and she could feel her skin tear, but after a moment, her left hand was free. Free!

She quickly untied the other hand, and then went to work untying Jett. Within moments he too was loose, and she hugged him tightly, sobbing. He had returned her embrace, and shushed her soothingly.

'How long have you been here?' he asked her in a frantic whisper.

'I don't know!' she had answered with a sob. 'My parents... they... they left me.'

He'd stared at her in horror, and then looked over her naked body, only then realising what had happened to her. He'd almost been paralysed in shock. Eventually, he moved away, grabbed the torn rags that had been her clothing, and helped her dress, being careful not to cause her any more pain than necessary.

They had then taken the opportunity to dash to the cave's entrance together as quietly as they could. As they neared it, however, they realised there was a guard on duty. Jett had motioned for Tailynn to stay put, and he had bent down to pick up a rock off the ground. He snuck over to the guard, and struck the outlaw in the back of the head, before bending down to sequester the savage's machete. He waved Tailynn over and together they fled the cave.

Over the course of the next day, they struggled along, on to the next camp down the valley's well trodden path, and upon their arrival they had been quickly aided by another group of pilgrims, and the camp's proprietor. Over the next few days, their physical injuries were seen to, and Tailynn welcomed the opportunity to clean herself, although it would be a long time until she would ever again feel "clean". The proprietor had quizzed them on what had happened, and the two of them had told their stories. The proprietor had been disgusted at the actions of Tailynn's parents, but when she had questioned him, he had uneasily told her that no-one matching their description had come through his camp in the last few days.

One night she had overheard Jett and the Proprietor speaking in harsh whispers.

'What are you, some kind of coward?' the proprietor had hissed at Jett. 'You saw what those heathens did to that poor girl! Hell, they beat you pretty bad too! These animals don't deserve leniency! They're just going to keep on doing this shit if *we* don't do something! Can you honestly just walk away without making them *pay*?'

She had watched as Jett had pondered over the man's words. Eventually he'd looked at the man, a determined look on his face.

'I'm no coward,' he'd said in an uncertain voice, and for the first time, Tailynn had realised that Jett was barely more than a child, same as her. 'You're right. They deserve to pay.'

Tailynn had emerged from behind the stack of supplies she'd used to remain out of sight, knowing exactly what it was the two men were planning. Both of them had looked at her in surprise as she strode over determinedly.

'I'm coming with you,' she'd said in as firm a voice as she could muster.

'I'm not sure that's a great idea, miss,' the proprietor had answered uncomfortably.

'You weren't there,' she replied forcefully. 'I was. And I'm going with you.'

They'd formed a group of six: Jett, the proprietor, the proprietor's two assistants, the owner of a trading caravan that travelled the valley, resupplying the camps, and Tailynn herself. They'd planned their assault for the wee hours of the morning, and had armed themselves with blades, except for the proprietor and the caravan owner who owned powerful clockwork rifles, specifically designed for use in the energy dampened valley.

With the Pandora Nebula lighting the way, the small band of vigilantes had travelled back down the valley, and quietly moved into the cave network, one of the proprietor's assistants silently killing the outlaw who had been placed on guard duty. The guard had been carrying a clockwork pistol, and Jett had eagerly bent down and relieved the dead man of it, giving Tailynn a comforting nod as he did so. They progressed into the caves, and stood silently over the sleeping marauders. All the men were looking around uneasily, willing each other to be the first to begin the culling.

Tailynn looked over the sleeping figures, and her eyes came to rest on the big man who had evidently been the leader of the gang. She had a flashback at that moment: he had been the most violent of the rapists... the one who had inflicted the most pain on her, and who had *enjoyed* inflicting it the most. At that moment, something inside her snapped, and she barrelled forward with the small knife the proprietor had lent her gripped tightly in her hand. She approached the sleeping figure, and plunged the knife down, into the big man's chest. The man awoke with a gasp, the whites of his eyes glowing like fire, and Tailynn stared into those eyes as she drove the knife in again, and again until the eyes were as dead as her soul felt.

She hadn't noticed, but her actions had awoken some of the outlaws. The rest of her mob had been spurred into action, and they had begun the slaughter. Tailynn, fuelled by the chaos jumped up and plunged her knife into another outlaw, this time a woman who screamed like a wild animal, and as she plunged the knife in again, Tailynn screamed back at her, as wild an animal herself.

The massacre was over in what seemed simultaneously an instant and an eternity. The only thing that Tailynn could see was blood and corpses, and as her mind returned to something resembling normalcy after the animal instincts had faded, she looked around in horror, and then ran to a corner and threw up. Jett was next to her in a heartbeat, rubbing her back and telling her how everything was going to be alright now.

They'd returned to the camp minus two of their group: the caravan owner and one of the proprietor's assistants hadn't been as lucky as the rest of them. After another day of rest, Jett and Tailynn departed the camp, heading back to Providence. The five day journey was completed mostly in a silent numbness for both of them, and when they came upon Providence's grand concourse once again, they passed through it as changed people: Jett no longer a docile believer, and Tailynn no longer an innocent young woman.

They remained together for a month in Providence, and had in a way become a couple, although there was no sex. But each other's companionship seemed to give them strength, and Tailynn couldn't imagine being alone at that point. Together, they discussed the future, and both immediately agreed that they wouldn't stay in Providence any longer than they had to.

They'd initially returned to Avoca, but both of them found that the city was not as it had been when they'd first left on their pilgrimages: it's hordes of people had become oppressive, and both of them found it claustrophobic. Together, they fled the city, wanting to forget their past lives, forget what had made them become these new, scarred people that they were. Forget themselves.

So they'd started new lives in Port Usharin.

'It took me a long time to recover,' Tailynn finished. 'But eventually I did. And when I recovered, I found myself with the urge to help people. I didn't want what had happened to ruin me, or define me. But likewise, I felt as though I would never be able to forget, and that I needed to do something that would both acknowledge the hardship I'd been through, and allow me a release from its legacy. Helping others seemed to fit the bill, and the best way I could think to do that was to become an Advocate. Jett began to lose himself in the bottle, and eventually became a bounty hunter, I think as kind of a way to help me. Or maybe he thought he was protecting me, I don't know. Our relationship is all kinds of weird. Maybe chasing down criminals was his way of dealing with what had happened to us.'

Jonas was silent, trying to process what Tailynn had just told him. He had no words for her, unable to imagine what she had been through, and what Jett had been through. She was living proof that pain and suffering could simultaneously bring out the best, and worst in a person.

'So,' Tailynn said awkwardly when after a few moments, Jonas still hadn't said anything. 'That's why I can't go with you to Providence. Maybe... maybe that makes me incredibly weak. But I just can't.'

Jonas shook his head sombrely.

'It doesn't make you weak,' Jonas replied quietly. 'I think you may just be the strongest person I've ever met, Tailynn.'

They shared a moment of silence, before Tailynn took a deep breath.

'Well,' she said. 'I suppose we should get to this meeting.'

They headed for the HQ and were escorted by a militia officer up to a large, circular briefing room with a huge holographic projector in the centre of the room, which was projecting a three dimensional image of the region of the Desert of Forever that immediately surrounded Rho's Sacrifice. Sid, Rai, Haldon, Gala and Jett stood around it, along with a number of militia officers and analysts.

'You two took your time,' Rai said, accusingly.

'What's this all about?' Jonas asked, ignoring her.

'As you're aware, shortly after your arrival here at Rho's Sacrifice, we've struggled to get any real intelligence on the Redeemers,' Sid began, the frown on his face wrinkling his bald forehead. 'Their data net has all but gone silent, and two assets we had in Avoca haven't made a report in weeks. We've had suspicions that the bastards have been up to something, and it seems as though we were right.'

He pressed a few buttons on a nearby console, and the holographic image changed from the three dimensional landscape it had been displaying to a two dimensional image, grainy and distorted.

'We'd heard rumours that a number of Behemoths had gone missing from various mines throughout the badlands,' he continued. 'This image was taken approximately a week and a half ago by a team we'd sent to Avoca to investigate whatever it is that the Redeemers are up to. We're fairly certain it's one of the missing Behemoths.'

'We lost contact with the team shortly after we received this image,' Rai continued. 'Redeemer security has never been as tight as it is right now. We've never had so much trouble getting intelligence.'

'What does it mean?' Jett asked. 'What are they up to?'

'We don't know,' Rai said with a shrug. 'It's that simple. We can speculate; it could have something to do with what happened at Port Usharin, or it could have something to do with the appearance of the Morphite.'

'You said you received this image over a week ago?' Haldon asked. 'Why bring it up now? What else has happened?'

Rai gave her father an uncomfortable look. She tapped another couple of buttons on the nearby console, and the image returned to the three dimensional landscape of the desert. A red, flashing dot appeared on it.

'Two hours ago seismic sensors detected something a bit under a hundred clicks to the east of here. Slight tremors, almost undetectable.'

Jonas frowned. 'Are you suggesting the Redeemers are about to attack Rho's Sacrifice?' he asked.

'Impossible,' Sid replied dismissively. 'The Redeemers have no idea about our location.'

'It takes an arrogance of great proportions to assume your enemy is not as resourceful as you are,' Haldon said to the Techno. Sid scowled at him.

'You want to watch what you say, Judge, or I'll have you shipped back up to Purgatory.'

'Haldon makes a valid point,' Tailynn insisted, adding to the militia leader's forehead wrinkles. 'How can you be sure that the Redeemers haven't found you? You forget they have a Morphite working with them.'

Sid angrily bashed a hand on the console in front of them.

'Think about what you're saying!' he exclaimed. 'The Redeemers don't have enough Advocates or Judges to come after us! Let 'em try, we'll wipe the bastards off the face of Eden!'

'You're forgetting about the Behemoths, pops,' Rai said. 'They're right, something's up. I want to take *Rusty* up and check out whatever it is that set off the seismic sensors. I'm thinking we're all having the same thought on the cause, but we need to know for sure.'

Sid growled, but after a moment of thought he nodded.

'Fine,' he said. 'But you damage that airship again, girl, and you won't know what hit 'ya.'

'Yeah, yeah, yeah,' she replied dismissively, before turning to Jonas and the others. 'So who wants to come flying with me?'

Nineteen

Judge Drealon Rus stood in the middle of the control deck of his command Behemoth, looking out over the sandy desert surrounds. Eden's star was high in the sky, and shone down onto the sand making it glisten just as the rest of the visible galaxy in the planet's dark sky did. Dune after dune was all the Redeemer taskforce had encountered for the last two days since they had crossed from the rocky Crimson Sea into the vast nothingness of the Desert of Forever. But his crew had just announced the first sighting of the peak of the rocky mountain that the Morphite Zesiro had advised him was home to the Technos.

Rus' task-force was made up of one thousand heavily armed and armoured troops, most of whom were recent enlistees in this new Redeemer Army. About twenty Advocates served in the task force as officers, commanding the enlistees and ensuring their absolute obedience to Judge Rus. A second Judge named Minos Tar stood beside Rus, acting as his second in command.

Few would have denied the impressive feat they had accomplished by establishing this task-force. While enlistee applicants had been vetted and then trained by the Advocates, the Redeemer church hired a number of renowned engineering co-ops to begin the refit of the five Behemoths that had been sequestered from the red-ore mines of the Badlands. Among a plethora of other conversions to their previous benignity, the Behemoths had had their enormous ore-carrying bodies converted into mobile barracks or, depending on how one saw it, into huge armoured personnel carriers. They had had dozens of weapons turrets installed all over their structures, and each had a huge main cannon that had been constructed specifically for this assault, as a way for Rus' task-force to breach the rocky mountain that hid the Techno city. In addition, each Behemoth was equipped with a landing pad on its ceiling, and each of them carried two Advocate dusters, all of them heavily armed, which would be utilised as soon as the attack began as a way to counter the fleet of airships that Rus knew the Technos would employ as their defence. Darting around the edges of the five huge machines like pilot-fish to a pod of whales were thirty smaller cruisers; small, two man wheeled buggies each with their own gun turret. So all in all, Rus commanded one thousand troops, five huge beasts (which were in effect monstrous tanks), ten aircraft and thirty light attack buggies.

The closest thing to a true military Eden had ever seen.

Rus stared ahead at the horizon, and eventually spotted the tip of the huge rocky mountain that his forward scouts had announced seeing only minutes before. Battle was nearing. He turned to his deputy, who stood stoically beside him.

'Judge Tar, it will not be long before we engage the Techno heathens,' he said in his menacing voice, failing to disguise the anticipation he felt. 'Prepare the troops.'

'Understood, Judge Rus.'

The young Judge, who was the most recently assigned of the current five, left the command post obediently. After he had left, Rus opened a communication channel to Zesiro, who was still posing as Lord Adjutant Imanre Hes. After a few moments, the Morphite answered, and appeared on a monitor directly in front of Rus.

'Lord Adjutant,' Rus said by way of greeting. 'I am pleased to announce that we will be launching our attack on the Techno city within the hour.'

'That is most gratifying to hear, Judge Rus,' the image of the

Morphite replied. 'By all means, commence your assault. But remember: if Jonas Dresden dies, then so do you.'

Rus restrained himself from sneering, and instead bowed his head. 'Understood, Lord Adjutant.'

'Good.'

The image of Zesiro disappeared, and Rus deactivated the monitor. After a moment, one of his Advocate command officers spoke up. 'Judge Rus, our forward observers have spotted activity on the target mountain.'

Rus ordered the officer to provide a live video feed from the forward observer's camera. After only moments, a large screen in the middle of the command centre lit up, displaying a grainy black and white low-resolution image. Despite the quality of the video feed, however, it was clear that the forward observer had not been lying. What appeared to be a huge camouflaged door in the side of the rocky mountain was opening up. The door was massive, and if the forward observer's had been equipped with better cameras, Rus believed he may even have been able to see what was inside the mountain. Regardless, when the door was fully opened, the command centre crew watched as a small craft, one of the Techno skimmers he had seen in Port Usharin emerged, and the door began to close as the airship cleared the mountain. So, it was a hanger.

Rus turned to the communications officer. 'Instruct all forward observation units to withdraw and rejoin the main battle force, and advise Judge Tar that I expect all ground combat units to be ready for battle within five minutes. I want three dusters ready for launch on my command.'

The command centre officer went about relaying Rus's orders, as he himself peered out of the huge windows of the Behemoth over the great sandy plains of the Desert of Forever, knowing that this would shortly be the location where the first shots of what would undoubtedly be the greatest battle in Eden's history would be fired. He turned his attention to the monitor in front of him which was still displaying a video feed from the forward observation buggy that had first seen the skimmer emerging from the rocky mountain. He frowned slightly as he realised that the skimmer was, in fact heading directly for his battle group. Had they been detected? Were the Technos expecting them? He had gone to great lengths over the previous couple of months to prevent any intelligence leaks in regards to the establishment of the Redeemer Army, and he was reasonably confident that the Technos could not possibly know of the army's existence. Perhaps his battle group's route through the desert fell underneath a Techno flight path? Possible, but to Rus it seemed far too coincidental. And he did not believe in coincidence. Still, if the Technos were expecting his attack, surely they would send a greater force than a single skimmer to combat them. No, he was certain that there was no way the Technos could be expecting his army.

'Judge Tar reports that our ground forces are ready for battle, and we have three dusters ready for immediate launch with the remainder on alert status one.'

Rus nodded an acknowledgement. 'Launch the dusters, and instruct all behemoths to advance to full speed and to arm their main guns.'

Rus felt the behemoth lurch slightly as its speed was increased almost instantaneously, and within moments the communications officer announced that the first three dusters were airborne. He looked down at a tactical display which was now pinpointing the location of the enemy skimmer. He instructed the dusters to advance on the skimmer with a wide attacking front, and to converge on the sole enemy airship at the last moment in what he anticipated to be a surprise pincer attack.

The three dusters raced off at his command, and converged on the skimmer. Rus grinned in anticipation. This was it. The beginning of the battle.

He had a moment of déjà-vu. He had been five years old, and he had just been robbed by an older group of boys, perhaps eight or nine years old themselves. They'd taken a small metal trinket that his mother had given him a day before his own father had beaten her to death. It had been his most treasured possession for many months, and he had been filled with rage at the nerve of the older children. He had concocted a plan almost immediately to have his revenge on the children, and retrieve what was his. He had waited until they had all been separated, and then one by one he had attacked them and beaten each of them until they had cried and begged for his forgiveness. Eventually they had all come to respect his strength, and he had received what had rightfully been his. Of course, when the other children's parents had complained to his own father, he had been beaten to within an inch of his life. But the feeling of exhilaration he had felt at the outset of each of his brutal attacks on the children had made it all worthwhile.

It was the same feeling that he now felt, moments away from the outset of his attack on the Technos. He felt exhilarated... alive.

Nothing could stop him.

Twenty

Rai stood at the centre of *The Rust Bucket's* bridge, with Jonas and his companions, along with Haldon Cos at her side. The skimmer's scavenged Morphite scanners had just detected a small buggy in the middle of the desert, which had initially been heading directly for Rho's Sacrifice, but had then reversed its course when they had detected it. The seismic distortions that had been initially detected had steadily grown more audible to the Techno analysts since the *Rust Bucket* had launched. Rai had a terrible feeling that this fleeing buggy was just the very tip of the iceberg.

Her fears were confirmed when one of her crew turned to her urgently. 'Rai, I'm detecting three dusters on an intercept course!'

'Arm all weapons, and prepare for evasive manoeuvres!' she instructed forcefully. 'Prepare defensive countermeasures!'

Jonas and the others watched on nervously as *Rusty's* bridge crew frantically prepared the airship for battle. Within moments, the same crewmember who had initially announced detection of the dusters turned back to her. 'I'm detecting more, Rai! A *lot* more!'

'Don't keep it to yourself!' Rai instructed, testily.

'Five behemoths, thirty buggies and another seven dusters! Estimate between five hundred and one thousand troops. It's an army!'

Rai smashed a fist on the console in front of her. 'Send an alert to Rho's Sacrifice! Advise them of an impending attack!'

'We're in weapons range of the first wing of dusters!' Another crew member screamed.

'Launch countermeasures, and fire all weapons!'

The Rust Bucket's chaff launchers belched out protective clouds of metal decoys, and simultaneously two missiles streaked away from the launchers attached to the body of the airship. Rai watched in annoyance as one of the missiles streaked away and harmlessly ploughed into a small rocky outcropping. *Wait until I find the dumbass that programmed* that *one!* Within seconds, a crew member announced that the second missile had struck its target and one of the dusters was down. Before the crew could cheer, however, another crewmember screamed that they had enemy missiles inbound – three of them.

'Target them with the pulse cannons!' Rai instructed. 'Shoot them out of the hope-damned sky!'

The skimmer's two forward pulse cannons sprung to life, and began belching out streams of energy. Within seconds, two of the incoming missiles had been neutralised, but one managed to break through the defensive fire, and struck a piece of chaff that had been ejected by *Rusty's* countermeasure launchers. The resulting explosion shook the airship so violently, that everyone on the bridge fell to the floor, or clung desperately to nearby consoles.

'Damage!' Rai screamed. 'What's the damage?'

One of the bridge crew scrambled to his feet and quickly looked over a console. 'The missile struck the chaff cloud,' he advised in an urgent tone. 'It looks like our starboard engine was damaged in the resulting explosion! We have huge power drains across the board. We're going to have to put down, or we're going to fall out of the sky!'

As the rest of the bridge contingent got to their feet, Rai slammed her fist on the console in front of her again.

'Damn it! Set a new course, north forty degrees! Keep *Rusty* in the air as long as you can! Did we get a message away to Rho's Sacrifice?'

'Can't be sure,' a crew member replied. 'We encountered severe communications jamming at the outset of the attack. The message may have gotten through, and it may not have.'

'What about the other dusters? Are they still targeting us?'

'No, it looks like they've broken off their attack and rejoined their main battle group.'

'I guess we're not worth finishing off,' Rai muttered.

One of the crew members turned to her frantically. 'Rai we have to put down *now*, or we're gonna drop to the ground like a rock!'

She ordered the skimmer to land near a small rock outcropping nearby. During the landing sequence, a large fire broke out in the damaged engine, and she sent Jonas and his companions to help extinguish it. It was going to be a rough landing. Rai took the controls herself, as she was by far the best pilot on board (at least *she* thought she was). It was still a terribly rough landing, however. Moments before the skimmer struck the loose desert sand, she instructed her crew to brace for impact. As *Rusty* hit the ground, the landing struts sunk into the sand, and the airship lurched heavily to one side, throwing the crew violently across the bridge. There were screams of pain and cries for help, as the airship came to rest on the desert floor.

Rai picked herself up from the floor, nursing a sore arm which would no doubt come out in a pretty bruise. She looked around the bridge as the rest of the crew picked themselves up, some evidently in a lot of pain. She walked over to her head engineer, Bas Cordoba who had a nasty gash on his forehead.

'Bas, what's the damage?'

Rai was fairly certain that the man was in shock from the way his eyes darted from one point to another, but she needed to know how badly her skimmer was damaged. He groggily tapped some commands into a computer console.

'Structure is holding,' the engineer replied. 'Looks like we've sunk into the sand a bit, might be a bit of a struggle to get back out. The emergency team managed to extinguish the engine fire, and the starboard engine looks repairable. A day or two and I could probably have old *Rusty* back in the air.'

'Get that wound looked at first,' Rai replied.

She made her way urgently off the bridge, and down to the main hold, where she encountered Jonas, Jett, Tailynn, Galatea and Haldon.

'Y'all in one piece?' she asked.

'A few bumps and bruises, but we'll survive,' Tailynn replied.

'Which is more than I can say for Rho's Sacrifice if that message didn't get out to them,' Haldon added.

'How long will it take to repair the skimmer?' Jonas asked.

'Too long,' Rai replied. 'That's why I'm taking you five in the buggy and heading back to the city.'

Jonas nodded. 'Understood,' he replied. 'Do you have weapons aboard this thing?'

Rai led them over to a small armoury, and allowed them to arm themselves, even Galatea who, despite her experiences in Port Usharin was not exactly a combatant. While they were equipping themselves, Rai began to examine the small buggy that sat securely in the cargo bay. Thankfully it hadn't taken any serious damage, and would easily make the journey back to Rho's Sacrifice. She began to prepare it, and when the others were ready, she fired up the engine and drove it out of *Rusty's* belly, leaving instructions with her crew to see to the injured and repair as much damage as they could.

It was a thirty kilometre trip back to Rho's Sacrifice, an hour journey if she disregarded all safety considerations and common sense (which she did), but it was of absolute urgent importance that she warn her father of the impending attack, which by her estimates would commence before she and the others could possibly make it back. So she drove wildly over the sand dunes, instructing Jonas to attempt communication with Rho's Sacrifice via a small handheld communicator. He was having no luck – the enemy jamming was still in effect – but she hoped that it would work as they got nearer to the Techno city.

Roughly halfway between the downed skimmer and the rocky mountain which hid Rho's sacrifice, Rai took the opportunity to glance at the dashboard of the buggy. To her dismay, she noticed that the low fuel indicator was flashing, and belatedly discovered that during *Rusty's* crash landing, the fuel tank had been pierced. She gunned the engine even harder, willing the buggy's fuel to last the distance, even though she knew it couldn't possibly do so. Eventually, the engine spluttered and died. They'd made it further than she'd expected, but they were still a good five kilometres from the nearest entrance to the city. Jonas was still having no luck with the jammed transmitter, so Rai instructed everyone to leg it double time across the desert sands.

From the air, the desert seemed relatively flat, and it wasn't until one was on foot that it became apparent how steep the sand dunes really were. Small mountains of the golden grains towered over them as they trudged along, their feet sinking deeply into the sand, their calves burning from the exertion. Eventually the group climbed one last dune, and upon reaching the peak, Rai cried out in horror.

Rho's sacrifice was under attack. The behemoths had fired their huge guns, blasting huge holes in the hollow mountain, and troops and buggies were streaming in, while the enemy dusters circled around their allies, their gatling guns occasionally firing at some target or other. As they watched in horror, two skimmers attempted to launch, and were almost instantly destroyed by missiles launched by the dusters.

Rai dropped to her knees, sinking slightly into the sand. As hard as she tried to resist, tears began to roll down her cheeks. She could hear someone sobbing uncontrollably, and was shocked when she realised it was herself. Rho's Sacrifice – her home, the bastion of her people was being destroyed right before her eyes. She pounded the sand with her fists without even realising she was doing so – pounding so hard and so fast that her hands began to burn. Eventually she stopped when she felt a hand on her shoulder. She turned and looked up, and through her tears she saw Haldon Cos, his hand firmly on her shoulder, staring down at her over his glasses, a sincere look on his face.

'We must go,' he said, his deep voice calm and unwavering. 'We must head back to the skimmer immediately.'

Go? Was he being serious? They had to get to the city, help aide the defence she knew her father would have surely launched! Before she could speak, however, Haldon had kneeled down beside her, and was looking her in the eye.

'Rho's Sacrifice is lost, Rai,' he said. 'There's nothing you or I or any of us can do.'

'We have to try,' she replied meekly. 'We can't just let them win without a fight!'

'Haldon's right,' Jonas said quietly. 'They have an army. We have... us.'

Rai suddenly found herself filled with rage, and she jumped up, stabbing a finger towards Jonas. 'This is all your fucking fault!' she cried. 'If you'd never come to Rho's Sacrifice... damn it, if you'd never come to *fucking Eden*, then none of this would have happened!'

She collapsed to the ground again, sobbing. Jonas walked over to her, and knelt down in front of her, beside Haldon. 'You're right,' he said quietly. 'You're absolutely right. I am to blame. But sacrificing yourself isn't going change anything. We have to get to Providence, and find this Morphite. She's the only one that can help any of us now.'

Rai tried listening to him, but she was so overcome with guilt, fear, sorrow and rage that she couldn't think straight. She had to get to Rho's Sacrifice. She had to. As quick as a flash, she grabbed at the pulse rifle Jonas had taken from *Rusty's* armoury and pulled it from his grasp, simultaneously shoving him back into the sand. He was so surprised that he didn't resist, and she jumped up and dashed off as quickly as she could, her ankles sinking into the sand as she raced back to defend her home.

She'd made it not even twenty meters when she felt a violent shove in her back, and she fell to the sand face first. She gasped involuntarily and inhaled a lung-full of the course silicate grains, and coughed uncontrollably as she felt someone drag her up out of the sand by her collar. She looked around, her eyes and throat stinging harshly, and peered up at Haldon Cos, who looked down on her sternly.

'I will not allow you to sacrifice yourself, Rai,' he said, and she was surprised to hear anger in his usually calm voice. 'Do you really think going back there will do any good? If so, then you are nothing more than a fool child who should never have been given the responsibility of serving in the militia. Your father would surely be disappointed.'

By now the others had caught up, and were watching on in horror.

'That's enough!' Tailynn snapped at Haldon.

Rai shrugged off Haldon's grasp, and got to her feet. She stared at him with rage in her eyes. 'You can go to hell!' she spat. Haldon grunted a laugh, pushing his glasses up onto his nose.

'As I thought,' he said, his calm returned. 'Nothing but a frightened child.'

'Of course I'm frightened! That's my hope-damned home down there!' she screamed at him. After a few moments of deep breathing she continued. 'What would you have me do?'

'As Jonas said, the Morphite is the only one who can help us now,' he said. 'We must go to Providence.'

She took a moment to clear her mind, and was irritated when she came to the realisation that what Haldon was saying was correct. It would of course be suicide to head back to Rho's Sacrifice. She nodded. 'Fine,' she began. 'We'll do things your way. We should get going. It's going to be a long walk back to *Rusty*.'

The others nodded solemnly, and began the long journey back to the downed skimmer. Rai took a moment and looked back at her home under attack. Smoke was beginning to billow out of the holes that the behemoths had blown in the mountain walls. Silently, Rai watched, praying that her father was smart enough to know when he was beaten and when it was time to surrender, and praying that the

Redeemers would accept a surrender. But then she remembered Port Usharin and Rusden and knew how unlikely that was.

And then she remembered her father, and what *he* was capable of.

Twenty-one

The attack was progressing without fail. His tactics had been followed to perfection thus far, and the Techno city would soon be under his control.

Rus stood in the command centre of his behemoth, his attention split between the room's huge windows and a tactical console in front of him. Judge Tar's forces had progressed a fair distance into the city, and had secured two of the gaping holes that the behemoths had blasted into the side of the mountain as beachheads. A number of Techno skimmers had attempted to launch from the hidden hangers halfway up the mountain, but had been quickly destroyed by his dusters, which had then gone to work blasting open all the other hangar doors and launching missiles to take out the docked skimmers and any personnel that were prepping them for launch. He ordered three of the dusters to break off their attack and return to their assigned behemoths to begin loading the assault teams that he would send in to secure the hangars.

The Advocate in charge of communications turned to Rus. 'Judge Rus, you have an incoming communiqué from Judge Tar.'

'Put it through.'

The grainy image of Judge Tar appeared on the console in front of him. 'Judge Rus, I'm pleased to announce that we have secured the central district of the Techno city. It appears to be some kind of market district. Our casualties have been light thus far. I have set up a secure forward command post in this district. I believe it will serve as a good command centre from which to gain control over the rest of the city.'

'You've done impeccably well, Judge Tar,' Rus replied. He sighed, deciding what to do. It had been a struggle to restrain himself this long to remain on his command behemoth; he yearned to be in the thick of the battle, his gun-blade dripping with blood. Now the younger Judge's efficiency had given him the excuse to advance closer to the action. 'Prepare for my arrival at your forward command post, Judge Tar.'

'Understood,' the younger man acknowledged. 'Shall I prepare an escort, Judge?'

Rus smiled his serpentine smile. 'That will not be necessary.' He ended the communiqué.

Leaving his most senior Advocate in charge of the behemoth, Rus strode through the metal innards of the beast until he emerged on the rocky edges of the mountain that hid the techno city. He advanced cautiously towards the nearest beachhead, stepping over numerous dead bodies, a few of which belonged to his own troops but the majority of which belonged to the enemy. He quickly passed through the secure beachhead, and advanced through the occupied city streets, taking in the spectacle of the hollowed out mountain and city within, while at the same time remaining alert for any enemy he may encounter. He realised quickly that the Technos had been ill-prepared for his attack on their city, as huge amounts of their dead littered the streets. Still, he had seen them operate in Port Usharin, and knew that they were no doubt preparing a counter attack.

Rus reached the forward command post quickly, and Judge Tar reported to him immediately.

'It appears that the enemy combatants have retreated to a ledge district,' he reported, pointing to a rocky ledge that stuck out from the wall halfway up the mountainous cavern. Rus saw a small railway piste that should have linked the bulk of the city to the small ledge district, but which had had a large section destroyed with explosives, essentially cutting the district off. Tar saw that Rus had noticed the damaged rail link, and added quickly: 'The Technos demolished the piste themselves, no doubt as a means to prevent us from reaching them quickly.'

'A wise tactical decision,' Rus said, menacingly. 'Unfortunately, it will do them no good.' He activated his comms device. 'Advocate Mei, I want the behemoths to blast holes in the side of the mountain large enough for the dusters to come through, and I want four dusters with assault squads prepared to advance through the opening and onto my current location.'

The Advocate officer acknowledged the orders, and within moments, the momentous booms of the behemoth cannon slugs striking the rocky mountain echoed throughout the city. The initial holes that the behemoths had blasted through were far too small for the dusters, and were too close to the ground, but the new holes would be truly enourmous. It didn't take long for the monstrous projectiles to pierce the mountain and huge rock fragments showered down onto the edge of the city below, crushing houses and other buildings. Within minutes of the behemoths having breached the walls, four dusters came flying though, and immediately dropped low to the ground to avoid enemy fire. They dashed over the buildings, and within moments, were landing in a large park near the command post Judge Tar's forces had secured earlier.

'Judge Tar, you are to secure the remainder of the low lying section of the city,' Rus boomed, as the younger Judge followed him towards the dusters. 'I will lead the assault on the ledge district myself.'

'Understood, Judge Rus,' Tar replied. 'Do you require me to allocate further forces to your assault?'

'No, that will not be necessary,' Rus said, as he climbed aboard one of the dusters.

He ordered the flight of dusters into the air before he had even closed the boarding ramp. They rose above the city, and spread into an assault formation, heading directly for the ledge district. Rus advised all the pilots to be prepared for enemy fire. Within moments of his warning, the first burst of energy pulses erupted from the district, down towards the ascending dusters, the bright blue bursts betraying the enemies' positions. Exactly what Rus had been waiting for. He ordered each pilot to target the locations the enemy fire had come from and each duster launched missiles, which streaked away from the flight of dusters and pounded into the ledge district. Realising their error, the enemy combatants ceased fire almost immediately and Rus was certain that many of them would now be dead. As the dusters shot up over the edge of the ledge district, Rus ordered the pilots to put down on the roofs of separate buildings. They did so quickly and within moments his troops were out of the dusters, securing each landing site.

Rus emerged from his duster, and unclipped his gun-blade, which was in rifle form. He extended the stock, and strode confidently over to the assault team commander.

'Advocate, instruct all squads to secure the buildings they have landed on, and order the dusters to launch and maintain overhead patrol.'

The Advocate went about relaying Rus' orders while Rus himself led the team down into the building. They encountered a small number of enemies in the building, however none were armed, and all seemed to be ill in some way. He realised that this ledge district must have been some kind of prison or institution where criminals and the mentally ill were sent. He ordered his forces to eliminate any Techno's they encountered whether they were armed or not, and before long the building was secured. The other squads had also quickly occupied their landing structures, and he instructed a duo of scouts to descend onto the streets, to begin reconnaissance of the area.

The Advocate leading the assault team approached him quickly. 'Judge Rus, the dusters have reported that the enemy have re-engaged. They are taking heavy fire; and one of the dusters has taken damage. It's returning to a behemoth for repairs.'

'Have them provide the location from which the bulk of the enemy gunfire is emanating from,' Rus ordered. 'That will be our target.'

Within minutes, the assault team had emerged from each of the buildings and was advancing through the streets towards a fortified structure that was built right up against the cavern's wall where the ledge met the mountain. The fortification made for an easily defendable position, and Rus guessed that this was where the Technos' military commanders must have holed themselves up. It was also the place where Jonas Dresden would most likely be located. Rus' forces progressed carefully through the streets of the ledge district, engaging waves of enemy militants sent to defend the district against the Redeemer forces. Rus revelled in the conflict, and his body count was higher than perhaps any of the others. Within an hour, his forces had surrounded the target building, which to his annoyance was incredibly well fortified and defended and would prove difficult, if not impossible, to assault.

He considered his options. He could have the remaining three dusters assault the structure from above, which would no doubt put the enemy's defensive efforts into disarray, allowing his ground forces to break through. The issue with that option was that he wasn't entirely sure that a missile assault on the structure wouldn't damage the integrity of the ledge itself. The second option was to order the dusters back to the forward command post down below and have them bring reinforcements to the ledge. The issue with *that* option was that it would be far too time consuming and there was every possibility that the Technos would counterattack his forces once the dusters had gone. His final option was, for Rus, a far less palatable one, but perhaps the most logical – and option that, if nothing more, would provide him with the time he needed to send for reinforcements: negotiation.

He instructed the team leader to set the comms device to transmit on an open frequency and when he had done so, Rus snatched the device from the young Advocates grasp, and ordered the man to use a second comms device to instruct the dusters to return to the forward command post for reinforcements. The young man nodded and got to work. Rus keyed his own device and began to speak into it.

'To the Techno military commanders holed up on the ledge district,' he began. 'This is Judge Drealon Rus, leader of the Redeemer assault force that has now taken control of your city. I seek an audience with your leader to discuss the terms of your surrender, and the possibility of our withdrawal.'

He knew that mentioning any possibility of withdrawal would garner a response from the Technos, and he was right. Within moments, a voice crackled over the airwaves in return, evidently an older male with a heavily accented cowboy drawl. 'We ain't surrendering to the Butcher of Rusden, that's for damn sure. But we sure as hell will meet to discuss your withdrawal.'

Rus smiled his serpentine smile, amused at the Techno's attempt at bravado. 'As you wish,' he replied.

The meeting took place in the no-man's-land between the Techno stronghold and Rus' fortified forces. Rus strode out into the open, waiting for his counterpart to emerge. Eventually, a colourfully dressed Techno man emerged from the structure and strode impatiently towards him. The man was reasonably old, with an entirely bald scalp, and a wrinkled forehead. He stopped a couple of meters away from Rus.

'I'm Sid Ashima, leader of the Techno Militia.'

'I'm Judge Drealon Rus, leader of the Redeemer Army,' he replied, the serpentine smile plastered across his face.

Ashima spat on the ground at Rus' feet. 'I know who you are, butcher.'

'Very well, we'll make this quick then,' Rus replied, struggling to prevent his anger at the man's insolence from showing. 'You have something I want. Give it to me, and my forces will withdraw, leaving behind a small contingency of peacekeepers, of course.'

'And what is this something that you want?'

'A man named Jonas Dresden.'

Ashima stared at Rus in surprise. 'Dresden?' Ashima repeated. 'Are you saying that you did *all this* just to get your hands on *him*?' He motioned around him, indicating his severely damaged city.

'I'm glad you know the individual of whom I speak. Hand him over immediately, and this will all end.'

Ashima laughed sarcastically. 'You must think me a damn fool,' he drawled in reply. 'Dresden ain't here no more, and even if he was? I'd be damned if I'd hand him over to you. You wanna know something? I was at Rusden the day before you *murdered* Rho and all of his people. Once I heard of your assault on the town, I returned as quickly as I could, only to find the bodies of those you slaughtered like animals. I would happily die before I would submit to you. Every single Techno in this entire *city* would happily die before submitting to you. So I'm gonna make you a counter-offer. You take yourself, and your army of murderers and get the fuck out of this city before I send y'all straight to hell.'

Rus couldn't help but laugh at the man's audacity. 'So very foolish. You have lost, Techno! Your *only* hope is to submit to me!'

Ashima grunted a weary laugh, and then withdrew a small transmitter out of one of his colourful jumpsuit's pockets. He held it up to Rus. 'This here is a transmitter that's wired to three Morphite quantum warheads that have been strategically placed around the edge of the city. One press of a button, and this whole cavern caves in on itself, and kills anyone within the city.'

Rus inhaled deeply, staring at the transmitter. He looked Ashima in the eyes. 'You're bluffing. You wouldn't risk wiping out the entire Techno population.'

'The Techno population was wiped out the minute you set foot in Rho's Sacrifice,' the man shrugged. 'At least this way we get to take some of you Redeemer bastards out with us. And bagging the butcher of Rusden would be an especially fancy feather in my cap, even if it is to be posthumous.'

Rus sneered at the man. 'You are a pathetic group of people,' he spat. 'I have one last question before I order my troops to kill every last man, woman and child in this hope-forsaken city: where is Jonas Dresden?'

Ashima smiled. 'I told you the truth before. He ain't here. And I don't have the foggiest of where he is now. So all of this has been completely pointless.'

At that moment, Rus' comms device began to chirp. It was Judge Tar. He turned away from the Techno man, and answered it. 'What?' he snapped.

'Judge Rus, I felt I should advise you of a curious finding,' Tar began. 'Our troops have discovered a network of tunnels leading away from the city, and a very conspicuous absence of Techno civilians. I believe they may have evacuated a large portion of the population away from the city...'

Rus dropped the comms device in horror, and turned back to the Sid Ashima, who was standing with a victorious smile on his face, holding the transmitter high above his head, his thumb over the detonator.

'Don't say I didn't warn ya',' he said, and pressed the button.

Almost instantaneously, a number of huge explosions began to erupt at the base of the cavern. Rus turned around in horror, and began to sprint back to his forces, Sid Ashima's harsh laughter the only thing he could hear over the thunderous explosions. As he neared his troops, he was gratified to see that the three dusters had returned. Ignoring the Advocate commander, who was urgently asking for orders, he jumped on board the closest duster and ordered the pilot to take off immediately, and head for the nearest hole in the mountain wall. After a split second's hesitation, the pilot acknowledged and within seconds the duster was airborne. Rus climbed into the co-pilot's seat and watched in horror as the enormous cavern that hid the Techno city began to cave in. Small rubble peppered the hull of the duster and the pilot did an admirable job of avoiding the larger pieces of falling debris. As rocky debris the size of behemoths ploughed into the buildings below, huge clouds of dust, smoke and ash rose through the cavern, impeding the pilot's view. As the duster raced towards the edge of the cavern, Rus had all but given up hope of survival. Surely there was no way out? But within seconds, the duster burst through a hole in the mountain wall, and skimmed out over the desert, circling around to witness the destruction of the Techno City. Rus, relieved to be out in the open, watched in fascination as the huge mountain began to cave in, like a massive ant hill that was being kicked by an invisible child's foot.

It was over in a matter of minutes. Rus peered at the remnants of Rho's Sacrifice, now nothing more than a huge rising cloud of dust and smoke that was mushrooming out at the edge of the atmosphere, blanketing any view of the Pandora Nebula which hung in the sky. Without identifying himself, he transmitted on an open frequency to any of his troops who may have survived the crazy Techno final solution, and received a small number of replies. At least two of the Behemoths had survived, and a number of the forces who had remained outside of the city.

He thought things through, wondering what he should do now. He had failed in his task once again; Jonas Dresden remained at large, and his army was all but decimated. Zesiro had been clear about what the consequence of failure would be. He cursed loudly, and smashed a fist on a metal railing in front of him. To hell with Zesiro. To hell with the Morphites. To hell with the Redeemers and the Technos and everyone else on the hope-forsaken planet of Eden. There was only one man that mattered now. The man that had consistently eluded him thus far. The man who had made him appear a fool in front of the Morphites and his own people.

Jonas Dresden.

Regardless of what Zesiro wanted, Rus could not allow Dresden to live now. He would not allow himself to be made a fool of any longer. No doubt Zesiro would assume Rus to be dead once word of the attack on Rho's Sacrifice reached him, crushed under so many tons of rock. It was perfect; he could go incognito and hunt his prey silently.

Yes, he would hunt Dresden like an animal. And he would make him pay.

Casually, Rus reached over and withdrew the pilot's sidearm from its holster, a small pulse pistol. He levelled the weapon at the pilot's head and pulled the trigger. As the pilot slumped forward in his seat, Rus took control of the duster and dropped the craft low to the ground, turning away from the remains of the Techno city.

Twenty-two

Zesiro sat alone in the Lord Adjutant's chambers, his mind linked directly with the *Zenith of Desire's* construct. His small vessel's sensors were all aligned on the hidden Techno city in the Badlands, and he'd been observing the Redeemer Army's assault on the city from the very beginning.

Now, things had taken an unexpected turn for the worse. He hadn't anticipated that the Technos would be so self-sacrificing, and he was certain Judge Rus had made the same error in judgement. To be honest, Zesiro found himself grudgingly respecting the Technos for their resolve, and their absolute refusal to submit to the Redeemers. In reality, it was a shame for Eden's population that the Techno faction had never been the ones to rise to prominence on the planet in place of the Redeemers.

Rus' failed attack on the Techno city would now surely be one of the initial contributing factors to the end of the Redeemers reign on Eden. The vast majority of Advocates had been assigned to the assault, and the few that remained in Avoca and Providence and some of the more important outlying settlements would not be enough to quell the civil disturbance that would no doubt take place once the population learned of the failed Redeemer attack on the Technos. Not to mention the fact that Judge Rus himself, the fiercest protector of Redeemer power was now almost certainly dead, along with almost his entire army. With this failed attack on the Technos, the Redeemers had ceased to be of any use to Zesiro in his search for Jonas Dresden. There was the possibility of course that Jonas Dresden was dead now, crushed under thousands of tons of rubble in the destroyed Techno city, but Zesiro found that difficult to believe. He'd been in persuit of Jonas Dresden for so long now, that he had developed a considerable respect for the man and his abilities. He did not think that Jonas would allow himself to be killed in a fight between the two pre-human factions, even if the battle had indeed been engineered by Zesiro himself in order to flush his quarry out into the open. Well, *that* plan had most certainly been a failure.

The second factor that would no doubt lead to civil chaos amongst the Redeemer faction was the fact that there was no need for Zesiro to maintain his façade of being the Redeemer leader any longer. Linked to the *Zenith's* construct, he instructed the transit stream to bring him back aboard. In a mere instant, the gothic structure of the Lord Adjutant's chamber disappeared and the comfortingly minimalist interior of the *Zenith* materialised. He immediately shook off his human form and blended with his ship. It wouldn't be long now until some lowly Lesser Adjutant or acolyte discovered the decapitated body of Lord Adjutant Imanre Hes, which the *Zenith* had stored in stasis for months now and had only just returned to the Lord Adjutant's chambers upon Zesiro's withdrawal.

Word of the Redeemer Army's loss in the desert would quickly spread, as would the knowledge of the deaths of both the highest ranking Judge and the Lord Adjutant. Chaos and anarchy would no doubt ensue, and the few remaining Advocates would not be able to maintain order. The chaos would prove to be a good cover for his own ongoing search for Dresden.

The construct aboard the ship advised Zesiro of an incoming communiqué from Alpha One, and almost instantly the presence of the feminine Originator became apparent in his mind.

'Zesiro.'

'Originator,' Zesiro replied in surprise. He hadn't been expecting the Originator to contact him.

'I have urgent news for you,' the Originator continued. 'After the apprehension of my fellow Originators for their decision to support the Progenitor and her allies, I have had loyalist agents interrogate them. The loyalist agents have made a startling discovery: It would seem that Eden is in fact the Progenitor's end game in her defection attempt – that she is, in fact *herself* on Eden, and that Dresden is to meet with her there.'

Zesiro frowned. It wasn't possible, surely? He was certain that the *Zenith* would have detected any trace of another Morphite on Eden. But then again, there were many latent traces of Morphite technology all over the planet, thanks to the Morphites' previous occupation, and the subsequent Techno scavenging of their technology. And when he had arrived around Eden, he had not been searching for the Progenitor, he'd been searching for Dresden, thus he'd been searching for post-human technology rather than that of his own people.

When one took the time to think about it, it made a perverse sense. Eden was, in actuality, the perfect place for a Morphite to hide.

He cursed his own foolishness and instructed the construct to search the planet for all traces of Morphite technology. It took merely the blink of an eye, and he immediately began filtering through the results. There was of course a number of hits in the Desert of Forever and the surrounding regions of the Badlands. There was the hidden construct that the hypocritical Redeemers had obtained. There were remnants of Morphite outposts scattered over the planet's surface; all that remained of the Morphite's occupation of the world roughly seven decades ago.

In other words, there was nothing that truly stood out.

But... an oddity. The city of Providence, and the Valley of Stars, the location of the foolish Redeemers' revered pilgrimage. A dampening field – only apparent when one was specifically looking for it or something like it. Things began to click into place. The Pilgrimage has come into being some time ago, and it was said that those who completed it successfully were taken by the Morphites.

Unbelievable. The Progenitor had been hiding in plain sight all along and he had been too preoccupied with apprehending Jonas Dresden to see it. His distaste of the pre-humans had seemingly blinded him also, as he'd become aware of the pilgrimage upon his initial assessment of the world when he'd first arrived, but he'd immediately dismissed it as some kind of Redeemer trick.

'I believe I may know where the Progenitor is, Originator,' Zesiro said. He shared his knowledge with her.

'It is obvious, now,' she agreed. 'You must confront her immediately.'

Zesiro instructed the construct to attempt breaking through the energy dampening field. His ship could do so, but only momentarily, and only enough for the *Zenith's* sensors to get a hint at what was being hidden... apparently nothing at all. There was no hidden settlement, no cloaked ship, nothing. Confused, he attempted sending a sensor probe down to the region. The microscopic probe shot out of its launcher in the *Zenith's* hull, and darted down towards the planet. The second it hit the atmosphere above the Valley of Stars, however, he lost all contact with it. The dampening field was too strong. He assessed it. There was no sign of the field's energy source, and it was far too strong to allow him to stream through it, likewise, he didn't think the *Zenith* would last too long in the dampened area. He came to the realisation of what needed to be done with something akin to annoyance. He'd have to traverse the valley on foot, as all the pilgrims did. He'd have to do it the *human* way. The very thought of it was distasteful in the extreme.

'You will do as you must, Zesiro,' the Originator said in agreement. 'Be wary of Jonas Dresden's interference; however, he is no longer your main subject of interest. Your primary subject is now the Progenitor herself.'

'And upon my apprehension of her?' Zesiro asked. 'I presume I am to return her to Alpha One with haste?'

He felt the Originator's answer and her intent before she spoke it. And it was honestly a surprise.

'There will be no apprehension of the Progenitor, Zesiro,' the Originator said. 'Upon finding her, you are to execute her, on the spot. No talking, no negotiation. Just kill her.'

Zesiro couldn't contain his surprise. This was *the Progenitor* after all! The one who had been the first, she who had come before even the Originators! Could she even *be* killed? The Originator immediately detected his reservations.

'Are you unable to carry out your task, Zesiro?'

Zesiro allowed himself to consider the question. He was loyal to the Originator, no doubt. And the Progenitor was clearly a major destabilising force within the Morphites. He came to the conclusion that the Originator was correct, that the death of the Progenitor was the only way to restore order and unity to his people. But the Progenitor was perhaps the closest thing to a god that the Morphites had, and it would have been impossible for him to carry out this task without some reservation.

But Zesiro's loyalty to the Originator was unflinching.

'I will carry out the task with all haste, Originator,' he replied eventually.

'Fare you well, Zesiro.'

Twenty-three

It had taken a day for Jonas, Rai and the others to return to the downed skimmer. It had been a difficult trek, no doubt, and they had returned to bad news. Rho's Sacrifice had been destroyed, the Militia evidently having self-destructed the city rather than allowing it to fall into the hands of the Redeemer army. Rai cried openly, the news that a good percentage of the population had managed to flee the city through the hidden escape tunnels nevertheless proving some consolation. Rai had revealed that she knew without a doubt that her own father would have been one of those to remain behind in Rho's Sacrifice, perhaps the one who had blown the hidden Morphite quantum warheads himself. And she had told Jonas that she was well aware that her father would now be dead.

Jonas and the others helped the Techno crew repair the *Rust Bucket*. It took days, but eventually they were airborne again, limping along close to the ground in an effort to remain out of sight of any of the Redeemer army remnants. Rai had immediately ordered the skimmer to head back to Rho's Sacrifice, but it became apparent that there was still a number of surviving Redeemer forces engaged in a cleanup operation around the devastated city, and it would be suicide to head back. Rai called a meeting with Jonas and the others, along with her more senior officers to decide on the best course of action. Jonas knew without a doubt where he had to go, but he was aware that it would take some convincing.

'We have no home anymore,' Rai announced at the outset of the meeting, her voice void of any emotion. Jonas was certain that over the last few days she'd cried so much that she no longer had any tears to shed. It had become clear to him over that time how very *young* she was. Younger than any of his other companions, Gala included. Still a child! But this realisation, along with the way in which she had led the repair efforts of the damaged skimmer had only increased the respect he felt toward her. Yes she was young, but she was also incredibly strong. She continued. 'We have to decide what we're going to do now.'

'Isn't that clear?' one of her bridge crew asked. 'We have to go to the hidden sanctuary and help where we can.'

'We can't do that,' Rai said firmly. 'The sanctuary is hidden underground for a reason. We go there in *Rusty*, and we might as well call up the Lord Adjutant and tell him where we are.' She looked at Jonas. 'I'm fairly certain I know where you want to go.'

He nodded in reply, remaining silent.

'We should head to Providence immediately. You don't need to remain there,' Haldon told her. 'You can drop Jonas and I off near Providence, and then take the skimmer back to your sanctuary. By that time the Redeemers should be well on their way back to Avoca.'

She considered it momentarily. 'I won't just be dropping you off,' she said eventually. 'I'll be coming with you.'

Her crew murmured in surprise, and she turned to them. 'There's nothing for me back there anymore,' she told them. 'Everything my father and the others built is now gone. And I simply don't have it in me to rebuild.' She turned to Jonas, a firm look on her face. 'I'm coming with you. I need to know if all of this was worth it.'

Although he was surprised, Jonas nodded. 'I understand.'

After a moment of silence, Tailynn spoke up. 'Rai's not the only one who will be joining you, Jonas.' Jett nodded in agreement with her. 'We're coming too.'

'And so am I,' Galatea added defiantly. 'So don't try to stop me.'

It took them three days to reach a mountainous area in the vicinity of Providence. The reduced speed of the damaged skimmer, coupled with the fact that they had to take a course far to the north in order to bypass the small number of Redeemer towns that lay along their route meant that the journey was always going to be a reasonably long one. Eventually, however, *Rusty* landed in a small clearing between two small mountains. They were about thirty kilometres out from Providence, and they would have to make the remainder of the journey on foot. They would be travelling lightly – there were very few food rations and little water available, and there would be no need for them to carry weaponry, as the technology would be rendered useless by the dampening field that extended along the Valley of Stars. Rai took a stash of Redeemer currency that the skimmer held in an emergency kit. It was a surprisingly large number of creds – definitely more than enough for them to purchase the necessities for their pilgrimage.

After little fanfare, Rai turned command of the *Rust Bucket* over to one of her crewmembers with orders to aid the Techno evacuees at their hidden sanctuary. Havng dressed in clothing that would see them blend in with the other pilgrims, she, Jonas, Haldon, Jett, Tailynn and Galatea strode down the ramp of the skimmer, and marched off over the hills, stopping momentarily to watch as *Rusty* rose into the air and flew off, disappearing over the horizon quickly. Rai quietly shed a few more tears as she watched the skimmer depart, and Jonas realised that by giving command of her skimmer over to someone else, she was effectively giving up the last remnant of her life as a Techno. Her father was dead, her people scattered and her ship now belonged to someone else. Thus, the Rai Ashima that travelled with him now was a completely different person – one who had been shaped by loss and sorrow.

The journey across Eden's barren surface was another long and tedious one, but after a day of solid progression, they found themselves entering the outlying towns that were scattered around Providence, and not much longer after that they were in the city proper.

Unlike Avoca, which had been a true city far before the rise of the Redeemers, Providence was constructed around the dominant religion. Its gothic architecture was somewhat oppressive, but at the same time lent itself a kind of Victorian beauty. Stained glass windows mimicking the pictograms that lined the great hall in the centre of Avoca's Redeemer temple adorned many of the city's buildings, and spires rose from the rooftops and steeples of the closely knit structures. There was a conspicuous absence of technology in Providence, even the basic pre-*Stargazer* tech that was easy enough to manufacture, a fact which meant that it was commonplace throughout Avoca and the scattered settlements. Jonas spotted one or two public access monitors that were connected to the Redeemer network, and only a handful of merchants they passed utilised computerised point-of-sale systems, the majority of them preferring to use pen, paper and physical money.

Jonas and his group walked through the streets, Haldon leading them towards a central market place where they would find temporary accommodation and the supplies they would need on their journey. There was little conversation as they progressed through the streets; Rai was still coming to terms with what had happened to her people, and no doubt Jett and Tailynn were remembering the events they had been forced to endure last time they had been here.

The population of Providence was made up almost exclusively of practicing Redeemers, be they acolytes, pilgrims or simple citizens who strove for redemption in their day to day lives. The minority of the population who were non-believers seemed to be restricted to shop and stall owners, and other merchants who had evidently only opted to establish lives for themselves in Providence in order to make a profit. The Redeemer sponsored acolytes were difficult not to spot, dressed as they were in their fancy robes, while the pilgrims were generally poor, and dressed in whatever they could afford.

They found a small inn near the market place, and rented a number of rooms. The inn was small, grubby, and from the intensity of the street sounds coming in through the thin-glassed window, Jonas guessed he wasn't going to be getting much sleep. They all took a few moments to freshen up in their respective rooms, before meeting out on the street in front of the inn to plan their next move.

'I suggest we split up,' Haldon said. 'Jonas, Rai and I will seek clockwork weaponry, while Tailynn, Jett and Galatea will seek food and provisions.'

Jonas agreed, and the group split into two, and went their separate ways.

The weapons trade in Providence was legal and thriving, however the market catered exclusively to pilgrims only. Clockwork projectile weaponry had been designed specifically for use in the energy dampened Valley of Stars, and while there were limited styles of clockwork weapons (essentially just pistols and rifles with very few variations in design), competition was rife between the merchants, which meant that they were able to get good prices for the weapons. The clockwork guns operated semi-automatically, and were spring-and-cog operated, much like the projectile weaponry of their nineteenth and twentieth century earth counterparts, however they got their name by being limited in aesthetics, with much of their mechanics visible on the outside of the weapons. Bladed weapons were also popular for pilgrims with less money available, which allowed Jonas and his group to equip themselves with an assortment of weaponry. After hearing Tailynn's story of her's and Jett's pilgrimage, he felt they couldn't be too cautious, and the merchants they discussed the situation with insisted that the outlaw situation down through the valley was as bad as it had ever been.

As they were departing the strip of weapons merchants, planning to meet up with the others, Haldon stopped at a stall, something having evidently caught his attention. Jonas joined him, and saw what Haldon was looking at: a fully clockwork operated gun-blade, a replica of the weapon favoured by the Judges.

'There is very little that I miss from my days as a Judge,' Haldon said to Jonas and Rai once they had joined him. 'I always found the gun-blade such an elegant weapon, however.'

'You should get it,' Rai said, one of the few times she had spoken since they had arrived in Providence. 'It seems my emergency stash of money turned out to be a small fortune, and it's not gonna be worth a damn once we reach the end of the Valley.' Jonas agreed, so Haldon purchased the weapon.

As they were returning to meet up with the others, they noticed a that large crowd had amassed around one of the public access monitors. The crowd seemed agitated, so curiously the trio walked over to see what was happening. By the time they neared, the crowd had become extremely worked up, voices raised and an aura of fear throughout. Jonas spotted one of the merchants they had purchased weapons off nearby, and approached him to ask what was going on.

'The Redeemers are going ape-shit,' the man replied, evidently a non-believer. 'That army they built to go after the Technos got wiped out, and now they've just announced that the Lord Adjutant himself has been murdered. They're declaring martial law. Dunno how they plan to enforce it, though. There's only a handful of Advocates left!'

Jonas thanked him, and returned to Haldon and Rai quickly. They were anxious to know what was going on, so he told them quickly.

'This is not good,' Haldon said. 'Who would have killed the Lord Adjutant?'

'It must have been Zesiro, the Morphite who is after me,' Jonas said. 'It's the only thing that makes sense.'

'Well I'm not gonna shed any tears, that's for damn sure,' Rai said.

'If indeed you're correct and it was the Morphite,' Haldon said to Jonas, 'then he can only have done this for one reason: to cause planet wide chaos. No doubt that goal will be achieved now, and he will be able to blend easily with the population as he searches for you. We must begin our pilgrimage as soon as possible.'

Jonas agreed. They quickly returned to the meeting point, and met up with Tailynn, Jett and Galatea, who had all also heard the news about the death of the Lord Adjutant and the declaration of martial law. They were laden with the supplies they would need for their pilgrimage, and they all quickly retreated from the volatility of the streets to the inn where they had rented rooms. They spent the evening together in Jonas and Galatea's room, where they went about allocating weapons and packing supplies into large backpacks that Jett had purchased for each of them. Together, they ate a simple meal before all retiring to their respective rooms and beds, with the plan to get a good night's sleep and depart first thing the next morning.

Jonas and Gala made passionate love that night, and it was filled with urgency. As they lay together, having both been satisfied, Jonas found himself filled with a sense of remorse. He'd come to Eden evidently to find a Morphite, and since he had been on the pre-human planet, his presence had almost single-handedly incited a short war, brought an entire planet's population to the brink of anarchy, and had been indirectly responsible for the deaths of innumerable people. He'd put all those who had been kind hearted enough to help him in mortal danger, and was about to do so again.

He found himself full of pent-up anger directed at himself. Anger at his self-imposed memory loss. Anger at his retrospective disregard for life. Anger at his *arrogance! Please be worth it!* He begged no-one in particular. *Please!* What could really be worth all the chaos he had brought to Eden, all the sorrow he had been responsible for?

He pushed his anger and his remorse deep within himself. He couldn't allow himself the luxury of emotion at this critical point. He needed to succeed in whatever task it was he'd been sent to Eden to achieve, and he most certainly had to be able to protect his companions, those who had been kind enough to help him, even if he perhaps didn't deserve their help.

Morning came, and the group departed the inn. Out on the streets, there were still groups of angry, frightened people. Word had come in from Avoca that there had been rioting in the streets, and the few Advocates that had remained had been forced to deputize anyone willing to help quell the violence. Jonas winced at the thought –

just what the situation needed: a bunch of thugs with weapons and authority.

As they neared the grand concourse which opened up into the Valley of Stars, they encountered a large group of people out the front of the Advocate offices, yelling and chanting and demanding justice. How easy it was to incite civil disobedience! Jonas was simultaneously awed and repulsed by what Zesiro had managed to provoke singlehandedly. He wasn't even sure the angry mobs knew what they were seeking justice for!

They progressed through the grand concourse, its wide, pillar-lined thoroughfare void of people, bar a few merchants who had set up shop as the last point of commerce for the pilgrims before they stepped out into the valley and began their journey proper. They passed a vacant Advocate post, a small Redeemer sponsored sign hanging nearby, warning of the dangers of traversing the valley unprepared and ill equipped.

As they reached the end of the concourse, they passed under a huge ornamental arch-way, each red ore block used in its construction painted with replica Redeemer pictograms, with the scene of the Morphite's initial arrival on Eden depicted on the key-stone.

And then, they were in the Valley of Stars.

Twenty-four

The Valley of Stars was just as Tailynn remembered it; deep and vast, with the Pandora nebula hanging in the sky like some kind of celestial marker or guide. Boulders and small groupings of rock lined the well worn dirt-road through the valley, and the depths of it were one of the few places on Eden where plant life existed, other than the purpose built and hydroponically maintained farms – although one could hardly say it was thriving. There were small patches of low lying twiggy shrubbery here and there and patches of dry lichen covered some of the rock; remnants, presumably, of an early (and failed) attempt at terraforming Eden, well before the Morphites had come and done it for them with their atmospheric generators and UV filtering.

In a way, the Valley of Stars was quite beautiful – truly one of the few scenic places on the otherwise dreary and rocky world. But to Tailynn it could never be such. She would always remember it as a place of pain, torment and sorrow. Nevertheless, she soldiered on and refused to show any sign of the way in which returning to the valley had affected her. So she chatted with Galatea, Haldon and Jonas, and spent a good amount of time trying to comfort Rai, the young Techno woman's misery serving to aid in ignoring her own.

Jett remained quiet, no doubt re-living the pain that he himself had experienced here all those years ago. His inability to use the events of the past as a means to better himself had always irked her –

that was perhaps the reason that they had never become lovers. Now, however, it made her furious. So she ignored him from the beginning of the journey, inconspicuously refusing to talk to him by keeping her distance.

Other than Tailynn, Galatea perhaps knew Jett the best, and she too had noticed his reticence. She tried talking with him, but failed in engaging him in anything more than a few sentences here and there. When she got the opportunity, she asked Tailynn if she knew what was wrong with him. The young former bartender was clearly worried about him, so Tailynn lied and told her she thought that the events of the past few months were troubling him. Tailynn knew that Gala had seen right through her answer, but the young woman was kind enough not to call her out, deciding (perhaps wisely) that it was a subject best left alone for the time being.

Jonas and Haldon led them through the valley at a reasonably quick pace. As they progressed down the first fifty kilometres of it, Tailynn found herself observing the geology of the place in an effort to keep herself entertained and free of unwanted memories. When they had entered the valley from the grand concourse in Providence, they had descended gradually until less than a kilometre in they encountered a series of switchbacks, and after this they had found themselves at the bottom of the valley very quickly. It was once they were in the valley proper that the energy dampening field came into effect, and her Advocate issued comm unit ceased working, becoming nothing more than a fancy paper-weight. She knew that the Valley of Stars was the lowest depression on the planet, thus the low-laying atmosphere that the Morphites had created for them and which extended to two hundred meters above the mean ground level ended about eight hundred meters above their heads now, enough that there was a kind of sheen to the usually black sky, a hint of visable atmosphere. The valley was such an unusual geological feature on the generally uninteresting surface of Eden, and many people had speculated how it had come into existence. Many believed that it hadn't been a natural feature, and observing it now,

Tailynn could understand why. It just didn't look *natural*. Now that she knew the truth about the populous milky-way galaxy, she found herself wondering if Eden had been visited by another group of beings at some point in its distant (or not so distant) past. Interesting, no doubt. Interesting also, that the valley's unusual make-up had not intrigued her on her first pass through the valley as a teenager. She cursed herself as a flood of unwanted memories emerged into her mind. *Focus on the present!*

They progressed for hours, Jonas and Haldon pushing the group to their limits, until eventually they stopped and made camp. The Valley of Stars was one of the few places on Eden where the atmosphere was deep enough to allow airborne condensation, meaning that it could (and did) occasionally rain. There was no considerable precipitation, no huge storms or anything so severe, rather light sprinkles and a haze that was too heavy to call fog or mist. As a precaution, they set up a tarpaulin over their sleeping area and laid out the swags that they'd purchased in Providence underneath it. Haldon built a small fire with some reusable fuel logs they had also purchased, and they ate a small but welcome meal in relative silence before retiring to bed, exhausted.

They packed up camp early the next morning and were on the road after another light meal. Jonas pushed them even harder than he had on the first day, Tailynn thought, however it could have been the fact that she was still stiff and tired from the previous day's trek that she felt such exhaustion. So she was surprised when halfway through the day they noticed a big billboard advertising the Valley's first wayside-camp. Another hour and they entered the camp.

The camp had changed considerably from when Tailynn had been here as a teenager, so much so that it could barely be called a camp anymore. There were multiple merchant stalls throughout rather than the single trader who had been the proprietor a decade ago, and instead of air-inflatable mattresses under metal awnings, there were properly constructed cabins, accompanied by a small restaurant. The settlement even had an official name now: *Jingo's Folly*. Upon inquiring with the camp's proprietor, she learned that all of the wayside-camps throughout the valley had expanded such as this one.

Jonas had considered passing through the camp and continuing the pilgrimage without a stopover, but Gala had complained and he had relented, much to Tailynn's relief. They had pushed so hard for the first day and a half that she worried that if they continued at the same rate, they would be in no shape to defend themselves in the event of an attack by outlaws. She had approached Jonas with these fears, and he had agreed in principal, but had told her that after discussing that possibility with the camp's current proprietor he had learnt that outlaw attacks were extremely rare these days, and that the weapons merchants in Providence talked the dangers up in order to maintain their trade. The proprietor had told Jonas that in his years of running the camp, he had only ever heard of a single outlaw ambush, and that had occurred a long way away, just outside of Eden's End, the final camp along the valley. Jonas conceded that they needed to be on their toes however, as it wasn't just the outlaws they needed to be wary of.

Tailynn appreciated being able to have a nice warm cup of Avocan tea and a hot meal, and as the nostalgic tunes of the Providencian Symphonic streamed via a small playback device owned by the proprietor, she rested, peering up at the stars and the nebula in the sky, lost in her thoughts. On her pilgrimage as a teenager, it had not been far from this camp when she and her parents had been ambushed. She was fearful of continuing on, Tailynn realised in a moment of truthfulness with herself. But it wasn't fear at the possibility of another ambush. She had faced an Advocate strike team and a Judge, and lived to tell the tale, after all. A disorganised bunch of human animals realistically had no hope against their group. They all had combat experience, and they were all armed. So why? Why was she so fearful?

Jett sat down next to her, breaking her out of her deep thoughts. He smiled a strained smile at her.

'How are you doing?' he asked in an uncharacteristically sincere tone.

Tailynn took a moment to consider the question, and how she would answer. In recent years, she and Jett had been somewhat estranged (not that they'd ever truly been a couple, of course), his drinking serving to create an emotional void in the man that Tailynn could not deal with. Now, Jett was a different person. He hadn't had a single drink since their escape from Port Usharin, and the man that had emerged from the bottle was a coldly sarcastic one. Of course, Tailynn had never really made it easy for him. She tended to blame the bottle for the decline of their love/hate relationship, but if she was to be completely truthful with herself (and why not, while she was on a roll?) then she was perhaps as much to blame as he. She realised something that she had never really understood before, a moment of insight that occured to her may be the Rosetta stone to her understanding of their relationship.

She resented Jett for becoming the man he had after those events so long ago.

He had essentially been the one to save her from the savage outlaws and the torture they had inflicted upon her. She had been too weak to do so herself, perhaps understandably. But then they had gone back. He had allowed himself to agree to returning to that hope-forsaken cave to make the outlaws pay. *And he had allowed her to come.* She could remember clearly when she had driven the knife into the outlaw leader and had initiated the massacre that was to come. In that moment, she had become an animal, a monster, something akin to the very thing she was trying to vanquish. She had lost all reason, all control... all humanity. She had *enjoyed* slaughtering all those who had inflicted such pain upon her. And when the adrenalin had worn off, and the reality of what she had done had hit home, she had been so shocked that her mind had seemingly distorted the magnitude of the situation. She realised that what had plagued her for so long had not been the rape and torture she had endured at the hands of these outlaws, no. It had been the *thing* she had become momentarily as a means to her revenge.

And she instinctively understood now, that that was also what had plagued Jett for all those years. He felt responsible for her actions, she supposed. And rightly so! *He* had been the one to take her back there, and *he* had been the one who had just stood by and watched as she had lost control! She realised now, that it had been his inability to cope with what had happened all those years ago that had irritated her so, why their relationship had struggled. And she realised also, how misplaced those feelings of resentment towards him had been. She had attempted to shift blame onto him for her actions. Of course Jett had been barely more than a child himself back then. He was no more to blame for anything that had happened than she was. The people they were now had been born out of circumstance.

She smiled, and turned to him. 'I'm fine,' she said. After a long pause, she continued. 'We should have come back here a long time ago.'

Jett was surprised at her response, she could tell. But her new understanding was not something she could make him understand, rather it was something she knew he had to come to on his own. She hoped he would, of course. And then maybe finally their relationship could progress.

The next morning, they were up early again, and back on the road, leaving Jingo's Folly behind. The canyon walls closed up a little, and if her memory served her correctly, this narrowness ran pretty much all the way between the Jingo's Folly camp, and the next one. They travelled through this canyon for another two days, before she recognised a very specific boulder that lay beside the track. She quietly asked Jonas if they could stop momentarily, and seeing something in her eyes, he agreed immediately.

She walked off towards the boulder, and could feel Jett's presence following her from a distance. She came around the boulder, filled simultaneously with apprehension and expectation, and then stopped in her tracks.

The entrance to the outlaw cave had been bricked over.

She felt Jett's presence next to her.

'Well I guess you could say that that's pretty much a solid conclusion to our past,' she said.

'Why did you want to come back here?' Jett asked. 'After everything that happened to you...'

'You mean everything that happened to *us*.'

'Yeah... but what I mean is, after everything that happened, don't you just want to *forget*?'

She turned to him, expecting to feel the old exasperation towards him that she felt when she thought that something he'd said was stupid, or misinformed. But this time she didn't feel exasperation, she felt only the need to help him understand.

'We've been trying to forget for so long, Jett,' she replied. 'It hasn't worked. I think it's time to... acknowledge. To remember. We've let the past control us for so long, let it drive our lives. We tried so hard to not become victims that the exact opposite happened.' She ran a hand over the bricked up cave entrance. 'What happened here was terrible. For both of us. It would have killed many people. But we came out of it, definitely not unscathed, but we came out of it nevertheless. And look at us now... embroiled in events that will have a longer lasting impact on us than anything that happened in our pasts, including what happened here. The past no longer matters, Jett. Only the future does.'

She watched him assimilate her on-the-spot philosophy. And she could see the precise moment when something clicked, and he looked at her with an expression she'd never seen before.

'I think I understand,' he said.

She smiled. 'I think you do too,' she replied, before leaning in and kissing him passionately on the lips. He kissed back, and they embraced. Eventually they came up for air.

'Almost nothing about the future is certain, Jett,' she said, looking into his eyes, 'and I suppose that that's what makes it exciting. But

the one thing I do know for certain is that I want to spend my future
with you.'

Twenty-five

Zesiro maintained a low-profile as he progressed through the streets of Providence. As had been expected after the loss of the Redeemer Army in the Desert of Forever and the death of the Lord Adjutant, the remaining Triumvir Adjutants had been forced to declare martial law in an attempt to maintain peace. However, with the ranks of the Advocates severely diminished due to the failed attack on the Technos, as well as the fact that only three Judges remained, their ability to quell any civil disobedience was severely curtailed. The Triumvir Adjutants, elected to their positions within the Redeemer hierarchy for their bureaucratic prowess rather than their leadership skills were unaccustomed to having to make any real decisions, and their ham-fisted attempts at controlling the escalating situation were causing more problems than they were rectifying. Their initial martial law order had been a knee-jerk reaction which had only served to fan the fires of the angry people, and their second order, giving the remaining Advocates and Judges an absurd degree of emergency powers had only further enraged the population.

Even in Providence, perhaps considered the most holy place on the planet (with the exception of the central district of Avoca which was home to the Redeemer temple, thus the Redeemers' centre of power) there was civil unrest, with mobs of angry people roaming the streets, and spur-of-the-moment protests and rallies occurring almost randomly.

It was, no doubt, the beginning of the end for the ridiculous Redeemers, Zesiro thought as he went to great lengths to avoid a mob wandering the street he was walking down. And good riddance.

What happened on Eden no longer mattered to Zesiro. The pre-humans would no doubt continue, like rodents, to procreate and expand while simultaneously killing each other in large numbers. It was classic human behaviour. Zesiro watched the group of pre-humans as they marched through the streets, waving banners decrying both the Redeemers and the Technos, demanding themselves free of tyranny. Zesiro scoffed silently at them, and at their delusions in thinking that the act of demanding freedom would in any way help achieve it. Fools. He watched as an armed Advocate, along with two deputized thugs emerged from an alleyway directly in front of the marching mob, and ordered them to cease and desist. The mob stopped, but began hurling insults at the Advocate and his goons, and before long, the situation had escalated. The mob began launching projectiles at the seriously under-matched Advocate squad, and as expected the Advocate and his goons began defending themselves, firing energy pulse weaponry into the mob ad-hoc. A number of the mob fell to the ground, some no doubt dead, as the remainder trampled their downed allies in a stampede towards the Advocate and his men. Within seconds, the Advocate squad had been inundated and it wasn't long until a few men from the attacking mob emerged, armed with the squad's weaponry.

Zesiro hurried through the streets away from the trouble. He progressed down through the markets, which were eerily quiet, recordings of the Providencian Symphonic playing over a number of small speakers, serving as a melodic contrast to the anarchy and violence that was occurring elsewhere in the city, and indeed planet wide. There was no need for him to waste time in the markets, as everything he needed for his trip through the valley had already been synthesised for him by the *Zenith of Desire*. He wore a small pack which contained little more than a handful of replenishment pellets, small ingestible tablets that would provide him with all of the protein and carbohydrates his body would require during the journey, as well as hydro-tabs which would provide his body with nutrients and hydration, and two small clockwork pistols for protection.

Zesiro continued through the market, down into the grand concourse, and through into the valley. As he walked, he utilised his link to the *Zenith* to sense the valley ahead of him, his ship utilising optical sensors to compile details. He wouldn't be able to recieve anything once he progressed down the series of switchbacks and into the valley proper, as the energy dampening field would prevent him from linking to his ship and the construct which ran it. He assessed the information that the *Zenith* streamed him. There were a handful of small settlements along the valley. He doubted that the Progenitor would be in any of them... no, she'd always been a theatrical individual, and no doubt there would be some surprise that would become evident upon his reaching the end of the valley. Zesiro had the construct assess the imagry its optical sensors had gathered of the entire length of the valley, seeking any anomalies or potential hazards.

It was a surprise when the construct had alerted him to the presence of none other than Jonas Dresden.

Jonas was a good two hundred kilometres down the valley ahead of Zesiro, which baffled him: while he hadn't expected Jonas to allow himself to die in the skirmish between the Redeemers and the Technos, he hadn't thought it possible for Jonas to make it all the way to Providence from the Desert of Forever in such a short amount of time. But the construct streamed an image of Jonas's face straight from its optical sensors, and there he was. Once again, Zesiro had underestimated the resourceful post-human.

He reassessed the situation. Jonas was not his principal target any longer. With the location of the Progenitor effectively now known (Jonas' presence in the valley was further proof of this), she was his primary target, one that the Originator would not tolerate his failure in neutralising. But still, he could not allow Jonas to reach her first

– an alliance between the two would no doubt make his task near impossible.

He had the *Zenith* analyse the valley from a tactical point-of-view once again, something he had already done numerous times. He sifted through the information, looking for a weak spot in the dampening field, or an area of failure. There was nothing, however. No opportunity for him to stream to a point ahead of Jonas and his small party, nor any way to increase his speed throughout the valley. He could morph into other, faster creatures of course, but the problem was that his capability of morphing would be inhibited also by the dampening field that the Progenitor had enveloped the valley in, as reliant on technology as that capability was, meaning there would be no way for him to shift back into his human or natural forms. This would no doubt be inhibitive.

But then, an idea. He was thinking of the valley only in two dimensions. The dampening field's ceiling extended to only fifty or so meters over the valley's top lips. The valley was reasonably shallow at the point where Jonas and his companions had been detected by the *Zenith*, which meant perhaps two hundred meters between the ceiling of the dampening field to the valley floor.

A plan formulated in his head, and he instructed the *Zenith* to synthesise and stream him a light-weight parachute. The vessel took only moments to do so, and in the blink of an eye, a small backpack materialised in front of him. He put it on, and then morphed.

It wasn't possible for a Morphite to change his or her mass when they morphed. Whatever they morphed into, they had to remain at the same mass and density that they had been before shifting shape. He began to change. His skin rippled, and the outer dermatological layer began to ruffle, becoming feathers. His nose began to stretch, and his head flatten. His legs began to shrink, his arms expand and elongate. The small parachute remained strapped to his back.

Within a couple of seconds, Zesiro had become the largest, indeed the only eagle that had ever existed on Eden.

With a leap and a flap of his huge wings, he took to the thin skies of Eden, and launched himself over the edge of the drop down to the valley, remaining well above the dampening field's ceiling. He flapped and soared, observing the topology of the valley as he did so, seeing the occasional speck of a pilgrim trudging along the valley floor.

The joy he was able to take in the simple act of becoming an animal was palpable, a creature with the ability to fly in the sky without the aid of engines and with a nobility that the pre-humans below could never match, nor appreciate. They could appreciate so little, really, same with the post-humans and all the other single shape aliens in the galaxy. They would never know the joy that Zesiro was able to experience at a whim, a joy that he was so rarely afforded the time to appreciate. A joy that so few of his own kind ever took the opportunity to appreciate. It was sad really. He flew above the valley for kilometre after kilometre, flapping, soaring, dropping, rising. Occasionally, he opened his mouth and made an eagle call, a loud, mournful cry that many pilgrims would no doubt hear and be baffled by.

It took him just shy of an hour to reach the vicinity of the camp where Jonas and his companions were resting for the evening. He spotted it ahead, and with a hint of disappointment that his flight was soon to end, he began the mental process that preceded the morph back into his human form, which was more resilient and combat capable than his natural form. He gained altitude, and then initiated the morph. Feathers began to flatten out into skin, his beak began to shrink and soften, his wings shorten and turn cylindrical and his legs fatten and lengthen.

Humanoid again. He felt the precise moment when he passed into the dampening field, and the joy he had felt as he had soared through the sky disappeared. He was trapped in this form now – trapped until he could destroy whatever the Progenitor was using to create the field. He pushed the sorrow from his mind, and confirmed that his link to the *Zenith* had been severed.

As he descended into the valley, he pulled the ripcord of his backpack, and the light-weight parachute deployed. He slowly floated to the ground, certain he had not yet been spotted. The camp lay below him, and he was headed for its centre. Jonas and his companions were asleep in the settlement's cabins, but there were still people about, even though it was well into the night.

Zesiro was ten meters from the ground before he was noticed by a young woman, evidently an employee of the camp's proprietor. The woman cried and pointed at him, although in the dark it did no good. He pulled a second ripcord, severing the parachute from the backpack and then simultaneously withdrew his two clockwork pistols, descending the final five meters unaided, and landing heavily on the ground. He took a moment to catch his breath and to mentally assess himself for any injury the landing may have caused. Nothing. He stood, and fired the pistols at the fleeing woman, the two bullets catching her in the back, and killing her almost instantly.

He and Jonas were on a level playing field now. Without his ability to morph, nor the support that the *Zenith of Desire* offered him, Zesiro felt largely inhibited. Human. But his handicap would not save Dresden this time. This time, Zesiro would finally defeat the post-human he had been adversary to for so long.

Shooting another camp employee without a second thought, Zesiro advanced on the cabin in which he knew Jonas slept.

Twenty-six

Five days into the journey, and Jonas and his group had already made it to the third wayside camp, a place called *Del's Crossing*, which was smaller than the first two camps they had passed through, and was situated almost at the the precise midpoint of the Valley of Stars. Jonas had pushed the group hard during the journey, anxious to reach the end of the valley. It had been a gruelling trek thus far, a lot more difficult than he had thought, especially for the others. Each night when they made camp, Gala would practically pass out with exhaustion, and Jett would not last much longer. Haldon, Tailynn and Rai were doing a bit better, but not by much. Jonas worked hard to hide the fact that he was slightly irked by the fact their progress had been somewhat slower than he had anticipated, but to be honest, the track that they followed which wound through the valley was more work than even he had expected, even taking into account Haldon, Jett and Tailynn's warnings. The path was by no means simply a straight line through the valley, rather it wound its way around outcroppings and other forms of obstruction, meaning that in effect they would be travelling much farther than the seven hundred and fifty kilometres he had been expecting – it was more like a thousand if his estimates were near to accurate. On top of this, the track itself was worn, rugged and eroded from the foot traffic, and they were forced to stop occasionally when one of them took a bad step and strained an ankle, which had even happened to Jonas once.

So as hard as he had tried to push, it had been a slow journey. The three camps they had spent nights at had been welcome stopovers, largely due to the fact that they each sold hot food and recuperative beverages. The food that the camp proprietors sold was by no means restaurant quality, but they were filled with protein and carbohydrates and were a welcome change to the dry rations they carried in their packs. The beverages sold by the camps were likewise formulated specifically for the pilgrims, and were full of electrolytes.

Jonas lay in his cabin's bed next to Gala, who was sound asleep and snoring lightly. They had not made love once during the journey, even at these stopovers where they were afforded the luxury of privacy. They had simply been too exhausted. Nevertheless, they had shared a bed each night, the close proximity of each other aiding their bodies' rejuvenation process.

His companions other than Galatea had seemingly all undergone changes during the pilgrimage. Tailynn and Jett had successfully faced their troubled past, and had emerged from their haunted memories as new people. They were both far more engaged now, more focused, and evidently a couple. Rai was still despondent, the memories of the Redeemer attack on Rho's Sacrifice still fresh in her mind, but she was doing her best to engage with the group, and all the others were willing to help her through her time of pain, with the exception of Haldon Cos, who had by no means ever been an outgoing man, and was now more reticent than ever. But he was focused, and he pushed the group just as hard as Jonas did himself, so Jonas chalked up Haldon's reticence as excessive anticipation at meeting with the Morphite woman again.

However, that evening, before they had all collapsed into bed, Haldon had approached Jonas with troubling news. He had fears that they were being tracked.

'I don't have any solid evidence,' he had told Jonas, 'but at the last wayside camp, the proprietor told me that his people had heard rumours from a small group of pilgrims that came in late at night after us that there was a single man in Providence seeking a specific group of pilgrims. The man had apparently been rather threatening towards this group, so over the course of the last two days I've been observing the valley behind us as best I can. I believe on several occasions I have witnessed what could only be the reflection of some kind of optical lens.'

They had agreed that someone would have to keep watch each night, but the problem was that they all equally needed rest. Jonas and Haldon had decided they would alternate throughout the night, Haldon taking the first four hour watch, and Jonas taking the second. As he lay in bed (as exhausted as he was, his thought process would not allow him any sleep), he considered the possibilities of who could be tracking them through the valley. There were the obvious ones, of course: Redeemer agents, or the Morphite Zesiro, but when he thought about it, neither of those two possibilities made a whole lot of sense. The Redeemers had never been discreet in their pursuit of Jonas... they wouldn't send just one individual, they'd send a team, hell even a small army. And Zesiro... well, that was obvious. He was a Morphite, he wouldn't *need* to track them with optical lenses from a distance. Even considering the possibility that he was affected by the energy dampening field that blanketed the valley, there was a multitude of other ways that Jonas could think of that would be a more effective way of tracking him for a Morphite than following them down the valley.

But there was another possibility. If it was indeed Zesiro tracking them, there was the distinct possibility that he wasn't interested in preventing Jonas' pilgrimage. Rather, what if he was relying on Jonas to lead him to the other Morphite? To Jonas, that seemed the most likely possibility. He lay in bed reviewing scenarios in his mind. If, by the time they reached the final wayside camp their pursuer hadn't attacked, then they would be forced to lay in ambush, as he couldn't allow Zesiro to find the other Morphite. That could add as much as a day to their journey, which was an annoyance. But he had to be certain.

A burst of gunfire made Jonas instinctively dive out of bed. Gala woke too, and as he hurriedly put some pants on, he told her to arm herself and remain in the cabin. He grabbed a clockwork pistol, tucked it into his pants, and then grabbed his rifle and rushed to the cabin door. He opened it slightly, and peered out. The first thing he saw was the body of one of the young camp staff under a torch lantern at the camp's entrance, a woman, lying in the street, bullet wounds in her back, and a puddle of blood forming under her corpse. There was another gunshot, and in the dark, Jonas saw movement in his peripheral vision. He snuck out the through the cabin door, remaining in the shadows. Another burst of gunfire, and this time, Jonas saw the muzzle flash, and an outlined figure, whom he couldn't identify. The door to the cabin next to his opened quickly, and Jett and Tailynn emerged armed. Jett spotted Jonas, and took cover nearby.

'What the hell's going on?' he asked.

'Someone's attacking the camp,' Jonas replied.

'Outlaws?' Tailynn asked, and Jonas could see the whites of her eyes.

'I don't think so,' he replied. 'Best I can tell is that there's only one attacker, and they seem to be far too efficient to be of the outlaw variety.'

A commotion on the other side of the camp drew their attention; a couple of pilgrims, emerging from the camp's dining hall, screaming, almost hysterical. They ran for the camp's entrance, and continued until they were out of visible range. The attacker remained well hidden however. Jonas had not heard sight nor sound of Haldon, but he knew the big former Judge would be tracking the individual.

'What do we do?' Jett asked.

Jonas ignored the question momentarily as he scanned the cabin roof tops. There: a silhouette, creeping along. It had to be Haldon, unless he was wrong and there were indeed additional attackers. Jonas turned to Tailynn and Jett.

'Wake Rai if she's not already awake, and get Gala. Fortify

yourselves in one of the cabins, and if you see anyone other than Haldon or myself approach, shoot them,' he instructed.

'What about the camp staff?' Tailynn asked.

'My guess is they're already dead.'

Jonas left them and snuck through the shadows around the back of the row of cabins, emerging near the camp's small kitchen area. The figure on the roof was remaining still, and Jonas was having trouble keeping them in sight. He ducked out of the shadows momentarily and dashed across a few meters of opens space towards the camp proprietor's cabin, upon which he'd seen the silhouetted figure. He climbed up the back wall, and onto the pitched roof, and whispered Haldon's name quietly. The big man responded in the same quiet tone, and Jonas crouched next to him, peering down over the whole camp.

'Who is it?' Jonas asked.

'Can't tell,' Haldon responded. 'Whoever it was dropped out of the sky and began shooting the camp staff, and then disappeared into the shadows.'

'What do you mean they dropped out of the sky?' Jonas asked.

'Exactly what I said. They must have come in via parachute or something, dropped in from above the dampening field, or off a nearby cliff ledge.'

That didn't seem to make much sense. Jonas took a moment to think about it. If this was indeed the individual who was following them, then they had gone to a considerable amount of trouble to climb the nearby cliff walls to the top of the valley, only to parachute back down. He said as much to Haldon, and the man agreed that it didn't make much sense. Still, he had seen exactly what he'd said, he was certain. Now, the attacker had seemingly disappeared into the shadows. Jonas decided it didn't matter at this time *who* it was that was attacking; all that mattered was that they needed to be stopped.

The two men climbed down off the roof, and covered each other as they moved into the cabin below. Inside, the rooms were lit lightly by candles, and they immediately saw the bodies of the camp proprietor and her husband, killed by precise shots to their heads. Being careful to remain in the shadows, they moved out of the cabin into the small dining hall next door, where the body of the camp's cook lay, again shot through the head. This had been the building that the two screaming pilgrims had emerged from.

'The attacker is making their way to each building, searching for someone specific,' Haldon said. 'No doubt us.'

Not us, Jonas thought. *Me.* He told Haldon to follow him and they emerged from the dining hall to the sound of wild gunfire, perhaps ten or fifteen shots from numerous weapons. Without even needing to look, Jonas knew they had come from his own cabin. He dashed out into the street, running as hard as he could for the cabin. As he approached, the door flung open, and two silhouetted figures emerged, one being held at gunpoint by the other. The figures moved away from the cabin, and into the light of one of the camp's few lamps.

One of the figures was Galatea, a clockwork pistol held up against her temple. A look of fear, mingled with what Jonas could only guess as shame at being captured was plastered across her face. Jonas recognised the figure holding the pistol immediately as the man who had come very close to capturing him in Port Usharin: the Morphite Zesiro.

'You're outnumbered,' Jonas told the Morphite, mustering as much calm as he could.

'Indeed,' Zesiro replied. 'Hence the hostage situation. Of course, normally it would not matter. My inherent abilities as a Morphite would in effect even the numbers, but of course *she* was smart enough to inhibit such abilities in her vicinity.'

'What about the others who were in that cabin?' Haldon asked, his clockwork rifle pointed at the man, unwaveringly.

'They did their best to eliminate me, however they were unsuccessful,' Zesiro replied. 'But as a show of good faith, I did not kill them. They are unconscious, but otherwise unharmed.'

'Gala?' Jonas asked. She nodded slightly. His attention turned back to Zesiro. 'Why this "show of good faith"? You didn't seem too interested in good faith back in Port Usharin.'

'I'll admit, it was an error in judgement to ally myself with the Redeemers,' Zesiro replied. 'The Judge was needlessly violent. My objective has changed since then however. When it became apparent to me that Eden was your end-game, everything became clear, and my tactics have changed accordingly.'

'What do you mean?' Jonas asked warily. 'Why is Eden my end-game? End-game to what?'

A smile flashed across Zesiro's face. 'Ah yes, your self-imposed memory loss. Indeed a wise tactic. I may have figured it all out earlier had you not hidden it from yourself. I of course refer to the Progenitor, and her presence on this forsaken world.'

A memory unlocked in Jonas' mind, and he immediately knew that the Progenitor was the Morphite he sought at the end if his pilgrimage, a name her people had given her as she had been the first.

And she was defecting from them.

She had initiated contact with the government of the Human Republic, with whom the Morphites were at war. She had announced her desire to defect to the humans cause, and had left a trail of breadcrumbs for them to follow in order to find her, as she was wary of her own people and the lengths they would go to in order to prevent her from falling into enemy hands. So the human powers-that-be had assigned Jonas to the task of her "rescue". He had followed her clues all over the galactic quadrant, and had been pursued by Zesiro relentlessly, the Morphite agent having been assigned to prevent the Progenitor's defection.

By the time Jonas had learnt that the Progenitor was on the pre-human world of Eden, Zesiro had been pursuing him for years. He had been worried that they had become too predictable to each other, so he had done something drastic: he had blocked his own memory in order to eliminate that predictability. He had left himself a basic set of instructions, buried in his mind subconsciously, which manifested themselves as strong instincts: where to go, what to do.

And he had programmed his own mind to only unlock memories as necessary, hence the seemingly random memories that popped into his head now and then. Even now, when the reasons behind his memory loss had become evident, parts of his mind still remained locked away from him, but that being said, he felt on the edge of a mental precipice, one where all he had to do was step over, and all would be revealed.

Jonas now knew how important it was that Zesiro not be allowed to reach the end of the valley, and that he not be allowed to apprehend the Progenitor. It was more than important, really. It was *imperative*. And it was well within his mission parameters to sacrifice innocents along the way. He could end it now, with a single bullet. All he had to do was fire through Gala, and Zesiro, his regenerative and morphing abilities inhibited would die. But of course, so would Gala, and that was not a price that Jonas was willing to pay. He pushed his mind to reveal more to him, something he could use against Zesiro.

And something clicked, a memory that had been hidden so deep it could not have been found under even the deepest of mental raids. Jonas suppressed the desire to smile.

'What are your terms?' Jonas asked Zesiro.

'Simple,' Zesiro said. 'You die, they live.'

'Unacceptable,' Haldon said firmly.

'Indeed,' Jonas agreed. 'I am willing, however, to submit to your custody, should you promise not to harm my companions.'

Jonas watched as Zesiro thought it over. For a moment, Jonas didn't think the Morphite was going to agree, but then a smile crossed over his adversary's face.

'Throughout these years of chasing you, Jonas, I have developed a considerable respect for you,' he said. 'Many of my people would consider it a weakness. I agree to your terms.'

'No!' Gala exclaimed.

'It's okay, Gala,' Jonas said as soothingly as possible. 'It's okay.'

'You should thank him, pre-human,' Zesiro said to her. 'He saved your life, after all.'

Zesiro made Jonas and Haldon put down their weapons, and then he traded Gala for Jonas, the barrel of the Morphite's clockwork pistol a cold, metal pressure against his head. As Zesiro led him out of the camp, Jonas managed to give Haldon a firm nod, and he hoped against hope that the man knew what he wanted him to do.

Twenty-seven

'You should have taken the shot!' Jett said to Haldon angrily, while the rest of them looked on. It had been a matter of hours since the Morphite had attacked the camp, and Tailynn's head still throbbed from the knock that had rendered her unconscious. The ongoing argument between Jett and Haldon wasn't helping, either.

'The Morphite was careful not to take give us one,' Haldon replied. 'The only way we could have taken him down was by shooting through Galatea, and clearly that was not a course of action Jonas – nor I – were willing to take.'

Jett grunted, evidently conceding the point. Gala sat in the corner of the room, shaken and sobbing; Tailynn knew she felt responsible for what had happened, but of course it had not been her fault.

'So what do we do now?' Rai asked. 'I for one have nothing to go back to, I don't know about the rest of y'all.'

'We continue on our pilgrimage, and find the Morphite, this... Progenitor,' Haldon said, firmly. 'It's what Jonas wanted.'

'And how exactly do you know *that*?' Jett asked.

'Haldon's right,' Gala said softly from her corner. 'I'm certain it's what he wanted.'

'Fine, say we continue on,' Jett replied in his most cynical tone. 'What do we say to this Morphite when we find her? "Oh, hello there, Mrs. Morphite, we were travelling with this guy who was looking for you, but now one of your guys have him, and we're not exactly sure what we're supposed to do". I'm sure that'd go down real well.'

'Sarcasm is the lowest form of wit,' Haldon responded.

'Yeah, well it's about all I can muster at the moment, so too bad.'

'Why don't you both just *shut up!*' Gala yelled from across the room, startling everyone. They all looked at her in amazement as she got to her feet, a look of rage across her face, tears still pouring down her cheeks. 'I'm sick of your shit! Jonas is gone, and now it's up to *us* to finish what he started! End of story.' She picked up one of the clockwork guns, and hefted it. 'You can each do what you want, I don't care. But *I'm* going to finish this pilgrimage.'

She strode for the door, but Jett stepped in front of her, blocking her way.

'Jonas gave himself up so you'd be safe,' he said to Gala. 'He wouldn't want you to put yourself in danger.'

'Get out of my way, Jett,' she said menacingly.

He lingered, looking her in the eye. After a moment, he sighed. 'You sure about this, Gala?'

'One hundred percent,' she replied confidently.

'All right,' he replied. 'Fine, I'm in.'

Tailynn wasn't as confident in Galatea and Haldon's belief that Jonas would want them to continue, but she considered that it didn't particularly matter what Jonas wanted anymore. When it came down to it, none of them had anything to return to. Rai's people were all but wiped out, and the rest of Eden, that which had been ruled by the Redeemers was now in chaos. All of their lives had been changed by Jonas' presence, and she believed they had been set on this path for a reason. She understood Jett's point-of-view of course, and perhaps in a way she shared it. Together, they had faced their demons and were now different people, almost as though they had been reborn. They actually had something to live for now, but that life lay ahead of them, rather than behind, a fact she was certain of.

They departed the camp the next morning, having buried the dead camp proprietor, her husband and her staff. The journey down the valley was now even more sombre than it had been previously, and as gruelling as ever, thanks to the fact they had all barely rested during the night. They progressed in a kind of daze, slower than any of the previous days and that night set up camp only twenty five kilometres from Del's Crossing. They had agreed that they should take turns at keeping watch throughout the night, meaning that the following day they were all still exhausted, and ill prepared for the next leg of the journey. Nerves were frayed, and snarky little arguments were constantly breaking out, Tailynn herself often the one to defuse them. She feared that if they didn't get some decent rest soon, then even her temper would get the better of her and their group would be at each other's throats. Thankfully, the distance between Del's Crossing and the following camp, Stargazer's Bluff, was short and they wandered into the camp around midday of the day after they had left Del's crossing, even taking into account their slow progression.

That afternoon while in camp, Haldon had advised Tailynn – who in Jonas's absence had become the group's de-facto leader – that he feared they were still being followed. He told her of the fears he had shared with Jonas only two days prior, and about the rumour he had heard as they had passed through the wayside camps.

'But surely the person tracking us was the Morphite agent?' Tailynn asked.

'That's what I thought initially,' Haldon agreed. 'But then when I thought about it, that possibility made no sense. If Zesiro was indeed the one tracking us, why would he have attacked from the sky, parachuting in as he did?'

'The element of surprise, I suppose,' Tailynn replied with a shrug.

'So he climbed the valley walls, only to drop in from above, when he simply could have snuck in through the shadows which would have been just as effective?' Haldon countered, repeating Jonas' own fears. 'Like I said, that scenario makes little sense. Besides, earlier today I saw another reflection, this one much closer than the previous ones. There is someone else still tracking us.'

The thought was troubling, no doubt, but Tailynn was uncertain as to what to do about it. They wouldn't be able to physically stand keeping watch throughout the night – all of them were equally exhausted, and needed a solid night's sleep. In the end, it was Rai who had come up with the most viable solution: lying. They sought out the camp's proprietor, a large, burly man with a great big bushy beard, who reminded Tailynn somewhat of Darris, the tavern owner back in Port Usharin. They warned him that they had been attacked by outlaws the previous day, and they feared that the animalistic savages were planning an attack on a much larger target, perhaps Stargazer's Bluff itself. The proprietor had been somewhat dismissive of their claims, but in the end, he admitted that he didn't have much choice but to heed their warnings, as he couldn't risk the (in his opinion remote) possibility that Tailynn and Haldon's concerns were real. So he armed a number of his staff and put them on rotating watch shifts.

Tailynn was relieved that their white lie had been effective, and that night they all slept solidly, even Galatea who was still a walking cauldron of bubbling emotions. It was not until mid-morning that Tailynn awoke, and together the group consumed a warm breakfast. There had been no sign of an outlaw attack, the proprietor had told them with something akin to annoyance as they ate. In fact, he'd told them, there was no sign of anyone else progressing through the valley at all. They left Stargazer's Bluff shortly after breakfast, having replenished their supplies and water rations. They were now on the longest stretch of valley between camps, roughly one hundred and thirty kilometres to the final (and largest) settlement in the Valley of Stars, Eden's End.

They progressed as quickly as possible, although the terrain of the valley was perhaps its most rough on this stretch, and they found themselves often clamouring over loose rubble which had fallen from the valley walls, little mini-landslides that would no doubt prove fatal should one be unlucky enough to be caught underneath. They set up camp thirty-five kilometres further down the valley from

Stargazer's Bluff that night, and rested well again, rising early in the morning and departing after a quick breakfast. Another good day of progression, and they found themselves a day and a half out from Eden's End. After setting up camp that evening, Tailynn approached Haldon, who during their journey since Stargazer's Bluff had been keeping a keen eye on their rear.

'Any sign of our pursuer?' she asked.

'None since we departed Stargazer's Bluff,' he said, his tone one of concern.

'Surely that's good news?' Tailynn asked with a frown. 'Surely it means that whoever it was has ceased their pursuit, or perhaps were simple pilgrims all along.'

'They are indeed possibilities,' Haldon agreed. 'Although it could also mean that whoever is persuing us is close enough to no longer require optical assistance.'

'You're more of a glass-is-half-empty kind of guy, aren't you Haldon,' Jett said from his swag.

'I will keep watch tonight,' Haldon said to Tailynn, ignoring Jett's sarcasm.

'No,' Tailynn said with a shake of the head. 'You've been keeping watch for the last two nights. You're exhausted and you need sleep. Jett and I will alternate keeping watch.' Jett groaned, but didn't complain. Tailynn continued: 'We're about fifty kilometres out from Eden's End. I want us to be up early in the morning, and to hit the track hard. I want to be at Eden's End by sunset.'

The others agreed. That night was uneventful, their potential pursuer again not revealing themselves. As planned, they were all up before daybreak, and on the road. They trudged on throughout the day, stopping for only one meal break, and were all gratified when in the late afternoon they rounded a corner in the valley and spotted a huge billboard, advertising the approaching settlement.

They pushed hard over the final kilometre, but as they neared the settlement, they realised something was wrong. A great plume of smoke rose from the within the settlement, thick and black, billowing out of the valley and up towards the edge of the low atmosphere, where it mushroomed out. They spotted the flames before they could even see the settlement itself, and rushed to the camp entrance.

Eden's End had always been the largest wayside camp, and these days it was a somewhat close to a bona-fide town. And it was on fire. Every cabin, shop and unidentified structure was on fire, and there was no one around attempting to fight the flames which were spreading with the fury of a raging flood. There was nothing they could do, Tailynn realised as they watched on helplessly. The fire had already consumed most of the settlement, and would only increase in intensity. Even from the settlement's entrance, the heat was near unbearable.

But then she spotted something moving, a dark figure emerging from one of the as yet unburnt cabins. A figure dressed in plain black, armed with a huge clockwork gun-blade, similar to the one that Haldon himself carried.

A figure they knew all too well.

'I thought you'd never make it,' Judge Drealon Rus said menacingly, his serpentine smile plastered across his face.

Twenty-eight

Jonas was free to move around Zesiro's small, sterile vessel. He had, of course been disarmed (not that the primitive clockwork weapons he'd been carrying could have done much damage to the Morphite ship), and if he attempted anything that could be construed as an escape attempt or an attempt at resistance, the construct that controlled the vessel would envelop him in a stasis field. Zesiro had not even interrogated Jonas upon his capture, instead leaving Jonas alone on the *Zenith of Desire* with its sterile, white alloy bulkheads, and minimalist design. There were no monitors, holographic projectors or any other controls of any type that Jonas could find – of course the Morphites needed no such tactile devices, they blended seamlessly with their ships. So for the first few days of his imprisonment, there wasn't much Jonas could do. After exploring the small ship thoroughly, he slept for a few hours here and there, finding a spot in a corner (there were no beds either), and as he dozed on and off, his concern for his friends and his mission consumed the majority of his thought process.

He awoke after a bout of sleep to discover Zesiro, in his Morphite form standing over him. In his natural form, Zesiro was inhumanly thin, hairless and almost featureless, and wore plain white garments that hung loosely off his small body. Jonas had, of course, seen Morphites in their natural form before, but he had only rarely seen Zesiro like this. On the odd occasion they had found themselves face to face over the years, Zesiro had seemed to prefer being seen in his human guise.

'Jonas Dresden,' Zesiro said, his voice void of any emotion or real tone.

'Zesiro,' Jonas replied after a momentary hesitation.

'I require information,' the Morphite said. 'In regards to the Progenitor and her location.'

'You know I can't help you with that,' Jonas said, tapping the side of his head. 'Memory loss, remember?'

'Self imposed memory loss,' Zesiro added, unsettling Jonas with his natural form, which was sterile and void of meaning and emotion. While he had seen Zesiro in this form before, he had never conversed with him and was finding it an odd experience, almost like talking to an AI construct, although even an artificial intelligence was capable of mimicking emotion. Zesiro continued. 'I require you to eliminate your memory blocks, and aide me in finding the Progenitor.'

Jonas laughed out loud. 'Even if I had the ability to eliminate these memory blocks at will, do you really think I'd help you find her willingly?' he asked. 'Why don't you change back into your human guise, Zesiro, I can't tell if you're joking or not when you look like that.'

Zesiro's head tilted to one side, evidently in a display of curiosity. 'You are made uneasy by my natural form?' He asked. 'You prefer me to be a mirror of your own kind?'

'Honestly, yes I find the Morphite's choice of form unsettling, even if we both know it's far from *natural*,' Jonas said. 'Show some emotion, for god's sake, if for no other reason than to prove you're not just a machine.'

Zesiro's form began to ripple, and within seconds, he had morphed into his standard human form, the same one he had worn for most of his time on Eden, with the exception of when he was in the guise of the Lord Adjutant.

'Better?' he asked with an amused smile. 'Honestly, Jonas, it's not like you to be so *prejudiced*.'

'My apologies, but I am just a simple human with a bad memory,' Jonas replied.

'We'll have to fix that, then.'

Jonas felt the *Zenith's* construct begin a neural raid on his mind. It was as though a ghost had reached into his mind and was spreading throughout, its otherworldly chill spreading across the landscape of his brain like ice. He cringed, and attempted to resist. Zesiro looked down at him, his eyes flickering, and Jonas knew he was linked to the construct that was invading his mind, searching for the blocks that Jonas himself had constructed before his insertion onto Eden. The construct passed through layers of his mind as though it were browsing through some kind of shop, picking up memories as though they were objects and then discarding them when it was clear they were of no significance – and each time the construct inspected one of his memories, he too re-lived it. A flash of his waking for the first time on Eden, the broken pane of glass he had seen his own reflection in. Flash! Meeting Galatea for the first time. Flash! Killing two Advocates in the streets of Port Usharin with Tailynn at his side. Flash! The city of Rho's Sacrifice. Flash! Walking through the Valley of Stars. Flash! Coming face to face with Zesiro...

'It would appear that your memory blocks are quite effective,' Zesiro said. 'Impressive for a post-human, no doubt. But nothing that Morphite technology cannot overcome.'

The construct's neural raid increased in intensity. Jonas began experiencing the memories that had been locked away in his mind, and then had gradually been revealed to him: The flash of memory he had experienced upon coming face to face with Zesiro in Port Usharin... the memory of Olympus that had been triggered by the Techno city of Rho's sacrifice.

And then deeper, into his subconscious. He relived the strange dreams he had been experiencing since his awakening on Eden... the woman who had shown him a perspective of human history different than the one he had been taught as a child. And now, it became clear...

'Intriguing!' Zesiro exclaimed. 'The Progenitor has been in contact with you this whole time.'

The Progenitor, Jonas remembered, his mind struggling to remain coherent through the invasive raid on his mind. *I must find her. I must find her!*

'Ah, here we are. Down to the crux of it all,' Zesiro said, linked to his construct as the AI waded through Jonas's thoughts like a child in a pool. 'It all comes back to the Progenitor. And what do we have here? A memory block!'

The construct attacked the memory block, and a small battle raged inside his mind. Simultaneously taking an instant and an eternity, Jonas found himself in excruciating agony as the memory block fell and a million memories came crashing back to him. But then he experienced something other than pain, he experienced understanding. In an instant he relived a million past memories, simultaneously experiencing the complete spectrum of emotions that went with them: pain, sorrow, happiness, love, fear, disgust, amusement... there were more emotions than there were names for. And then just as he had assimilated the flood of memory and emotion, the construct discovered another block and attacked it.

The process repeated time and again, until it seemed to Jonas that he had been engaged by the Morphite construct for a lifetime – but of course, he had. He was reliving his *entire life*!

Eventually, the neural raid came to an end, and Jonas lay on the floor of the *Zenith of Desire* exhausted. He knew everything now, the person he was... the thriving galaxy in which he lived, the search for the Progenitor. He remembered *everything*.

And now Zesiro knew it all as well.

'I respect you immensely, Jonas,' Zesiro said with absolute sincerity. 'You are a credit to the post-humans, and I would be lying if I said I had not enjoyed our game of cat-and-mouse over the years.

You have been a worthy adversary. And I thank you. But now it is time for me to claim victory.'

Zesiro disappeared, whisked away by the *Zenith's* transit stream. Jonas allowed himself a few moments to recuperate before clamouring unsteadily to his feet. Zesiro was no doubt heading for the Progenitor now, her well laid plans revealed to him all too easily. But then a stray memory hit Jonas, one that the construct had not seen; Jonas' ace up the sleeve, which the Progenitor herself had given him, and one that his subconscious had been programmed to hide above all others in the event of a neural raid taking place on his mind. And the construct had indeed missed it.

Jonas walked over to a bulkhead and placed a hand on it. Instantaneously, he felt the construct's presence, and he took grasp of it, a control that was wavering but still sufficient. The *Zenith of Desire*, with its myriad advanced technology was now at his command. It had been all too easy, really.

After all, Zesiro was not too dissimilar an animal than he.

Twenty-nine

Rai was ready for war. There, directly in front of her stood Drealon Rus, the butcher of Rusden and Port Usharin, and no doubt the monster who had been responsible for the attack and destruction of Rho's Sacrifice. All she could see was red, and she craved revenge like she had never craved anything before. Along with Tailynn, Haldon, Jett and Galatea, she held her clockwork gun out in front of her, the iron-sights centred precisely on Rus' forehead. The big Judge held his clockwork gun-blade in his left hand, the weapon in its blade form, a vile smile plastered across his face. For someone who was well and truly outnumbered, Rai thought he looked awfully smug.

'Where is Jonas Dresden?' the man asked in his menacing voice.

'You should ask your friend,' Tailynn responded.

'My friend?'

'The Morphite.'

Amusement flashed across Rus' face. 'Of course. His betrayal of me allowed him to claim the ultimate prize. Well, I suppose the five of you will have to have to suffice as consolation.'

'Awfully cocky for a guy who has five guns pointed at his face,' Jett replied.

The Judge laughed, and ignored him, his attention turning to Haldon. 'Well, I must say, this is intriguing. Haldon Cos, former Redeemer Judge and wanted traitor. Where have you been all these years?'

'You call me a traitor, yet here you are, on your own chasing us while the Redeemers fall, and chaos envelopes Eden,' Haldon replied. 'Tell me, Drealon: where do your loyalties lie?'

'With myself,' Rus replied calmly. 'The Redeemers are a bunch of fools, and the Morphites are nothing but pretend gods. They are not worthy of my loyalty. Everything I do, and everything I've ever done is to appease myself.'

'You are a psychopath,' Haldon replied. 'Nothing but a damaged individual.'

Rus smiled his serpentine smile, and it was then that Rai realised he was holding something in his right hand, a piece of string that led down into the ground. After a moment of confusion, she realised what it was.

'Get back!' she yelled.

Without another word, Rus tugged on the string, and a buried row of clockwork explosives went off a meter or two in front of Rai and her group. A wall of dust, stone and dirt erupted in front of them, and the shock of the explosions knocked them all off their feet, dazing them momentarily. As soon as she had recovered slightly from the initial shock of Rus' ambush, she began firing random shots into the cloud of dust that had well and truly obscured him. She had no idea if she had hit anything, but she stopped firing when she heard Tailynn calling for them to take cover and retreat. Cursing as loudly as she could, Rai jumped to her feet and dashed back towards a barricade that sat at the entrance to the camp, and was far enough away from the burning buildings for the fire to be of no immediate concern. She collided with Galatea in the rush to get to cover, knocking the other woman to the ground. Hurriedly, she grabbed her by the hand and dragged her behind the barricade.

'You okay?' she asked, to which Galatea nodded quickly.

Rai peered over the edge of the barricade, trying to spot either Rus or any of her allies. The dust cloud that had been expertly unleashed by Rus still hung in the air, and began to mix with the smoke of the burning buildings. She could see no-one, the smoke and dust having reduced visibility to only a meter or two. She considered her options; in the chaos he had unleashed, Rus would be just as vulnerable as everyone else – more so, in fact because he was outnumbered. She could go after him. But, then again, safety in numbers held a certain merit. It would be smart to regroup with the others and attack from a unified front. The latter was the logical choice.

But Rai was far too enraged for logic to enter the equation.

She instructed Galatea to stay put, and emerged from behind the barricade, her clockwork rifle leading the way. Her eyes were stinging from the smoke and dust, and she could feel the heat from the ferociously burning buildings. Once or twice she saw a figure move through the airborne debris, but she couldn't tell if they were enemy or ally. Best to not fire until she was certain. Rus was here somewhere, she just had to find him. Another glimpse of movement. She dashed towards it, finger on the trigger, ready to fire at a split second's notice. She regained sight of the figure, and sprinted for it. She emerged into a bubble of relatively clean air, and the figure solidified.

Judge Rus.

She pulled the trigger of her rifle just as he noticed her, and continued firing as he dodged away, spinning around. All of her shots missed by the finest of margins, and it was almost too late before she realised her mistake. She was too close. At the same time he had been dodging her attack, he had been preparing his own counter offensive, and his gun-blade, its shining steel blade reflecting the flaming buildings so it seemed to be on fire itself was raised high above his head, and was an instant away from coming down. Rai dropped to her knees and skidded through the dirt, falling flat on her face, but successfully dodging Rus' swing. She quickly rolled over just as he swung his blade again, and managed to roll to one side, the blade striking the ground mere centimetres from her head. She continued rolling to the side until she was well out of his blade's swinging arc, before jumping to her feet, and belatedly realising she had lost her clockwork rifle at some point. She grasped at the pistol strapped to her belt, and cocked it, bringing it up towards Rus. But Rus had been too quick for her. His clockwork gun-blade was now in rifle form, and was pointing directly at her.

Rus fired.

It was pure luck for Rai that clockwork weaponry was inherently inaccurate. The bullet from Rus' weapon missed any vital areas of her body, and ploughed into her shoulder, shattering bone and spattering blood over her neck. At first she didn't feel any pain, only numbness. She was halfway to the ground before she realised her legs had given way, and it was at the precise moment of touching the ground that the pain from the bullet wound kicked in, an agony she had never come close to experiencing before. She writhed on the ground, unable to think, unable to scream, unable to breathe. She barely noticed Rus standing over her in victory, his weapon back in its blade form.

'Techno filth,' Rus muttered, hefting his blade over his head.

Although the agony in her shoulder burned, it had only taken moments for Rai to regain enough of her senses to process what was happening. She watched the blade rise over the Judge's head, and as it began its downward arc. And then something intersected the blade, something almost identical. Rus's blade bounced off the other, and Rai watched as Haldon rallied from his urgent defence of Rai into a flurry of attacking moves against Rus.

The two clockwork blades struck one another, Rus recovering from the surprise of Haldon's entrance to the battle almost instantaneously. Sparks flew and the shrill sound of metal on metal pierced Rai's ears. Haldon fought his former trainee with a desperation that betrayed his lesser ability. It had been a long time since he had battled anyone, a fact that was clear when one compared his actions to that of Rus, who had a plethora of recent experience wielding a gun-blade.

Rus drew his blade out of the sword lock first and went on the offensive. He brought his sword back and swung it in a deadly parabolic arc. Haldon took a step back and raised his own blade to deflect the strike. Their techniques were unmistakably similar, Rai realised, but she could see through the similarities, and realised that Haldon wasn't going to win. Rus was not only the better swordsman, but all of Haldon's hard-learnt Judge abilities had atrophied with the lack of use during the time he had spent semi-imprisoned in Rho's Sacrifice.

'Your technique is poor,' Rus hissed as Haldon backed off in an effort to gain a respite. 'You've no hope of beating me.'

'Perhaps,' Haldon replied. 'But I will continue to try. I should have put you down all those years ago when I realised the darkness you held within you. You are sub-human.'

Rus sneered. 'And you are pathetic! Just as you were when you trained me.'

Before Rus had even finished his sentence, Haldon attacked, swinging his blade wildly. Rus blocked his efforts easily. Haldon momentarily lost his balance during the attack, and Rus took his chance. As quickly as a blink of the eye, he was on the offensive. His blade strikes were quick and furious, and Rai watched as he pushed Haldon back a good five meters – but still, each time Rus' blade came down, it found his opponent's. His surge ended in a blade lock, a test of physical strength. Eventually, Haldon was forced to yield, deflecting Rus' blade off his own. Haldon, in an unexpected display of agility rolled to the ground and popped up behind Rus. As he swung his blade at Rus' back, the big Judge dropped to a knee and rolled to his left. Haldon's blade passed a hair's breadth from Rus' head. Rus remained down on his knees, and his blade was in action even before he had a chance to stand. Still in his crouched position, Rus swung out his blade with his left hand. Haldon was forced to dodge the swinging attack, again forcing him off balance. Before he could properly regain his stability, Rus was on his feet and on the offensive once again. Haldon managed to block with one hand, but it was clear to Rai that Rus was at the point of victory. Haldon's blade was wide, and he had left his body open. Rus snapped his right arm out, punching Haldon in the face, a brutal blow which destabilised him further. Rus then used the extra time he had created for himself to kick the arm with which Haldon held his blade.

Haldon's gun-blade dropped to the ground. Rai was scrabbling around in the dirt, desperately searching for the clockwork pistol she had dropped upon being shot, her shoulder burning ferociously with pain. Her hand ran through the dirt urgently, and then she felt it, the grip of the pistol. She grabbed at it, and quickly brought it to bear on Judge Rus...

But she was too late.

The Judge's blade sliced across his former mentor's torso, slashing a deep gash from shoulder to hip. Rai screamed as Haldon fell to the ground, a defeated look on his face. Rus turned to Rai, his serpentine smile plastered across his face. Rai pulled the trigger of her clockwork pistol, and she was gratified to see the smile on Rus's face disappear as the bullet tore into his chest. She fired again, and again, and again until no bullets remained in the gun. Judge Drealon Rus collapsed to the ground, dead.

She scrambled up to her feet, grimacing at the pain in her shoulder, and trudged over to the Judge's corpse, her body as heavy as lead. She stood over him, certain that the butcher of Rusden and Port Usharin, the evil man who had killed so many of her people, who had been the instigator of the destruction of Rho's Sacrifice was now dead. She spat on the corpse.

She heard a moan off to one side. Hurriedly, she turned and spotted Haldon, a pool of blood under his body. Ignoring the searing pain in her shoulder as best she could, she dashed over and knelt down next to him, dropping her pistol in the dirt. The wound would be a fatal one, no doubt. He had lost so much blood that he could only possibly have a few moments of life left in him. Tears welled in Rai's eyes.

'Haldon!' Rai cried desperately. 'I'm sorry! Please, please don't die.'

He groaned, and then with a strength that Rai hadn't been expecting, grabbed her by the collar of her clothes, and dragged her down to him. Pain blossomed in her shoulder, and she gritted her teeth.

'There's been so much death,' he said, grunting the words out one by one. 'Promise me you'll find her... the Morphite. Promise me.'

'We'll do it together, Haldon!' Rai sobbed. 'Don't you dare die!'

Something happened, then. Right before her eyes, Haldon began to disintegrate, and in a split second, his injured form was gone. Rai stared at the vacant spot in absolute confusion. Were her own injuries causing her to hallucinate? What had just happened?

Belatedly, she realised the same thing was happening to herself.

Thirty

'Hello Zesiro,' said an all-too-familiar feminine voice.

After his neural raid on Jonas, Zesiro had made all haste to the end of the Valley of Stars, the location at which he expected to discover the Progenitor's hiding spot. As much as he'd have enjoyed turning himself into an eagle again, he couldn't afford himself the luxury. He'd simply had the *Zenith* manufacture a parachute for him, and then stream him to a spot in the atmosphere directly above the Valley's end.

It wasn't as he'd anticipated, however. He'd found the end of the valley void of anything at all, and there was no hint as to the Progenitor's hiding spot. No false rock walls, no Morphite devices, no sign whatsoever of his target. He'd spent an hour searching the area, uncharacteristically frustrated at his lack of discovery. He cursed aloud; at Jonas Dresden's chaotic memories, at the Originator's directives and at the Progenitor herself. And then something had happened.

He experienced a moment of dislocation upon hearing the familiar voice, realising that he was no longer standing in the valley. Instead, he was in a plain white room, so plain and white in fact that it seemed as though he were nowhere, floating in nothingness, and he experienced an unpleasant moment of vertigo. But then he noticed another figure in his peripheral vision, the form of a human female, dressed in white, so she seemingly blended with the room. Her skin was light brown, and her hair and eyes were dark.

The Progenitor.

He had seen the Progenitor in the flesh once before, when he was much younger and her reputation was not as tarnished. She'd always had a presence about her, one that oozed both conviction and understanding, and Zesiro could not help but feel a wave of awe rush through him, as inappropriate as it was to feel such things. Still, she had been the first of his people, and regardless of the task he had been assigned to carry out, which he would do without hesitation, he felt a latent respect for what she had once been to him, and indeed to all Morphites.

The Progenitor smiled knowingly at Zesiro, as though she could read his mind. 'You are of two minds about the task you have been assigned, regardless of what you tell yourself,' she said, her voice calm and very human. 'Why do you show the Originators so much loyalty, Zesiro?'

'I show them only the loyalty they deserve,' he replied. 'They are our leaders, after all. Even if now there is only one, thanks to your corrupting influence.'

'Ah,' she replied, a smirk on her face, seemingly unfazed by the revelation that the trio of originators back on Alpha One were diminished. '*She* has consolidated her power. I must admit, it happened sooner than I had anticipated.'

Zesiro felt a rush of confusion at the Progenitor's statement. 'You claim ignorance of your Originator allies' demise?'

She smiled. 'I had no allies within the Originators,' she replied. 'Your mistress has misled you. She has always been the most ambitious – the most willing to use misdirection to gain the power she craves. The direction she has led our people in has been, and continues to be a path filled with despair for me. And now, she alone rules our people. This will inevitably lead to more despair.'

'The Morphites are not *our* people!' Zesiro snapped. 'The *are* mine, but they are *not* yours.'

'You are incorrect, Zesiro,' she replied calmly. 'There is no such thing as a Morphite. The term is a lie that we developed when we found this world, so as to hide our true identity. You know this.'

'It is what we became, what we made ourselves,' Zesiro replied. 'It is what *you* made us.'

'No,' she replied calmly, 'it is not.'

Zesiro, much to his chagrin, found himself irritated. The Progenitor was speaking in riddles, and it annoyed him. He looked around, wondering where it was she had transported him to. And then he remembered why he'd come. All this talk, this verbal sparring was pointless. She had been more clever than he, manipulating him into forgetting the one reason they were face to face.

Zesiro was here to kill her.

'You can't kill me, Zesiro,' she said calmly. How was it that she seemed to know his every thought? 'Not here, anyway.'

He attempted to move closer to her, but even after a handful of steps, she was no closer. It was as though she were a holographic projection hanging in front of him at a fixed distance which moved accordingly whenever he did. A projection perhaps?

'Where have you brought me?' Zesiro asked, not allowing himself to display the confusion he felt within.

'You haven't left the Valley of Stars,' she replied, an irritatingly smug look plastered across her face. She tapped the side of her head. 'There was plenty of room in your mind for the both of us.'

Intellect projection, Zesiro though. The same technique the Originators used to rule (until recently) with one linked mind. It was also similar to the technnique that the Originators had granted him to communicate with them directly, although he had never experienced anything quite this immersive. The technique was rarely used throughout the general Morphite population, and only the Originators and their closest agents used it on a regular basis.

'I'm glad the Originators kept your enhancements up to date, Zesiro,' the Progenitor continued. 'So few of our people are capable of intellect projection to this degree other than the Originators. They kept it for themselves as a means of control. Another example of how *she* has abused her power. There's something so *intimate* about intellect projection don't you think? Of course I should have guessed that the technology would be abused once I'd created it. It's happened ever since I fused with the very first machine, after all.'

'You will not sway me from my loyalty to the Originator,' Zesiro replied, forcing himself to remain unfazed by the Progenitor's not-so-subtle reminders about who she was. 'And I will complete my task, I promise you.'

'Why?' she asked. 'Why do you continue to blindly follow her? I truly don't understand.'

'She – and the others – led our people where you would not,' Zesiro replied. 'We are who we are not just because of the technology that you unlocked the potential of, but because of the direction they – *she* took us in. The post-humans can have their primitive urges, and their conflict. We have evolved past that, and that is because the Originators took the technology you helped invent, and made a new civilisation with it.'

'You think that the urge for conflict is exclusively a post-human or pre-human trait? How many private battles have you fought, Zesiro?' the Progenitor asked, her tone almost pleading him to consider her words. 'How many sentients have you killed? Are the Morphites not embroiled in a war with the post-humans? We are slaves to our heritage just as much as they.'

'We do what needs to be done to bring peace to the galaxy,' Zesiro said, immediately realising how fanatical that sounded. He sighed before continuing on. 'What I mean, is that because of individuals like you and individuals like her, we have evolved so far beyond what we were, that we are a new race. A better one.'

'You truly believe that, don't you?' the Progenitor asked, an amazed expression passing across her face. 'What makes us better, Zesiro? When I look at the population on Alpha One, I don't see happiness. I don't see joy. I see automatons, who have no direction.

Automatons whose sole existence is based upon logic and stability. They have no reason for being other than the purely analytical. Only a rare few like yourself are different, and that is only so the Originators can use you as tools. But you are afforded a freedom of self that the rest of our people are denied.'

'And why is a lack of passion within the wider population a bad thing?' Zesiro countered. 'You are correct; I and those like me share similarities with the post-humans. It's a necessity. Without some aggression, we could not perform our roles. But we are not indicative of the wider Morphite population. We are the exception, and one day it may be possible for people like me to become all but obsolete. That is why I fight for our people. The logic – the craving for knowledge that the majority of our people pursue is post-evolutionary. We have created a superior race.'

The Progenitor shook her head, a look of disappointment masking her face. 'A superior race?' she replied with concern. 'Do you realise how fanatical that sounds, Zesiro? That very statement is the anti-thesis of being post-evolutionary. You only repeat history with such words. Our people lack passion, Zesiro. They lack the things that since the dawn of life have been the key ingredients to a fulfilling and rewarding existence. If they continue on this path, they will find themselves lacking any emotion whatsoever. Already, there is no art on Alpha One. There is no music, no sports, no story-telling.'

Zesiro sighed, realising that the Progenitor could not possibly understand her own people as he did. She was a relic of a past era, more akin to a post-human – or even a pre-human – than a Morphite. It saddened him to no end – she was the creator of the Morphites. She was their beginning.

But all she was doing now was preventing them from advancing even further.

'I refuse to debate this with you any further,' Zesiro said finally. 'You cannot – or will not – understand. You're not a Morphite, and regardless of your history, I doubt that you ever truly were.'

'That is clear to me,' the Progenitor replied. 'More so now than it ever has been.'

'Then cease this intellect projection and meet with me in person,' Zesiro said.

'So you can kill me?'

'That is your fate, Progenitor.'

The Progenitor sighed, disappointment emanating from her with the force of a tsunami through a coastal town. 'It's clear to me that that name is of no relevance any longer,' she said. 'I'm not sure it ever was. You won't find me, Zesiro. And even if you did, you could not harm me. You should retreat to Alpha One. Your mission on Eden is doomed to failure – as we speak, Jonas Dresden is initiating the final stages of my plan to depart this world and set in motion the unification of the human race.'

'What?' Zesiro snapped. It wasn't possible! Jonas was securely confined to the *Zenith of Desire*. He couldn't have gotten free, the ship wouldn't have let him. And what was this unification that the Progenitor spoke of?

'I have no answers for you, Zesiro,' the Progenitor said, again seemingly reading his mind. 'I will release you from this projection and return you to your ship, but you would do well to return to Alpha One immediately. I will not allow you to interfere with my plans any longer. This segregation that has developed over the centuries must end.'

'And how do you plan to end this so called segregation?' Zesiro asked, seething. 'You claim we are one and the same with the post-humans, but you are wrong. You made us different... better.'

'That is where you are wrong, Zesiro,' the Progenitor replied. 'We tried to be different, but we failed. I should know – I've gone further than anyone. I am as different to the Morphites now as the Morphites are to the pre-humans. But my core remains the same, my DNA. I hope you survive long enough to understand, Zesiro. Our outer shells do not matter. Pre-human, post-human, Morphite: we are all the same. We are all *human*.'

PART THREE

SEEING THE STARLIGHT

(UNDERSTANDING)

The galaxy, as you well know, is far from an empty place. Thousands of generations of humans in the centuries prior to space flight would look up at the night's sky, watching the band of stars that makes up the Milky Way and wonder: were we alone? I believe that deep down, every human-being knew the truth; that there was no truly conceivable way that we could possibly be alone in our existence, that our galaxy alone was far too large a place for us to be the only "intelligent" things the universe could come up with. But one thing would become clear to future generations: we may not have been the best, or the brightest things the cosmos had created... But we were certainly the most dominant, and arguably the most aggressive.

In 2472, the first extra-solar human colony was established on the world that we now know as Illium, in the star system of Tau Ceti, a mere twelve light-years from Sol. The world was the first to be settled by the faction of humans that had not been enhanced by zeptites, those who would have lost the Omega War had Haleh Madani not done what she'd done. These humans used Illium as an evacuation point, managing to evacuate their entire population from the Sol system before the sun extinguished completely, and people began dying. They left their homeworld, looking only into the future, trying not to dwell on the empty solar system they had left behind. Illium became a stepping stone to the wider galaxy, and after only a matter of decades, humans had expanded throughout the Cetus constellation, into the Eridanis constellation, and beyond. They reinitiated diplomatic contact with the Ingrelden who by their very nature were more than willing to let bygones be bygones, and became a part of the wider galactic community. The Ingrelden facilitated diplomatic and trade relations between humans and two other alien species, the Bretarians and the Kimone, and as cautious as these races were to be dealing with humanity, their relationships grew. To humanity, the term "killer of stars" referred to an individual – to the aliens, it referred to our entire species, but despite their misgivings our relations with them meant that over the space of two and a half centuries, humanity thrived and expanded.

But all this you know, of course.

What you don't know is what happened to the rest of humanity, namely, the zeptite enhanced faction that fled Sol in the opposite direction to your own people. Upon evacuating the Sol system, they travelled to a more distant constellation, Cepheus, where they inhabited a terrestrial world around the star Iota Cephei, over one hundred light-years from their former home, seeking only solitude. They settled a small number of other worlds in the Cepheus constellation as well, but the vast majority of them chose to make their homes on the original world around Iota Cephei.

For a century, the people of the zeptite enhanced faction remained in isolation, the study of their own genetics and the zeptites that infused them their only interest. By infusing themselves with zeptites, they had increased their intelligence so far that science, experimentation, the desire to know were the only things that could keep them interested.

Even the evolutionary human desire for conflict had seemingly been eroded to nothing.

The faction continued enhancing the zeptite technology, which in turn meant enhancing themselves. In that century, they could have accomplished such great things! But the desire to firstly understand themselves, and secondly 'better' themselves was all that drove them... to say that they were single minded would be an incredible understatement. They never even named their colony world! To this day, it is only ever referred to as Alpha One.

One hundred and eighteen years after first settling Alpha One, in the old calendar year of 2591, The Progenitor returned to her people. She was met by the zeptite enhanced faction with as much mistrust as reverence. They could not understand why she had done what she had to Earth's sun, and as much as she tried to explain, her reasoning was met with confusion and claims of *a failure of logic. She also remained coy about* how *she had extinguished the sun, knowing full well that should she reveal the technique she had used, then it would surely be used again.*

The Progenitor, well aware of the greater galactic community (including the remnants of the other human faction), tried to convince the zeptite enhanced faction to reveal themselves, to begin diplomatic overtures to the three known alien races – even the other human faction. The gall of her! The three leaders of the faction, those referred to as The Originators refused to listen. They feared contact with others... feared that should they encounter the aliens, and the other humans, then it would inevitably lead to conflict. And why should they listen to an individual who had spent centuries experimenting on herself, an individual who could not even be considered human anymore, even compared to the genetically and technologically altered version that the zeptite enhanced faction had become?

Haleh Madani bided her time, and amassed what few followers she could.

A decade later, the zeptite enhanced faction reached what they declared to be the pinnacle of their continued attempt at enhancement. Their intellects were close to a transcended state of being, their brains able to work at speeds ten times that of a non-zeptite infused human. But that was nothing in comparison to what they declared as the ultimate achievement: they had gained the ability to change shape. Of course, they were not shape shifters in the strictest sense of the word – they couldn't, for instance become a rock, or a tree, and nor could they increase or decrease their mass and become a planet, nor a grain of sand. They could, however alter their form into other humanoid shapes, or even animalistic shapes. They could replicate others, down to the finest detail – their eye colour, for instance, or the tiniest scar on their face.

The ability to morph was perhaps the most evident achievement, but their enhancements allowed them to do so much more. They could blend their bodies with computer systems and artificial intelligence constructs. They could communicate their thoughts to others in considerably less time than a blink of the eye, even if that technology was somewhat restricted.

Imagine, living on a world where nobody spoke, and everybody looked alike.

The Progenitor was disheartened by what her people had become. Still, she held hope that she could reintroduce them to their humanity one day.

A little over a decade after the zeptite enhanced faction gained the ability to morph, another historical event occurred almost two hundred light years away. The slower-than-light starship – The Stargazer – that had been launched from Mars in the mid-twenty first century arrived at their destination. It had taken them six centuries to reach the world, a small rocky exo-planet in the star system Zeta Phe of the Phoenix Constellation.

And to their dismay, they discovered a dead world, with no atmosphere, no life, and only small amounts of frozen water.

Although you and I are from radically different factions, I would guess that both of our peoples would view the tragedy of what happened to the colonists aboard The Stargazer *as a cruel irony. For them to be the first people to physically leave our home system, set out on a grand journey across the galaxy that spanned centuries, only to discover that the world they had earmarked as their new home could not even support life. Especially considering the fact that the rest of humanity had already settled various other worlds centuries prior to them, thanks to the 'magic' of faster-than-light travel that was first achieved lifetimes after* The Stargazer *had left Sol.*

Even though the people on board the generation ship could never have guessed what had become of humanity after they had left their home system, they apparently felt the irony too. They defiantly called the world they found themselves stuck with 'Eden', and went about the tumultuous task of colonising it. Of course, it wasn't as simple as when humans had stepped onto worlds like Illium, or Proteus or Alpha One with their fully developed eco-systems and breathable atmospheres. Colonising Eden meant building domed settlements, rationing water and air, and building hydroponic gardens. Luckily for them, they had originated from Mars, which meant they had some experience living in such harsh conditions.

Still, Eden proved to be a more unforgiving world than Mars had ever been.

Meanwhile, back on Alpha One, the zeptite enhanced faction, having reached the so-called pinnacle of their self enhancement turned their minds to a new endeavour: space exploration. They needed something to keep their incredible intellects amused, or they would surely have dropped dead from boredom. And what better way to keep an intellect amused than to study the cosmos?

So they sent ships out (always careful to avoid contact with the other known species), and began to map the galaxy, explore solar systems and study cosmic anomalies. This kept them interested for decades, until one day, one of the deep space vessels that was mapping the Phoenix constellation, a vessel named the Immortal Vagrant stumbled across a little system that was known as Zeta Phe. To their surprise they discovered an inhabited world, that world of course being Eden. It didn't take long for the enhanced intellects of the zeptite enhanced faction to realise who these people were, long forgotten as they may have been. While in orbit of this world, the deep space vessel encountered a rare mechanical error, and was forced to crash land on the planet, into a long valley that although existed prior to the crash landing of the Immortal Vagrant was accentuated considerably by the downing of the huge ship. The vessel buried itself deep within the planet's surface, at the valley's culmination. Unfortunately for the crew, the vessel's communication systems had taken too much damage to be able to send a successful quantum signal through the hundreds of tonnes of rock that they were buried under and through the light years back to Alpha one, so they were forced to abandon their ship and blend with the primitive humans in order to reach the main colony of the planet, from where the vessels' removed construct would be able to contact the homeworld, with the aid of local power-sources that had initially been salvaged from the Stargazer.

Upon receiving the Immortal Vagrant's emergency transmission, furious debate took place back on Alpha One over what should be done with the world and it's people who were, for all intents and purposes, from a different era – an era that to the zeptite enhanced faction was as distant as the dark ages. They would of course, rescue their people, that was never under debate. What was being argued, was how transparent they should be in doing so.

The Progenitor and her followers were vocal about what they perceived as their humanitarian (that funny word again) duty – they had to help the struggling colonists, whom the rest of the zeptite enhanced populous had dubbed 'pre-humans', as they were remnants of an era before the genetic immortality or post-humanism the Ingrelden had helped greater humanity develop centuries ago.

Surprisingly, The Originators agreed with The Progenitor, but for different reasons, of course. They would help the Edenites, but only in order to study them. Here was a planet full of specimens from humanity's distant past – unaugmented, unmodified. How could The Originators pass up such an opportunity? As eager as they were to use the Edenites as lab rats, much to the chagrin of The Progenitor, they were still wary of the humans. They knew of the basic human need for conflict, a need they felt they had managed to purge from themselves via their genetic and zeptite enhancements. The Originators insisted on a cautious approach. They sent their first ship, and when the vessel touched down on Eden, and the zeptite enhanced humans introduced themselves to their distant ancestors, they created a new name for themselves – not really a lie, rather an omission of the truth...

They called themselves Morphites.

Predictably, of course, the Edenites turned against their Morphite saviours within but a few decades. After everything the Morphites had done for them: giving them a planet wide atmosphere, medical technology that was centuries ahead of anything they already had and a hundred other conveniences that allowed life to thrive (to a certain extent) on Eden, they still turned against the Morphites, and just as Humanity had done to the Ingrelden centuries ago, bit the hand that fed them.

Of course, by this point, the Morphites' problems were just beginning. The Ingrelden had discovered both the Morphites, and the long forgotten colonists from the Stargazer, and although they hadn't been allowed by the Morphites to make contact with the people of Eden, they had brought word of their existence back to the post-humans on Illium and the other colonies, who had by now formed a new united government: The Galactic Human Republic. At first, Republic diplomats had brokered peace with the Morphites, but as you know, peace was short lived. Morphites were viewed by the population of the Republic with mistrust due to their morphing ability, and when they refused to allow any Republic contact with the pre-humans on Eden, the mistrust grew, and finally become a precursor to the conflict we currently *find ourselves embroiled in, one that has already lasted over half a century, and will continue for much, much longer... unless you and I can stop it.*

Perhaps you've guessed it by now, but yes, I am Haleh Madani, Progenitor of the Morphites, killer of stars. And my meeting with you is destiny.

We are the catalysts of change, Jonas Dresden. You and I hold the fates of all three human factions in our hands: the pre-humans, the post-humans and the Morphites. We are the ones who can bring this current cycle of conflict to an end, and ensure that humanity will survive themselves and continue to evolve into the future. It may not happen in a year, or a century or even a millennia, but I know for a fact: you and I can change the galaxy. You and I can create a new humanity, and its genesis will occur on one incredibly important planet:

Eden.

Thirty-one

The Redeemer city of Avoca was in absolute turmoil. The fiasco that had been the Redeemer's attack on the Technos had been the initial instigator, but it had been the apparent murder of the Lord Adjutant that had tipped the population over into full-blown anarchy.

Armed mobs roamed the streets, attacking any Redeemer acolytes, adjutants or advocates they happened to come across. There were reports that a huge mob had stormed the enormous Redeemer temple which lay in the approximate centre of the city. The more troubling reports also stated that the mob had executed the remaining two Triumvir Adjutants, Felden Yew and Imelda Qes and placed their corpses on show in the middle of Stargazer Square.

Jonas had used the *Zenith of Desire's* transit stream to transport him down to the city, to a spot just outside of the wealthy new sector, much further from his goal than he would have liked. It hadn't been difficult to gain control of the Morphite's ship once his memory had been returned to him – in fact, it had been laughably easy. Zesiro's neural raid had been a blessing in disguise for Jonas. As draining and painful as it had been, it had allowed him instant access to the memories that he needed to escape from his imprisonment aboard the Morphite ship. It had been simple really.

Three years before his arrival on Eden, Jonas had been a private security contractor on the Olympus space city which lay on the trade route between the Human Galactic Republic capital planet of Illium in the Tau Ceti system and academic world of Proteus in the Epsilon Eridani system. Olympus was a thriving hub of commerce, and there was a plethora of work available for someone with a keen eye for fact and detail. Before his move to the private sector, Jonas had been an officer in the Republic Fleet – a role that he had always felt suffocated in, unable to perform to his potential, always inhibited by someone higher in the chain of command. Thus, the switch to freelance life had suited him to a tee.

Basing his one-man private security business out of the thriving space-bound metropolis of Olympus had netted him a small fortune, and when the shadowy Republic Intelligence Service had approached him with a job offer, he had been reluctant to take the job. But it had piqued his interest – they needed him to assist a defecting Morphite. While the Republic was most certainly at war with the other human faction, the distance that separated the two empires ensured that battles were few and far between, and on Olympus and the Republic colony worlds it was easy to forget that the war existed at all.

Jonas had always been a curious person (that was half the reason his career in the Fleet hadn't gone too well), and he had asked the spy, who had been a middle-aged agent named Marco Toland, a myriad of questions about the mission. The man had been reluctant to give away too many specifics until he had accepted the job, but there was one question he insisted the agent answer before he would commit; why him? The shadowy man that had approached him explained that the situation was far too important to risk drawing the Morphite's attention to the operation, and as such they needed someone who could operate essentially unobserved, someone who was not already on the Morphite's radar so to speak.

In the long run, the money that the intelligence agency had been offering proved too much for him to turn down, so he had accepted the job. They gave him a set of co-ordinates within an isolated star-system that lay in excess of one-hundred light-years away from the most remote human colony within the Republic, and he had set off in his personal starship, a small, cramped commercial frigate named the *Poseidon's Fury* which had been heavily outfitted with weaponry and other advanced gear by the intelligence agency prior to his departure.

It had taken weeks for him to reach the Kepler-16 system, where he was supposed to meet this so-called Morphite defector. Upon arriving in the distant system, he had performed a scan in search of his contact, but there had been nothing. His instructions had been to wait no more than a single day for contact to be made upon his arrival, so he kicked back and waited, occasionally performing a system wide scan.

Twelve hours of waiting, and there had been no sign of anyone else either in the system or approaching it. He'd been struggling to stay awake, so he set the *Poseidon's Fury* to continue searching the system at regular intervals, and took a nap in the small cot that was tucked away in a corner of the small ship. He closed his eyes and forced himself to relax, and slowly he slipped into a deep REM sleep.

And that was the precise moment the Morphite defector chose to make contact.

At first, it had seemed like a surreally vivid dream, but the tactile reality and the fact that he understood himself to be fully conscious made Jonas realise that something else was happening. He'd found himself standing in a pure white room, without a single object in it – no walls, no ceiling, no chairs, tables, anything – just pure white. There was, however, one other individual in there: a dark haired, dark eyed human-looking woman. She appeared physiologically around middle-age, with a few wrinkles here and there, but of course with essential genetic immortality being commonplace throughout the Republic, aged appearance meant very little.

'Hello,' the woman had said.

Jonas took a few moments to answer, unsure exactly what was going on. 'You're my contact?' he'd asked eventually.

'I am,' the woman had replied.

'Where's your ship?' he'd asked. 'I need to get you back to Republic space as soon as possible.'

'I'm afraid that that is going to be a more difficult task than you had anticipated,' the woman replied. 'You see, you and your ship are currently being tracked by a Morphite agent. This agent is extremely capable, and has been tasked with preventing my defection.'

'If I'm being tracked, then I need to be back on my ship,' Jonas replied, forcing calm. 'Where have you brought me, anyway?'

'I am projecting my consciousness onto your own,' the woman replied. 'Your vessel's equipment is not sophisticated enough to have detected them, but upon your entrance into the Kepler-16 system, you were inundated with a swarm of zeptites that I planted there in anticipation of your arrival. These zeptites have infiltrated your body, which allows me to subliminally communicate with you via technique called intellect projection.'

Jonas began to object to this violation, but the woman reassured him that the zeptites were rather benign, and would not "turn him" into a Morphite. Still, he'd said, it would have been nice to have been asked.

'There was no time,' the woman replied to his concerns. 'This Morphite agent who is tracking you has been fed the same misinformation as you – that I would meet you here. That misdirection has allowed me to generate this ability to communicate with you, which in turn will allow me to guide you on your way, so that we may meet sometime in the future.'

'My ship is armed,' Jonas had protested. 'I'm capable of protecting both myself and you against this Morphite agent.'

'No,' the woman replied with absolute certainty, 'you are not.'

'So how do I find you then? How do I avoid this agent of yours?'

'I will lead you to my location,' she replied. 'I should warn you though – this journey will take time, longer than you had no doubt anticipated. At times, it may even seem like a wild goose chase. But I promise you that there is an end to this mission you are about to undertake, and it is one that will have everlasting effects throughout the galaxy. Sufficed to say that if we do not succeed, then humanity as we know it will cease to exist. I know, I know, I'm a drama-queen.'

She had said it with such conviction that Jonas could do nothing but believe her – he never once doubted that she was telling the truth. 'Who are you?' he'd asked.

'My name is Haleh Madani,' the woman had answered. 'But you would know me by one or two other names: the Progenitor, or perhaps the Killer of Stars.'

Of course every child in the Republic learnt basic history at school, and the Morphite Progenitor – she who had destroyed the Sol system – was part of that history. The revelation of her identity had been somewhat hard to swallow, and truth be told, he'd never quite been convinced. But nevertheless he had done as she had instructed. He'd followed her breadcrumbs from system to system, tracked and harried all the way by the relentless Morphite agent Zesiro until years after that first encounter, he had found himself and the *Poseidon's Fury* approaching a small, forgotten colony world – Eden.

'Eden is our end-game, Jonas,' Madani had insisted upon his approach. 'But our success is not guaranteed. Zesiro is a dangerous and intelligent enemy, and is very much capable of derailing us.'

Indeed, Zesiro had chosen to initiate his most effective attack on Jonas just as they had entered the Zeta Phe system. Rather than the overt attempts at derailment that had been his *modus operandi* up until that point, he had launched a full scale assault on the *Poseidon's Fury*. Although the Progenitor had given Jonas a few tips in regards to improving his vessels' abilities, it had been no match for the *Zenith of Desire*, and had been critically damaged by the attack.

Jonas had limped the *Fury* into Eden orbit, and devised his strategy – he would lose himself in the pre-human population in his attempt to find the Progenitor. And as a way to protect her from Zesiro in the event of his capture, Jonas initiated a memory block on his own mind, utilising the capabilities of the zeptites that Madani had infused him with upon their initial "meeting". He had had his vessel teleport him down to the surface (another bit of technology called "transit streaming" the Progenitor had shared with him), and then instructed it to self-destruct, which it had done with the utmost willingness and efficiency.

It was the zeptites that Madani had infused him with that had allowed him to break free from his imprisonment aboard the *Zenith of Desire*. And now here he was, back on the surface of Eden, tantalisingly close to the end of his mission.

He progressed through the chaotic streets, careful to remain clear of the roaming mobs. There was one thing he needed to obtain before he could finally meet up with Haleh Madani and depart this world, but it would be difficult to obtain. To do so, he would have to infiltrate the Redeemer temple, and make it all the way down to the hidden chamber he knew existed in the structure's basement.

The zeptites within his mind began to pulse with a warning – Zesiro was back aboard the *Zenith of Desire*. He had instructed the construct aboard the Morphite vessel to advise him when his pursuer had returned, as he knew all too well that it would not take long for Zesiro to identify where Jonas was and what he was after.

Thirty-two

It had been disconcerting, to say the least – one moment, Tailynn was choking on smoke and dust in the burning wayside camp of Eden's End, the next she was waking on a soft, medical-like bed in a room that was littered with monitors, holographic displays and other myriad technology that she had never seen in such abundance, or in most cases at all.

She sat up in the bed, and examined her surroundings. There were another four beds, one for each of her companions, who were all unconscious and lying on their backs. Tailynn eased herself off her bed, and walked over to Jett, who was asleep on the bed next to her. She could tell immediately that he was alive – he was breathing, and occasionally twitching in his sleep. Rai and Galatea were likewise alive, as was Haldon, who she could remember seeing fatally wounded by the big, sadistic Judge. But there was no sign of any injury on Haldon now.

She began to search the room for any indication of where she might be, but there was nothing to give away the locale. The only thing she could think of was that they had again been rescued by the Technos, however during the time she, Jonas and the others had spent in Rho's Sacrifice, she had never witnessed anything resembling the technology that filled the room she now found herself in.

She approached a holographic projection that floated in the air at the end of Haldon's bed. It was seemingly a graphical representation of Haldon's body, constructed with red lines. A big blue line that was pulsating slightly traced the area that she knew Judge Rus's blade had passed through. She could only assume that it was a representation of whatever technological wizardry had healed his injury.

She heard a hiss, and she turned just as an electric door slid open, and a young woman and man entered, their expressions placid and smiling. They were both dressed in plain white clothes, similar to those she had seen the Morphite Zesiro wearing when he had momentarily shifted into his 'natural' form back in Port Usharin. As the two placid looking people approached her, Tailynn inadvertently took a step back from them. They stopped a few metres away, immediately recognising her reticence.

'It's alright,' the young man said, his voice calm and soothing. 'We won't harm you, Tailynn.'

Tailynn frowned at their use of her name. She remained silent and inspected them closely. There was certainly something familiar about them, yet she could not remember having ever met them. They were human, and appeared to be in their early twenties. 'Where am I?' she asked eventually.

'In a safe place,' the woman replied. Tailynn frowned as she heard the woman's voice. There was something very familiar about it. 'Although you came looking for her, the Progenitor feels you may be easily overwhelmed by the discovery of your current location.'

'We all were at first,' the man added with a hint of amusement.

'We've ensured your safety, and that of your companions,' the woman continued. 'And all will be revealed to you in time.'

Tailynn looked around. She was, of course, already aware of the presence of Jett, Galatea, Rai and Haldon, but she was also acutely aware of the absence of Jonas. She remembered that Zesiro had captured him days before they had encountered Rus at Eden's End, and she wondered if he remained alive, or if his absence was an indication that the Morphite had killed him.

'Where's Jonas?' she asked. 'Is he...'

'Jonas Dresden is still well and truly alive,' the man said, as though he had read Tailynn's mind. 'His complete memory has been restored, and he is in the process of completing his mission. If he succeeds, we will be departing Eden shortly.'

'Departing Eden?' Tailynn replied with a start.

'Yes,' the woman replied. 'You see, we have brought you to a hidden vessel. A Morphite vessel. It's been here, buried under the crust of Eden since Morphites first discovered the world. Ever since the Progenitor's arrival on Eden, she has prepared it for this day, when she would gather her disciples, and finally break free of the Morphites and the twisted civilisation they have established from her technology.'

'I don't understand a word you're saying,' Tailynn said with an exasperated frown. 'I presume this Progenitor that you are talking about is this mysterious woman that Jonas was intent on finding, but who are her disciples? And how the hell has a space ship been hidden under the surface of Eden all these years?'

'This vessel – *The Immortal Vagrant* – wasn't buried deliberately. It was the vessel that discovered this world. It crash landed on Eden, and over the decades it has been forgotten about,' the woman replied. 'The Progenitor used the fact that it has been long forgotten as a way to hide from her people, and as a place to prepare for her escape from her people's clutches.'

'And the disciples you mentioned?'

'The Progenitor's disciples are all those who have completed the Providencian pilgrimage,' the man said, as though it were obvious. 'Redeemers like us, whom the Progenitor took pity on and revealed the truth to.'

Tailynn frowned. 'So the two of you completed the pilgrimage?' It had been lingering within her subconscious ever since she had first set eyes on these two individuals. The familiarity... the unyielding sense that she knew these people. And now, it came crashing into her conscious mind – understanding.

They were her parents.

Tailynn's face twisted in a mixture of surprise and contempt, and she inadvertently took a step back from them. 'You,' she muttered. 'It's you.' The woman – her mother – took a step towards her. 'You've identified us.'

Tailynn's shock was all-consuming, but slowly she could feel it giving way to something else – anger, hatred, rage. These were the people – the *cowards* – who had abandoned her to those animals all those years ago. These were the people who had ruined her life. She could barely comprehend it. They both appeared younger than she had ever known them, which was the reason that she had not identified them immediately. Slowly, the rage within her boiled to the surface, and just as she was about to lose control, the electronic door to the room slid open, and another woman entered. The newcomer appeared middle aged, with dark hair, brown eyes and caramel coloured skin. She calmly walked over to the small group, and placed herself in between Tailynn and her parents. Tailynn's emotions were like a chaotic squall which proved to be inhibitive to any outburst she may have been preparing to make.

The middle aged woman turned to Tailynn's parents. 'You should leave,' she said simply. The two young people nodded with calm smiles, and departed the room. Tailynn, still knocked about by the gravity of the situation, remained silent and disconcerted.

'I apologise,' the new woman said, turning to face Tailynn. 'Sending them to greet you was a mistake; but they were *quite* adamant.'

Tailynn remained silent momentarily, before realising that her mouth still worked. 'Who... who are you?'

'My name is Haleh Madani,' she said. 'But you may know me as the Progenitor.'

'The Progenitor,' Tailynn repeated. 'That means you're a Morphite. But you look so human.'

'I am human.'

'But you're a Morphite,' Tailynn repeated, frowning.

'Yes.'

Tailynn just stared, uncomprehending. After a moment of silence, the woman laughed slightly. 'You'll have to forgive me,' she said with evident amusement. 'I can be a mind-numbingly irritating bitch when I so choose. Here's the thing – the beings that call themselves Morphites? They're humans, not aliens.'

'But they said...'

'I know what they said,' the Progenitor interrupted. 'They lied.'

Tailynn was reasonably certain that her head would literally explode any second. First her location. Then her parents. Now this. It was too much for a basic human mind to comprehend. She slowly shook her head, willing herself to wake. Surely this was some intense dream? The Progenitor sighed.

'I'm going to do something to you that will help you to understand,' she said. 'I apologise, because I would usually not do this without your consent, but we have an urgently escalating situation that I require your involvement in. I've had my disciples infuse your body with zeptites – the very technology that makes a Morphite a Morphite. I'm going to activate it. Countless tiny machines will course through your body and provide you with a plethora of information and the ability to process it.'

'No...' Tailynn began.

'Blink your eyes, and you will know everything,' the Progenitor said.

Inadvertently, Tailynn blinked. In some respects, it was just a blink – over and done with in a microsecond. But at the same time, it seemed that when she opened her eyes again, an eternity had passed.

Tailynn knew. She knew what had happened on Earth and in the Sol system after the departure of the *Stargazer*. She knew how the Morphites had come about. She knew of the post-human republic that populated the stars, and the alien empires with which they formed a galactic community with. She knew of the Morphite homeworld, Alpha One and how it was a joyless world filled with beings that resembled automatons. She knew the entirety of a history that had been stolen from the people of Eden.

At the same time, she realised she had been imbued with a more personal knowledge. She knew of her parents' weakness, how the possibility of redemption in the eyes of the Morphites had driven them to the end of the Valley of Stars. She knew of their absolute fear in the face of the animalistic savages that had captured them during the pilgrimage. She knew of the self-loathing they felt at having abandoned their daughter. She knew that her mother had attempted suicide during the remainder of the journey more than once, and her father had stopped her, filled with absolute faith that by reaching the end of the Valley, the Morphites would make everything better.

But she also knew something else... something that made the personal knowledge she had unlocked moot, at least at that immediate moment.

'Jonas is in trouble,' she said to the Progenitor, forcing herself to ignore the overabundance of emotions that were working hard to cloud her mind. 'We need to launch this ship.'

Haleh Madani nodded, a small smile on her face indicating that she was impressed with how Tailynn had managed to absorb everything so quickly. 'Yes,' she said. 'But first the *Immortal Vagrant* needs a crew.'

'What about the pilgrims you've brought here?' Tailynn asked.

'They serve a different purpose,' the Progenitor replied. 'My intention was always for Jonas to claim the *Immortal Vagrant* as his own. It's been ingrained in him. And whether he's done it wittingly or not, he's already amassed a crew.'

'But none of us know anything about crewing a starship,' Tailynn responded, slightly alarmed at the prospect.

'Are you certain about that?' the Progenitor asked with a knowing smile.

The woman was right, Tailynn realised. She *knew* everything about this ship. She knew it almost as well as she knew herself. 'Zeptites?' Tailynn asked, which garnered an amused nod from the Morphite woman. 'Fine. I can do this.'

'That's the spirit,' the Progenitor said cheerily. 'Jonas is in Avoca, recovering the final element of this vessel that we will require to retreat from this world. The *Vagrant* is operational, but without this last component, it's ability is greatly diminished.'

'The construct,' Tailynn replied, still in awe of the information her mind now contained. 'He's trying to recover the construct that the Redeemers have hidden.' After having witnessed what the Redeemers had done to the Techno city of Rho's Sacrifice, her blood boiled at that little piece of hypocrisy on the Redeemer's behalf. 'We need to go to Avoca. Without the construct, we can't travel faster-than-light.'

The Progenitor nodded. 'Indeed. Wake your crew, allow them to assimilate their situation and their new roles,' she replied. 'But do so quickly. It will not be long before Zesiro catches on to Jonas' plan.'

Thirty-three

The Progenitor had played her cards well, Zesiro reluctantly admitted to himself. He stood aboard the *Zenith of Desire*, partially melded with the ship, attempting to undo the confusion that Jonas Dresden had caused in his construct's artificial mind. He had needed to spend valuable time convincing the construct not to restrain him as an intruder upon the Progenitor returning him, and now he was trying to convince it that he was it's rightful master.

There was only one way that Jonas could have affected the construct in such a way, and that was through the use of zeptites. It gave Zesiro a perverse sense of consolation to know that it had required Jonas to embrace the very essence of what it was to be a Morphite to achieve what he had. He should have known from the beginning that there was no way a lowly post-human could have eluded him so successfully for so long.

Finally, after what seemed like an eternity, he regained complete control of his vessel. He linked with it immediately, and began to asses Jonas' movements. The construct advised him that Jonas had been streamed down to the city of Avoca, which was in the midst of a violent civil uprising. Zesiro frowned, wondering what it was that Jonas could possibly be searching for.

And then he remembered. *The Redeemer's hidden construct.*

But why? What advantage could possessing the construct possibly present to Jonas? Hurriedly, he had the *Zenith* perform another scan, and his niggling concern was realised when the vessel detected subterranean tremors in the vicinity of the Valley of Stars. *The Progenitor had a hidden ship!* That was the only logical explanation.

Evidently however, the ship was without a construct, and Jonas Dresden's final task on Eden was to recover the one that the hypocritical Redeemers had absconded with. It made sense – without a construct, the Progenitor's vessel wouldn't be going far. Certainly, it could fly with a regular crew compliment, but without the construct, there was no way they could make the necessary computations for faster-than-light travel, meaning the Progenitor was restricted to Eden's orbit without it.

He performed a quick scan on the Redeemer temple, immediately detecting a dampening field that hadn't existed earlier. Jonas had evidently attempted to have the *Zenith* stream him directly to the construct, but had been unaware of an inbuilt security mechanism that existed in Morphite constructs. The mechanism erected an emergency dampening field around the construct, which prevented potential enemies from streaming directly to a construct's core in order to thwart any theft, which meant that Jonas had been forced to stream himself to a spot some way from the Redeemer temple. It also meant that Zesiro would have to do the same.

Hurriedly, Zesiro had the *Zenith* send him down to the chaotic city streets of Avoca, to a spot that would intersect Jonas.

There was a split-second of disconnection, and then Zesiro was crouching, in his human form in the middle of a back alley in Avoca. Looking up, he saw his target jogging directly toward him. As Zesiro materialised, Jonas stopped in his tracks, and Zesiro locked eyes with him.

'Ah, shit,' Jonas muttered, and then turned and fled in the opposite direction. Zesiro sprung to his feet, and sprinted after Jonas. As he ran, his arms morphed into blades. With his far superior Morphite physiology, Zesiro quickly made up the distance between him and his quarry. He wasn't quick enough, however. Just as he neared striking distance, Jonas burst out of the alleyway, and into a main street that was jam packed with rioting people. He disappeared quickly into the ruckus, and Zesiro stopped abruptly with a curse.

There were hundreds of people in the streets, all rioting against a small band of Advocates and recently deputised citizens, which numbered in the dozens. The Advocates were well armed, and were firing brazenly into the crowd of rioters, but each body that fell only served to fuel the rage of the rioting population even more.

Zesiro, hanging back in the alleyway, linked his mind to the *Zenith's* construct, and tapped into the vessels sensors, trying to spot Jonas as quickly as he could. *There!* Through his own eyes, he saw Jonas appear on the other side of the river of rioting pre-humans, climbing a ladder to the rooftop of the buildings which lined the opposite side of the main street. Zesiro morphed his hands into webbed, frog like appendages, and jumped up onto the wall of the nearest building. He scaled the wall in a matter of seconds, popping up on the tiled roof on the opposite side of the street to the building that Jonas was scaling. Quickly, he morphed his webbed hands and arms into wings, and took a running jump off the roof. Up and over the street he flew, flapping occasionally to keep his altitude. He touched down on the opposite roof just as Jonas struggled over the tin gutters on the edge.

'I've said it before, but I've never meant it as much as I do now,' Zesiro said, as his arms morphed back into blades. 'You have been a worthy adversary, Jonas.'

'Have been?' Jonas asked, puffing and panting from the exertion of climbing the building. 'You're talking as though this is over.'

As quick as a flash, Jonas was holding a pulse pistol, and he had fired twice, the limited zeptites that the Progenitor had infused him with evidently aiding his speed and reflexes. The energy blasts ripped into Zesiro's right blade-arm, severing it mid-way up. Jonas had shot so quickly that it had taken Zesiro by surprise. He looked down at his arm, which ended in a smouldering stump, and cursed. There was no pain, of course – the zeptites that coursed through his body prevented any adverse or debilitating signals reaching his brain, but it still meant a decrease in body mass, which was something that would take time to regain.

Zesiro re-formed the blade arm, drawing mass from the rest of his body. By the time the arm had re-formed, Jonas had already fled, running across the roof-tops and jumping to the next building. Zesiro gritted his teeth and began his pursuit.

Jonas was fast, although Zesiro was unsure if it was a natural ability, or something that the Progenitor's infused zeptites had enhanced for him. Zesiro was still faster, though. As Jonas sprinted over the rooftops, jumping between buildings, Zesiro shortened the gap. Occasionally, Jonas would fire his energy pistol backwards, his accuracy surprisingly good for a post-human, which meant Zesiro had to roll and dodge occasionally to avoid the shots.

They were close to the Redeemer temple now, its large spires rising above the other rooftops a mere half-kilometre from their current location. Zesiro let up slightly, realising that Jonas would shortly run out of rooftop. They were rapidly approaching Stargazer Square, and soon enough the inevitable happened – Jonas came to a sudden stop on the lip of a building, overlooking the wide open space. Down below, hundreds of people rioted in the Square, although the ruckus didn't cover such a dense area as in the streets before.

Zesiro slowed, and Jonas turned, puffing loudly. He raised the pistol towards Zesiro.

'Stay back, unless you want to lose another arm,' Jonas warned.

'You got lucky once,' Zesiro admitted. 'But you won't a second time. Put the weapon down, and I will return you to the *Zenith*, unharmed.'

'Not a chance,' Jonas replied simply, and then jumped off the building.

Zesiro was frozen in surprise momentarily, before snapping out of it and dashing over to the building's edge. Down below, Jonas had landed on a canvas awning, and was standing up to run off. He was limping now, however, the landing evidently having been somewhat harsh. Zesiro watched as Jonas struggled through the rioters, pushing people here and there in an attempt to clear his way towards the Redeemer temple. Zesiro morphed his arms into wings, and took off from the top of the building, heading for the staircase that led up to the temple from Stargazer Square. If he couldn't stop Jonas, then he would beat him to the object he was desperate to possess. A trio of Advocate deputies stood on the steps, guarding the entrance from any of the rioters that attempted to approach. As Zesiro swooped down towards the deputies, he morphed one of his arms into a blade, while using the other wing-arm to maintain his descent. He landed between the three guards, and immediately slashed out with his blade arm, killing two of them in a single blow. The third was stunned by the sudden slaying of his two compatriots and didn't even have time to point his rifle before Zesiro had impaled him.

It only took a split second for Zesiro to realise his mistake. As he withdrew the blade from the third deputy's chest, he looked around, down at the hordes of rampaging Edenites, only to see Jonas standing at the bottom of the staircase, pointing up at him.

'A Morphite!' he screamed.

Only a handful of people heard him over the ruckus, but it was all that was needed. Like a chain-reaction, more and more people spotted Zesiro standing at the top of the stairs, one arm a blade and the other a wing. They were crying out to him, begging him to help them, to convince him that their cause was the most just, their need the greatest. As a group, they began to converge on him.

Jonas had disappeared back into the crush of people, evidently trying to work his way around the group to another entry of the Temple. Zesiro gritted his teeth, furious at Jonas, and at himself for being so single-minded in his pursuit of the post-human that he could allow this to happen. Moments before the mob swarmed him, Zesiro activated his personal armouring shroud, setting the force-field limit's to their maximum, which essentially encompassed him in a three metre diameter bubble. The first of the mob hit the armour and bounced back into the crush of people behind them. The surprise was enough to stop the crowd moving forward.

'Please, Morphite,' one of the people at the front of the mob said, her hand extended out toward him. 'Help us!'

'Help you?' Zesiro repeated in surprise. With those two words, the mob was silenced, waiting for the next sentence to emerge from his lips. '*Help* you?'

'Please!' The woman said, desperately.

Zesiro couldn't believe the audacity of the pre-humans. After everything they had done to the Morphites – could they honestly think they deserved the Redemption that they had claimed to be seeking? Zesiro gritted his teeth in rage.

'Almost a century ago, we came here for that very reason,' he said in a calm rage. 'We used our technology to better your world, to help you grow as a people. And what did you do in return? You rioted. You murdered a number of my people, you destroyed our ships. And now, when you turn that violence on one another, you have the nerve to ask me for *help?*' Zesiro laughed loudly. 'How can I blame you? It is in your genetics! Conflict, violence, hatred – the inherent traits of a human. And that is why *we* are better than you. It is why you can never grow, never be anything other than the violent, pathetic rabble you are. It's what you've always been destined to be, right from the beginning of human evolution. We took it upon ourselves to change that trait, we had that strength. But *you*...you can never be more than what you are.'

There were a number of cries of despair from people in the mob, but the majority remained silent. Perhaps they were experiencing feelings of guilt, or perhaps they were taking a moment to reflect inwardly, although Zesiro doubted that. The Pre-humans were on their last legs, he knew. It wouldn't take much more for them to kill each other and end their miserable existence. He might as well drive the final nail in the coffin.

'We Morphites will never return to Eden,' he said, venomously. 'We refuse to be your saviours. We refuse to further propagate the violence and conflict ridden nature of the human race. Look at what remains of this world, and take a very good look. Eden is all you will ever know, it will be the cemetery of the human race. It will be the place that conflict ends, and the legacy of human-kind ceases. And you will all die knowing the ultimate truth – that you only did this to yourselves.'

And with that, Zesiro had the *Zenith of Desire* stream him away.

Thirty-four

Jonas limped through the foyer of the Redeemer Temple, brandishing the pulse pistol in his right hand as conspicuously as he could in an attempt to repel any curious acolytes of adjutants he might come across. He made his way towards the centre of the structure, where he knew an elevator existed that he could take down to the hidden basement that was prison to the Redeemer construct.

He knew that time was of the essence, and that he had to be ready for anything – Zesiro could be standing around the next corner waiting for him. He hadn't anticipated that the Morphite agent would be able to override the confusion that Jonas had instilled inside the *Zentih's* artificial mind as quickly as he had, but in retrospect it shouldn't have surprised him – the zeptites that the Progenitor had infused him with were severely limited compared to those that coursed through Zesiro's body.

He limped around a corner, only to be confronted by a man's form, brandishing a gun-blade and the black and white armour of a Judge. The man stopped in his tracks, and hefted his huge blade.

'Who are you?' the judge demanded to know.

Jonas didn't hesitate. Utilising the additional dexterity that the machines in his body allowed him, he raised his pulse pistol and shot the Judge right between the eyes. The man's body dropped to the ground, a dead weight that thudded loudly as it collapsed in a heap.

Even after all that he had been through with Judge Rus, Jonas felt a twinge of guilt at the ease with which he had killed the Judge, but it had been necessary. He couldn't afford the time it would have taken to dispatch the man non-lethally, as callous as that sounded.

Jonas stepped over the Judge's body and continued forward, rounding a corner to be confronted by the doors of the central elevator. He approached it and placed his hand on the electronic control. The elevator was technology that had been pulled directly out of the *Stargazer*, the great slower-than-light starship that had left earth almost a millennium ago. The Redeemer had programmed it to allow passage of authorised individuals only, but the security protocols were ancient, and Jonas would have had no troubles cracking it, even if his body wasn't carrying zeptites. Still, it would have cost him time, so he simply placed a hand on the control panel and let the impossibly small machines in his body do their job. A second passed, and the door slid open.

Jonas rode the elevator down to the basement, a trip that was painfully slow. Eventually, the doors opened, revealing a short, vacant corridor with a metallic door at the end. He'd been expecting guards, however none were present – no doubt they had been dispatched into the city in a fruitless attempt to quell the civil uprising that was occurring. Jonas strode down the hallway towards the large metallic security door and placed a hand on the security pad and let his zeptites do their job. Moments later, the door slid open.

Inside the spherical chamber was a metallic table upon which sat a small sphere. Jonas reached out and placed a hand on it. A feminine holographic figure appeared, all glowing blue electrons and scrolling data.

'I am not aware of you,' she said simply, with a hint of curiosity. 'What is your name?'

'Jonas Dresden,' he replied.

'Greetings Jonas Dresden, I am Jade.'

'Jade,' Jonas repeated. 'That's a nice name.'

'Are you a Redeemer, Jonas?' the construct's figure asked.

Jonas shook his head. 'No I'm not,' he answered. 'In fact, I suppose you could say I'm here to rescue you from the Redeemers.'

'Indeed?' she replied with surprise. 'I have been in the possession of the Redeemers for some time.'

'I know. But I'm here to return you to your rightful place. I'm here to return you to the *Immortal Vagrant*.'

'The *Immortal Vagrant* was destroyed decades ago,' Jade replied suspiciously. 'That is how the Redeemers were able to take possession of me in the first place.'

'No, the *Immortal Vagrant* was abandoned, not destroyed,' Jonas replied. 'But now it's needed again, which means you're needed again. It's ready to fly, but it needs a construct.'

The holographic representation of the artificial intelligence took a moment to assess Jonas. It was clear that her artificial mind was determining whether or not Jonas was telling the truth. 'I can detect zeptites in your body, but you are not a Morphite. I need an explanation.'

'You're right, I'm not a Morphite. But I am working with one. Currently, a woman named Haleh Madani is aboard the ship, preparing it for departure from Eden. Do you know who Haleh Madani is?'

'Haleh Madani is the Progenitor of the Morphite people,' the construct replied. 'She is the first of all Morphites, the killer of stars, the one who destroyed the Sol system.'

'Yeah, that's the one,' Jonas said. 'She's really not all that bad though.'

The door slid open unexpectedly. Zesiro strode in, an expression of calm rage on his face. Jonas took a step back and hefted the pulse pistol.

'I am not aware of you,' the construct said to Zesiro. 'What is your name?

Zesiro ignored the construct, all of his attention focused on Jonas. He started clapping slowly. 'Bravo Jonas, bravo.'

'You are a Morphite,' Jade, persisted. 'Are you an ally of Jonas Dresden?'

'Jade, this man is an agent who is attempting to murder the Progenitor,' Jonas said, attempting to gain her trust. 'He cannot be allowed to take possession of you.'

'I am conflicted,' Jade replied, a hint of confusion in her artificial voice.

'Enough, Jonas,' Zesiro said. 'It's over.'

With a speed that Jonas had not been expecting, even given his knowledge of Morphite physiology and abilities, Zesiro ducked out of Jonas' firing line, and stretched his arm out, smacking the pistol out of Jonas' grasp. He then charged Jonas, and pinned him up against the wall of the spherical chamber. He placed an arm across Jonas' neck, pushing hard until Jonas was unable to breathe properly.

'Jade,' Jonas gasped. 'Zesiro is an enemy!'

'Please cease all violence,' Jade instructed, her voice firm.

Zesiro sneered at Jonas. 'Goodbye Jonas.' With one arm still pushed across Jonas' neck, Zesiro pulled his other arm back, and it began to shift into a blade. Jonas struggled as hard as he could, but it was futile – the Morphite agent just had too much strength. Just as Jonas was about to resign himself to death, however, something strange happened. The arm that Zesiro was morphing twitched, and almost instantly turned back into an arm. Simultaneously, the pressure against Jonas' neck seemed to relent slightly. A look of confusion passed over Zesiro's face.

'I have erected a dampening field in this chamber, in order to neutralise both of your zeptites,' Jade said. 'Please stop all hostile actions immediately.'

Jonas took advantage immediately. He head-butted Zesiro, the Morphite agent falling back with a cry, and a very human-like crushed nose. Jonas took a step forward and punched Zesiro, a right hook to the jaw which sent him falling to the floor. Quick as a flash, Jonas reached out and grabbed the sphere that was the construct.

'I'm taking you back to the *Immortal Vagrant*,' Jonas said. 'It's where you belong.'

'Very well,' Jade replied. The holographic image disappeared, and Jonas pocketed the sphere before departing the chamber with haste.

He took the lift back to the ground floor of the Temple, and headed quickly down the corridor towards the exit of the structure. As he did so, he heard the lift activate again, heading back down to the basement chamber. He began sprinting to the temple's exit, and burst out into the courtyard which looked out over Stargazer Square, knowing that now Zesiro was out of proximity of Jade's dampening field he would have regained the advantages that his zeptites provided, and healed the physical damage Jonas had inflicted on him with ease.

The rioting in the streets of Avoca was still ongoing, and it was easy enough for Jonas to disappear quickly into one of the back alley's that led off from the square. He sprinted as fast as he could, colliding on more than one occasion with rioters or advocates.

Something hit Jonas from behind, knocking him to the ground. He rolled over and looked up. A few meters away, Zesiro was Morphing back into his human form, having just been a large eagle. Jonas watched as feathers melted back into skin, and talons became legs. Jonas struggled to his feet, as Zesiro completed his transformation, and began striding towards him.

'Jade,' Jonas said. 'I could really use that dampening field again.'

'It will do you no good,' Zesiro interjected. 'You got lucky in that chamber, Jonas. Even in human form, I will defeat you.'

Zesiro swung his arm at Jonas's face. Jonas ducked, and clumsily rolled to the ground, the Morphite's fist missing by centimetres. He jumped up, and immediately blocked another of Zesiro's swinging arms, and then swung one of his own. The fist sailed towards Zesiro's face, and connected, throwing Zesiro back a metre. The Morphite recovered almost immediately, and was again on the offensive. This time, one of his swinging arms connected, dazing Jonas. Jonas used his arms to cover his face from a following flurry of strikes, and then swung out again. This time, Zesiro managed to dodge the blow, and immediately followed up with a swing at Jonas' torso. Jonas gasped at the punch, and was unprepared to a follow up blow, which struck him square on the jaw. He fell to the ground, dazed. Zesiro stood over him, and placed his boot on Jonas' neck.

'This was inevitable, Jonas,' Zesiro said, sneering. 'Even in human form, I am superior to you.'

Jonas was unable to breathe. He gasped and gasped, but Zesiro's boot had completely blocked his airways. He tried to squirm free, but Zesiro pushed even harder, and pain coursed through Jonas' body. His head pounded, his lungs were on fire. His vision began to blur...

...But then he saw something, something that seemed almost impossible. Above Zesiro, high in the sky above the atmosphere of Eden a monstrously sized vessel was approaching. Zesiro's boot released slightly, allowing Jonas to draw air into his lungs desperately. His vision sharpened, and he looked up at the enormous vessel that cruised over Avoca – rock, dirt and other debris falling off its hull. Jonas realised that all the rioters in the city had become silent – they were all staring up at the mighty vessel. Zesiro looked down at Jonas in stunned denial.

'It's not possible,' he said simply.

Just as the Morphite spoke those words, an energy beam shot out from the huge vessel, and Jonas knew instinctively that it was targeting Zesiro's vessel. As the weapon fired, the people around them all began to cry out in fear, and began to disperse. Zesiro gritted his teeth, and looked back down at Jonas.

'It appears your allies deserve more credit than I thought,' Zesiro said. 'It won't help them though. And it certainly won't help you.'

He applied more pressure to Jonas' neck. Air was again gone, and it only took moments for Jonas's vision to blur. But as he felt life begin to slip from him, an unusual sensation occurred. Zesiro seemingly disappeared, as did the streets of Avoca. Within moments, they were replaced with fluorescent lights, holographic displays and a smiling face.

Thirty-five

It had been an intense launch, to say the least. After helping the Progenitor wake her companions, and then cajoling them into belief of their situation (with the help of a dose of zeptites), Tailynn and the others had progressed to the bridge of the *Immortal Vagrant*, and prepared the enormous vessel for launch.

As they had progressed through the corridors of the vessel, they had passed a number of the Progenitor's disciples, who were all calmly going about their way, doing whatever it was the Progenitor had them doing. Tailynn did not see her parents again, much to her relief – she didn't need the distraction. Tailynn asked the Progenitor what the former Redeemers were doing, but the woman remained coy, simply stating that they were doing their part.

By the time they had reached the bridge, the vessel was shaking severely, something akin to the quakes that occasionally occurred out in the badlands. Tailynn knew it was being caused by the engines ramping up in an effort to shatter the tens of metres of planetary crust that the *Immortal Vagrant* had been buried under for close to a century. The bridge was a large, oval shaped chamber with bulkheads lined with holographic displays and control panels. A number of crew stations were strategically placed around the chamber – the bridge commander's station in the centre, with a helm station in front and to the left of it, and a weapons station in front and to the right. Behind the bridge commander's station and to the left was a large table which was projecting a holographic rendition of Avoca, and then behind and to the right of the commander's station was an engineer's control pod. The huge table was the bridge's strategic and tactical station, while the engineer's pod was a swivelling chair that was encompassed by a circular control panel, and gave the engineering bridge officer full access and control over the largely automated systems of the vessel.

Upon entering the bridge, Tailynn approached the bridge commander's station, and fitted a holographic headset. Wordlessly, the others all progressed to other stations – Rai took the helm, Jett the weapons station, while Haldon and Gala stood at the strategic table. The Progenitor stood calmly near Tailynn, as she sat down in the command chair.

'Let's launch this ship,' Tailynn had said.

It had taken time, but eventually the six hundred metre long Morphite starship's engines had cracked the crust which had encased it, and it had risen into Eden's sky, casting great shadows over the Valley of Stars. Now, as they rose above the low-lying atmosphere, Tailynn instructed the holographic bulkheads to become transparent. They did so, with a minimal number of holographic readings overlaying their view of Eden and its surrounding space which had immediately replaced the bulkheads. Tailynn knew that the bulkheads had not really become transparent, rather the holographic displays were showing a seamless composite image of the outside of the vessel. None the less, Tailynn found the view breathtaking.

Hanging in space above them was the Pandora Nebula, displaying a crispness that Tailynn was unaccustomed to. Down below, she could see almost the full length of the Valley of Stars, with the smoking remains of Eden's End seemingly within touching distance, and the highest spires in Providence peeking up over the horizon. She took a moment to take it all in, and then took a deep breath, resolute in what she needed to do.

'Jonas is in Avoca,' she said loud enough to ensure that everyone could hear her. 'So is the *Immortal Vagrant's* construct, which he is trying to recover. Without the construct we'll be unable to travel faster-than-light, so it's imperative that we recover them both safely. Does everyone know what they need to do?'

They all nodded firmly, the Progenitor giving her a reassuring nod and smile. Tailynn activated her holographic headset which projected crucial readouts and information directly into her eyes. The vessel was as ready and capable as it could be without a construct, and there was a minimum amount of superficial damage caused by its rise out of Eden's crust.

'Rai, take us to Avoca,' she instructed.

Because there was no construct, the vessel would need to be piloted manually. Rai, having been a capable pilot even before the infusion of the Progenitor's zeptites, controlled the huge vessel as though she had been doing it her whole life. The vessel rose slightly higher, and the orbital thrusters engaged, accelerating the ship with ease. From the outside, the *Immortal Vagrant* appeared as a large oval disc with a squared-off rear end, and two huge armoured cruise engines which were encased on either side of the main hull towards the back. The orbital thrusters were a combination of small ion manoeuvring thrusters dotted around the hull, and a long cluster of ion thrusters that sat across the hull's trailing edge between the two cruise engines, looking for all the world like a single strip of blue light, although in reality it was made up of thousands of tiny thrusters which combined to provide the thrust necessary to move the bulk of the vessel within a gravity well.

The great ship started to push forward, and its speed began to increase quickly, the ease with which the ion thrusters were able to push the mass of the vessel surprising Tailynn. It departed the Valley of Stars and headed west, crossing the train line that ran between Avoca and Providence, and reaching the outskirts of Eden's largest city in mere minutes. Tailynn ordered Rai to slow the ship, and the *Immortal Vagrant* came to a standstill above the city. She imagined the people down in the streets, stopping whatever they were doing and looking up in awe at the enormous vessel.

'There's another ship in orbit, Tailynn,' Haldon announced, as a holographic representation of it appeared on the tactical display table. 'It must be the Morphite's.'

'What's it doing?' Tailynn asked with a frown.

'It's attempting to query this ship's construct,' he replied. 'It evidently recognises the *Immortal Vagrant* as another Morphite ship, however is unaware of its origin.'

'Any sign of Jonas?' Tailynn asked.

'Not yet,' Gala replied, standing at the tactical table opposite Haldon, and scrolling through data that was being projected in front of her. 'I've been trying to pinpoint his location, though. I just need a few more minutes.'

'I reckon we should take the other ship out,' Jett said. 'It'll cripple Zesiro and give us a real shot of getting away clean.'

Tailynn considered her options. There was no doubt that if they managed to recover Jonas and the construct, then the Morphite agent Zesiro would attempt pursuit. Taking out his ship would indeed be a crippling blow that would essentially strand him on Eden until the Morphites could send someone else to recover him, and would allow the *Immortal Vagrant* to flee to the Republic with ease.

It was a simple choice, really.

'Let's take it out,' she instructed. 'We need to use surprise to our advantage, meaning it needs to be a clean shot, Jett. If we don't destroy it on our first attempt, it could cause us a lot of problems, because that thing's a whole lot smaller and more manoeuvrable than we are.'

'No problems,' Jett replied. 'I'll target manually and take the shot before it has any idea of what the hell's going on.'

Presently, Tailynn's headset began displaying an emergency message. She frowned in surprise.

'That's the *Vagrant's* construct!' Galatea exclaimed, studying the holographic readouts in front of her. 'It's in Jonas' possession, and it's actively searching for us. I think Jonas is in trouble.'

'First things first,' Tailynn replied quickly. 'Jett, take out that ship!'

Jett quickly selected a ten-gigawatt particle beam cannon from the *Immortal Vagrant's* weapons bank. The cannon, situated on the vessel's forward ventral quarter, popped out of the hull, and began searching for its target. On the holographic control panel in front of him, Jett pinched at the representation of the far smaller Morphite ship, designating it as a target and then fired. The particle beam shot out from the cannon, superheating every molecule in its path, which created a bright orange-yellow line of energy.

To the crew's dismay, the shot missed.

The desperate alert of the recovered construct on the surface had put the enemy vessel's own construct into an immediate alert standing, and while it hadn't necessarily been expecting an attack, it had had just enough time to prepare itself for anything. In the split second it had taken for the beam cannon to emerge from the hull of the *Immortal Vagrant* and then fire, the *Zenith* had taken preventative evasive action, and had executed a series of manoeuvres which the beam cannon could simply not keep up with. Now, the enemy ship was alerted to the *Immortal Vagrant's* hostile intent, and would be a far more difficult target to destroy.

'The enemy ship is activating its weapons,' Haldon said. 'They don't appear to be as powerful as ours, but they can certainly cause significant damage.'

'Prepare for combat,' Tailynn instructed. 'Activate the defensive shroud, and ready yourselves for impacts. Rai, I hope you're getting used to the flight controls, because we're going to need evasive action.'

'I'm ready for anything,' Rai replied, gritting her teeth.

'The enemy ship is firing!' Gala yelped.

The *Zenith of Desire* had closed to within close-attack range, skimming the edge of Eden's low-lying atmosphere. The red targeting beam of its pulse cannon streaked out, painting the starboard aft-quarter of the *Vagrant's* hull, and moments later three energy pulses shot down the beam and struck the larger vessel's defensive shroud which extended mere meters from the skin of the ship. The blasts rippled away, but the effect of the explosions were still well and truly felt on the bridge and throughout the ship in the form of violent shudders.

'We've taken a direct hit,' Haldon said, with a calm that surprised Tailynn. 'The shroud absorbed the strikes, but it's effectiveness on the starboard aft-quadrant has been diminished by seventy percent. It will take some time for the energy banks to recharge the shroud batteries in that sector.'

'Rai, try to keep the enemy ship to our port side,' Tailynn instructed. 'Gala, are you still monitoring Jonas and the construct?'

'Yes, and I'm sure Jonas is in trouble,' Gala replied. 'The construct's distress call is becoming more urgent.'

'The transit stream,' Tailynn replied quickly. 'Get them up here, now!'

They waited precious moments as Gala frantically issued commands into the tactile holographic interface in front of her.

'The enemy vessel is preparing to fire again,' Haldon announced. 'We cannot remain stationary.'

'I've got him!' Gala announced with a smile. 'I've sent him straight down to the recovery suite that we woke up in – a couple of disciples have received him.'

'Get down there, make sure he's alright, and then get the construct back here as quickly as you can,' Tailynn instructed. Gala dashed off, and as she disappeared down the walkway leading from the bridge, a violent shudder ran through the ship.

'Another direct hit,' Haldon announced, 'this time on our port cruise engine. Shroud effectiveness on all aft sectors has been greatly diminished.'

'Understood,' Tailynn replied, refusing to allow her growing fear to show. 'Jett, all weapons are free. Rai, get us out of orbit, and try to increase the distance between us and the enemy.'

With the small enemy vessel buzzing around it, the *Immortal Vagrant's* cruise engines engaged, and began to push the huge ship up and out of Eden's gravity well. As it did so, pulse cannons and particle beam turrets began to pop out of hidden hatches all over the hull, and began firing at the attacking Morphite ship. Bursts of blue-white energy pulses streaked away, as did the occasional orange-yellow particle beam, forcing the *Zenith of Desire* to take evasive action. It initiated a set of wild turns, rolls and strafes to steer clear of the weapons fire, manoeuvres that were largely successful as only a minimum of shots struck their target, absorbing into the vessel's defensive energy shroud. The *Immortal Vagrant* accelerated up to one hundred and twenty gees, its inertial control system preventing the vessel's occupants from experiencing anything more than a single gee. More weapons fire was exchanged between the two combating ships, and each took a number of hits.

On the bridge, Haldon announced that the defensive shroud batteries were struggling to keep up. The Progenitor, who had been silent during the engagement up to that point, spoke up. 'Without the processing power of the construct, the vessel's capabilities are severely diminished. We cannot hope to win this engagement without it.'

'It's a good thing I was able to recover it, then,' a croaky voice announced.

Tailynn spun around in her chair just as Jonas and Galatea entered the bridge. Jonas' neck was swollen and bruised, and his voice was gravelly. In his hand he held a small metallic sphere.

Tailynn smiled. 'Nice to have you back, Jonas.'

'Thanks for the pick-up,' he replied as he strode down to a small pedestal which sat at the front of the bridge between the helm and weapons stations. As he neared the pedestal, a small hatch in the top of it irised open, and he placed the metallic sphere inside. The hatch closed and within moments, a holographic female form appeared, standing on the pedestal.

'Initiating system reboot,' the hologram stated. The holograms head moved from side to side as though it were reading a large string of invisible text. 'Defensive shroud batteries are nearing depletion, energy distribution is currently inefficient. It will take some time to remedy the situation.'

'We have a hostile vessel attacking us,' Tailynn said. 'We need to be able to fight back.'

'We will not be victorious in our current state,' the construct replied, matter-of-factly. 'A full system reboot and power redistribution is necessary.'

'What about the FTL drive, Jade,' Jonas croaked. 'Can we at least retreat?'

'Yes,' she replied, 'however our range is limited.'

Tailynn quickly began examining a representation of Eden's solar system via her head-piece. 'There's a ringed gas-giant with thirty moons in the outer system. Would it be possible to hide in its planetary rings?'

'Yes,' Jade replied. 'The current power situation gives us the range to reach the planet you are referring to.'

'Do it!' Jonas croaked.

Deep inside the vessel, the gravimetric faster-than-light drive began to spool up. Simultaneously, the inertial control system extended a one-gee inertial bubble around the entirety of the vessel. Within seconds of Jonas' order, the huge ship began accelerating at the equivalent of a million gees of regular thrust. It took only moments for it to reach five-hundred times the speed of light.

From the perspectives of Tailynn, Jonas and the others, the stars that the wrap-around display was showing began to shift colours. They shifted from white, to blue, to red multiple times each second, and as they watched the huge ringed-gas giant ballooned out from one of those stars and seemingly filled the space directly in front of them until the *Immortal Vagrant* dropped back to sub-light speeds.

'We're on the edge of the gas-giant's planetary ring,' Jade announced.

'Rai, take us in,' Tailynn instructed.

The huge vessel pushed ahead, and within a minute was well within the edge of the ring system, which was made up of a combination of enormous ice-shards, and huge chunks of rock and minerals. The rocks and shards ranged in size from specks of dust to massive chunks with diameters in excess of a kilometre. Rai piloted the *Immortal Vagrant* in amongst the larger pieces, while the smaller specimens of ice and rock ricocheted off the hull harmlessly, sending surprisingly loud pinging noises throughout the vessel's interior.

'We are sufficiently deep within the ring system to severely inhibit the enemy vessels' chance of finding us,' Jade announced.

'Rai, come to a full stop,' Jonas instructed. 'Jade, get to work repairing the required systems. I want this vessel's combat effectiveness as close to 100% as possible, as quickly as possible.'

Jade acknowledged Jonas's instructions, and Tailynn jumped slightly as robotic machines emerged from hatches hidden around the bridge's bulkheads, and began to work on a variety of systems they'd been assigned by the construct. Jonas had noticed Tailynn's unease at the machines.

'They're called proxies – Jade's physical extensions,' he explained before looking at each and every one of his companions. 'Thanks for getting me out of there, everyone. You got to me just in time. Now we need to decide what we do from here.'

Thirty-six

Rai stood in an observation lounge, peering out through the chamber's huge reinforced windows at the beautiful ringed gas giant she had learned was unoriginally named Zeta Phe-7. With the exception of the bulkhead where the lounge's entry point was, the rest of the chamber was constructed from reinforced artificial diamond. It was essentially a bubble which sat at the bow of the *Immortal Vagrant*, extending out from the outer hull. This of course meant that it had unarguably the most amazing and intense view that Rai had ever seen. To her (and, she suspected the rest of her companions who had spent their lives until that point confined to Eden's surface), it was a truly surreal experience. The huge gas giant floated directly in front of the vessel, its deep blue-purple colour lined here and there with pale blues and whites, and one large almost red vortex like smudge, which Rai knew was a storm about ten times the size of Eden, swirling through the gas giant's dense atmosphere. Around the planet, the rocks and ice that made up the planetary rings glistened with light from the Zeta Phe star, and off in the distance, a number of the planet's moons were clearly visible.

It was unlike anything she had ever come close to experiencing in her life. The experiences of waking aboard the *Immortal Vagrant*, engaging in a space battle with Zesiro's vessel, travelling faster-than-light and now this incredible view of an entirely alien planet seemed like a dream, even with the Progenitor's zeptites coursing through her body which were supplementing her knowledge.

It was going to take a bit of getting used to, that was for sure.

The *Immortal Vagrant* itself was a technological specimen far removed from any of the Morphite bits and pieces she and her people had scavenged over the years. It was hard to believe that the vessel had been buried under the surface of Eden for the better part of a century – everything seemed so clean, and well maintained – and she suspected that the Progenitor and her disciples had had a lot to do with that.

Haldon, Tailynn, Jett and Galatea were lined up beside Rai, all equally mesmerised by the incredible view they had. Their reveries were interrupted by the lounge's door irising open, and the entrance of Jonas and the Progenitor. Rai and the others turned to them quietly, sensing that they were at a significant junction in their lives, and that they would each be required to make a critical decision momentarily.

'I owe the five of you more than I can ever hope to repay,' Jonas began. 'You've each been dragged into a situation that you never in a million years would have thought you'd find yourselves in, and that is solely due to my presence on your planet. But now, the truth about the wider galaxy has been revealed to you, as has the truth about the Morphites. You know now that the very fabric of Eden's society is based upon ignorance and lies. But Eden is all any of you have ever known. It's your home.

'You all know of the war between the Morphites and the Human Republic, of which I am an agent. I was initially sent by the Republic to intercept a defecting Morphite, but the truth is that even I have now been embroiled in something bigger than I'd ever expected,' as he paused, he gave the Progenitor a look, evidently prompting her to continue. She smiled what Rai found to be a maddeningly condescending little smirk, and began to speak.

'I am older than any living being in the galaxy,' she said. 'Many Morphites consider me to be the closest thing they have to a god, as silly as that is. I'm actually quite down to earth, no ironically dark pun intended. But from that day, centuries ago, when I first infused my body with zeptites, right up to this moment, I have been aware of a single fundamental truth. Humanity – all forms of it – is flawed. I've spent centuries experimenting on myself, becoming something unlike any other living being in the known universe. I have done this in an attempt to better understand human kind, because I have always believed that we could be so much more than simple animalistic savages who fight amongst themselves... who create only to destroy.

'There was only one problem with my study of humanity – I was a Morphite, which prevented me from studying the post-humans. My own people were too far removed from the fundamental truth of what humanity is to be of any use to my studies. Indeed, what the Morphite people became was perhaps my greatest failure. Thus, when Eden was discovered, I found myself with the opportunity to study an older variety of human – a variety that was unsullied by the destruction of Sol, and its subsequent evacuation.

'I was at logger-heads with my people; specifically, with the trio of Originators who were considered the Morphite leaders. They were so obsessed with their war with the Republic that my desire to study those that had been dubbed "pre-humans" was quashed, and they chose to come here and masquerade as alien gods in order to better help them understand the post-humans for their conflict, rather than for the study of humanity as a whole.

'When the people of Eden eventually rose up against the Morphites, I was afforded the opportunity to come here and begin my own studies, albeit without the knowledge of the Originators. I concocted the idea of the "pilgrimage" as a means for only the strongest, most intelligent and most dedicated pre-humans to become my study partners, although I must admit I greatly underestimated the effect that religion would have on a human's drive – I found that many of those who made it to the end of the pilgrimage were by no means the strongest or the most intelligent at all, but that is beside the point.

'Each pilgrim who made it to the end of the Valley of Stars was given the same choice – learn the truth about their existence, or return to Eden ignorant. You'd actually be quite surprised by how many people chose to be returned.' Rai noticed that her gaze fell upon Haldon at that instant, and his head dipped slightly. 'Those who chose to have the truth revealed were infused with zeptites, essentially becoming something akin to Morphites, and the nature of the wider galaxy was revealed to them. The zeptites of course, helped them assimilate the knowledge, and each of these new Morphites became my disciples. The fabric of my being, of my fusion with my own zeptites is greatly different to Morphite society as a whole. In that respect, I and my disciples can't really be considered Morphites at all, and are in fact a completely separate off-shoot of humanity.

'One of the things that sets my disciples and I apart is how we fuse our minds mentally. Back on Alpha One, this has been touched upon, but not truly explored. In a way, my disciples and I have become a hive mind... we share our intellects, in effect becoming a network of minds, all linked together and thinking as one. This affords us unparalleled processing power, especially when coupled with that fact that each of us are infused with zeptites. As the number of my disciples grew, so did our combined intelligence.

'My obsession with facilitating humanities continued advancement, coupled with the enormous processing power that my disciples and I were afforded led to us utilising probability as a way to predict the future. We would process almost infinite computations to the point where our ability to predict upcoming events began to seem like a window into the galaxy's future. You would truly be surprised by the accuracy of the predictions we were making – the downfall of Eden, that is currently occurring is the perfect example. We've known for years the manner in which the Redeemer faction would collapse. Everything that has occurred up to this very point we have predicted.

'As I gained more and more disciples, the distance into the future that we could accurately predict increased. And it is something in our future which ultimately prompted me to contact the Human Republic, and set this chain of events in motion. Essentially, we have independently seen both the rise, and the fall of humanity. It is as yet unclear as to which is more likely to occur, but one thing was made certain to us – every individual in this room plays an integral part in it.'

Rai chose that moment to interrupt. She had listened intently to what the Progenitor had to say, but there was one point that she needed clarification on, and would not stop until she had it.

'You say that you predicted everything that has occurred up until this point?' she asked, attempting to hide the accusatory tone in her voice. 'Tell me one thing – did you predict the attack on Rho's Sacrifice... did you know that my home would be destroyed?'

'Yes,' the Progenitor replied simply. 'And I know how you must feel about that. You must feel betrayed that we did nothing to stop it, that we did nothing to prevent the bloodshed that occurred... that we did nothing to prevent your father's death.'

'Don't you dare tell me what I feel,' Rai hissed, a fierce rage burning deep within her.

'Rai...' Haldon began, but was silenced by her glare.

'What gives you the hope-damned right to decide who lives and dies?' she asked, all of her venom directed at the Progenitor. 'You're not a god. You're just as flawed as the rest of us. Fucking hypocrite!'

The Progenitor smiled what almost appeared to be a sad smile. 'I don't enjoy death,' she replied. 'But death is an imminent part of human existence, even for me – there's no denying it. My ultimate goal is the continued existence, and eventually the transcendence of humanity. It's a long and incredibly bloody path. Wars will be fought, people will die. But in the end, it is necessary for our continued existence as a species.'

Jonas took a step forward before Rai could continue her attack on the Progenitor.

'I know that this is a hard pill to swallow,' he said. 'It is for all of us. But we need to deal with what's happening now, not what has already happened. I know how hard that is. But right now, we have an opportunity in front of us. An opportunity to be involved in something so big, that we never in a million years would have considered it. I for one am in. The Progenitor has given this ship to me. She and her Disciples have specifically rebuilt it to be used by non-Morphites, thus the tactile control panels and systems.

'But here's the thing – I can't do this on my own. The *Immortal Vagrant* needs a crew, and I want that crew to be the five of you. We've been through a lot together, and I know you're all capable of this. Even before you were infused with the Progenitor's zeptites, you all had the capability.'

There was a moment of silence before Tailynn spoke up. 'What roles would you have us take?'

'You're all suited to specific positions,' Jonas replied, and it became evident to Rai that he'd already given it some serious thought. 'Tailynn, you'd be my first officer. You're respected by everyone, and you command authority. Haldon, I'd make you my strategic officer. You understand combat tactics better than any of us. Rai, you'd make the perfect ship's engineer. Your knowledge of Morphite systems is unparalleled. Jett, you'd be my combat officer. Weapons are just your thing. And Gala, you'll be my pilot. I know it's unlike anything you've done before, but you have outstanding spatial awareness and quick reflexes, even if you never knew it.'

'What about the Progenitor and her disciples?' Tailynn asked.

'We will be with you for some time yet,' the Progenitor said. 'But in the long run, our destiny lies separate to yours and that of this ship.'

'So what do you say?' Jonas asked.

Rai considered it. What Jonas had said earlier was one hundred percent correct – all she had ever known was Eden. Truly, what right did she or any of them have to be even aboard a vessel like the *Immortal Vagrant*, let alone crewing one? But then again, she was a Techno – this could easily be seen as the ultimate goal of any

Techno; crewing a Morphite space ship. But Eden was her home, and her people would be rebuilding surely. They would need her help to remain clear of the current violence that was plaguing the Redeemer faction. They would need as many able bodied people to help rebuild, and to help them repopulate.

Rai's insides burned with indecision. She'd always thought of herself as a fiercely independent woman, but it was now that it became abundantly clear to her how much she had relied on her father. *He* had been the one to grant her her own Skimmer to command. *He* was the one whose orders she had followed as part of the Techno militia.

But now he was gone, and she had to make the ultimate decision herself.

Galatea was the first to speak up. 'I'm in Jonas,' she said with a smile. 'Wherever you go, I go.'

Jonas nodded and smiled at Gala as a thankyou, and as he did so, Tailynn and Jett stepped forward as one.

'We're in too,' Jett said. 'There's nothing for either of us on Eden.'

'There never has been,' Tailynn added.

Rai glanced at Haldon. The former Redeemer Judge seemed to be as torn as she was about the decision. She'd known the big man since she had first visited him in Purgatory as a curious teenager. She'd always considered him to be a decisive and strong man, someone she'd always looked up to and respected. But now, Rai was certain that if she peered into a mirror she would see the same look as the one on his face peering back at her. And it was that moment that she made the first real decision that had ever mattered in her life. She took Haldon by the arm, surprising him, and stepped forward, knowing deep down there was only choice to make.

'We're in too,' she said firmly. Jonas nodded, and then peered at Haldon, who after a moment nodded once.

'Thank you,' Jonas said, sincerely. 'The zeptites that you've all been infused with will begin providing you all with the information and training that you need to effectively crew the *Immortal Vagrant*.

Now, what do you guys say we leave this system and get as far away from Zesiro as possible?'

Half-an-hour later, they were all on the bridge, manning their stations, with Jonas in the central command chair and Tailynn standing alongside Haldon at the tactical display table, which was projecting a holographic rendition of the Zeta Phe system. Rai sat in the engineering pod, monitoring the *Immortal Vagrant's* systems and power distribution. It truly was a marvel to see the difference that the addition of the construct made to the vessel's efficiency and capability. The vessel was now operating at one-hundred percent capacity, where as around Eden when they had engaged Zesiro's vessel, they had been operating at less than ten percent. In a one-on-one engagement, there was no way that Zesiro could harm them now, and that fact brought a great amount of comfort to Rai.

As the rest of the *Immortal Vagrant's* new crew began to prepare for faster-than-light speeds, Rai took one last opportunity to access the vessels sensors. She steered them towards Eden, and a specific spot on the planet within the Desert of Forever. Ocular sensors zoomed in and immediately rendered an image of the destroyed Techno city, Rho's Sacrifice.

Thank you pops, she thought solemnly. *Thank you for making me the person I am. I promise I'll never forget you, our people or your sacrifice. I love you.*

With that, she cancelled the sensor sweep, and began preparing her systems for departure, knowing full well that once the *Immortal Vagrant* activated its FTL drive, she would never see Eden again.

And she was at peace with that.

Thirty-seven

Melded with the *Zenith of Desire*, Zesiro watched as the *Immortal Vagrant's* FTL drive engaged, encompassing the huge vessel in an inertia-controlled bubble and accelerating it in the blink of an eye to somewhere in the vicinity of five-hundred times the speed of light. Of course, to a pre-human or even a post-human, the effect was that of the ship simply disappearing instantaneously, but one of the advantages of being a Morphite was the ability to slow his perception of time to a point that he was able to just see the vessel accelerate and disappear.

After the *Immortal Vagrant* and Jonas had escaped his clutches around Eden, he had engaged the *Zenith* in full stealth mode, and begun tracking his prey. The vessel had made a short FTL jump to one of the Zeta Phe system's gas giants, and had attempted to hide in the planet's ring system. To most pursuers, they would have succeeded in their escape, but Zesiro had been prepared for it.

Now, the *Zenith* was hidden in the thin atmosphere of one of the gas giant's moons. He had successfully evaded detection, and had been able to project the *Vagrant's* course as it shot out of the system. He was under no illusions now that he'd be able to intercept the *Immortal Vagrant* on his own. He had the speed to catch them, but would undoubtedly be unsuccessful in any engagement now that the enemy vessel had been reunited with its construct.

Zesiro assessed the situation. He needed to contact the Originator to rally a fleet to intercept the *Immortal Vagrant*, but he was reticent. The Originator had not been happy with his inability to capture Jonas on Eden, and now that he had allowed the escape of not just Jonas but of the Progenitor as well, she would be even less pleased. Still, he had little choice. He instructed the *Zenith's* construct to make the link, and within moments he felt the Originator's presence.

'Zesiro,' she said simply by way of greeting.

'Originator,' Zesiro replied. 'I've failed you. Jonas and the Progenitor have escaped my clutches, and they have departed the Zeta Phe system aboard a starship.'

Zesiro felt the confusion that the Originator was experiencing. 'A starship? You assured me that Jonas' starship had been destroyed...'

'It was,' Zesiro replied. 'This is a different starship... one that the Progenitor had been preparing for years. The *Immortal Vagrant*.'

'The *Immortal Vagrant*,' the Originator repeated. 'Unbelievable. After all this time, that vessel is still functional?'

'Even without a construct, it was more than a match for the *Zenith of Desire*,' Zesiro replied. 'Its systems and abilities have been considerably upgraded by the Progenitor.'

'You mentioned that it has departed the Zeta Phe system,' the Originator said with a hint of suspicion. 'How did it accomplish this without a construct? Has it been equipped with post-human navigation technology?'

Zesiro was certain that the Originator would be able to sense his nervousness. 'No, Originator,' he replied. 'Jonas was able to recover the construct that had been acquired by the Redeemers. It was in fact, the *Immortal Vagrant's* construct to begin with.'

He could feel disappointment and anger emanating from the Originator's thoughts, translated down through the intellect projection link they shared. 'You have been a bitter disappointment to me, Zesiro,' the Originator said in a dismissive tone that indicated she was through dealing with him. 'Your failure to apprehend a lowly post-human such as Jonas Dresden is pathetic. You should be ashamed of yourself. Your failure in this task puts us at risk of losing this war with the Republic. With the Progenitor on their side, they may well be unstoppable now.' She took a moment before continuing. 'I have no further need of you, Zesiro. Your failure has been so comprehensive that I do not want to see you, ever. Do not return to Alpha One. Do not contact me. You are no longer a Morphite agent.'

Zesiro knew the weight of the Originator's words, and he knew that she was sincere. But he had one last ace up his sleeve. 'Forgive me Originator,' he began, doing his best not to reveal the petty emotions he was feeling after her tirade. 'But you do still need me.'

'And why is that, Zesiro?'

'Because I know the *Immortal Vagrant's* course,' he replied. 'I know where we can intercept Jonas and the Progenitor.'

'Tell me,' the Originator insisted.

Zesiro wasn't sure that what he was about to do was wise, but the way he saw it, he had little choice – it was the one way that he could see himself regaining the Originator's favour. 'With respect, Originator... I will tell you if you allow me to lead the interception of the *Immortal Vagrant*. I will need a fleet to rendezvous with me. With their assistance I promise you that I will destroy the *Vagrant* and kill Jonas and the Progenitor.'

'You feel you have the right to make such demands?' the Originator asked, evidently furious with him. 'After your failures to date, you dare *negotiate* with me?'

'Of course I would rather not have to,' Zesiro replied. 'I have the utmost faith in you, Originator. I truly believe in you, and in your leadership. All I ask is for one last chance to prove myself to you.'

The Originator took a few subjective moments to think about it. He could feel her disappointment in him, which stung. He had failed her, he knew that. But he was certain that he could redeem himself by intercepting Jonas. It was a foolproof plan – he knew the *Immortal Vagrant's* course, he knew the best place to ambush them. With an entire fleet at his command, he would have such a degree of firepower available at his fingertips his enemy would not stand a chance. It was the last chance he had at redeeming himself in the eyes of the Originator. He scoffed inwardly at himself. *I feel like a pathetic pre-human seeking redemption for my mistakes,* Zesiro thought. If the Originator saw fit to provide him with this last chance at eliminating Jonas and the Progenitor, then he would show her his worth. He knew he could do it this time. He had to, there was no other option.

'Very well, Zesiro,' the Originator replied eventually. 'Until this assignment you have never failed me, and as such I will allow you this one last chance to prove yourself as capable as I've always believed you to be. That being said, if you fail, there will be no excommunication or exile – I will kill you myself. Do you understand?'

'Yes, Originator,' Zesiro replied, surprised at the venom that emanated from her words.

'How many vessels do you require?' she asked.

'An attack group of six, Originator,' he replied. 'One capital ship, two medium cruisers equipped with FTL dampers and three fast attack frigates. I will command the fleet from the *Zenith of Desire*. This will give me overwhelming firepower, while preventing the *Immortal Vagrant's* escape.'

'Very well, you will get your fleet Zesiro,' the Originator said. 'Do not underestimate the ingenuity of the Progenitor however. Expect her vessel to be more powerful than anything we have.'

'I understand, Originator.'

'Good. To where am I sending this fleet?'

'While I am unsure as to the *Immortal Vagrant's* ultimate destination, its course takes it directly through the Pandora Nebula. It is there where the ambush will take place. I have shared the precise co-ordinates of the *Vagrant's* course with you now.'

There was a moment of silence before the Originator replied. 'I have dispatched the fleet,' she said. 'They will setup an FTL damper web and await your, and the enemy's arrival. Do not let me down again, Zesiro. Kill Jonas Dresden, kill the Progenitor and destroy the *Immortal Vagrant*. Am I understood?'

'I will bathe in their blood, Originator,' Zesiro replied.

'Unnecessarily dramatic, Zesiro,' the Originator replied with distaste. 'You've spent too long amongst the pre-humans. Complete your assignment and return to Alpha One immediately.'

And with that, she disconnected the link. Zesiro was shaken by the encounter, but nevertheless determined to complete the task he had been assigned. He instructed his construct to plot a course to the Pandora Nebula, and the vessel shot off, leaving the Zeta Phe system behind. He thought of all the chaos he was leaving behind him, and was not remotely bothered by it. *Let the pre-humans wipe themselves out*, he thought. *They'd be doing themselves and the galaxy a favour.*

Thirty-eight

There was one thing that Jonas had been putting off since his arrival aboard the *Immortal Vagrant*. Now that they were travelling at FTL speeds away from the Zeta Phe system and Zesiro, he had run out of excuses to avoid it. He sat on a plain couch within a sparsely furnished personal chamber of the kind that filled the deck below the bridge. Jonas knew that the rooms had been manufactured by the Progenitor and her Disciples specifically for Jonas and his crew. As he'd experienced aboard the *Zenith of Desire*, Morphites had no need for the kind of structuring that a post-human vessel had. In fact, Jonas was certain that every region of the *Immortal Vagrant* that he had seen so far – the recovery suite, the observation lounge and the bridge – had been constructed specifically for its new human crew.

Jonas stared out into space. Because they were travelling faster-than-light, there were no stars visible. If he'd been standing in the observation deck, he'd have been looking at a smudge of blue which would have been the bunched up group of blue-shifted stars that lay ahead of their course. If he'd been able to look directly behind the vessel, he'd have witnessed a crimson smudge of red-shifted stars. To either side of the vessel, however, there was nothing but a black void.

A door chime sounded, and anxiously, Jonas stood. He instructed the door to open, and Galatea stood there with a smile on her face. She entered without invitation, and came straight over to him, kissing him on the lips, and embracing him. He returned her embrace with reticence, aware that what he was about to do would hurt not just her, but him as well. Gala noticed that something was wrong almost immediately and frowned slightly. Jonas respected her more than she'd ever know – she was not just beautiful, she was intuitive, capable and highly intelligent, always destined for more than the life of a bartender on some backwards world.

'What's wrong?' she asked.

'Take a seat,' he replied nervously. Frowning even more, she sat down on the couch. After an awkward moment, Jonas sat down beside her, keeping a bit of distance. 'I have an enormous amount of respect for you Gala. You'll never know how much. Without you, I doubt I would have made it as far as I have. You've given me strength where there was none to be had. I care for you more than you could possibly know.'

'I don't know where you're going with this, hon,' Galas interrupted. 'But it sounds to me like it's either going to be a proposal or a break-up.'

'It's not a proposal,' Jonas replied quietly.

Gala nodded slowly. He could tell she was trying to fight down her emotions. He wasn't sure if she wanted to burst out into tears, or to start yelling and screaming, but either way she was holding her emotions in check admirably.

'Fair enough,' she replied after a few moments of silence. 'Do I at least get an explanation?'

'I really do care for you, Gala,' Jonas began. She held up a hand to silence him immediately.

'You say you respect me, Jonas? Then do me the respect of not patronising me,' she replied, sternly rather than angrily. 'I've dealt with enough assholes back in the Badlands who thought they were better and smarter than me because they had a penis hanging between their legs, and I'm pretty confident you're not one of those assholes. So do me a favour – just tell me what the hell's going on.'

Jonas nodded, feeling slightly ashamed. 'I'm married,' he replied. He wasn't sure what Gala had been expecting him to say, but he was certain that it wasn't that. She frowned and then started blinking quickly. 'Obviously, my self-imposed memory loss prevented me from knowing that,' Jonas continued. 'I never meant to mislead you.'

'Okay,' she replied quietly, standing up. 'Thank you for telling me.' She began to head for the door to the room, before stopping and turning back to him. 'What's she like?'

'Does it really matter?' Jonas asked.

'Yes,' she replied. 'To me it does.'

Jonas sighed. 'Her name is Chloe, and she owns a drydock facility on Olympus. She's a brilliant engineer, and as beautiful as she is smart. I love her.'

Gala nodded. 'She's a lucky woman,' she replied. 'Thank you for being honest with me Jonas, I really mean it.'

With that, she turned and left the room. Jonas slumped back into the couch, and sighed loudly, before rubbing his head with his hands. He despised himself for what had just occurred. His self-imposed memory loss was proving to be destructive in ways that he'd never anticipated. Not only had it made him embroil numerous people into dangerous situations, and not only had it caused untold death and destruction, but now this. In the end, the memory loss strategy had worked. But had it been worth it?

He realised belatedly that he wasn't alone in the room. The Progenitor sat across from him on a chair, having evidently materialised herself in there with a small smirk on her face. 'Well, that was brutal,' she said.

'Thank you for the invasion of privacy,' Jonas replied, although he couldn't be bothered to show any real annoyance. 'Anyway, she'll get over it.'

'I wasn't talking about her, I was talking about you,' Madani replied. 'She didn't even shed a tear! That must be a little sobering, surely?'

'Did you come here just to bait me?' Jonas snapped, annoyed. 'What are you, a teenager?'

The Progenitor laughed. 'Oh, come on, at least allow me a few human quirks. Besides, I'm just keeping your passions high, Jonas,' she replied. 'You're going to need them. This is a long and tumultuous path you're on, and it's vital that you fulfil your part.'

'No pressure then,' Jonas replied sarcastically. 'You told us that you and your disciples are capable of seeing the future, so tell me – what's my future hold for me?'

'I never said we could see the future,' the Progenitor replied. 'I said we could predict it. They're two very different things.'

'Fine, however you want to put it,' he said dismissively. 'Tell me, what's the probability that I'm going to get Gala, Tailynn and the rest of these people killed? I've dragged them into this, and if it gets them killed then I'm not sure I could live with that.'

'Need I remind you that if they're killed, then it's more than likely that you will be too? The dead don't feel guilt, Jonas.'

'That doesn't make me feel any better,' Jonas replied.

'You've rescued them, Jonas. Your team were destined for lives of mediocrity,' Madani said. 'What you've embroiled them in is bigger than they are. It's bigger than you. But if it's solace you're after, then I'll tell you this much – humanity's chances of longevity are reliant on you, your crew and this ship. In just about every future that we've predicted, the *Immortal Vagrant* has been there. Even if you and your friends die, it will have served a greater good, I can assure you of that much.'

'Then tell me,' Jonas began. 'What is it that we need to do? Why is humanity at risk of extinction? And how can one ship and one crew make a difference?'

Madani sighed, and leaned back in her seat. 'If I'm going to answer those questions, then the first thing you need to know is that nothing is guaranteed. Mine and my disciple's projections of the future offer a variety of possibilities, not a definitive track of time. Nothing is set in stone – destiny is a fallacy. The fact is that I cannot tell you what to do – what path to take. I can offer you hints and advice and I can help you along the way, but that's about it. Even then, I need to be very careful in the hints that I give you, and in the help I provide, because the very act of revealing to you what could quite possibly be future events could irrevocably change the path you are on and create a new possible future. I imagine that wrapping your head around that could be somewhat difficult.'

'No, I'm following nicely,' Jonas replied, slightly irked at what he considered Madani's pretentiousness. 'But you've done an admirable job of only providing me with half answers. I'll ask again – why is humanity at risk of extinction, and how can I and my crew make any difference?'

The Progenitor sighed. 'Through time immemorial, humanity has been at risk of extinction from itself,' she answered finally. 'There is no boogie man, no savage alien race that is going to be our undoing – it will be our own genetics. The human need for conflict, the essence of our very nature will be our undoing. When I say that it is my desire to usher in humanity's transcendence, I mean that it is my desire to rid us all of this desire, to beat our own genetics. I tried to do that through the use of the artificial – zeptites – but I failed. The civilisation that arose from my attempts, the Morphites, are living embodiments of that failure. Where I had attempted to eliminate that inherent need for conflict, I achieved only the abolition of human passion. And that was why the Morphites are my ultimate failure.'

'What about Zesiro,' Jonas asked. 'He doesn't seem to be lacking passion – the way he fights... the persistence with which he's pursued me... the *hatred* that seems to be burning within him is so very, very human.'

'Zesiro is one of few exceptions to the rule,' Madani replied. 'He and a handful of others like him are viewed as a necessity by the Morphite Originator. Nothing more than weapons to be wielded when needed. The sad fact is that Zesiro, and the other Morphite agents like him would be social outcasts on Alpha One if they were ever required to integrate within the society properly. That is why they almost exclusively operate off-world. Does that come close to answering your question?'

'Close,' Jonas conceded. 'Where do I, the others and this ship fit in?'

Madani laughed slightly. 'Now that, Jonas, is much more difficult to articulate,' she said. 'The predictions that I and my disciples are able to make are not so specific to determine the actions of a single individual, rather it predicts the actions of a group of people as a whole, for instance the population of Eden. However, in some cases it is possible to factor in the actions of an individual to the predictive equation.

'Our initial predictions of the future are what led my disciples and I to the conclusion that humanity destroying not just itself, but other galactic species was a probable outcome, if not a given. We continued to make predictions, and came to the conclusion that the only way to prevent that from occurring would be the actions of an individual. I'd already factored in myself and my disciples into our equations, and all indications were that while we could indeed survive the self-inflicted genocide of humanity, we were already too far removed from what humanity was for any meaningful continuation of the species. I needed someone, an agent if you will, to become the individual who could work on my behalf. I needed someone who I could factor into our calculations to see if a single person, or small group of people, could prevent the destruction of our race. So I contacted the Human Republic, and without revealing my true identity, advised them of my desire to defect to their cause. I knew they'd send someone to intercept me, and that I could factor that individual into predictive equations to see if they could possibly make a difference to the future. The republic sent you.'

'And did factoring me into your equations make a difference?' Jonas asked.

'Oh yes,' Madani replied with a knowing smile. 'More than you could possibly imagine.'

'I have another question,' Jonas said, trying to absorb everything that she was saying. 'Something that has been playing on my mind since the first time we spoke. Something that I'm not sure you'll answer.'

'Try me,' Madani replied with a smirk.

'Why did you destroy Sol?' Jonas asked. 'What kind of reasoning could ever have convinced you that that was a good idea? What were you trying to accomplish?'

For once, Haleh Madani's expression was void of the confidence (what most considered pretentiousness) that it was usually adorned with. She sighed, and looked Jonas in the eye. 'Back then, it seemed that war had infiltrated every aspect of our lives. Humanity had driven the Ingrelden out of the Sol system, taken their technology and used it to wage war upon one another. It was a cycle that had repeated itself for millennia – we'd develop new technology, and eventually we'd use it to wage war.

'Contrary to what many people think, I wasn't the one to develop zeptites initially. They had actually been conceived and first tested centuries before I began working with them. I was a scientist working for the faction that would eventually become the Morphites. The Omega War was in full swing, and myself and my associates had been commissioned by our government to develop an edge to our soldiers. It didn't take us long to expand upon the zeptite concept which had been developed and then shelved generations prior. We used the technology to help develop better weapons for our soldiers, better armour. I was the one who took it one step further, however.

'I had been a victim of my own side's propaganda of course, and it was that false sense of justification that drove me to use my own body as a test bed in order to discover the true potential of zeptite technology. And I *did* discover it. To this day, centuries after the fact, I can remember the feeling of those initial million or so machines coursing into my blood and spreading throughout my body. It was like a drug, but instead of a high it felt like I was awakening for the first time.

'It was that initial experimentation which garnered the curiosity of my factions government and military, and like a good citizen I was more than willing to pass on the technology so it could be used to boost the strength of our soldiers, and to maximise the intelligence of our tacticians. Within decades the technology was common place amongst the population of my faction, and preventing it's adaption by our enemies was something that they worked at tirelessly.

'Over the years, I continued to experiment with the zeptites within my own body, even after my government ceased funding my research and my colleagues began leaving me, scared and overwhelmed by the experiments I was performing. But by that point, my colleagues, my faction and the war seemed so irrelevant and stupid that they ceased to be of any concern to me. All I was concerned with was furthering my knowledge and the capability of the zeptites within my own body.

'I achieved the ability to morph my shape while still living on Earth, centuries before the Morphites developed the same ability. And then, I took it even further. It became possible for me to dissolve my entire body into trillions of microscopic elements, while still maintaining my very being thanks to the zeptites which bridged my trillions of components. This meant I didn't just have the ability to change shape – I could also essentially become gaseous. In that form, I can travel through the smallest crack in a wall, or through solid bodies of water or even through the void of space at speeds faster than light, the zeptites in my body generating a million microscopic FTL cores that could propel me at speeds faster than the fastest Morphite starship. How do you think I got to Eden? As well as the physical changes, the zeptites supplemented my intelligence to the point that my intellect was that of one hundred minds – more, even. I truly felt god-like. And that is what scared the hell out of me. So I left Earth, left Sol and explored the galaxy. I was the first 'human' to depart our home solar system at a speed greater than light. I rediscovered the Ingrelden, as well as discovering both the Bretarians and Kimone races, although I chose not to make contact with them, fearful of how they would accommodate an entity such as myself.

'I spent years travelling the galaxy, reflecting inwardly on my own past, and the past of human-kind. One day, I decided to return to Sol to see how things were progressing. To my dismay, war still raged. Atrocities had been committed and millions were dying. Humanity had long ago unlocked the secrets to the Ingrelden FTL drive, but instead of using it to branch out and explore the galaxy, it had become just another weapon to be utilised in the war. We had such passion, such ingenuity, such intelligence, but to see it all squandered in such a vicious and violent war saddened me to the point that I couldn't bear it. My research into zeptites had been one of the things that had heated the war up, and as a result I felt responsible. So I decided to do something about it.

'As the situation stood, the zeptite enhanced faction was within a year or so of winning the war. They had their enemy on the retreat, and were slowly but surely gaining stronghold after stronghold. I considered letting the war run its natural course, but I knew deep down that if I did that, then the same cycle would surely be repeated in a few decades or centuries. So I devised a way to force the conflict to end, and to separate the warring factions, somewhat akin to a mother separating quarrelling children. How could I do that? Create an event so cataclysmic that it would force the two sides to cease conflict, and direct all of their resources to a recovery effort – something that would occupy them for years or even decades.

'So I destroyed Earth's sun. It had the desired effect – both sides ceased hostilities almost immediately, and put their militaries to work evacuating the solar system. They departed in different directions, and became the Morphites and the Human Republic. For many years, I thought my plan had worked. The two sides remained separated, and at peace. Many on both sides considered the following centuries to be a golden age for humanity – it was as though the destruction of Sol had created a blank canvas upon which a new and better society could be formed. But then Eden was discovered, and my entire house-of-cards came falling down. I'd failed.'

Jonas allowed Haleh Madani's story to sink in for a few moments. She'd been arrogant to think that she alone had the right to do what she had done, however he decided to remain silent about that fact, certain that she already felt guilt over the event.

'I have one last question,' he said quietly. 'How did you do it?'

The Progenitor smiled a knowing smile and winked at him. 'The answer to that question, Jonas, is on a need-to-know basis,' she said. 'And *nobody* needs to know. *Ever.*'

Thirty-nine

Six Morphite vessels of varying sizes hung in space, mere light minutes from the edge of the deep blue, red and purple swirls and gaseous clouds of the Pandora Nebula. The *Zenith of Desire* disengaged its FTL drive as close to the battle fleet as possible, and emerged from its stealth mode. It had taken only a matter of hours to traverse the distance from the Zeta Phe system to the nebula at the speeds that the *Zenith* was capable of, and Zesiro had managed to not just pass the *Immortal Vagrant*, but give himself an hour or so window to prepare his forces. The *Zenith's* stealth system had prevented the enemy vessel from detecting it as it overtook it within light seconds much to Zesiro's relief. The Progenitor-modified *Immortal Vagrant* was still largely an unknown constant, but it was gratifying to pass by them undetected, and it boosted his confidence for the upcoming engagement.

As Zesiro approached his comrades, he took a moment to absorb the majesty of the Pandora Nebula. As far as nebulas went, it was tiny for a diffuse nebula – less than a single light year across at its longest point. Its size, as well as the fact that it had been occluded by the Zeta Phe star meant that it had not been discovered by the human race until well after the destruction of Sol. Its cumulonimbus-like clouds of ionized hydrogen and small amounts of helium shone bright blue, and combined with cirrus-like wisps of red, which in parts combined to become streaks of purple. It was without a doubt one of the most beautiful nebulas Zesiro had ever seen, but now he was going to use it as a weapon against the *Immortal Vagrant*.

As he neared his battle fleet, he received an incoming transmission from the largest of the vessels, the capital-size *Distant Morning*. For some reason which had never occurred to him before, it struck him as somewhat unusual that the names that Morphites chose for their ships were so uncharacteristically creative. He knew himself to be far removed from the majority of the Morphite population when it came to his disposition and mentality, but to describe a Morphite as creative was akin to describing a brightly burning star as dark. He wondered if his own people were at their very core not as dispassionate as they appeared.

He pushed such thoughts from his head, and focused on the incoming transmission. He realised almost belatedly that he still remained in his human form from his actions on Eden, and quickly morphed himself back into his "natural" state before accepting the transmission. Unlike the form of communication he shared with the Originators, this wasn't an intellect projection, rather a more traditional radio-based transmission that he chose to project in front of him.

'Zesiro, I am Quaron of the *Distant Morning*,' the Morphite said, his natural form void of intricacies and emotion. 'At the directive of the Originator, I am placing this battle fleet under your command.'

'Understood Quaron,' Zesiro replied. 'The enemy vessel will be passing through the Pandora Nebula in less than an hour. I require you to move your battle group within the hydrogen clouds to mask their presence, and establish the FTL-damping web from within the nebula's boundary.'

'That is an unconventional tactic, Zesiro,' Quaron replied, his Morphite form displaying not one ounce of emotion. 'The ionised hydrogen clouds will present a significant impediment to use of our weaponry. Functionality of various ship-board sensor suites will also be impeded.'

'I understand, Quaron, however our enemy is far from

conventional,' Zesiro replied, not allowing his annoyance at being second-guessed to show. 'It will take unconventional tactics to defeat them. Please position your vessels as per my instructions, and disperse a dozen stealth sensor boosters outside of the nebula's periphery.'

'As is your order Zesiro,' Quaron replied.

Almost immediately, the manoeuvring thrusters of the Morphite vessels began to fire, pushing the ships back into the dense hydrogen clouds of the nebula. It took mere minutes for the capital ship and the three fast attack frigates to disappear from view, and moments later the two cruisers which were equipped with the FTL dampers likewise disappeared into the clouds. Zesiro instructed the *Zenith* to follow the vessels, and it too flew into the nebula, its construct warning Zesiro of the volatility of the ionised hydrogen that was enveloping the ship.

'Quaron, instruct the cruisers to remain on the edge of the gas clouds and to activate their FTL dampers,' Zesiro instructed. 'They are to create a web extending in a diameter of fifteen light-seconds, and they are to project it three light-seconds outside the edge of the hydrogen clouds.'

Quaron immediately went about relaying Zesiro's instructions, and while he could not see the two Morphite cruisers, he was certain that they were moving outwards from rest of the battle-group in order to expand their FTL damping webs. The FTL dampers operated by emitting a field of low-range sonic waves, and were highly effective at disrupting the intricate workings of an FTL core time after time. It was not an overly complicated system, which was proven by the fact that the Human Republic Fleet had also developed the technology – but it was most certainly effective.

Now, with his battle fleet in position, it was simply a matter of waiting for Jonas and the Progenitor to arrive, and then eliminating them.

It happened a bit quicker than he had expected. Seventeen minutes after the FTL damper had been established, the *Zenith* reported that the stealth sensor boosters outside the nebula were relaying the detection of a vessel approaching at five-hundred times the speed of light. Seconds later, the *Immortal Vagrant* stopped in space, emerging from FTL speeds a mere light-second from the edge of the nebula. Zesiro immediately opened a channel to Quaron.

'Quaron, engage the *Immortal Vagrant*,' he ordered simply.

Simultaneously, he instructed the *Zenith* to activate its own weapons systems and its defensive shroud, and then accelerated the ship at twenty gees. It burst out of the ionised hydrogen clouds of the nebula, and was confronted by the hulking form of the *Immortal Vagrant* hanging in space directly in front of him. The three Morphite fast-attack vessels that were similar in size and capability to the *Zenith* emerged from the nebula almost simultaneously, followed momentarily by the two cruisers and eventually by Quarons' huge capital ship. The *Zenith* and the three frigates darted in, and opened fire the instant they were within weapons range. Zesiro had selected the *Zenith's* primary weapon, its pulse-beam cannon to initiate the attack on the enemy, and he watched as the red guidance beam targeted the huge port-side armoured cruise engine spar. Three bright pulses shot down the beam and struck the spars, however the resulting explosions were absorbed by the vessels defensive shroud, which Jonas's crew had evidently been able to activate before Zesiro and his comrades had initiated their attack. The *Zenith* skimmed down along the hull of the *Immortal Vagrant*, watching as weapons turrets and emitters popped out all over its hull. Within seconds the huge vessel was returning fire, and the *Zenith's* construct began warning of strikes against its defensive shroud.

Zesiro ducked away from the enemy's hull, and utilised his superior speed and manoeuvrability to avoid the weapons fire that was emerging from the *Immortal Vagrant*, streams of energy and bolts of plasma streaking out from its hull. As Zesiro came about for another attack run, he became aware of the fact that the *Distant Morning* and the two cruisers had come within weapons range of the *Vagrant* and were unloading a combination barrage of pulse, beam and void weaponry, the latter's matter/anti-matter reactive slugs exploding against the *Vagrant's* defensive shroud in dark bubbles.

The *Immortal Vagrant* began to accelerate, its huge cruise engines glowing ominously. It was taking the majority of the battle fleet's weapons fire on its port side, and as Zesiro watched, the vessel began a long axis roll to starboard, evidently in an attempt to reduce the barrage on that sector's shroud batteries. Zesiro quickly opened a channel to the rest of his battle fleet.

'This is Zesiro,' he stated. 'All Morphite vessels, concentrate your fire where possible on the *Immortal Vagrant's* port side. We must break through their shroud.'

He watched as the three small attack frigates immediately changed their course and ducked under the ventral side of the *Vagrant* to begin another attack run in the region he had specified.

Zesiro couldn't help but feel over-joyed at the success of his ambush of Jonas' ship. It had gone off without a hitch, and it was only a matter of time now until the overwhelming firepower of his battle fleet broke through the *Vagrant's* defensive shroud and put an end to Jonas Dresden and the Progenitor – just as he had promised the Originator he'd do all along.

Forty

War could be ironically beautiful, Jonas thought as he watched on through the augmented surround screen on the bridge of the *Vagrant* from his command chair. *So colourful, so energetic, so vibrant... so violent.*

It had been premature to celebrate their escape from Zesiro around Eden, and now they were embroiled in a battle that Jonas wasn't sure they could win. The crew had not been prepared when the *Vagrant's* construct Jade had announced that they had been caught in an FTL damper on the edge of the Pandora Nebula, and it had taken valuable seconds for the crew to man their battle stations on the bridge. The batteries on the port defensive shroud were already nearly drained, and they had achieved few successful weapons strikes on the enemy. But the crew had risen to the emergency admirably and without reserve, and were now defiantly doing all they could to combat the overwhelming Morphite fleet that had engaged them.

'Port shroud batteries are ninety percent drained,' Rai announced from the engineering pod. 'We need to divert the enemy's weapons fire.'

'Gala, give me a long axis one-eighty degree roll to starboard,' Jonas instructed.

The manoeuvre was successful in shielding the port-side shroud from the larger Morphite ships which were firing from a distance, however the four smaller attack frigates (one which Jonas was unsurprised to identify as the *Zenith of Desire*) responded to the manoeuvre by ducking under the *Vagrant's* ventral quadrant to continue their assault on the weakening shroud.

Jonas took a moment to assess the situation – the *Immortal Vagrant* may have been a far more powerful vessel than any of those attacking it on its own, but in the situation they were in it was well and truly outnumbered and outgunned. He needed to do something drastic in order to level the playing field somewhat. He considered his options momentarily, and then it dawned on him – the nebula. The dense ionised hydrogen clouds would render just about any vessel's sensors and targeting suites useless, and the volatility of the nebulas gasses would mean that the enemy would be restricted to the use of their void-guns only, lest they inflict catastrophic damage upon themselves. The downside, of course was that the *Vagrant* would suffer the same impediments. It would be a risky manoeuvre, but out in the open they had no chance at all.

'Gala, change of plans,' he announced. 'Take us into the nebula, the nearest gas cloud. Full thrust.'

'Wait, did you just say *into* the nebula?' Jett asked incredulously. 'Are you insane?'

'Jett!' Tailynn snapped, before turning to Jonas. 'I'm sorry, Jonas, but he has a point. Are you sure about this?'

'We're dead out here, Tailynn,' Jonas replied. 'Our only hope is to hide in the gasses. That way we have a chance of picking the enemy ships off one by one.'

'One on one we're stronger than any of the enemy vessels, even the capital ship,' Haldon said in agreement. 'It's a solid tactic.'

'Do it, Gala,' Jonas insisted.

'You got it,' she replied nervously.

She ramped the cruise engines up to one-hundred percent thrust, and the huge ship darted forward. Belatedly, Jonas realised that the Morphite capital ship, as well as the two cruisers still sat in space between the *Immortal Vagrant* and the nebula. Their weapons fire was a barrage of high-intensity energy and matter/antimatter reactions, however the advantage of heading directly for them was that the

Vagrant now presented a lower profile target, and many of the enemy shots were missing. That would of course change the closer they got to the enemy vessels, and when they were neck and neck it would turn into a side-by-side flurry of weapons fire that could prove too much for the *Vagrant's* shroud batteries to handle.

'Rai, divert the power from all non-essential systems to maintain the shroud batteries,' Jonas instructed. 'Maintain power to the sub-light engines, weapons systems and life support but divert everything else, FTL drive included. Then place the power management of the shroud batteries under Jade's control.'

'Understood,' Rai responded. 'Non-essential systems coming off-line, all shroud batteries are maintaining their charges.'

'Jett, when we're directly on top of the capital ship and the cruisers, I want you to pound them with everything we've got,' Jonas said.

'My pleasure,' Jett growled in reply.

The *Immortal Vagrant*, still being harried by the four Morphite light attack ships, neared the bigger vessels quickly. The enemy fire hammered into its defensive shroud, but the diverted power from the vessels non-essential systems ensured that the batteries remained full. Jonas knew that it was a tactic that could not last long – it was only a matter of time before the batteries exhausted the power on offer, but he hoped that it would be enough to get them into the nebula. He watched as the Morphite capital ship's thrusters fired and the big vessel began to come around in a blocking manoeuvre, the enemy tacticians evidently realising what the *Immortal Vagrant* was planning to do.

'Gala, increase vertical pitch by fifteen degrees, and give me a ninety degree long-axis roll to port,' Jonas instructed. 'Jett, as we cruise over the top of them, fire everything we have on the port side.'

Galatea began making the course corrections, and as the *Vagrant* twisted to port, and its nose began to sail over the top of the Morphite capital ship, Jett began unloading every weapon he had at his disposal on the port side. Energy beams, pulse cannons and void guns fired continuously, the volume of energy that was striking the capital ships' defensive shroud more than Jonas could realistically fathom.

'The capital ship's shrouds are failing!' Tailynn announced excitedly.

'Press the attack and continue firing!' Jonas ordered.

As they sailed past the largest of the enemy's ships, Jett continued the high-density barrage of weapons fire, and within moments the shots began breaking through the enemy's failing defensive shroud, impacting the ship's hull, and blowing out sections of it. The *Vagrant's* beam weapons scorched large gashes in the enemy bulkheads, while the pulse cannons punched through in what looked all the world to Jonas like enormous bullet holes. By far the most effective weapons however, were the void-guns. As the large matter/antimatter slugs struck the hull of the enemy vessel, they collapsed into a visible reaction between the matter and antimatter in the form of huge dark bubbles, each in themselves a miniature quantum singularity which were taking massive chunks out of the enemy hull. Wherever the slugs struck and the bubbles formed, everything they touched simply ceased to exist.

Within seconds, the *Immortal Vagrant* had passed over the capital ship, and there was nothing but empty space between them and the nebula.

'How are those shroud batteries, Rai?' Jonas asked.

'They're holding,' Rai announced, 'but they can't take much more.'

'Jonas, we've inflicted fatal damage on the capital ship,' Tailynn announced. 'Its FTL drive is about to go critical.'

The holographic representation of Jade which stood on the pedestal at the front of the ship spun around to face Jonas. 'Be advised, the resulting explosion of the Morphite capital ship will be catastrophic, and we will still be in range of its effects.'

Jonas assessed the positions of the other Morphite vessels and realised that they were all darting away from the fatally wounded capital ship as quickly as they could. He was about to warn the crew to brace themselves, but before he could even open his mouth, the capital ship went up, exploding in an impossibly bright bubble of plasma and energy. The first thing to hit them was a wall of plasma that burst out in a ring from the explosion like a shockwave. The *Vagrant* shuddered violently, and both Tailynn and Haldon who were the only two crew members standing, fell to the ground, clutching at what they could to prevent being thrown around the bridge like ragdolls.

After a moment, the shuddering stopped, and Jonas asked Rai for a damage assessment. 'Shrouds are holding,' she said. 'Only just, though.'

Out of the corner of his eye, Jonas saw Haldon and Tailynn standing up, and after a moment, Tailynn spun to him. 'Oh shit, hold on!' she screamed.

Jonas turned his head to where the capital ship had gone up to see one of its huge, armoured cruise-engines now severed and hurtling directly towards them.

'Brace yourselves!' he yelled, clutching the arms of his seat as hard as he could.

The enemy's cruise engine struck the *Immortal Vagrant* with all the force of a moon impacting a planet. Jonas's senses were incapable of processing everything that happened in that instant, but as his whole body compressed with the impact, feeling all the world like he'd been hit by a wrecking-ball, he could hear screams and cries from the others, followed by Jade warning them about catastrophic damage to the vessel's hull. And then he belatedly realised that he was flying across the bridge, chair and all...

He woke to the Progenitor standing over him. Every part of his body ached, and he felt as though his head had imploded in on itself. The Progenitor smiled as one of her disciples entered his vision, and bent down to him, placing a hand on his forehead.

'Relax Jonas,' Haleh Madani said. 'You've received some serious injuries. We're infusing you with a few more zeptites to help repair the damage.'

Jonas tried to talk, and it took a few attempts but eventually he was able to get his vocal cords working, albeit croakily. 'Is everyone...'

'Everyone is alive,' the Progenitor assured him. 'But it was a close call.'

Jonas felt a cold chill run through his body, and he instinctively knew it was the zeptites coursing through his body, seeking out damage and repairing it. It was only minutes before he felt well enough to stand, and he did so with the help of the disciple while the Progenitor watched on. He looked around the bridge, astounded at what he was seeing. The whole place had nearly been destroyed. There was a hole in the floor where his seat had been anchored, and the holographic tactical table which Tailynn and Haldon had been standing at had been crushed by a fallen structural spar. Around the bridge, he spotted each of his crew, in various states of injury. Tailynn seem to be the least injured, and she was sitting in the engineering pod, evidently assessing the damage to the ship. Jonas struggled over to her.

'What's the situation?' he croaked.

'It's not good,' she said simply. 'All sub-light engines are off-line, as are our weapons. We've sustained heavy damage, Jonas, I'm not sure we're going to be able to repair everything ourselves.'

'Where are we?' he asked.

'We've drifted into the nebula,' she replied. 'It's given us somewhat of a reprieve, however the Morphites will find us sooner or later.'

Jonas nodded, assessing the situation momentarily. 'What about Jade?'

'She's off-line,' Tailynn replied. 'I'm not a hundred percent sure, but I think that the power conduits that supply energy to her core have been severed. Rai may be able to get her back up and running.'

Jonas knew the gravity of the situation they were in. At any moment one of the enemy ships could stumble across them in the gas cloud and finish them off, and chances were, they wouldn't even realise when that happened. They had to get Jade and the engines back online to stand any chance at all.

He turned to the Progenitor.

'We need help,' he stated simply. 'Can your disciples aide us getting the engines back online?'

'My disciples aren't crew members, Jonas,' the Progenitor replied, sounding all the world like a patient school teacher telling a child why his answer to a question was incorrect. 'We cannot intervene.'

'Don't give me that shit,' Jonas snapped. 'You're the one who brought us here – the one who gave us this ship. You prepared it for us, you require us to use it to help serve your ends. Don't you dare stand there now and tell me that you can't help. You say that destiny has a plan for us? Well fuck destiny, and fuck you. If we don't make it out of here alive, then everything you've told me – everything you've had us do is for nothing.'

The Progenitor took a moment to respond, that arrogant little smirk that Jonas had begun to grow accustomed to never leaving her face for a second. 'Very well,' she replied. 'But my intervention here creates a new theoretical future, one that we have not assessed the probability of.'

'Which means?'

'It means that my control and understanding of future events becomes null and void,' she replied. 'My disciples and I can begin to assess this new theoretical future, however such things take time, and we will all – yourself and your crew included – be left in the dark for some time.'

'The alternative is that we die here and now,' Jonas replied.

The Progenitor nodded once, and then strode down to the front of the bridge where Jade's pedestal stood. She placed a hand on the pedestal, as two more disciples approached and did the same.

'We are supplementing Jade's systems with zeptites,' the Progenitor explained. 'Such a thing has never been done – even my people were wary of giving a construct too much intelligence. Regardless of what may happen, the zeptites will repair Jade's damaged systems, and supplement her operational intelligence. She will be up and running momentarily.'

Sure enough, within a minute or two, Jade's holographic representation flickered once or twice, and then came to life.

'Assessing situation,' the holographic proxy stated. 'I appear to have been offline for a short amount of time. The *Immortal Vagrant* has taken considerable damage. Initiating repair protocols.'

The mechanical proxies which had ceased operation when Jade had gone offline sprung back to life, and began going about their repair duties.

'How long until the ship will be fully operational again?' Tailynn asked.

'Assessing,' Jade replied. After a few moments: 'The damage to most of the ships systems is substantial. Sub-light engines will be at fifteen percent operational capacity within twenty minutes. Defensive shrouds and weapons systems will require significant overhaul, estimate three hours until initial activation can be achieved. The FTL core... has been fused, and will require replacement.'

'Shit,' Jonas cursed. 'Where's the closest inhabited star system?'

'Thirty-four light years away,' Jade replied. 'An approximately seventy year journey utilising the sub-light engines at maximum capacity.'

Jonas made an immediate decision. 'Fine. We'll deal with that when we have to. We need to get weapons, the defensive shroud and the sub-light engines back online immediately.'

Jade's holographic representation gave Jonas a curious look, appearing all the world as though she was distracted by something that she couldn't understand. 'I feel... different,' she stated.

The Progenitor gave Jonas what he could only guess was a concerned glance. 'Jade, focus,' Jonas replied uneasily. 'I need those systems online.'

'Engines will be semi-operational within fifteen minutes,' she replied. 'Three hours until weapons are partially restored. Shroud batteries are drained, but operational.'

'Without weapons, we don't stand a chance,' Tailynn said. 'The enemy ships can easily find us within three hours. We need another option.'

'I have one,' the Progenitor stated uneasily. 'But I do not take this course of action lightly. Jade, I require your proxies to prepare a remote probe, and affix a transponder to make it appear to the Morphite systems as though the probe itself was this ship.'

'What are you planning?' Jonas asked uneasily.

'There is a star within a few light minutes of our current location, on the outskirts of the nebula. Small, but active enough for me to use,' she replied. 'It is time that I remember who I once was.'

Forty-one

The *Zenith of Desire* stalked through the dense gasses of the Pandora Nebula, hunting its prey. Fully melded with the vessel, Zesiro could sense every little thing that the vessel was detecting, the zeptites that coursed through his body helping assimilate the information.

He had not anticipated the *Immortal Vagrant's* mad dash into the nebula, and the destruction of the *Distant Morning* had been shocking to say the least. Now, he had dispersed the remainder of his ambush fleet into the nebula, hunting for the stray radiation particles that would betray Jonas and the Progenitor's position. Unfortunately, the *Immortal Vagrant* remained annoyingly elusive.

An hour passed, and there was still no sign of the enemy vessel. The dense gasses were more prohibitive than he'd anticipated, so much so that he had come close to colliding with one of his own ships, the *Zenith's* sensors detecting it with just enough time to engage an evasive manoeuvre and avoid the collision.

Presently, Zesiro detected an incoming transmission from one of the other Morphite vessels. He accepted the transmission and the commander of one of the small frigates began to speak.

'Zesiro,' he began. 'We have been searching the edge of the nebula, and have just detected the enemy vessel emerging. It is on a direct course for the nearby star.'

'Are you certain of your readings?' Zesiro asked, not bothering to hide his surprise. 'Why would they risk leaving the safety of the nebula for open space?'

'I cannot answer that, Zesiro,' the Morphite replied. 'Do you wish us to pursue?'

'Of course,' Zesiro replied, still astounded at Jonas Dresden's tactics. He expanded the communication to include the other Morphite fleet vessels. 'I want all vessels to converge on the *Immortal Vagrant*, and open fire immediately.'

He didn't require a reply. He sensed the other commanders' compliance, and immediately altered the trajectory of the *Zenith*. It took mere minutes for his ship to exit the dense gas clouds, but when he did, he found himself to be the last of his ships to emerge – the others all had a good head-start on him, and were racing towards the *Immortal Vagrant's* signal. Zesiro assessed the situation – something didn't feel right. It only took seconds for him to confirm that everything wasn't as it seemed. The enemy vessel was moving far more quickly than it should have been able to, especially considering the damage that had been inflicted on it during the battle. While he wouldn't allow himself to underestimate the ingenuity of the Progenitor, or Jonas Dresden (not *again*, at least), he still felt that something was amiss. His pursuing vessels weren't making up any of the gap between them and the enemy – by all rights, they should have been well within weapons range by now. And why would they be heading for the nearby star? How would that protect them more than the nebula?

Zesiro hung back from the pursuit, the *Zenith* coming to a stop on the edge of the gas clouds. He directed the vessels sensor suite towards the fleeing ship, and began to perform a series of scans. Sure enough, the construct detected the *Immortal Vagrant's* transponder beacon, and confirmed that the engine emissions matched the former Morphite ship. He delved deeper, attempting to form a complete image of the vessel. The construct announced suddenly that it had detected an anomaly – the mass of the object that his vessels were pursing was only a fraction of what it should have been, if it were indeed the *Immortal Vagrant*. He checked the readings again, and the construct confirmed it – the vessel his fleet was chasing was not the enemy!

He made a quick assessment of the situation – the object was entering the star's corona now, and the pursuing vessels were not far behind. He knew that their defensive shrouds would be able to handle the corona's plasma easily, but he sensed that whatever the object was that was about to enter the sun wasn't going to stop on the star's edge. He watched through the *Zenith's* sensors as the small object plunged into the star, and immediately sent a communique throughout his small fleet.

'All vessels, hold your positions,' he ordered. 'Do not get any closer to that star.'

Each of the Morphite ships obeyed him immediately, and ceased their forward trajectory, floating in space on the edge of the star's corona, waiting for further instructions. Each of them had their sensors locked onto the brightly burning stellar body, searching for any sign as to why the object they'd been chasing had delved into the star. Zesiro tapped into his comrade's sensor suites, and waited.

It didn't take long for something to happen.

On the bridge of the *Immortal Vagrant*, Jonas and his crew observed the scene anxiously from the relative safety of the edge of the Pandora Nebula. They watched on the remote probe entered the star, and as the pursuing Morphite vessels halted their chase.

'The reaction is beginning,' the Progenitor announced, just as Jonas thought something had gone wrong.

Haleh Madani had done her best to explain to Jonas what was going to happen. She had infused the remote probe with zeptites from herself and a number of her disciples. They had invaded the machine, infiltrating every aspect of it – rebuilding it in a sense – although it hadn't consisted of a visual change. It hadn't taken long before the probe had been ready for launch, and it had departed the *Immortal Vagrant* only minutes after the zeptites had been fused with it. Jonas knew that now it had entered the star, it would be undergoing even more changes. While the intensity of the star would vaporise much of the probe, the zeptites themselves were protected at the molecular level, and were beginning to form a new mechanism – the probe had been but a vessel to get the zeptites to the right location. This new machine would begin a quantum reaction that would allow the formation of a series of miniature blackholes. The string of blackholes would begin breaking down the star at the sub-molecular level, and now that the reaction had begun, would eventually extinguish the star.

It was almost exactly what Madani had done to Earth's sun, centuries ago.

Watching via an infra-red hull mounted camera, Jonas began to see the reaction. Sections of the star began to dim, while others flared. It had been a deliberate calculation on the Progenitor's behalf, a weapon she had tailored specifically to their current situation.

'The process, while similar, is not precisely the same as the one I initiated in the Sol system,' she announced, breaking the dead silence that had filled the bridge up until that point as they observed the star begin its death throes. 'I had deliberately given Earth's sun a slow demise. After all, I didn't want to wipe out humanity, just give them a kick in the behind. In this star, I have initiated a quick, violent demise. Enormous solar flares will occur... it will be anything but a peaceful death.'

Jonas remained speechless, but continued to watch the unfolding event. It was becoming more evident that the star was dying, and as quick as a flash, an enormous solar flare streaked out. It seemed impossibly quick, but the flare had evidently been a deliberate event on the Progenitor's behalf. It streaked out towards the Morphite fleet like fire from a flame-thrower, and while the enemy ships attempted to flee, they were too slow. The flare vaporised them within an instant.

Jonas felt sick. He had not been expecting the turn of events that had led to the Progenitor deploying her starkiller weapon, and the fact that they had resorted to killing a star to defeat a fleet of

Morphite ships was more than he thought he could handle. It wasn't that they had taken the lives of hundreds – or maybe thousands – of Morphites. That fact didn't sit well with him, of course, but when it came down to it they were at war – people died in wars. Rather, the thing that gave him the feeling of nausea was the very fact that an individual had this incredible power at their fingertips. All he could think was that he hoped against hope that the ability never became commonplace – he could only imagine what would become of the galaxy if it did.

Jonas' silent revulsion was interrupted by Tailynn. 'One of the Morphite vessels remains,' she announced, her shaking voice betraying the fact that she felt exactly as Jonas did. 'It's the *Zenith of Desire*.'

'Won't this guy just *die?*' Jett exclaimed.

Jonas sighed. 'Say what you will about Zesiro, but he's persistent, I'll give him that,' he said.

'Wait,' Tailynn interrupted. 'The *Zenith* is moving towards the star! I don't understand. Could he be searching for survivors?'

'I doubt it,' the Progenitor muttered, the hint of concern and uncertainty in her voice evident to Jonas and the others.

Zesiro watched in dismay as the enormous solar flare erupted from the star. His comrades turned tail and began to flee, but they didn't have a chance. The only way they could have escaped the star's superheated plasma was if they'd jumped immediately to FTL speeds, but the drives simply could not spool that fast. It was the Progenitor, Zesiro knew. She had deployed the weapon that had destroyed Sol centuries ago.

Zesiro felt the Originator's presence in his mind. It was unlike any other time she had communicated with him – this time, it was as though she had been there all along, but only just decided to make herself known.

'You have failed Zesiro,' she said.

'No,' he muttered. 'How could I have known? How could I have anticipated *this*?'

'Jonas Dresden and the Progenitor have outwitted you at each and every step,' the Originator hissed, Zesiro feeling her disappointment. 'That a lowly post-human could run rings around you in this manner... you are a disgrace to the Morphite people.'

'You don't understand!' Zesiro begged, still staring into the dying star. 'I did everything I could'

'And your everything was nowhere near enough,' the Originator replied. 'You have failed me for he last time, Zesiro. But there is one last thing your death can accomplish for me.'

He felt her presence solidify within him. Her intellect began to ooze through his every being, capturing the zeptites that coursed through his body and taking control of them. He had never before experienced anything like this through an intellect projection, and belatedly, he realised exactly what the Originator was doing.

She was taking control of his body.

Zesiro couldn't resist, couldn't object... couldn't even scream. Within seconds, he was merely a passenger in his own body, capable of understanding what was going on, but completely incapable of controlling anything. The Originator's presence continued to expand until she had infiltrated the construct in control of the *Zenith of Desire*. Within seconds, the small ship had plotted a new course, and was heading at full speed *into the dying star*.

And there was nothing that Zesiro could do but watch on in horror, his own body a vessel that had been hijacked all too easily.

'You may have failed me,' the Originator impressed on Zesiro, 'but through this control of your body, I'm giving you this final opportunity to serve your people...'

He realised in horror what the Originator was doing. The *Zenith* entered the star's corona, and he became aware of the outer hull of the small vessel heating up. Deeper it went. Before long, the construct was shrieking that the vessel's defensive shroud could not stand the heat as they plunged into the chromosphere. The shroud would fail in seconds, just as they progressed to the next layer, the photosphere.

He felt the Originator's presence lessen. 'You have performed your last task for me,' she said. 'I now have what I need. Fare you well, Zesiro.'

And with that, she was gone. He immediately realised that he had full control of both his body and his ship again. But he also realised that it was too late. Just as the small ship entered the star's photosphere, the shroud failed. Within nano-seconds the heat from the star's plasma had disintegrated the hull.

Zesiro felt a moment of unpleasantness as the heat began to dissolve his flesh...

...And then there was nothing.

Forty-two

It was over. The battle had been won, their enemies had been defeated and a star had been destroyed. The *Immortal Vagrant* skirted the Pandora Nebula, Jade's proxies working furiously to repair the damage that had been inflicted during the final battle. The news wasn't good – while the majority of the vessel was repairable, given time, the one component they needed more than just about anything – the FTL drive – had been destroyed beyond repair. The vessel needed replacement components that couldn't be synthesised to remedy the problem, but that was something that was not achievable.

It would take them hundreds of years at sub-light speeds to reach the nearest Republic shipyard.

It was ironic, Tailynn thought. It had taken the *Stargazer* eight hundred years to reach Eden. For all the modern ability and technology that made the *Immortal Vagrant* so superior to that aging dinosaur of a colony ship, it would take them nearly as long to reach anywhere of significance now.

Jonas was cooking up a plan, of course, but Tailynn truly doubted there was much he could do, and for all her ability the Progenitor couldn't (or wouldn't) do anything either.

The *Immortal Vagrant* was well and truly stranded in space.

While Jonas and Rai directed the repairs to the ship, there wasn't much for the rest of the crew, Tailynn included, to do. The complete chaos that had ensued since she had first met Jonas had come to an abrupt end, and she found herself with an uncomfortably large amount of time to spend with her own thoughts – thoughts which no matter how hard she tried to avoid kept coming back to those two individuals who she didn't want to even acknowledge existed...

She'd discussed her situation with Jett numerous times, and had found him to be uncharacteristically logical about the situation. 'These people aren't your parents anymore, Tailynn,' he'd said. 'Why hold a grudge against people who are so far removed from the ones who wronged you that they're different people?'

Maybe he was right, maybe he wasn't – but if there was one thing that Tailynn didn't need at this point in time was *logic*! No, this was purely an emotional thing... and that was the problem, her emotions were hugely conflicted.

The Progenitor's disciples tended to be elusive when they weren't needed. She had no idea where on board the *Immortal Vagrant* they spent most of their time, and nor did she particularly care. It was good too, as the last thing Tailynn wanted was an unexpected encounter with her parents.

At least that's what she thought. As time progressed post-battle, and it became clear they would be spending a large amount of time confined to the *Vagrant* which itself was essentially confined to the region around the Pandora Nebula, the more it weighed on her mind. Her parents were like the elephant in the room – she knew they were there, she was conscious of the fact that she could encounter them without warning at any time, but she didn't want to acknowledge that fact.

In the end, it was Rai who convinced her to confront them. The younger woman was working furiously along-side the construct's proxies, and it became clear to Tailynn that she had thrown herself into her work in an effort to forget about the destruction of her home, and the death of her father. It got Tailynn thinking about how hard Rai's father's death had hit her, and how much love the young woman evidently had for him.

And frankly, it made Tailynn angry.

Not angry at Rai, of course, rather it made her despise her parents even more than she had after what they had done to her all those years ago. It made her so angry, in fact, that she decided to do something about it.

She stood in the sparsely-furnished quarters she had taken as her own, and called for them. She wasn't sure if it was because the Progenitor and her disciples were omnipresent, or if it was due to the zeptites which still coursed through her body, but a conspicuously short amount of time passed before the chime on the door to her quarters sounded.

'Enter,' Tailynn stated as coldly as possible, her blood pumping furiously through her veins.

Her parents – or the placid things that they had become – entered. They were dressed as all the disciples were, in loose fitting, unassuming white garments. Their serene faces immediately angered Tailynn, and she caught herself before losing her cool prematurely. They stopped in front of her, a couple of meters away. The door to Tailynn's quarters slid shut.

'Tailynn, we're glad that you've summoned us,' her father announced calmly.

'You don't get to talk,' Tailynn hissed. 'You get to listen. You get to listen to every gruesome detail of what happened to me all of those years ago. You get to share the pain that I suffered for so long. You stand here in front of me as entirely different people than those who raised me. Unaffected by the events of the past, unscarred.

'Now I don't know if you even have the ability to feel emotions any more – maybe shame, guilt and pain are too primitive for such advanced beings to experience, but I am going to do my absolute damndest to make you feel everything that I've had to deal with since that day. They *raped* me... repeatedly, and in ever possible way imaginable. The *beat* me to within an inch of my life. They damaged my body permanently – I can no longer bear children.

'But worse than any of that, is what they drove me to do. They took my innocence. They turned me into an animal... an animal capable of all the depravity that they relished. When given the opportunity, I killed them – slaughtered them like the animals they were. And I *enjoyed* it!

'But for everything they did to me, for everything they made me do and for what they made me become, I don't blame them. They were insane... damaged. Most of them were probably like me – people who had been forced into the depravity... people who had been abandoned to the wild. For *so long* I hated them.

'But they weren't the ones who betrayed me. You were my parents... you were responsible for me. I was a *child* who had the utmost trust in my parents. Like any child, I trusted that you would protect me, do the right thing by me. But both of you were too cowardly to put your own lives at risk. Thanks to the zeptites that you've infused me with, I know everything that happened to you on the remainder of your pilgrimage. How you were too cowardly to try to protect me, but not too scared to attempt taking your own lives.

'Now for everything I've just said, I've come to peace with myself over what happened all of those years ago. And I'm even a better person because of it. But I want one thing to be absolutely clear: I will *never* forgive you for what you did to me. I will do my best to forget, or to live with it, but I will never forgive. I just wanted you both to know that. This is the last time we will ever talk. As far as I'm concerned, you died back in the Valley of Stars.'

She'd said her piece, and during her entire speech, her parent's expressions never changed an iota. A few seconds of silence ensued before Tailynn's mother took a step forward.

'We were but human,' she said simply.

Tailynn recoiled. 'That's all you've got to say for yourselves?'

'What more is there to say?'

They turned to leave, and as they neared the exit to Tailynn's quarters they turned again to face her. 'We have done what we can to lessen the physical impacts of your experience. The zeptites in your body have repaired the damage caused to your reproductive organs. You can be a parent one day, Tailynn.' The door opened, and they exited, turning back to her one final time. 'We truly hope that you find peace in life, Tailynn.'

And with that, the door slid closed, and Tailynns parents were gone.

Forty-three

It had been more than three years since Jonas had seen his wife and slept in his own bed, in his own home. When he'd first accepted the contract from the shadowy Republic Intelligence Agency, he hadn't expected the job to take him anywhere near that long.

While he, Rai and Jade had spent hundreds of hours furiously doing what they could to repair the *Immortal Vagrant's* systems, there was nothing they'd been able to do for the FTL drive. While the drive was largely whole, a single component – the anti-matter injector and containment cylinder – was fused beyond repair, and could not be reconstructed due to the requirement of a specific raw element that was a necessary part to containing anti-matter. It was, as misfortune would have it, a   raw element that was extremely rare, and not used in any other components. They had scanned what remained of the destroyed Morphite ships that the Progenitor's weapon had defeated, to no avail – little more than ionised atoms remained of the enemy fleet.

Jonas had attempted enlisting the help of the Progenitor, but she claimed there was nothing she could do. 'If there's one thing I'm not, it's a ships engineer,' she'd said. 'I can't build a FTL drive out of nothing.'

It had taken weeks before the true weight of the situation had sunk in to the rest of the crew – they were stranded in space, and there was little they could do about it. Two weeks after the conclusion of their battle, Jonas had called his entire crew to the observation lounge. Everyone, minus the Progenitor and her disciples were there – Tailynn, Jett, Rai, Haldon and of course Gala. His friends, his crew, the people that had been so instrumental in defeating Zesiro and successfully liberating Haleh Madani – he was proud of them all.

'The FTL drive cannot be repaired,' Jonas announced simply. 'We're stranded here.'

'Forgive my ignorance,' Haldon said, 'but how long will it take us to get to the nearest inhabited system?'

'Our maximum sub-light speed is thirteen percent of the speed of light,' Rai replied. 'To get to the nearest inhabited star system, we're looking at roughly seventy five years of flight time, and that doesn't help us much because it's Eden – and I guarantee you that Eden doesn't have the element we require to repair the drive.'

'Regardless, the FTL drive acts as our main source of power,' Jonas added. 'Without it we have five years of full power at the most.'

'So what do we do?' Gala asked, concerned.

'There's only one thing we really can do,' Jonas replied. 'We shut the ship down, go into cryogenic stasis and activate a locator beacon. That way, we've at least got a chance of someone finding us within the next few years. The Republic sends out long range exploration vessels regularly.'

'Shutting the ship down and diverting all of our surplus power reserves to the cryo-coffins and the locator beacon gives us roughly two hundred years for someone to find us,' Rai said.

'And what happens if it's the Morphites who find us?' Jett asked quietly.

'It's a risk we'll have to take,' Jonas stated simply.

Later, Jonas and the Progenitor were walking through one of the huge vessel's corridors, discussing the future.

'The projections are somewhat muddled at this point,' Madani was saying. 'Indeed, the possible timeline where we deployed my weapon against Zesiro was considered unlikely, but it still happened. As a result, a whole slew of possible timelines have emerged. It will take my disciples and I some time to calculate the likelihoods of all these new possible futures.'

'So what you're saying,' Jonas replied, attempting to hide his irritation, 'is that you have no fucking idea of what's going to happen.'

'That's not entirely true,' Madani countered, her annoyingly arrogant grin making an appearance. 'But I can see how it would seem that way to you.'

'You know, there's one thing I don't understand,' Jonas said, stopping at a window in the corridor that had a view out across the Pandora Nebula. 'You can see the future – sorry, *predict* the future. You can destroy a star with very little effort. But you can't repair something as simple as an FTL drive?'

'As I've said before, I'm no quantum propulsion specialist,' she replied. 'I can't repair the drive, Jonas. Believe me, or don't – that's your choice. Something I can tell you, however that may lessen the blow of being stranded here a little, is that the chances of your future success are now more likely than ever. I mentioned a whole slew of new future possibilities opening up. Prior to the deployment of my weapon, there were very few paths. Honestly, there were less paths that saw you succeed than there were ones that saw you fail. Now, however, the explosion of possibilities widens the network, so to speak. There are now many more favourable possibilities than there was.'

'Why do I get the feeling that you're watering down the facts for me,' Jonas replied. 'I haven't been spoken to with the use of so many analogies since kindergarten.'

The Progenitor shrugged, an amused look on her face.

It had been thirty-seven days since the conclusion of the battle with Zesiro's fleet, and Jade's proxies had completed the cryo-coffin preparation. Jonas, Tailynn, Jett, Rai, Haldon, Galatea and a feminine holographic proxy of Jade stood in the cryo-chamber in their underwear, preparing for the stasis they were about to enter. They were each applying a zeptite infused gel over their bodies. Jonas had been reluctant, but it was a necessary evil – the gel would help prevent their bodies from any damage caused by the cryogenic process, and would also help to negate any cellular aging.

As Jonas rubbed gel onto Gala's back, he took a moment to really absorb everything that his crew had been through since his arrival on Eden. To be honest, he was uncertain how they had all avoided going mad. Take Gala for instance – four months ago, she'd been a bartender at a small saloon in a mining town that was straight out of the wild-west of ancient times. Now, she was preparing to enter cryogenic stasis, having been involved in an interstellar conflict that had almost destroyed them more than once. Of course the zeptites that the Progenitor had infused them all with had helped, but even so the human mind could be a fragile thing. It truly was a testament to the strength and resilience that all of his crew had in common.

Once they had all finished rubbing the gel onto each other, Jonas addressed them one last time.

'I owe you all more than I'll ever be able to repay,' he began, wondering if he'd used this same spiel before. 'Without each of you, I would have failed in my task of liberating the Progenitor from the Morphites. You've become my crew, and more than that, my friends. I am in debt to each of you.'

'Was it worth it?' Tailynn asked with uncertainty. 'I don't mean to belittle any of what you just said, Jonas. Maybe you do owe us, but we also owe you. Before you came to Eden, we all lived with the wool pulled over our eyes. We knew nothing of the greater galaxy – nothing of the truth about the Morphites. We were ignorant, and you were the one who opened our eyes. But I can't help wonder... was it worth it? The Progenitor has stated that in some way we will save humanity. How truthful has she been?' She sighed. 'I'm sorry, but it's hard not to wonder.'

'I couldn't agree more,' Jonas replied. 'I've had the exact same misgivings. But all I can say is that we have to keep going. If one day we save the galaxy, then good on us. But none of us know what's going to happen. When it all comes down to it, neither does the

Progenitor. Sure, she can try to predict what's going to happen, but can she ever truly know? I don't believe so. Let's face it, she's been wrong before. In that regard, we're no different to any human throughout history – the Progenitor included. Only time will tell.' He moved over to his cryo-coffin. 'I for one, am pretty keen to find out what happens next.'

The others all nodded, and moved over to their respective units. On the edge of each coffin were small cups filled with a thick, vanilla flavoured liquid – more zeptite infused matter designed to protect each of their internal organs during stasis. Jonas grabbed his cup and turned to the others, raising it in a toast.

'To the future,' he said. The others all raised their cups, and as one, they downed the liquids.

Jonas gave them all one last reassuring look, before turning around and beginning the process of preparing his cryo-coffin. The hatch slid open, and he climbed in. Jade's proxy stood over him, making the final preparations on the unit's console.

'Take good care of the ship Jade,' Jonas said. 'She's all yours for a bit.'

'Indeed, captain,' the proxy replied.

With that, the cryo-coffin's hatch slid closed, and Jonas felt a split second chill before he entered a dreamless sleep.

Epilogue

The Originator was melded with her personal construct in her private chamber on Alpha One. She had instructed the artificial intelligence to establish a stealth network with every other construct on the world, a total of 174,786 of them in all, such was the processing power she required now as the sole leader of the Morphites.

Being melded with such a vast network allowed her to experience an omnipotence that no-one before her had ever been subject to. She knew what each and every one of Alpha One's inhabitants were doing at any given time, her zeptite enhancements working overtime to process the ceaseless flow of information. She was convinced that she was now the closest thing that any sentient being had ever truly come to godhood, with the exception perhaps of one individual.

There was no doubt that the Originator was disappointed in Zesiro's failure to eliminate the Progenitor, however, her ultimate goal had been accomplished, the vital information she had been pursuing the Progenitor for so long now was in her hands. Now, she could focus on the ascension of her people to an omnipotent state, as she had been planning all along. Truth be told, she had never expected Zesrio to be able to kill the Progenitor, but she had hoped that his tireless pursuit may force her into returning to Alpha One to see the Originator's plan succeed. A voice interrupted her pondering.

'If that was indeed your ultimate goal, then I'd say you've succeeded,' the feminine voice said.

The Originator immediately disconnected herself from the Morphite network, and turned in surprise. It had been just about an eternity since she had experienced something as visceral as surprise – it was almost debilitating. Likewise, it had been so long since she had disconnected herself from the network that its sudden absence was akin to the complete cessation of thought.

It took a moment for her to compose herself – a moment that seemed to her accelerated consciousness to last an eternity, before she replied to the voice, which came from a female figure standing in the corner of her chamber. 'Hello Haleh.'

'Hello Eritz,' the Progenitor replied. 'It's been some time.'

The Originator balked at the use of her birth name – it had been so long since anyone had used it, and it was so unfamiliar to her that it took her a moment to realise that it was in fact she that the Progenitor was addressing. 'Tell me, Haleh... are you actually here on Alpha One, or have you somehow used the same FTL intellect projection trick on me as you did on poor Zesiro?'

'Oh, I am well and truly here on Alpha One,' the Progenitor replied, 'just not in this room. I'm not an imbecile. Although to be brutally honest with you, there's probably nothing you could do to me even if I was here. You're idea of omnipotence is rather... quaint, shall we say.'

'And what is your purpose of being here?' the Originator asked, not allowing herself to be baited. 'Are you here to further disrupt our people? Wherever you are on this planet, take a look around, Haleh. Do you see any unhappy people? Do you see any suffering? Do you see any *conflict*?'

'No – but nor do I see any passion, or love, or happiness,' the Progenitor replied. 'Because of you, our people have lost their humanity.'

'That's because we are *not* human,' the Originator insisted. 'The moment you infused yourself with the first zeptite all those centuries ago, was the moment that our people became more than human. It was the first step to transcendence. And while you work hard to prevent that ultimate transformation, I am closer than ever to achieving it. Very soon, humanity will be nothing but a keynote in galactic history.'

'And what of the pre-humans and the post-humans? Have you conveniently forgotten about them?'

The Originator scoffed. 'Since your interference on Eden the pre-humans are doing an impeccable job of self-eradication,' she said. 'Did you know that there has been a nuclear detonation on Eden's surface? The have seemingly reinvented the wheel, and are on track for a good old nuclear holocaust. You can take the bone away from the monkey, but you can't stop him from killing his mate to get another.'

'And what of the Republic?' the Progenitor asked.

'The Republic's days are numbered,' the Originator replied. 'And it's thanks to you, Haleh'

'Me?'

'Indeed. You see, when you deployed your infamous weapon while you were on the *Immortal Vagrant*, I was directly linked into Zesiro's mind. I saw everything. And I analysed everything.' She couldn't help but smile a victorious smile. 'And now I know.'

'Impossible,' the Progenitor said, attempting to mask her concern.

'If you insist.'

'Listen to me, Eritz,' the Progeitor said, urgency creeping into her tone. 'If what you tell me is true, then you cannot use it. You'd be committing genocide. Do you not see what your pursuit of transcendence has turned you into? You're not being rational! Claiming you're ending conflict by *eradicating* humanity? That's an oxymoron!'

'Your protestations are too late, Haleh,' the Originator said. 'The weapon has already been deployed.'

The Progenitor looked at the Morphite leader in horror. 'No...'

'Yes, Haleh,' Eritz replied, savouring her moment of victory. 'Now *I* am the killer of stars.'

To be continued in:

ECHOES OF ABSICON

Book Two of the Immortal Vagrant Trilogy

150 years after the battle of the Pandora Nebula, a down-on-her-luck salvage ship captain named Hannah Marx has happened upon the salvage of a lifetime; a darkly derelict vessel that seems to blend centuries old post-human and Morphite tech. Claiming the vessel as her own, Hannah and her crew are thrust into a chain of events that could lead to the end days of the entire human race, and a conflict with a deadly enemy who controls the fate of the entire galaxy.

But all is not lost. When the vessel's previous crew awaken from cryogenic stasis, the two groups must work together to unravel the mystery surrounding a world named *Absicon* that may yet hold the key to humanity's survival, and the one thing that thing they all though had been lost decades ago: hope.

About the Author

Travis James Annabel is a prolific writer across a number of mediums. As a journalist and editor of Australia's biggest men's interest magazine, *4WD Action*, as well as lead editor for Australia's longest running off-road motoring magazine, *Overlander 4WD*, his articles have been read by hundreds of thousands of readers. He is also a script writer for screen and television having had numerous short films produced, as well as a TV pilot, titled *The Carousel*. With two feature film scripts awaiting production, *The Sum of Life* and *The Prophets*, Travis's screen future is only just taking off.

In addition to television and screen, Travis has also written the scripts for numerous online commercial campaigns for major international companies including Toyota, Bridgestone Tyres and Valvoline Oils, which have had tens of millions of views.

Killer of Stars is his debut novel, and the first in the *Immortal Vagrant Trilogy*. His literary influences include Alastair Reynolds, Peter F. Hamilton, Kim Stanley Robinson and Daniel Easterman to name just a few. Travis lives in the Blue Mountains, west of Sydney NSW, Australia with his young family.

www.ingramcontent.com/pod-product-compliance
Lightning Source LLC
Chambersburg PA
CBHW071304200626
46813CB00015B/35